Fate or Folly

DAROS CHRONICLES
VOLUME TWO

Sarah Ettritch

NORN PUBLISHING
TORONTO, CANADA

Contents

Caged and Free — 1

Friends Reunited — 59

Uneasy Alliances — 117

Snakes and Sycophants — 179

The Road to Darroth — 239

Some Live, Some Die — 307

Unforeseen Choices — 377

Epilogue — 413

Author's Note — 414

Caged and Free

The journey that had begun the first time Erryn whispered Zayvang's name had brought her to a secret underground temple and into the presence of a goddess. Those she'd trusted had spat on her, branded her forehead, torn her away from her dear sister, banished her from the only home she knew, and tried to kill her, but she'd refused to give up, had persevered, had come here knowing that even if she found an explanation for why she was a Beast Master, the wild folk would tear her limb from limb. Lying awake at night, she'd come up with all sorts of possibilities for what she'd find at the temple she sought. In her wildest guesses, she'd never imagined that she'd stand in the presence of one of the Seven, gaping at the woman she'd only seen stitched into tapestries and painted on altars.

Fearful that she was about to bear the wrath of Zhikinden, Erryn fell to her knees and lowered her head. *Zhikinden. Here. In Daros.* And kneeling before the goddess, a Beast Master. The Holy Texts condemned Beast Masters, teaching that they were reviled by the Seven for calling the Fallen into the physical plane, and in Erryn's case, for loving them. She'd believed, then questioned, then dismissed the holy words. But now, doubt set in. If she was wrong, she wouldn't leave this chamber, and could be condemned to a terrible fate.

"I am pleased that I am able to take this form again." The voice was melodious, yet firm; commanding, yet inviting. Erryn wasn't sure if the words had been spoken aloud, or had sprung into her mind. She kept her head lowered.

"Rise and lift up your eyes. I would see you, and have you see me."

Her stomach knotted. She slowly lifted her head. Zhikinden was standing; she had to be taller than a house. No wonder the tallest man couldn't touch the chamber's ceiling.

Zhikinden nodded encouragement. "Rise."

Erryn pushed herself to her feet. Asha and Yanik did the same. Realizing that Zhikinden was speaking aloud to all of them, Erryn forced her gaze to the goddess's face and tentatively met her eyes, then sucked in her breath. She knew those eyes. She'd looked into those eyes. *Zayvang.*

Everything Erryn thought she knew, everything she'd been taught, everything she'd accepted and believed . . . *Zhikinden is Zayvang.* Her world changed, and unbeknownst to every person in Daros, so did theirs.

What about the other Fallen? She instinctively reached out to them and felt both relieved and frightened when they answered. Sath must be Samshy, Lerxis must be Lleor, Cheturrak, Cesernys; Iss, Irnys; Quon, Queyris; and Rachagha, Roosad. What were they doing in her head? How could they be the Fallen?

Zhikinden looked down at those standing before her. "It has been so long, and I have grown accustomed to looking up at you. I had forgotten." She stepped off the altar—now only a small step—lowered herself to the ground, and crossed her legs. "Do as you choose, stand or sit, but come closer to me. I do not have much time, and there are things I must tell you."

Erryn approached her and sat down. The others did the same. Nobody made a sound.

"Know that I must leave this form if I am to slow the sickening of the land. I cannot stop it without my brothers and sisters. You must free them. There is a chamber like this for each of us, and one chamber for all of us. There is a book in the next chamber that will tell you where to go. Erryn, you must summon each of them, as you did me. The rest of you must protect Erryn." She surveyed those gathered before her. "Asha, Toe, Renn, Avere, Yanik. You must not hesitate to give your lives to save hers. If Erryn falls, it will be some time before the Called and Caller walks the land again."

Called and Caller? Is that who I am?

"Yes, it is part of who you are," Zhikinden said. "You have freed one of us. You may become Saviour. We shall see." She turned to Avere. "No, I cannot see the future, and I can see that surprises you. I tell you this: if we could see the future, we would not have agreed to be bound to our beloved companions." She raised her hand. "So many questions, but little time. The book explains it all. For now, I tell you this: Erryn is most loved, not most despised. The Fallen are not Fallen. There are no Fallen. But there is Zayvang, Sath, Cheturrak, Lerxis, Iss, Rachagha, and Quon. They have been with us since the beginning, and we with them."

Erryn cringed. She'd been calling and commanding the Seven all along.

Zhikinden focused on her. Erryn had to will herself to not shy away. "You must call them. You must do so. They want to help. If it aids you, do not think of them by their true names. Think of them as you did before. Refer to them as you did before. They are yours to command, and yours to free."

"But there *is* a Zayvang," Erryn said, then quickly followed it with, "I'm sorry," when she realized she'd spoken aloud.

Zhikinden smiled. "Speak it or think it, it does not matter to me. But know this: I can only hear your thoughts when I am in this form and near, or when you invoke my name. Otherwise, your thoughts are yours. But I will not answer you while I am sustaining the land as best I can. I have not been able to answer since I was bound."

"Do you mean all the prayers, the offerings . . ." Asha trailed off.

"I do, Young Mother. But that does not mean we did not care. We cared and suffered, and we will continue to do so until we are free." Her eyes settled on Erryn again. "You will still be able to call Zayvang, but it will not be me. It will be Zayvang. I will allow you to command her while she is in her physical form. I will introduce you to her."

A thunderclap reverberated around the circular chamber. The air shimmered. A saber-tooth cat leaped into existence and instantly sat next to Zhikinden. She reached out and ruffled the cat's fur, reminding Erryn of all the times she'd done the same thing—to Zhikinden.

"I have missed you," Zhikinden murmured. "This is Erryn, the Called and Caller. Please obey her when she calls you and while you walk the land."

Golden eyes met Erryn's—different eyes, but intelligent ones. Then the cat nodded to Zhikinden. "She understands you," Erryn breathed. "She talks to you."

Zhikinden's eyes danced with amusement. "Of course she does. She is my beloved, and this is the form she takes here, in the physical plane." Her expression grew serious. "But now I must leave you. I must do what I can. It is up to you to free us, and the rest of you to be her protectors. Asha, Toe, Renn, Avere, Yanik, you know what you must do. You are together in this." She paused. "I will leave you with one gift, Called and Caller. Come to me." When Erryn hesitated, Zhikinden beckoned. "Come."

Her heart hammering in her chest, Erryn rose and approached the goddess.

"You have done well. We hope you will become Saviour." Zhikinden took Erryn's face in her hands and kissed her forehead. A sudden searing heat made Erryn gasp. When Zhikinden released her, Erryn fell to her knees. "We must go," she heard Zhikinden say. "Come, Zayvang."

Erryn felt a sudden, palpable void, the lack of a presence where there had been one. She didn't have to look up to know that Zhikinden and her beloved had left them. She shivered and mentally called out, feeling more alone than she could ever remember.

The others must have felt the same, because some time passed before she sensed one of them next to her. "Erryn," Asha murmured. "Are ye all right?"

"I'm not sure." She was already starting to wonder if she'd dreamed Zhikinden's presence. "Did you see Zhikinden?"

"Yes."

Erryn looked up. Asha's eyes widened. So did Toe's, and Avere's. Renn met her eyes, then quickly looked away. Yanik's eyes were fearful. "What is it?" Erryn asked. "What's wrong?"

Avere crouched next to her and reached out. Her fingers lightly touched Erryn's forehead. "The brand. It's gone."

Erryn's fingers went to her forehead, knocking Avere's away. She ran them along smooth skin, not the rough ridges she'd grown accustomed to feeling when she accidentally touched the area.

"It's brilliant!" Avere said. "Of all the things she could

have done, this is brilliant. Think about it. Nobody will ever suspect you of being the Beast Master."

"The Called and Caller," Asha said.

"Everyone knows her as the Beast Master, and now she doesn't need a hat."

"As long as she doesn't call the Fall—" Asha caught herself. "Call them in front of anyone who lives to tell the tale of the woman without a brand."

"Nobody would believe them. The king branded the heathen. The guards are looking for someone with that brand. Erryn could walk up to them and say hello, and they wouldn't know it's her."

Erryn had no intention of doing that. She stood and felt her forehead again. She wished there were a mirror in this chamber, so she could see the smooth skin.

"We need to find the book Zhikinden told us about." Avere shook her head and looked around at them. "We all saw her, didn't we?" Nods answered her. "We've heard about her all our lives, and now we've seen her."

"And yet we have trouble believing." Asha was silent for a moment. "Why do we say we believe, when we really doubt? Will anyone believe us?"

"First things first. The book." Avere looked at Erryn. "If you agree."

They were all looking at her now, their eyes deferential. She'd gone from heathen to leader, from despised to respected. She had Zhikinden's blessing, and she was the Called and Caller, the one who could free the remaining Six. Fear and awe mingled inside her, but she couldn't let it go to her head. She was still Erryn, and she'd never free the Six without the brave people who'd journeyed with her. "We all freed Zhikinden. I'm not your leader."

"Ye're the most important among us," Asha said.

"I don't see it that way. I'm the only one who can free them, but without you, I'll never have the chance. I never would have made it here. I'm the same as when we arrived here. I don't want you to see me differently." She made a point of looking at Renn. The guarded expression on Renn's face concerned her, but it would have to wait until they were alone. "I hope you trust me now, at least."

Erryn had wanted to lighten the mood, but Asha, Avere, and Yanik appeared contrite and apologetic, making her feel bad. "You were only following the Holy Texts, and what your people believe," she said to Asha.

"Not all of us, and not really," Avere said brightly. "If we were following what we're supposed to believe, we would have killed you."

Erryn would have smiled, if not for the certainty that had they not stumbled upon this hidden temple, Avere would have planted a dagger in her to prevent everyone except Toe and Renn from torturing her to death. But they'd also stuck their necks out, and she wouldn't forget that. "We have to find this book so we can figure out what to do next."

"I don't think we'll have to go far. Zhikinden said it's in the next chamber, so it must be through that door." Avere pointed over Erryn's shoulder.

She turned around and saw the doorway that had appeared in the stone. "When did that happen?"

"Perhaps when she left us," Asha suggested. "There was a flash."

"Let's go see what's there." Avere darted past Erryn. "Me first. Remember, Erryn is gold. Nothing happens to her."

"I doubt Zhikinden would open a doorway that would kill her when she steps through it," Toe said, accepting the walking stick Asha handed him with a nod.

"We're not taking any chances." Avere stopped in front of the doorway and gazed through it. She ran her hands along its stone edges, then crouched and studied the ground. Yanik hovered next to Erryn, his eyes wary, but not because of her. Only one of the Seven could have turned him from calling for her torture and death to treating her like a treasure. She wished Renn were next to her, so she could give her a reassuring smile and touch her hand, but then she didn't. Renn might look away or stiffen, which would weigh on Erryn until they could talk.

Avere stepped over the threshold. Nothing happened. Erryn took a step forward. "Wait!" Avere snapped, making Erryn wonder if she had eyes in the back of her head. She stopped in the doorway and watched Avere circle the chamber. Apparently satisfied, Avere beckoned for everyone to step inside. "Erryn last, just in case."

When Erryn crossed the threshold she listened for the door to rumble closed behind her, but it didn't. She focused on the middle of the room, where a book sat on a small stone altar. Erryn stepped to—Avere was immediately at her side. "Let me," she said.

Wondering if Avere would want to feed her and pull

down her underclothes when she had to go, Erryn stepped back. Avere wiped her hands on her cloak and lifted the book. She opened it and flipped through its pages. "It's never easy, is it?" she murmured.

"What's wrong?"

The Ferret turned the open book around and held it in front of Erryn. "See for yourself."

Erryn's eyes went to the script on the pages. The writing was in a language she barely recognized. She could pick out one or two words, but . . . "Why would she leave us a book we can't understand?"

"This book has been here for a while." Avere motioned for Erryn to examine the altar. "There's a thin layer of dust." She turned the book back around. "I recognize a few words."

"So do I, but a few words on a page isn't going to help us."

"Asha," Avere called. "Come look at this book."

Asha, who'd been supporting Toe's elbow, came over.

"Can you read any of this?"

The priestess peered at the book, then shook her head.

"We could show it to those two scholars," Erryn said.

Avere cocked her head. "We'll show them a single passage we've copied. We're not showing them the entire book. They might keep it from us, or turn us in to the guard. You do realize that if we tell anyone about what happened here, they'll think we're deluded."

"Lale and Zheir and the ones who travelled with us won't," Asha said. "They saw." She jutted her chin toward

Erryn. "They saw the brand that now isn't there. May I touch it?"

The request surprised Erryn. "Yes."

Asha swallowed. She gently touched Erryn's forehead. Her eyes closed, and she drew a shuddering breath. "Zhikinden touched ye. She called ye Called and Caller."

"I call the Fallen—the Seven—the Six." Erryn grimaced. "The Fallen. I need to keep calling them the Fallen."

"Called could mean ye were called to be the Caller," Asha mused.

Erryn wished she'd asked Zhikinden why. Why her? Wasn't that why she'd come to this temple? To find out why? She'd been in the presence of one of the Seven! If only there had been more time, and she'd been calm enough to choose the questions that haunted her most.

"We know the Holy Texts are wrong about Beast Masters," Avere said, her eyes on the book. "I wonder if the originals were wrong, or if they were tampered with. Are other parts wrong?"

"We also teach that Falleners are despised," Asha said.

"Look." Avere tapped an open page. "Something I recognize. A map of Daros."

Erryn looked over Avere's shoulder. She recognized the map. There were no names on it, only eight dots. One dot was larger than the others.

"I think it's the temples Zhikinden told us about." Avere stabbed her finger onto one of the dots. "I believe we're in this one."

"They're scattered all over the place," Erryn said. It

would take them months, perhaps longer, to travel to all of them.

"I'm guessing this larger dot is the one that has altars for all of them. It would be safer and quicker to go to that one."

Erryn's heart sank. "Are you sure? If I'm right, that dot—"

Avere groaned. "I think you're right."

"What is it?" Asha said.

Erryn turned to her. "The temple with all the altars . . . it's in Darroth."

"The Royal City?"

Erryn nodded. "Not only will the guard presence be strong, it's the seat of the Primacy's power. And there will be more people there than anywhere else who'll recognize me on sight."

Avere snapped the book shut. "They won't be the problem. They'll do a double-take, then realize you're not branded. But primates, guards, and bounty hunters might be a little more persistent."

Erryn agreed. "Let's find out what the book says before we come up with a plan. It might turn out we'd be better served by going to the other temples."

Avere nodded. "Let's get going."

They didn't have to search for a second door, one that would hopefully lead to a passage that would take them to the surface. Erryn had spotted the other doorway when she'd entered the chamber. Apparently once they'd passed the test of getting to the chamber with the altar, no further tests were required.

Everyone followed Avere into the passage. She'd handed the book to Asha so she could carry a lit torch in one hand and use the other to feel for traps, though Erryn doubted there would be any. They all trudged along, using the torch as a beacon. It wasn't long before Erryn felt as if she were walking uphill. Only ten minutes after leaving the chamber, they came to a dead end.

"Not a dead end." Avere pointed upward. "Look."

A whip marked the stone above them. Erryn stood on her toes, reached up, and pushed it. The stone slid open. She shielded her eyes when light flooded the passage, then moved aside, guessing that Avere would want to go through the opening first.

Avere handed the torch to Erryn. "Give me a boost," she said to Yanik. He hoisted Avere upward until she was able to grab the edges of the opening.

Erryn's heart leaped when someone yelped. It wasn't Avere. Suddenly two of the wild folk they'd left behind were peering down at them. One helped Avere through the hole. Asha went next, then the others. Erryn emerged last. She looked around, bewildered. It wasn't possible, yet it was. They'd somehow just climbed through the same hole they'd entered.

The others appeared equally befuddled. Avere went back to the hole and stared down it. She looked up and shook her head.

"The sun shouldn't be here," Asha said. "How long were we gone?" she asked one of the wild folk.

"Only a minute, Mother. The stone slid shut, and then it opened, and you were there."

Erryn and those who'd gone with her exchanged glances.

One of the wild folk pointed at her. "The Fallener's forehead!"

Asha motioned for him to calm down. "We have much to tell ye. Come, sit with us."

Everyone gathered around Asha. Those who hadn't entered the temple gave Erryn a wide berth. Her mind racing, she sat cross-legged next to Renn and listened to Asha recount what had happened in the temple, a tale she wouldn't believe, if she hadn't been there herself.

Erryn pushed to her feet and stretched her arms and legs. Asha had finished telling her people what had happened, but had regretfully shaken her head at the many questions they'd asked. "There was no time to ask her questions," she explained. "Zhikinden left us as quickly as she came."

Many questions had run through Erryn's mind as she'd listened to Asha. Why had the Seven agreed to be bound to their beloveds? Who had bound them? Why were the Holy Texts so distorted on the subject of Beast Masters and the Fallen? What had happened to Fi? Where was she? There hadn't been time to ask Zhikinden, and the goddess might not have answered. "It's growing dark," Asha said. "Let's make camp here and return to Loring tomorrow."

Everyone murmured their agreement. Erryn lifted the bundle containing the tent she and Renn shared and claimed a spot near to where one of the hunters was starting to build a fire. She expected the others to do what they usually did: raise their tents a short distance away, leaving room between them and her. But when she crouched to unroll the tent, she sensed eyes upon her and lifted her head. The wild folk were gathering around her. One reached out—then snatched her hand back. Erryn wasn't sure what to do.

"They want to touch yer forehead," Asha said, joining those gathered. "They want to touch where Zhikinden has touched."

Erryn straightened and warily surveyed those around her. "I don't mind," she said, wondering if those watching her with deferential eyes would have believed Asha's story if she was still branded. Perhaps that was another reason Zhikinden had chosen to remove the ugly wound that had marked her as cursed by the Seven.

The woman who'd snatched her hand back took a tentative step forward. When Erryn met her eyes and nodded, fingers lightly touched her forehead and remained there for a few seconds. The wild woman bowed her head and murmured something under her breath, then stepped away with her head still lowered. Another hunter came forward and lifted his hand. Trying not to shift her weight, Erryn stood patiently as the rest came one by one. When nobody was left, she turned around to pitch the tent and discovered that someone had already done it for her. Renn?

"Ye'll have to get used to it," Asha said, leaning on her walking stick. "Ye've been touched by Zhikinden."

"But that doesn't make me better than anyone else."

"Of course it does." Avere strolled over to them, holding a piece of paper. "You've been chosen by the Seven."

"We don't know why I'm a Beast Master."

"Called and Caller," Asha said.

"We're the only ones who know that name, and none of us knows what it means."

"That won't matter. Anyone who hears the story will see you as being blessed by Zhikinden." Avere's eyes went to Erryn's forehead. "In the flesh. She touched you. And we have work to do." She waved the paper in her hand. "We need someone who can understand the book. I've copied a passage for Boren and Antony."

"And if they can't read it?"

"Hopefully they'll know someone who can." Avere folded the paper and tucked it into one of her many pockets. "I'll sleep better tonight than I have in a while." She walked away.

"Will you sleep better, now that you know you did the right thing in helping me?" Erryn asked Asha.

"This new knowledge has brought new worries. Six are still bound, and Zhikinden said she needs her brothers and sisters to heal the land. She has laid the fate of the land and its people on our shoulders." Asha's eyes grew distant. "But she lives. They are. No matter what comes, that knowledge will see me through."

The scent of cooking meat wafted by, making Erryn's stomach grumble. "Come and eat," Asha said.

Now she would be permitted to sit around the fire? She understood why the wild folk had shunned her but couldn't help resenting it. "I'll eat in my tent. I want—"

"Ye want to eat in peace, without the others watching ye."

That, too. The moment Asha turned away, Erryn searched for Renn and spotted her sitting alone on the ground some distance away from the fire. Erryn sat next to her. "Are you all right?"

Renn was as still as a statue. "Ye are the Called and Caller."

"Not what I was expecting."

"Ye have the Seven inside of ye. Now ye have six, but ye had seven. The Six are always with ye."

Erryn reached out to them and felt their presence as she always had. She couldn't wrap her head around the notion that they were the Six still bound. To her, they would still be Cheturrak, Lerxis, Iss, Sath, Quon, and Rachagha. It would be easier, less intimidating. She had to command them. She couldn't fear their wrath, and Zhikinden had assured Erryn that her siblings wanted to help free themselves.

"I don't sense Zayvang anymore," she said. "And I won't call her unless I need her."

"Will ye call the others and sit with them?"

She wanted to. She'd like nothing better than to call Lerxis and sit with her, ruffle her fur, and talk to her. But could she do that now? "I don't know." She gazed at the side of Renn's head. "What's wrong?"

"Ye are touched by Zhikinden and ye're the Called and Caller. Ye don't need me anymore."

Erryn bit back the first response that came to mind, that she needed all of them, that Zhikinden had said they were her protectors. That wasn't what Renn meant. "You think what happened has changed things between us. Why? Nothing's changed."

"Everything's changed, Erryn. We'll free the others, or die trying. If we free them, Daros will be at yer feet. Ye'll be able to have anything, and anyone. Ye won't have to hide anymore."

"That doesn't mean things have to change between us." Erryn picked up a stick and drew idly in the dirt. "The whole time we've been together, we didn't think it would last. We were expecting it to end."

Renn's jaw tightened. "So ye want it to end?"

"No, I meant that our feelings grew despite that, despite not being able to make any promises to each other. The only thing we expected from each other was . . . love. Our feelings were strong then, and they're strong now, at least for me. Unless you see me differently now? Is that the problem? You no longer want to be with me?"

"Ye are the Called and Caller."

"I've always been the Called and Caller. We're just using another name now. Before it was Beast Master. Fallener." She tossed the stick aside and gripped Renn's arm. "You saw past that, past the brand on my forehead. All that's changed is those we travel with no longer consider me an outcast. They see me as touched by Zhikinden."

Suddenly Erryn understood. She and Renn had both been outcasts. Now Renn saw herself as alone, and Erryn as one of the accepted who'd look down on her. She relaxed her fingers but still held Renn's arm. "Nothing has changed between us, not for me. I—"

Toe hobbled toward them. Erryn quickly let go of Renn.

"Come and get some supper," Toe said, beckoning to them.

"I'm going to eat in the tent. I think I'll do that until they get used to me—again."

Toe nodded. "Still, the others want ye to receive yer supper first."

Erryn inwardly groaned. This had better stop, and soon. For now, she'd go along with it. She didn't want to snub them. They might interpret it as a judgement from Zhikinden. *Madness.* "You come, too," she said to Renn.

"I'm not very hungry."

"We have a conversation to continue," Erryn said, sounding as firm as she could without sounding angry. "And you need to eat. You won't be much of a protector if you're weak from hunger."

That brought Renn to her feet. They walked with Toe back to the fire. "I'm going to eat in the tent," she said when Asha smiled at her, in case the priestess had forgotten.

"But let us serve ye." Her eyes flicked to Renn. "Ye no longer have to eat and sleep with the shamed."

Erryn sensed Renn stiffen and felt the eyes of the others around the fire upon her. She had to make herself clear now, and not only for them. "Renn is my friend," she said to Asha, but loud enough that everyone could hear. "She stood by me when nobody else did. She stood by me when you would have tortured and killed me. Zhikinden named her as one of my protectors. She didn't call her the shamed, or call her out in any other way. I know you see her as shamed, but I don't. I welcome her company, and I want things to be as they were. I choose to share a tent and eat with her." Let them read into that whatever they wanted to.

Asha frowned, but she inclined her head. "If that's what ye want."

"It is." And she wouldn't thank them for thinking they were doing her a favour.

Avere filled two bowls with meat and added a thick piece of bread to each one. As she handed a bowl to Erryn, she leaned closer to her. "You could have just said you love her," she murmured, making Erryn's mouth drop open. Was there anything Avere didn't notice?

"And here's yours," Avere said to Renn, her expression giving nothing away. "Enjoy your supper."

When they entered the tent, Renn sat and put down her bowl. "Ye see? They know I'm not worthy of ye."

Erryn almost flung her supper across the tent. She quickly crouched to put it down, then stood and glared at Renn. "Don't be so stubborn and stupid!" She wanted to throttle her, but tears sprang to her eyes and her fists clenched. "I don't want you to treat me this way. Don't treat me this way. First I'm despised. Now I'm touched by Zhikinden. I'm just a person. I've always been just a person. I thought you saw that, saw past it all, but I guess I was wrong."

Renn leaped to her feet, her face stricken.

"I was on my own, and lonely, until I ran into you and

Toe. And what's happened with you . . ." Erryn blinked away her tears.

"I'm sorry. I didn't mean to hurt ye."

"I'm just a woman, Renn, like you, and Avere, and Asha. I need you, most of all, to see that. If you care about me, then see me." Erryn pressed her hands against her chest. "Nothing should have changed. Nothing has for me."

"But things *have* changed. Not how I feel. But I wondered . . . since ye're no longer seen by the others as heathen, if ye still wanted this. What will happen when everyone knows ye're the Called and Caller?"

"I'm not with you because nobody else would have me. I'm with you because my feelings for you grew and I want to be with you." Erryn mustered a smile. "And everyone will only know if we succeed. If we don't, I'll still be the reviled Fallener."

"If we succeed, ye'll return to the Royal City."

"Fi isn't on the throne, and I don't understand why. The only thing I know for certain is that I'm not welcome in Darroth." She stepped closer to Renn and met her eyes. "Let's worry about what comes next when we know I have a future. We have more pressing concerns."

"I will stand with ye, no matter what comes."

"Because I'm the Called and Caller?"

"Because my heart belongs to ye."

Renn had stood with her so far, against her own clan, and perhaps against her own judgement at times. Erryn pulled her into an embrace and held her tightly, feeling safe within Renn's strong arms. "I should have asked her why I'm the Called and Caller. That's why I wanted to find the temple in the first place."

"Maybe the book will tell ye," Renn murmured.

Maybe. Right now, she closed her eyes and tried to forget, for a moment, that she'd been in the presence of Zhikinden, who'd kissed her forehead. The animals she'd come to love, who shared her mind, were the Seven, now Six. If she hadn't seen and heard Zhikinden herself, she wouldn't believe it. *There are no Fallen.* But she'd still call them that. It would make it easier for her to summon them, and to command the gods and goddesses she'd revered all her life.

Fi cracked open an eye when Jeena came into the tent and plunged her hands into the washing bowl. The water must be cold, but the wild woman always washed herself when she returned to the tent late at night. Fi always woke up. She couldn't sleep soundly on the hard ground and with her wrists in chains. She felt exhausted most of the time. Fortunately she rode in a wagon when the slaver's camp moved, and often managed to doze.

"What are ye looking at?" Jeena snarled.

"You. What do you think?"

Jeena's foot connected with Fi's rib. Pain stabbed through her. She grunted and struggled to keep her expression neutral.

Jeena muttered something under her breath and backed away. "If we didn't have to deliver ye with no marks, I would have pummelled ye by now."

"Why? You've said so many times you don't care about

the throne or who's on it. So you don't want to pummel me because I'm accused of assassinating my father. That's not why you're jealous of me."

"Jealous? Ha! Ye're a leashed dog."

"Yes, I'm leashed. And so are all those women in the cage. But you're not leashed. Yet you let them use you like a dog. Who was it tonight? Devon?" she asked, referring to the bald man who led the slavers. "Mac? Quinn? The one with the red hair who always grabs your bottom?"

"Shut yer mouth!"

"Those women have no choice, but you do. Why do you let them do it to you? Why don't you leave? You could take one of the horses right now and leave."

"And take ye with me?" Jeena picked up the washing bowl and tipped it over Fi's head. The icy cold water made Fi gasp. She sat up and coughed. "Ye have no reason to look down on me. Ye're the one they'll cut open and hang."

"And they'll be wrong, but I'll still have my dignity," Fi said, shivering. "They can't take that away from me."

"Dignity?" Jeena's laugh sounded forced. "Ye're a dirty rat in rags."

Dignity came from within. Fi had learned that lesson since escaping through the tunnel with Cedric and Enkelo. As they'd travelled, she'd noticed the quiet dignity of the merchants, farmers, and tradesfolk. She hadn't seen it before. Her new appreciation for them would have served her well on the throne, but the best she could hope for now was not giving anyone the satisfaction of seeing her pain and regret when they brought her before the people and humiliated her. Dann, Erryn, Cedric,

Enkelo . . . she'd give up the throne in an instant to be reunited with them. She prayed to the Seven every day, begging them to somehow let her know if any of them were alive, but she'd heard and seen nothing. She was alone and on the way to a traitor's death. History would not be kind to her.

Jeena made a point of drying herself with a rag while Fi tried to pat her hair dry, not an easy feat with shackled wrists. She inched away from the puddle until she could lie down without getting wet.

"If I didn't want ye to sicken, I'd make ye lie in it," Jeena said.

"How petty of you. But I suppose the only power you have is over me and the other women. We're the only way you can make yourself feel big. Otherwise you're just a small woman nobody cares about." The moment the words left her mouth, Fi felt a twinge of guilt. She'd promised herself she wouldn't stoop so low, but the wild woman constantly taunted her, and Jeena was a slaver. Still, Fi sometimes saw her as a victim. "How did you end up with these men?"

"Shut yer mouth and go to sleep." Jeena doused the lamp she'd left burning, plunging the tent into darkness.

Fi tried different sleeping positions until she couldn't feel anything digging into her. The rib Jeena had kicked ached. Fi would have a nasty bruise, but the pain would eventually subside. Nothing would take away the ache in her heart. Still, she would hold her head high, for Father and Mother, and Henrick and Surann, and Dann, and

Erryn. She would hold on to her dignity. It was all she had left.

Avere fished the copy of the book passage from her pouch and led the way into Antony and Boren's domain. She'd entrusted Toe with the book itself, not wanting the scholars to see it. She couldn't leave it with Erryn or Asha for safekeeping, because they were with her, and while she trusted Renn, the feeling wasn't mutual. Perhaps giving the book to Renn would have earned her more trust, but she'd done what was easier.

"Ah, you've returned." Boren clasped his hands on the wooden table. Antony had his nose stuck in a book, as usual. "Did you find anything?"

Avere wanted to laugh. They wouldn't believe her if she told them. When she'd stepped out of her tent that morning and blinked into the sun, she'd hardly believed it and had almost convinced herself it must have been a dream, or some type of mass hallucination, until she'd spotted Erryn with her smooth forehead. Yet another reason Zhikinden had performed that act out of the many she could have chosen.

"It was as ye said," Asha said. "There were ruins."

"And not much else." Boren gave them a sympathetic look. "I did try to warn you."

"We did find this." Avere handed him the copy. "It was etched into one of the fallen columns. Can you read it?"

Boren's brows drew together. "Hmm. This is . . . unexpected."

"Why?" Erryn asked.

"This language is ancient and not my area of expertise, but . . ." He nudged Antony. "Look at this." Antony slowly lifted his head. "They found this on a column," Boren explained, handing the paper to the other scholar.

Antony read the passage. "I can pick out a few words. Prove. No, demonstrate, or maybe show. Uh, bound. Final. The names of the Fallen."

Avere knew about the names. They were the only words she'd understood.

"Beloved. Faith, though it could also mean belief. It would depend on the context, and since I don't understand the rest . . ." He looked up. "You say you found this on a column. Who would have etched it into the column?" he mused.

Avere didn't respond. "You can't translate it, then?"

"I'm afraid not," Antony said. "You need a primate."

Fiddlesticks.

"They study the ancient tongue. Ideally, you'll find one who specializes in the ancient languages, but I'm sure every primate will know a few more words than I do." Antony gave the copy back to Avere.

"You found it on a column, you say?" Boren frowned. "We didn't see anything etched into a column when we were there, did we, Antony?"

"We were only there for five minutes," Antony said.

Boren nodded. "Oh, yes, I remember now. We only had a quick look around. Not our area of study."

Avere wished she'd come up with a better story. Then again, if Boren and Antony decided to see the column for themselves, she and the others would be long gone by the time they discovered the lie. "Ah, well. We were just curious about what the passage said, and since we had to pass through here on our way back to civilization, we thought we'd see if you two could translate it."

"Sorry to disappoint. Where are you heading now?"

Back to the Snowlake clan, and then they'd have to return to Stronghaven and find a primate, something Avere wasn't looking forward to. They had no idea what the passage said. The first primate who read it could accuse them of blasphemy, or worse, call for the guard. She'd tear away the part that included the Fallen's names before showing the passage to a primate. "I'll be returning to Denkirk," she said, saying the third town that sprang to mind, Darroth and Stronghaven being the first two. "So will my friend, here." She gestured to Erryn.

"I assume you'll return to your clan, Mother," Boren said. "Would you consider spending a few days in Loring with us? I'd be remiss if I didn't introduce you to my wife."

"I'm sorry, but I must decline," Asha said. "I don't want to be away from my clan any more than I need to be."

"I understand. Times are hard." He smiled. "I'm sorry we can't help you any further."

"Ye've been a great help. Ye told us about the ruin."

They said their good-byes and left the hut. "A blasted primate," Avere said. "We can't trust any of them."

"We need to know what's in the book," Erryn said.

She agreed but would prefer a way that didn't involve men with mitres. "We'll try one in Stronghaven."

"What about the map?" Asha asked. "Will going to

Stronghaven take us farther away from one of the six temples?"

"No. Even from here, they'd be quite the journey."

Erryn shifted her weight. "I'd say let's go to Darroth and find the one temple, but we'd be going straight into the vipers nest."

Yes, but also to Arrick and his resources. But would he help them? The Holy Texts hadn't changed, and the princess had been usurped. Who knew what the situation was? "There might be messages for me in Stronghaven that will help us decide what to do next. At the very least, we can try a primate there."

Asha nodded. "But first to my clan."

"Maybe Lale or Zheir can read this passage," Avere said.

"Perhaps. They've studied more than I have, but the language of the book is not our language." Asha's voice dropped. "I thought it would be."

"It doesn't mean the Seven didn't come to you first," Avere said. And what did it matter, anyway? The past was the past. They had to work together now. "Let's join the others. The sooner we get back to Stronghaven, the sooner we'll have a plan."

Fi sat sullenly in the covered wagon she always shared with Jeena, Quinn, and one other brute, wondering how close they were to wherever they were taking her. How much longer until she was sold like a sack of potatoes to the next person who'd humiliate her? She recalled seeing this Lord Millwood's name on a guest list for a dinner at the castle, but she couldn't remember meeting him. Father might not have introduced him to her, or he might have been one of the many lords who hadn't stood out. Nobles always bowed and said the same bland words. The only lords and dukes she'd cared about were the ones Father had mentioned in the same breath as "potential husband." Viren had won that honour and paid for it with his life. His youngest brother might have done the same. Fi's stomach clenched. Sometimes she cared about what would happen to her; other times she just wanted it to be over.

"How much longer will it be to wherever you're taking me?" she asked Jeena. "Where does this Lord Millwood live?"

"Ye don't know? What kind of princess were ye?"

The kind who hadn't kept track of every minor noble in Daros. "Whoever he is, he wasn't very important."

Jeena's eyes narrowed shrewdly. "He will be when he turns ye over to the Primacy. We know he'll pay a handsome sum for ye."

"Devon should hold out for as much as he can," Quinn said. "Going from minor noble to a seat on the Royal Council? Millwood will pay whatever we ask."

"He might not get a seat for capturing me," Fi said, but only to be argumentative. He probably would. "Where does he live?"

Quinn looked to Jeena, then shrugged. "Near Stronghaven."

"So that's where we're going."

Quinn barked a laugh. "Do you see us riding into

Stronghaven with a bunch of slaves? Don't be stupid. We'll camp near his estate. If he isn't there, we'll send word."

"But when he has ye, he'll want to march ye into Stronghaven for all to see," Jeena said. "Then he'll parade ye down to Darroth, where ye'll get what's coming to ye."

"Oh, so you won't be there to see me hang, then," Fi said, sounding as bored as she could. "Pity. I was looking forward to at least one friendly face in the crowd."

When Quinn snickered, Jeena glared at him. "Maybe I'll offer to guard ye down to Darroth."

"I suppose Millwood might want another whore."

Jeena snarled and drew back her hand. Quinn caught her wrist. "Down, girl. She's only trying to get a rise out of you."

"Because she can't do anything else." Jeena lowered her hand. "Look at ye, in chains. Ye talk too much. Millwood will shut that mouth for ye."

"I may be in chains, but I'm freer than you'll ever be," Fi snapped.

Jeena snorted. "Ye tell yerself that when they're cutting ye open."

Fi would. She bloody well would.

Erryn patted the hat on her head when the stronghold's walls loomed in the distance. When Avere had insisted she wear the hat, Erryn had gone along with her. She had no idea what would happen when the wild folk who knew about her realized the Fallener was still alive. Her only certainty was that those with her would defend her, no matter what came. Renn was glued to her left side, Yanik to her right, and the rest of the wild folk with her would fight their own people. Toe's ankle was still healing, so he wouldn't be as deft in a fight. Still, he'd cut down as many as he could. Asha would appeal for calm. During the commotion, Avere would spirit Erryn away. That was the plan if those within the stronghold attacked them on sight.

Minutes later, Erryn breathed a little easier. Wild folk hunters hadn't rushed from the gates, but she could feel wary eyes upon her. An eerie silence surrounded them as they closed the distance to the gates, Erryn's view now blocked by those who'd encircled her. They passed over the threshold.

"Ye have returned." Lale's voice.

"Yes, we have." Asha.

"The Fallener is with ye."

"We have much to discuss. Our journey was not in vain. The Fallener is not a threat."

Silence, then, "Ye found the temple she spoke of." Zheir. Erryn wished those around her would move, so she could see what was happening.

"It was a temple to Zhikinden. We have much to tell ye."

"Then let us go and speak." Lale raised her voice. "Take the Fallener and the shamed to the pen."

"No," Asha said firmly.

"No?" Erryn could hear the surprise—and anger—in Lale's voice.

"The Fallener must be with us when we speak. And the shamed . . . I believe she should remain with the others."

"Why?"

"I'll explain that to ye when we speak."

"Then we will speak," Lale said, her voice hard. "Come."

Those in front of Erryn parted, in time for her to see Lale and Zheir's backs. Asha beckoned for Erryn, Avere, and Toe to go with her. Erryn guessed that she wanted Toe there to have one of her own people back up her words.

Inside the priestesses' hut, Lale whirled. "Why is the Fallener still with ye? Why have ye insisted that she enter our hut?"

"She is not who we thought she was," Asha said. "We found the temple, and inside it, we found Zhikinden."

Lale frowned and turned to Zheir, who looked equally perplexed.

"She appeared to us. She told us the Fallen are the Seven, and they have been bound to their beloveds, who take the form of the Fallen when they enter the physical plane. The Fallener is the only one who can free the other six, though Zhikinden did not name her Fallener. She named her the Called and Caller."

Two incredulous faces stared at them. Lale lunged at Asha and grabbed her robe. "What has the Fallener done to ye? Ye are corrupted. Ye—" One of Avere's daggers was suddenly at Lale's throat.

"Let her go," Avere said.

Toe slid his sword from its sheath and brandished it.

"Ye threaten us, Toetril?" Zheir said quietly. "Ye have turned against the Seven."

Avere pressed the dagger tip against Lale's skin. The priestess released Asha's robe and stepped back. "Ye are all corrupt," she spat.

Avere also stepped away, but her dagger remained in her hand. Toe didn't lower his sword.

Asha swallowed. "We are not corrupt, but I understand yer skepticism. If I hadn't been there myself, I would react the same. But we tell ye the truth. Zhikinden came to us and told us the Fallener is the Called and Caller. Zhikinden spoke to her, touched her. We must free the other Six."

Lale's eyes burned into Asha. Zheir drew a deep breath. "This goes against much of what we know."

"How do we know it?" Asha said. "Because we were told it by others, not by the Seven. What I just told ye about the Called and Caller was told to us by Zhikinden herself."

"Ye lie," Lale said.

"How can ye say ye believe, but refuse to believe? Are the Seven only tales to ye? If ye believe they truly exist, why can ye not believe we saw Zhikinden, and she spoke to us?" Asha spread her hands in a pleading gesture. "Where do ye think our teachings came from? They may have changed over the years, but ye taught me they came from the Seven when they walked the land. If they could walk the land then, why can't they do it now?"

"Ye are asking us to accept what we have never heard or read," Zheir said. "How can we know what Zhikinden said to ye? Ye claim the Fallener is not a threat, but if ye went to a temple that serves the Fallener, how can ye know she did not trick ye?"

"Maybe that's why she wanted to go to the temple," Lale said. Zheir nodded. "Maybe—"

"It's time to take off your hat, Erryn," Avere said. "Take it off. Show them."

Erryn pulled off her hat and lifted the bangs that partially covered her forehead.

"It cannot be," Zheir whispered. Lale remained silent, but she stared at Erryn's forehead.

"Zhikinden kissed it, and it was gone," Asha said. "I saw this with my own eyes. I listened to her with my own ears. She spoke . . ." Her voice faltered. She gathered herself, but her eyes were moist. "She spoke to me. She called me Young Mother."

"She speaks the truth," Toe said. "I was there too. I saw too."

Zheir approached Erryn. "May I?" Erryn nodded. Zheir's touch felt like any other. She ran her fingers along Erryn's forehead, as Erryn herself sometimes did to remind herself that it was true.

"We will listen to what Zhikinden said," Lale said.

"Well, that's awfully big of you." Avere sat cross-legged on a woven mat. The others followed suit.

As Asha recounted what had happened at the temple site and inside the temple itself, Zheir glanced Erryn's way several times. Lale focused only on Asha, but her mild tone when she asked questions conveyed her shock, rather than masking it. The fight was gone. Erryn felt bad for her, Renn's mother. She could see the resemblance, now that she was looking for it.

"And she named us as Erryn's protectors," Asha was saying. "Me, Avere, Toe, Yanik . . ." she looked pointedly at Lale ". . . and Renn. We are to see that no harm comes to the Called and Caller. We are to give our lives for her. I'm sure Zhikinden expects the same of all who know the truth."

"Ye have been commanding the Seven all this time," Zheir said to Erryn.

"I didn't know," Erryn replied. "But I always knew the Fallen were intelligent. I always felt love from them."

"Ye should not call them the Fallen now," Lale said.

Erryn bit back the retort that Lale was the last person who should be advising her about how to relate to the presences in her mind. "Zhikinden said I could, if it helps me. If I see them as the Six . . . I have to be able to command them. I don't think they care how I refer to them, to be honest."

Lale's stricken look said she clearly disagreed, but she kept the thought to herself.

"May I see the book?" Zheir asked.

Avere fished it from her bag and handed it to Zheir. The priestess opened it and flipped through its pages, with Lale looking over her shoulder. "I can't read this. Can ye?" Zheir asked Lale.

The older priestess shook her head.

"The scholars in Loring told us to show it to a primate," Avere said.

Lale tutted. "The Seven came to us first."

"Be that as it may, the book is written in a language our ancestors used," she said, glancing at Erryn. "Primates apparently study it. Though if the book speaks of Beast Masters being blessed and denies the existence of the Fallen, any primate will chase us out of the temple. If he's really irritated, he may call the guard on some trumped up accusations. We don't have any choice, though. We need someone who can read this. We have to decide whether to visit each of the Six's temples, or go to Darroth."

"Hopefully the book will tell us where the temple is in Darroth," Erryn said. "I don't know where it would be in the city, and I've been to a lot of temples." When the queen was still alive, the king had made a point of dragging his family, including Erryn, to services around the city, so he could be seen by the people—and as being pious. "I've never seen an altar anywhere that depicts one of the Seven with one of the Fallen, let alone seven of them."

"We might decide going to Darroth is the wrong choice. Our first step is to go to Stronghaven and hope to find a primate who won't chase us away or throw the book into the fire."

"I must go with them," Asha said, a tremor in her voice. Standing up to Lale and Zheir couldn't have been easy.

"There must be something we can do," Zheir said. "We'll send more hunters and scouts with ye."

Avere shook her head. "We don't want to attract attention. With the throne under contention, nobles are twitchy. We don't want to be seen as any type of force."

"We have to do something. We must help ye free the Six."

"Ye already have," Toe said, his sword now sheathed. "Ye marked us, which I know was difficult for ye, because of what ye—of what all of us—believed."

Asha nodded. "It's true. Ye have already done much. But ye can do more. Ye should make a copy of the maps in the book and record what we've told ye. Zhikinden said if Erryn falls, there won't be another Called and Caller for many years. If we fail to free the Six, our clan must be ready to aid the next Called and Caller. Our clan must know and pass down this story."

The other two priestesses murmured their agreement. "We will record what Zhikinden said, and yer journey to the temple," Zheir said. "We will teach it to everyone here."

Lale frowned. "They might not believe us. They didn't see her brand."

That was true. Erryn had kept her hat on the whole time she was here.

"Everyone who travelled with her will support our words." Zheir gazed at Erryn. "When will ye leave for Stronghaven?"

Apparently the priestess now viewed her as the leader, but it was Avere who answered, and Erryn didn't mind. "As soon as possible," the Ferret said. "We want a primate to read this book, and there may be letters there for me that will explain why the princess isn't on the throne. The reason could help us to decide whether to risk the Royal City."

"We can stay for a couple of days," Erryn said. "It's

important we be here to help them convince others about what happened to us."

Avere's face tightened. "That will only matter if we fail, and I have no intention of doing that. With your brand gone, we're in a better position than we were before."

Perhaps, but Erryn didn't share Avere's confidence. They'd have to choose between travelling around Daros, a lengthy journey fraught with many dangers, and entering the Royal City. Her brand was gone, but that wouldn't prevent an over-zealous guard or primate from throwing her into the dungeon.

"We will gather the family heads together and speak for ye," Zheir said. "Tomorrow. The sun has set and ye must be hungry. Eat with us."

Erryn would have preferred to eat with Renn, and wondered where she was and how the others were treating her. She wasn't worried about those who'd travelled to the temple with her. They hadn't embraced Renn, but after hearing Zhikinden had said her name, they no longer ignored her existence.

As if reading Erryn's mind, Lale said to Asha, "Why did ye speak up for the shamed? Why did ye go against us?"

"Because Zhikinden named her as one of Erryn's protectors. I don't know what that means. Perhaps she is still shamed, but Zhikinden did not treat her differently than any of us. And the Called and Caller favours her."

Lale's brows rose. "Why?"

Erryn squirmed. "She and Toe helped me when nobody else would. I never would have made it to the temple without them. I would have died long before getting anywhere near it." She gave Toe a quick smile. "We're friends now. I've never seen Renn as shamed, but then I don't belong to your clan."

Lale grunted. Erryn shot Avere a guarded look. Avere's attention was on Lale.

"Let us eat," Zheir said.

She prepared supper for them and served Erryn and the others herself. As they ate, the two priestesses asked more questions about the brief encounter with Zhikinden, wanting every detail. They would record what had taken place, and they were curious.

After the meal, Erryn rose to leave. "I will stay here," Asha said.

"We will find ye somewhere to stay," Zheir said to Erryn. "Ye will not be in the pen tonight." The regret in her voice was clear.

"You didn't know," Erryn said. And her time in the pen hadn't been unpleasant. "Don't worry about finding me somewhere to stay. I want to camp with the others."

"Are ye sure?"

"Yes." She wanted to find Renn and make sure she was okay. "Perhaps you'll come and eat breakfast with us," she said impulsively. Would they refuse to share a meal with the shamed, and hence with the Called and Caller?

"We will do so," Zheir said quickly. "Thank ye. Ye humble us."

Outside the hut, Avere turned to Erryn. "From reviled to revered. Your fortunes have certainly changed. If only everyone in Daros had been in that temple." She paused. "You haven't called them since the temple. You used to call them every morning. I always thought you were being reckless, but you should call them soon. Better to do it when you're not under pressure."

Erryn nodded, but the thought of summoning one of the Six tied her into knots.

"Maybe it's time to tell them," Erryn said, sitting with Renn in the tent they shared. "They don't know how to look at you now. If you tell them why you killed Ian, I'm sure they'll embrace you and declare that you're no longer shamed."

Renn stared into the mug she held brimming with a type of cider made by the wild folk. Erryn had taken one sip of hers and poured the rest on the ground outside the tent. It was stronger than anything she'd ever tasted at the many banquets she'd attended. She didn't understand how Renn could enjoy something so vile. She'd grown up with it, but still. "Why don't you want to tell them?"

"I lied to them."

"You were protecting someone."

"But I lied to the Mothers. It was only Lale and Zheir, then."

"Did you and Lale have a close relationship before then?" On the journey to and from the temple, Renn had revealed a bit more about her family. Her father had been killed while hunting when Renn was only two. She had no brothers or sisters, and Lale had been a priestess before she'd pledged to Renn's father. Mother and daughter were both strong-headed and stubborn.

Erryn would love to know more about her own

mother. She only knew what others called her—a whore who'd charmed Lord Fyler. "You don't fall in love with the wenches," she'd overheard one noble disdainfully say, when he'd explained to a noble from outside the Royal City why the king had taken a dead noble's child into his own family. "Fyler was always a sentimental fool. He should have done what we all do—paid the bitch off, or taken her to someone to get rid of it. Half the time they don't survive it. Problem solved."

Instead, the sentimental Lord Fyler had supported the wench and claimed the babe as his own. Not only that, he'd somehow persuaded the king to take responsibility for his bastard daughter when he'd known he was going to the Seven. Could the Seven have guided him to protect the babe who would later free Zhikinden from bondage? No, according to the goddess, they hadn't been in a position to do anything since being bound to their beloveds. Was Erryn being the Called and Caller happenstance, then? Perhaps the book would answer the question she wished she'd asked Zhikinden.

"We were close," Renn said, bringing Erryn back to their conversation. "Which meant it hurt her more. I disappointed her. I turned my back on her, or so she thinks. I did what I think she would have done. If Anasi could have proven what Ian did, the clan would have killed him. But she couldn't, and making her pledge to Ian would have punished her for no reason, and rewarded him. My mother would have done what I did."

"Then tell her."

"Anasi is still part of the clan. She has two children now. Jory believes they're both his."

"Tell her as her daughter. She doesn't have to announce it to everyone. What purpose would it serve? Ian's dead."

"If I'm to no longer be shamed, she has to explain why. So I'll remain shamed."

"They didn't put you in the pen."

"Because Asha spoke for me, and she spoke for me because ye spoke for me. And that's enough. This is no longer my home. When we leave, I won't be coming back."

That didn't sit well with Erryn. Did Renn want to run contracts for the rest of her life? What would she do when she was older? Erryn wouldn't ask, because they could both die trying to free the Six. "This could be your only chance to tell her why you did it. I'd think about—"

Someone pulled the tent flap open. Lale stepped into the tent. Erryn and Renn scrambled to their feet. "Excuse me for intruding, Called and Caller," Lale said.

"Call me Erryn. Please."

Lale inclined her head. "I was told this is Renn's tent. I would speak with my daughter."

Erryn didn't look at Renn. "I'll wait outside." She went to leave.

"Stay," Renn said.

Lale scowled. "I'm sure the Called—Erryn wishes to return to her own tent."

For a moment, Erryn considered playing along, but that would be silly. "This is my tent."

"I'm sorry. Asha brought me to this tent when I told her I wanted to speak to Renn."

"That's because it's Renn's tent, too. On the way to the temple we were the two outcasts, so we were told to share a tent. We've continued to do so."

Lale blinked at her, then glanced around. Her eyes settled on the two bedrolls spread next to each other. "I don't understand," she said, more to herself than to them.

Erryn looked to Renn, who shrugged. "What don't you understand?" Erryn said.

"I thought ye killed Ian because he rejected ye," Lale said to Renn.

Renn's eyes bulged. "Why would ye think such a thing?"

"Because ye were always together, ye and Ian and Anasi and Jory." The priestess's eyes briefly closed. "Ah. I see."

"Ye don't know anything," Renn snapped.

"Ye're right. I thought I understood why ye killed him, but now I don't. It would make more sense to me now if ye'd killed Jory."

Mother and daughter stared at each other, measuring each other up.

"Why don't you tell her?" Erryn said. "She knows half of it now, anyway."

Lale rounded on her. "She told ye?" She harrumphed. "Did she tell ye before or after Zhikinden named ye?"

Erryn shifted her weight. "Before."

Lale gave her an appraising look and turned back to Renn. "Ye grew close to someone we believed worked against the Seven." There was no condemnation in her voice.

Renn drained her mug, making Erryn grimace at the

remembered taste, and dropped the empty mug to the ground. "I did what Toe does. I believed my eyes and ears and trusted my own judgement."

"And I suppose ye trusted yer own judgement when ye slew Ian, rather than coming to me and Zheir."

Renn remained silent, defiance in her eyes.

"Will ye tell me now what happened?" Lale said.

"I can't."

"Ye don't have to be shamed anymore."

"I can't tell ye. If ye no longer want me to be shamed, ye'll have to tell the clan."

Lale's eyes narrowed. "Ye're protecting someone."

Two people. No, more. It wasn't only Anasi and Jory who would be hurt. Their children would be too, especially their eldest.

"Zhikinden named ye as one of Erryn's protectors," Lale said. "I believe the clan will accept ye back, if ye wish it."

Renn's chest rose and fell. Erryn could see the battle raging within her. Did Renn want to return to the clan? Erryn had said they had more pressing concerns to worry about than the future of their relationship, but in her heart, she didn't want to say good-bye to her. She hadn't given much thought to the future because she hadn't expected to have one, especially not one in which she could return to the Royal City. But first things first. They must survive.

"I have carried this weight with me, begged for food, lived in rags, because ye shamed me," Renn said. "Toe saved me. He gave me a life. I don't know if I could come back here and live. Not with those who turned their backs on me so quickly."

Lale's mouth set. "Ye wouldn't tell us why."

"I did what I had to do."

"But ye won't explain yerself now?"

Renn shook her head.

"Will ye explain it to yer mother? So I would know why. I won't tell anyone."

Renn slowly exhaled, then dipped her head. Erryn wanted to go to her, but she wasn't sure if Renn would want that, with Lale here. The priestess relieved Erryn of making a decision by going to Renn herself and touching her shoulder. "I want to know why. Ye disappointed me because ye wouldn't tell me. I thought ye killed him because ye were lovesick, and I thought I'd raised ye to be stronger than that. I've carried pain too, the pain that my daughter didn't trust me."

"Ye were asking me as one of the Mothers," Renn said, her head still lowered and her voice barely a whisper.

"I asked ye privately."

"Ye would have told. The clan wanted a reason. Do ye deny that ye would have told?"

Lale took a moment to answer. "No."

"How can I be sure ye won't do the same now?"

"Because years have passed. We aren't judging ye, and I've missed ye. I've always wished I knew why. If ye're going to leave and never come back, tell me why. I want to understand. Tell me."

Erryn ducked out of the tent, certain that neither woman would notice. The wild folk she'd travelled with had all returned to their huts, except for Yanik. And Toe, who no longer had a place within the stronghold he called his own. The outsiders, as Erryn thought of herself, Avere, Toe, and Renn, had camped not too far within the stronghold's walls.

Yanik and Toe sat in front of the fire Yanik had built. He beckoned to her. She squared her shoulders and went over to him.

"When ye and the Mothers meet with the heads tomorrow, we don't know what will happen when they tell them ye're a Fallener. The Mothers know we'll all be there, all who travelled with ye."

"Will ye call them . . . the Fallen . . . at the gathering of the heads?" Toe asked.

Hopefully not. "Only if I have to, and only to prove I'm the Fallener. Do you think they'll believe Asha?"

"All the Mothers saw yer brand and now see that it's gone. Asha was at the temple. So was I. So was Yanik. Let us protect ye until everyone calms down. Don't call them."

"You sound like you're expecting trouble," Erryn said.

"I'm not. All the Mothers will vouch for ye. But it would be best if ye showed restraint."

So they wouldn't think she was an animal? "Don't worry. Unless I fear for my life, I won't call them."

She lowered herself to the ground and made conversation with Toe and Yanik until Lale emerged from her tent. Lale folded her arms. Erryn leaped to her feet and went over to her. "Did she tell you?"

Lale's expression was unreadable. "She did."

"Are you going to tell anyone?" Shock stabbed through Erryn when Lale's eyes teared up.

"No. But if she doesn't fall helping ye, I will do everything I can to bring her back into the clan." Lale's eyes raked Erryn from head to foot. "If she wants to come back." The priestess drew a deep breath and strode away.

Erryn stepped into the tent. Renn sat cross-legged on the ground. Her shoulders were stiff, but she met Erryn's eyes. It was clear that tears had been shed. "Are you all right?"

Renn nodded.

Erryn wanted to ask whether Renn would go back to the clan if she was no longer shamed, but she sat next to her and pulled her into a hug. She'd ask the difficult questions when the answers would mean something.

Arrick strode into the Ferret base's dining room and took the seat at the head of the table. Anticipation was in the air. The Ferrets he'd summoned to this meeting waited for him to speak. He clasped his hands on the table. "Does anyone have anything to report? Any sightings?"

His jaw clenched when everyone shook their head or murmured a no. Where was Avere? He normally didn't ask his people to report to him in person, and certainly not as a group. But he'd tasked these Ferrets with watching every approach to Darroth. They were to kill the Beast Master on sight and bring Avere to him, if she was with her. If she wasn't . . . Arrick couldn't bear to think about it. "Have the Westerfox primates left the city?"

"No, sir."

He'd already checked with the Ferrets who weren't here, the ones currently keeping watch. "I brought you here to remind you how important it is that we find the Beast Master and protect one of our own. You all know to send word the moment you spot the Beast Master, Avere, or a Westerfox primate. The future of Daros depends on your diligence." They were expecting more, but he'd called them here so he could look into their eyes and impress upon them that they must not fail in their tasks. "That's all. You can collect your wages on the way out."

His people silently filed from the room. Arrick stared at the empty table. He never should have sent Avere after the heathen. But at the time, he hadn't known the king would be assassinated and he'd desperately want her here.

He rose and threw a log onto the sputtering fire. He should remain detached and not worry about her, but he'd never managed to see his people as expendable. And when it came to Avere . . . he should have trained her to do something else. He'd always feared that one day it would happen, that she'd leave the base to do a job, and never return. He should have—

Jack burst into the room. "Message from Stronghaven, sir. You said to bring any to you right away."

Arrick's heart leaped. "Give it here." He snatched it from Jack and quickly broke the seal. It only took a minute to mentally decode the short missive. *Rumours that Lyos traitor captured. Travelling merchant ran into slaver with big mouth. Lord Millwood to claim her.* Arrick stared at the words.

"Are you all right, sir?" Jack asked.

He sank into the chair he'd just vacated. It was unravelling. Avere was missing. If the rumours were true, the princess would never claim the throne. He hadn't heard from Enkelo for too long. Cedric was alive, but caution meant his gathering of allies was slow. The Primacy was in charge. If Arrick's role in the princess's escape came to light ... His fate lay in her hands. She'd be interrogated and tortured. Would she divulge his name?

He steeled himself. It wasn't over yet. The Lyos dynasty may have come to an end, but while he still lived, someone would be working to expose the Primacy's role in the assassinations. The best thing the princess could do for Daros now was to keep her mouth shut.

Fi jumped off the wagon and almost crumpled to the ground. The wagons had rumbled out of camp early that morning and only stopped once. Her legs felt like jelly. The sun was already setting, casting shadows on the path that led to the manor house on the Millwood estate. Devon, the bald man who'd called her a little pig on the night the slavers had captured her, was swaggering up the path with Quinn. Fi glanced around and noticed the rest of the camp hadn't come with them. The women in the cage, the other men . . . they'd stayed behind. Did Millwood know he was dealing with slavers? Days ago, she'd overheard one of the men say a message had been sent ahead to Millwood. Who had they said they were? Bounty hunters?

Telling Millwood the truth would earn Fi nothing but

a slap. Millwood might not care, anyway. The disgraced princess, the Lyos traitor, was about to become his property. He'd march her into Stronghaven and through all the villages and cities between it and Darroth, showing off his prize. A sick feeling formed in the pit of her stomach. She'd hated being held captive by these men and Jeena, but she'd been safe. Now she didn't know what to expect.

Devon and Quinn had reached the entrance and disappeared inside the manor. Jeena grabbed a handful of Fi's hair and twisted it, making Fi cry out. "If Lord Millwood comes to see ye, ye'll keep quiet, ye understand."

Fi grunted. Her scalp burned. Tears sprang to her eyes. When Jeena finally let go, Fi squeezed her eyes shut, determined not to let a tear escape. She opened them when she heard approaching footsteps. Devon and Quinn were returning with a third man. The ring on the man's left pinkie finger and the cut of his clothes told Fi that Millwood himself was coming to see her. She didn't recognize him, even though she must have met him at some point. Two guards trailed after the three men.

Jeena pushed Fi to the ground. A stone on the path dug into her right knee. She bit her lip, but she would not lower her head.

Millwood and the others stopped in front of her. "So this is the Lyos traitor. I remember her. She looked prettier back then. And cleaner." Devon and Quinn guffawed. "To think my father once asked the king to grant me her hand in marriage. It could have been me on the rack, had she bewitched me as she did her unfortunate betrothed."

"A narrow escape, my lord," Devon said.

"And one I welcomed. I married for love instead."

Devon leered. "That doesn't mean you can't have a taste of what your father wanted for you."

Millwood's face tightened. "I am a pious man, and if I wasn't, I wouldn't touch such filth. You said you and your men hadn't spoiled her."

"We thought the Primacy would pay more if she was still pure, but we're only common men."

"No, I think you're right." Millwood smiled. "And I'm going to ask for quite a high price, indeed." He glanced over his shoulder at the two guards. "How did you manage to keep your men in line? I'm sure there were some who wanted to lie with her."

Devon jutted his chin toward Jeena. "She guarded her."

Millwood's eyes narrowed. "How much do you want for her?"

Jeena stiffened. "I'm not for—"

"Quiet, wench!" Devon scratched his cheek. "She's a wild woman, in more ways than one. They don't come cheap."

Millwood pulled a coin purse off his belt and tossed it to Devon. "Will this do?"

Devon loosened the string and peered inside. Quinn did the same. Their eyes widened. "We have a deal," Devon said.

"No, ye can't. Ye—"

Millwood backhanded Jeena across the mouth, making her stumble back a step. "You're mine now, woman. You don't speak unless I say you can speak. You're going to guard the traitor day and night. Your only purpose in life from this point forward is to make sure none of my men touch her. You have permission to kill anyone who tries. Do you understand?"

Jeena nodded. Millwood inclined his head to Devon and Quinn. "Our business is concluded." He turned to his guards. "Find a sword for the wild woman and put them both into the same cell." With one last disdainful look at Fi, Millwood whirled and strode up the path.

Jeena gingerly touched her bleeding lip. "Why have ye done this to me? I was loyal to ye." she said to Devon.

He jangled the coin purse. "I didn't let you go cheaply, darlin'. You can take pride in that. And let's face it, things were getting old. We both need a change." His eyes flicked to Fi. "Don't worry, once the little pig is dead and there's no one to guard, I'm sure Millwood will give you to his men. You'll still be wanted." He slapped a grinning Quinn on the back. The two men trudged back to the wagon.

Jeena took a step in that direction. One of the guards grabbed her arm. "Where do you think you're going? You heard the lord. Get her on her feet and come with us." The other guard rested his hand on the hilt of his sword.

Jeena's mouth pressed into a thin line. She grasped Fi's arm and hauled her to her feet, her fingers digging into Fi's skin. "Walk," she barked.

Fi didn't resist. Jeena would take Devon's betrayal out on her, but she couldn't help feeling sorry for the wild woman.

With one guard leading them and the other taking up the rear, they walked to the rear of the manor, continued down another path, and eventually approached a square stone building. The only window was barred. The dungeon. This would be where Millwood locked up criminals his guards arrested until they were moved to Stronghaven.

When they entered the dungeon, Fi's nose wrinkled at the scent of urine and stale sweat. *Charming.* There were only two cells. The lead guard ushered them into the one on the right, then swung the door shut behind them and locked it. "I'll stay here while you fetch her a sword," he said.

Jeena let Fi go with a shove. Fi stumbled, but she managed not to fall. She went to the back of the cell and sank to the stone floor. Jeena paced. She flexed her fingers. Fi glanced at the guard standing outside the cell. Anything she said would echo in here, so she waited until Jeena was walking right past her. "Don't do it," she whispered. "You won't make it very far."

"What did ye say?" Jeena bellowed.

The guard outside peered into the cell. *Stupid woman.* Fi should let Jeena get herself killed, but then there would be nobody to keep Millwood's men off her. "I said, look at you now, caged like me. You were always worthless to Devon and the others."

As she'd expected, Jeena crouched in front of her and grabbed her chin—tight. "Shut yer mouth. I'm not like ye. I didn't kill my own father."

"Don't try to cut down the guards," Fi whispered. "Even if you manage to do it, you won't get very far. Millwood would see it as a personal insult and hunt you down."

Jeena's eyes bored into Fi's. She abruptly let Fi's chin go and stood. They waited in silence for the other guard to return. It wasn't long before he marched into the dungeon, his boots ringing on the stone. He approached the cell and dropped a sword through the bars. It hit the floor with a loud clang, making Fi wince.

The guards left, swinging the thick metal door to the dungeon closed behind them, which cut off most of the light coming from the sun. Once it had set, she and Jeena would be sitting in the dark until dawn came. Jeena picked up the sword and turned it around in her hand. Her eyes glinted. She brought the tip of the sword to Fi's neck.

Keeping her voice even, Fi said, "Don't bother. Killing me will only lead to you hanging in Stronghaven, and after Millwood's men have done whatever they want with you. You're not going to hurt me."

Jeena's cheek twitched. Her knuckles grew white. Then she lowered the sword and turned her back on Fi.

"If you want to get away, do it when we're in Stronghaven, where you'll have a chance of losing yourself in the back alleys."

Jeena snorted. "What would ye know about it?"

"I was hiding from the guard before you captured me. And I've lived in a city all my life."

"In a palace."

"A castle, actually, but that doesn't matter now." She was in a cell with a wild woman who hated her, and she'd spend who knew how many nights sleeping on stone.

There was only one filthy pile of hay, and even if there were two, she wouldn't touch either of them.

Jeena sat cross-legged, her back still to Fi, and rested the sword across her legs. Fi could see the protruding hilt and tip. She inched backwards until her back hit the wall. Shadows encroached, snuffing out the sun. Fi's stomach grumbled. She closed her eyes, hoping to fall asleep and wake to the sound of the guard bringing them something to eat for breakfast. She was dozing off when a noise intruded on her infant dream. It sounded like . . . gasping. Her eyes flew open. She stared into the darkness and listened. Quick breaths. Gulping. She was about to ask Jeena if she was all right, when it hit her. Tears. Anguish. Jeena was weeping.

Fi hugged her knees to her chest, rested her head on them, and closed her eyes again.

Erryn ducked into her and Renn's tent and flopped onto a mat. "I'm glad that's over," she said to Renn, who hadn't attended the gathering.

Sitting on her bedroll, Renn looked up at her. "They accepted it. They grumbled, but they listened to the Mothers."

Erryn should have known. "You watched."

"Ye may have needed my help."

Fortunately, she hadn't needed Renn to rush in and save her from a mob. As Asha had recounted their trip to the temple and the reason they'd gone in the first place— she'd dramatically revealed that Erryn was a Fallener just before the point when she'd summoned Zayvang to stand on the altar—there had been rumblings of disbelief, and someone shouted the accusation that Asha was young and easily misled. But everyone respected the Mothers. Based on Lale and Zheir's words, and the corroboration of Yanik and the other wild folk who'd seen Erryn's brand and could vouch that it had existed, the family heads had come around and accepted the story.

The discussion had turned to what the clan should do. Some wanted all the hunters and warriors to go with Erryn to Stronghaven and then to whichever temple they'd visit next, but Avere had insisted that smaller numbers would be to their advantage, and Erryn had agreed with her. The priestesses had convinced their people a small group would be best. Only Asha, Renn, Toe, Yanik, the scout Timor, and the hunter Var would go with the two city folk. The rest of the Snowlake clan would ensure the truth about the Fallen and the story of what had happened in the temple was passed from generation to generation. If necessary, the clan would await the next Called and Caller.

That didn't mean everyone accepted Erryn with open arms, but when Zheir had ended the gathering, Erryn had endured many hands touching her forehead. Large, small, pudgy, bony, gentle, and light fingers, all wanting to touch where Zhikinden had touched. She'd borne their curiosity and awe with good humour.

"I have something for ye," Renn said.

Erryn propped herself up on her elbow. "What?"

Renn reached behind her, then lifted her hand. A necklace dangled from her fingers. "When I was banished,

I left the stronghold with my clothes and the sword on my back. I didn't know what happened to everything else."

"Did Lale keep everything?" Erryn asked, her eyes on the necklace.

"Not everything. What she knew was important to me. Including this. I made it." She handed it to Erryn. "I want ye to have it."

Erryn took it from her and examined the jewelry crafted from iron. Four animals hung from the chain: a bear, a fox, a rabbit, and a hawk.

"If I'd known, there'd be seven."

"No, it's beautiful." She looked up at Renn. "I didn't know you made jewelry."

"Running contracts . . . there's never time, and I'd have to borrow tools. I wouldn't want to be carting any around with me." She gazed at the necklace. "Are ye going to put it on?"

Erryn sat up and slipped the necklace over her head. She looked down at it and lifted each animal one by one. She wasn't one for jewelry, but this was different. There were no pearls, no glittering gems. "I love it."

"It suits ye."

"Thank you." She reached for Renn, held her close and savoured the peace that always came when they were in each other's arms. Someone pulled the tent flap aside. Her heart hammering in her chest, Erryn quickly let Renn go, then blew out a sigh of relief.

Avere gazed at them, her expression smooth. "Everyone's at the fire. We have to figure out what we need for our journey back to Stronghaven."

This time, the wild folk—no, Northerners. Erryn was determined not to use "wild folk" anymore. They were Northerners, and this time, Yanik, Timor, and Var would be her protectors, not her guards. Soon after dawn, they'd sling bags over their shoulders, receive a blessing from Lale and Zheir, and walk through the gates of the stronghold, perhaps for the last time.

Friends Reunited

Fi walked the perimeter of the small cell while Jeena sat sullenly watching her, the sword across her legs, as usual. The wild woman's hands were free. Fi's had remained shackled since arriving at the estate, which had been two days ago. What was Millwood waiting for? She would have thought he'd be eager to ride into Stronghaven and show off the traitor. At least they were being fed, if one could call the scraps a guard brought twice a day food.

"How long will it take us to get to Stronghaven?" she asked, not sure Jeena would answer her.

"Less than a week," Jeena said flatly.

"I wonder if you'll travel with us all the way to the Royal City." Would Fi see Otane? The thought made her jaw clench. She'd be humiliated and scorned by a hypocrite she was convinced had ordered the assassinations of Father, Henrick, and Surann, and had tortured Viren for no reason.

"I don't care about yer fancy city."

"I didn't say you'd care."

"The people there will cut ye up and hang ye. I don't care about kings and queens, but ye murdered yer own father."

Fi stopped walking and turned to face Jeena. "Not that it will matter, but I didn't do it."

Jeena snorted.

"I didn't! What purpose would I have for proclaiming my innocence to you? You certainly aren't in a position to sway anyone who matters. You're right. I'll be tortured and hung. But I didn't kill my father, or my brother and his wife. I loved them all very much." A tremor crept into her voice. She drew a shuddering breath.

"They wouldn't arrest a princess unless they knew for sure."

"Don't be so naïve." Like she'd been. "You've been betrayed by people you trusted. So have I. Coin and power. That's what it's all about. At least I know what will happen to me. Who knows what will happen to you?"

Jeena snorted again, but she avoided Fi's eyes. "Ye sound like ye don't care that ye'll hang."

She did, and she didn't. She cared because it frightened her. She didn't because everyone she cared about was gone, and likely dead. If any lived, they'd risked their lives for a futile cause. Were they searching for her, still hoping to put her on the throne . . . or because they cared about her? If she could, she'd tell them to forget about her and salvage a life for themselves in hiding. Dann, Erryn, Enkelo, Viren, her family . . . all gone. All condemned.

"I've had time to get used to the idea," she said to Jeena. And to go back and forth between wanting to harden her heart so she could bear the pain, and wanting it to remain raw, because those she loved deserved it, and she didn't want everyone who called her names and spat on her to take that away from them, or her.

The thick door to the dungeon swung open. Jeena leaped to her feet and brandished the sword. Fi stood behind her.

Two guards marched in, their armour clinking. One smirked at Jeena. "Easy, woman. We're here because you're leaving, not because we want to disobey the lord. We have standards. We wouldn't touch a traitor. Give me the sword."

Jeena hesitated, then turned the sword around and offered it to the guard through the bars. The other guard pulled out a key and unlocked the cell. "Come on," he growled.

Fi trailed after Jeena. When she stepped outside, she slowed down to savour the fresh air, not caring about the light drizzle. The guard who'd taken the sword shoved her from behind. She stumbled forward, almost grabbing Jeena for balance. But she managed to keep her footing on her own.

They trudged to the front of the manor and down the same path they'd walked when the slavers had given them to Millwood. A group of guards and several wagons stood in a line. Millwood sat atop a magnificent stallion, his standard flapping in the breeze. The guard who'd taken the sword from Jeena led them to an uncovered wagon. If the skies opened, Fi would be soaked, not that anyone would care. Millwood wanted to show off his prize, the reason for the wooden pole secured to the back of the wagon. The guard motioned for Fi to stand with her back pressed against the pole. Her hands were pulled behind her and bound to the rough wood. This was it. The beginning of the end.

Jeena sat in the wagon and looked up at her, then away. Fi stared at a withered flower bush, listened to the shouted orders, and watched servants scurrying from the manor with the last of the supplies they'd load onto another wagon. The one she was on lurched forward. Her arms were already sore, and she'd be in this position for hours every day until they reached the Royal City, where the Primacy would put her out of her misery.

Erryn wiped imaginary sweat off her brow and took a deep breath. Her stomach churned. She could feel the eyes of the others upon her. It didn't help that Avere, Renn, Toe, and Yanik were kneeling. What would they do when Erryn called the Fallen to fight? Drop their weapons and fall to their knees? *Focus.* She had to do it. They'd been on the road for almost a week, and she hadn't called them. This morning, Avere had insisted.

"What's the matter?" Avere hissed.

Erryn could hear the irritation in her voice. "Nothing."

"Zhikinden said they want to be called. They want to be free. You're doing it because you want to free them. She said—"

Lerxis, come.

The air shimmered. The dire wolf leaped into existence and gracefully landed on her four feet. She came to Erryn and sat in front of her.

Erryn reached out her hand, snatched it back, then reached out again and touched Lerxis's—Lleor's—no, Lerxis's head. She had to think of them as she had before, otherwise she wouldn't be able to command them. As it was, she was as taut as a drawn bowstring. *I missed you.* Warmth. Love. Erryn dropped to her knees and threw her arms around the wolf's neck. *I'll do all I can to free you,* she said, sure now that the Fallen could understand every word she uttered. If only they could talk back to her and tell her what the book said.

She savoured her connection with Lerxis a moment more, then shifted her gaze to the others. "You should stand. You could be fighting alongside the Fallen. You can't gape all the time."

They exchanged glances, then stood, their attention back on Lerxis. Erryn motioned for everyone to remain where they were. *Zayvang, come.* The saber-tooth cat entered the physical plane. At a glance, she looked the same. But her eyes were different. Someone else now inhabited Zayvang's form—the one whose form it was. Erryn sensed friendship, curiosity, gratefulness. *I won't call you unless I need to,* she said, suddenly wondering if she'd angered Zhikinden by calling the goddess's beloved when she wasn't in danger. *I wanted some time with you when it's calm.*

The cat gazed impassively at her. Erryn ruffled Zayvang's fur and didn't sense disapproval. Still, she didn't want to keep her long. *Return.* The cat disappeared.

Erryn gazed at Lerxis. *I'll free you, or die trying.* The weight of responsibility on her shoulders took her breath away. Every person, every creature, every plant, insect, stream... Daros *was* dying. She'd lost count of how many times she'd stepped around an animal carcass with its ribs protruding through its dull fur, and the few beasts she'd managed to glimpse before they ran away were more bone than flesh. There were also fewer herbs to pick, fewer berries on the bushes. Erryn and the others relied on the food in their bags more than they had in the south.

Death. It was all around them. If she didn't complete the task Zhikinden had set before her, there would be nothing left in the north, and Death would continue marching southward, swallowing everything in its wake.

Lerxis still sat obediently before Erryn. *Thank you. Return.* A dull ache radiated through her chest. She wouldn't call the others. It was even more painful to dismiss them now, knowing they were bound in the heavens. She didn't understand how, or why; she only understood that she could free them.

Erryn tried not to hunch her shoulders as she walked through one of Stronghaven's gates without her hat on. The guards were looking for a woman who covered her forehead and travelled alone. She was surrounded by Northerners, another reason the guards wouldn't give her a second look. But inside the gates, one guard's eyes narrowed and he approached the group, motioning for them to stop.

"You there," he said, pointing to Erryn. "Step forward."

Erryn sensed those around her tense and suspected a few had moved their hands closer to their weapons. She moved past Avere and Asha and stood in front of the guard. He studied her, then leaned in to look at her forehead. His breath stank of garlic. "Move along," he snapped, making her jump. She rejoined the others and let out her pent breath when the guard returned to his post.

"I need to check in with my people." Avere gestured at Renn. "I don't think you should stay at your usual rooming house. The guard might have figured out where you and Erryn were staying when you were last here. I'm sure someone at the base will know somewhere safe and discreet." She surveyed those they were with. "You all need to stick together and keep an eye on Erryn."

"Let's go to your base, then," Erryn said. "We'll wait outside."

"This way." Avere took up the lead. Asha fell into step with her and swivelled her head from side to side as she took in the stone buildings and shop fronts. Erryn couldn't wait to fall asleep in an actual bed. How long had it been? Fortunately the journey to Stronghaven had been uneventful. They'd only skirmished with one group of hunters, who'd quickly run off when one of Avere's daggers thudded into the leader's throat. Others had given them a wide berth. They were still marked. Before they'd left the stronghold, Lale had refreshed the faded ink. Now that they were in Stronghaven, Erryn would wash hers off and expected the others to do the same. The marks on their cheeks wouldn't stop guards from cutting them down.

She moved aside to let a woman and her two children hurry by and was struck by how foreign the city felt. The city folk wore clothing she'd see in the Royal City and the architecture had its roots in Darroth, but she still felt out of place.

They entered one of the numerous town squares. Erryn's eyes wandered to the public board standing— She sucked in her breath and broke away from the others so she could have a closer look, ignoring the alarmed exclamations from her protectors. The sketch hanging on the board was definitely Fi. Erryn read the words printed underneath Fi's likeness.

Filmona, formerly the princess, wanted for treason and murder. Any information leading to the traitor's arrest will be handsomely rewarded.

Shit! She read it again, and then a third time. Fi, wanted for treason and murder?

Avere stepped to her side and read the notice. "Now we know why she's not on the throne."

"There must be some misunderstanding. Treason? Murder?"

"Put those two together and we know who she's accused of killing. The king. The prince."

Erryn gaped. "They think Fi killed her father and brother? There's no way."

Avere shot her a warning look. Fortunately nobody nearby gave any indication of having overheard. Erryn lowered her voice. "Fi would never kill them. It doesn't make sense."

"Are you sure? If she'd managed to do it without drawing suspicion, she'd be on the throne."

"Fi had no interest in ruling, and certainly not if it meant murdering the king."

"What about her betrothed?"

"I didn't know him very well, but I know Fi. She wouldn't agree to any plot against her father."

"Perhaps she was inadvertently caught in someone else's game, then. There's probably a letter waiting for me that explains what happened."

"Let's get to your base, then," Erryn said, now eager to go.

They returned to the others and set off again. Many more guards patrolled the city than the last time they were here. Were they looking for her, or Fi? Murder? Treason? It couldn't be true. If they caught Fi, they'd hang her. Erryn gasped at the thought, turning Renn's head.

"Are ye all right?" Renn asked.

"Fi is in trouble. They think she was involved in the king's assassination."

"Could it be true?"

"No!"

Renn opened her mouth, then closed it. Erryn wanted to say more, but not here. To keep her mind off Fi, she played a mental game with herself, counting the number of people with green dresses or tunics. Where was Fi? Was anyone helping her? Oh, there was another green tunic. That made six so far.

"Here we are," Avere said, just as Erryn was tiring of her game. They stopped outside a two-storey stone building with a sign outside that read *R.L. Denton and Sons*.

"What are R.L. and his sons supposed to do?" Erryn asked.

"Arrange trade deals between merchants in different towns, I think. Someone mans a little counter and tells whoever comes in that regrettably they're unable to handle their business at the present time. Now, you wait out here. It shouldn't take me longer than ten or fifteen minutes to catch up on things and collect any letters." Avere glanced around, then pointed. "Go into that tavern. You'll draw suspicion if you hang around outside." She bounded up the stone steps and disappeared inside the building.

Erryn and the others went into the tavern. When many of the Northerners ordered the weakest ale, the barkeep shook his head but went to the appropriate barrel. They pushed two empty tables together, took the weight off their weary feet, and waited for Avere.

Avere strode past the counter and into the base's common room. Billy sat at a square wooden table, buttering a piece of bread. A plate of meat and cheese sat in front of him. Avere's mouth watered, but she'd eat with the others. Billy rarely ventured into the field these days; he was more a clerk than anything else, but even though his head was lowered as Avere approached him, he didn't jump when she spoke.

"How have you been keeping, Billy?"

He lifted his head. There was no surprise in his eyes. "You're back, mistress." He beckoned to someone. A man Avere had seen at the base once before came over to them. "Look who's back," Billy said. "We'd wondered what had happened to you."

"We did," the other man said. He nodded to her and slinked away.

"I've been busy," Avere said. "Are there any letters for me?"

Billy's head bobbed. "Let me finish my lunch first."

Avere inwardly sighed and pulled out a chair. "What do you know about the king's assassination? I saw a wanted poster for the princess."

"You don't know? You *have* been away." Billy put down the knife and bit into his bread.

Avere waited patiently for him to finish chewing, though she tapped her foot under the table.

"She and her betrothed killed them all. The king, the prince, the princess, two or three primates . . ."

For what reason? Had she hoped to get away with it and take the throne?

"They caught her right away, but she escaped. She had help. The royal primate and some guard."

Enkelo, the snake who'd sat in Arrick's study asking for Erryn's head, had thrown in with the princess? He must have thought she had a chance and would reward him with the grand primate's mitre. "Who's on the throne?"

"The Primacy."

"The Primacy?" Why was it occupying itself with ruling?

"Well, they're acting regent," Billy said. "Not that they're doing much except putting up wanted posters. They only took over because the only Lyos alive is a traitor."

Naïve man.

"They need to take that wanted poster down. The one for the princess—the Lyos traitor."

"Why?" Her fingers twitched when Billy took another bite of his bread and popped a bit of cheese into his mouth. At this rate, the sun would set before she got back to Erryn and the others.

He finally swallowed. "They got her. Millwood's bringing her here, to show her off, I expect. Then he's taking her to the Royal City and delivering her to the Primacy. He's after the throne now. Maybe they'll give it to him."

Millwood, one of the local nobles. "So he's bringing her here, to Stronghaven?" Avere asked, her wheels turning.

His mouth full again, Billy nodded.

Erryn would insist they rescue her, which would be foolhardy. They had to remain focused on what Zhikinden had directed them to do. Avere considered keeping the information to herself, but news like this travelled fast. Erryn was bound to find out. She might have already overheard someone talking about it in the tavern. Avere didn't want to lose her trust. "Was the former royal primate captured, too?"

Billy shook his head. "Nobody knows where he is." He popped another piece of cheese into his mouth.

"Can you chew quicker, Billy? I have things to do."

Billy brushed a couple of crumbs from the corner of his mouth. They landed on his shirt, making Avere wonder why he'd bothered. "I'll finish my lunch later. Come on, then. I locked them in one of the storage rooms upstairs, for safekeeping."

"Did you read them?"

Billy's eyes widened. "Would I do that?"

Yes, he would, and deftly reseal them. Arrick would have been careful with his words. She followed Billy up the stairs, eager to read the letters and find out whether the princess truly had killed her father. Surely Arrick would know by now.

Billy pulled a ring of keys from his pocket and unlocked the second door on the left from the stairs. "They're in here," he said, stepping inside.

The moment Avere crossed the threshold and entered the dark room, her skin prickled. She whirled. Two Ferrets blocked her way to the door. Her hands were grabbed from behind. Shackles were snapped onto her wrists. "What's the meaning of this?" Avere spat, as angry with herself as she was with them.

Billy grimaced. "I'm sorry, mistress, but I have to do this." He searched her and relieved her of her daggers, including the ones strapped to her calves, the one up her right sleeve, and the one strapped behind her left shoulder. Next, he found her lockpicks, including the one inside her left sleeve. They'd both learned from the same master.

"When the spymaster hears about this, he won't be pleased," Avere said.

"We're doing this because the spymaster ordered it," Billy said.

She quickly masked her shock. Arrick had ordered them to treat her like a common thief? She was a thief, but not a common one!

Billy unhooked everything hanging from her belt. "We're to take you back to the Royal City."

"You could at least take the bag off my back," Avere said, knowing he'd have to unshackle her wrists to remove it. She might be able to grab one of the daggers he'd set atop a crate in the corner before the two Ferrets at the door could stop her.

"I suppose I could."

Avere prepared to spring. Billy went behind her. She felt a slight tug, then the weight on her back lessened. Her bag thudded to the floor. Billy came into view again, holding her bag—with its straps cut.

"I like that bag!"

Billy shrugged.

"Billy, there will come a time when I'm not in these shackles and we cross paths . . .""You won't kill me. The spymaster won't allow it."

"Perhaps not, but you have bits I can cut off."

He froze for a second, then plunked her bag on top of another crate and flipped it open.

"You're making a terrible mistake," she said. "I'm on important business." For Zhikinden.

"You can tell it to the spymaster," Billy said calmly.

Avere held her breath when he examined the books, Malina's and the one from the temple. "I'd better get everything back, including my daggers."

"You will." He flipped through the books, then put them aside. All he cared about was whether she'd hidden anything among the pages. Avere seethed as he pulled out each item from her bag and examined it. When he was finished, he put everything back into her bag, and carefully placed each dagger and book inside it, too.

He tucked the bag under his arm. "We'll keep it safe, don't you worry. You'll leave for the Royal City in an hour or so. Until then, there will be someone outside this door." He motioned for the other Ferrets to follow him outside and locked the door behind him.

Cursing herself, Avere turned in a circle and surveyed the dim room. One window, but crates were stacked in front of it, allowing only a sliver of light into the room. She went to the door and examined the lock as best she could in the shadows. Fiddlesticks. Even if she had a lockpick and her hands weren't shackled, she wouldn't be able to pick this lock from inside. She continued to search the room with her eyes, but didn't find anything that would help her escape. The crates were too heavy to move, and she suspected the window would be barred. She was trapped, by her own stupidity. She'd sat there chatting with Billy, who'd delayed her long enough for the others to set their snare. If Erryn and the others didn't realize she was in trouble, she'd be on the way to the Royal City—with Zhikinden's book.

Fi tried to ignore her thudding headache and burning throat, but the pain was too great. She lowered her head and closed her eyes. Usually she kept her chin up despite the pain, not wanting to give anyone the satisfaction of seeing her suffering, but when Millwood and his men finished their meal, she'd be bound to the pole again. The afternoon sun would beat down on her, and if they passed through any villages, people would shout and point and call her names. One or two would throw fruit. Most missed because the wagon was moving, but a few apples had found their mark. She had bruises on her arms and legs to prove it, but no bumps on her head. Her headache was due to hunger and thirst. They only fed her at night. The rest of the day she had no food and water. By the time they hung her, she'd be so thin the drop might not break her neck. She could hang there for hours, with everyone watching and cheering her on to the Seven, a prospect that kept her awake at night. Not going to the Seven, but dying slowly, in agony, struggling for breath.

The wagon jostled, making her head ache more. Someone grasped her shoulder. Fi lifted her head and opened her eyes.

"Here." Jeena lifted a mug to Fi's mouth and poured. Half the water ended up mingling with the sweat on her dirty shirt before she managed to suck some into her mouth.

"Hurry," Jeena snapped, glancing over her shoulder.

After Fi had gulped down two more mouthfuls, Jeena yanked the mug away and leaped off the wagon.

If her lips weren't moist and her throat soothed, Fi would have wondered if she'd dreamed it. She quickly lowered her head, not wanting her gaze to draw attention to Jeena. A minute later, one of the guards was binding her to the pole again. Jeena sat in her usual spot, cross-legged, with the sword across her legs.

When the wagon was moving, Fi said, "Thank you."

Jeena's eyes flicked her way. "If ye get sick and die, they'll blame me."

"Thank you anyway." The wagon jumped as it went over a bump. Fi gritted her teeth. "Why did you leave the wagon when we were passing through the last village?" Jeena had suddenly leaped to her feet and jumped off the wagon. At first Fi had thought the wild woman was finally escaping, though doing it during the day, while in a village, would have been stupid. When none of Millwood's men had broken formation to go after her, Fi had wondered what was going on. She had limited movement and couldn't see behind her. A minute later, Jeena had returned to the wagon. It had been travelling slow enough that she'd been able to climb onto it easily. If not for the shouting and jeering that made it difficult for Fi to hear her own thoughts, she would have asked where Jeena had gone. Then her head had started to pound, and she'd forgotten about it—until now.

"Someone threw a stone," Jeena said. "There's to be no throwing stones, and no throwing at yer head. Millwood's orders."

"How did you know someone threw a stone?"

"It almost hit me."

A giggle bubbled up inside Fi. Suddenly the sun's heat didn't bother her. She was hungry, tired, dirty, in agony, and on her way to a humiliating end, but she wanted to giggle. In that moment, she'd never felt more powerful, or more free.

Erryn folded her arms and gazed at the Northerners sitting in the tavern with her. "Something's wrong. She's been gone too long." The barkeep had shot several glances at the group taking up space in his common room but not paying for more drink. In another five minutes he'd come over to wipe the table and suggest they move along.

"I agree," Asha said. "She should have returned by now. We should go and find her."

"No," Erryn quickly said. "If we all go into the building, they might think we're hostile. I'll go. I'm, uh . . ."

"Like them?" Asha didn't sound offended. "Ye're marked."

"But I'm still like them. Wait here. If the barkeep comes over, buy another round, or he'll kick you out." She rose and—

Yanik was instantly on his feet. "I'm going with ye."

"No, I'll go with her," Renn said.

Erryn folded her arms. "I can go alone."

"Ye can't go alone," Yanik said. "We're yer protectors."

"One of you, then," Erryn said, not wanting to waste time arguing. "I can say you're my guard."

"You go, Yanik," Asha said.

Renn's face tightened, but she remained at the table. Erryn caught her eye and gave her a quick smile, then left the tavern with Yanik. The Northerners didn't know how to relate to Renn now. She was still shamed by the clan, but Zhikinden had said her name and tasked her along with the others. Sometimes Asha treated her well, and other times she looked down on her, which confused those she led. But they all knew Erryn favoured Renn, so they didn't overtly disrespect her.

"Let me speak to them," Erryn said to Yanik. "I'll say that—"

A group of people emerged from the Ferret base. Erryn's breath caught in her throat when she recognized Avere. The Ferret's arms were pulled behind her and a hooded cloak sat on her head and hid her back. "They've shackled her," she murmured to Yanik, confused.

Avere's three escorts flanked her. They walked south.

"I'll follow them," Erryn said. "Go tell the others what's happened."

Yanik shook his head. "I won't leave ye alone."

Not wanting to lose Avere, Erryn held her tongue and trailed the Ferret group, which turned left at the first crossroads. She turned the corner, and . . . her nose wrinkled. Manure. The group was heading to the base's stable. She spotted Avere's bag in one of the Ferrets' hands. They must have Zhikinden's book!

"We have to do something now," she said as the group filed into the stable. "I'll distract them."

"How?" Yanik said.

Erryn shot him a look. He grimaced, but nodded. They

casually walked closer to the stable, then darted toward the stable's entrance when none of the Ferrets looked their way. Voices murmured from inside. Erryn closed her eyes and held out her hands. *Iss, come.*

The air shimmered. The six-foot snake appeared, draped across her hands. Iss raised his head and turned to look at her.

Go into the stables. Erryn placed Iss on the ground. The snake slithered away. A horse nickered. A stall door creaked open.

"I want my horse," Avere said.

"No, and you're not riding alone. You'll—"

A piercing scream made Erryn jump. "Where did that come from?" someone shouted. Horses whinnied. Wood splintered. Yanik rushed past her. Erryn hesitated, then peered into the stable.

A horse was rearing in the stable's alley. Its hooves crashed down, narrowly missing the head of one of the Ferrets who stood immobilized, his hands raised to protect his head. Avere barrelled into another Ferret distracted by the ruckus. Yanik sucker punched the third Ferret, knocking him out cold, then grabbed the Ferret Avere had knocked to the ground and pulled him to safety. He held his sword at the man's throat. The Ferret who'd raised his hands backpedalled away from the snake slithering toward him. He picked up a chair, then dropped it and raised his hands when the spooked horse reared again.

Avere stumbled from the stable and to Erryn's side.

"Get rid of it," she shrieked, sounding more rattled than Erryn had ever heard her sound. "Get rid of it."

"Ye're afraid of snakes?" Yanik said, his eyes bright.

"It's Iss," Erryn reminded her.

"With apologies to Irnys, I'm really not fond of the shape his beloved takes."

Erryn dismissed Iss. The Ferret still inside was occupied with avoiding the spooked horse while trying to calm it.

"Where's my bag?" Avere said.

Erryn had forgotten about the bag. It was on the ground just inside the stable. "Over there."

"Take one of the daggers from my bag. You know how to use it."

Avere knew she didn't, but Erryn went to the bag and dug out a dagger. She held it casually, trying to look as if she'd brandished one many times before, and waited for the Ferret still inside the stable to calm the horse.

A minute later, he came outside and bent over to catch his breath. "You're lucky nobody got hurt," he said, glancing back at the Ferret Yanik had sucker punched.

Avere glared at him. "If you hadn't jumped me, none of this would have happened. Now get me out of these shackles, or my friends will make you bleed."

Erryn scowled at him, but didn't try any fancy work with the dagger, afraid she'd drop it.

"We need to find that snake," the Ferret growled.

"Don't worry about the snake, Billy. Just get these cuffs off me."

He obliged. Avere rubbed her wrists.

"The spymaster isn't going to like this," Billy said. "You could have killed us."

"But we didn't. And when you send a message to the spymaster about all this, you'll tell him I'm all right, and I know what I'm doing. He's to stay out of my way and leave my friend alone."

"What friend?"

"He'll know what friend. Tell him the Seven are with me."

Billy gave her a strange look, then said, "I doubt the Seven will save you from him."

"Just tell him." She dipped into her bag and fished out two daggers. "I'll let you keep your bits . . . for now. But if you come after us . . ." She grimaced. "That goes for you, too," she said to the one Yanik still watched. "And take care of my horse."

Billy turned to go, then suddenly stopped. His eyes narrowed at Erryn. "You look famil—wait a minute. You look like—"

"The Beast Master?" Avere chuckled. "Yes, Billy, I'm travelling with the Beast Master. Does she look branded to you? Would I be strutting around the city with her? Don't be an idiot."

He gave Erryn's forehead another look, then skirted around her and bent over his unconscious man.

Avere picked up her bag and strolled back to the road. Yanik and Erryn glanced at each other, then followed her.

Once they were safely away, Erryn looked over her shoulder. Billy and the other conscious Ferret were helping the one Yanik had knocked out. She shook her head. They'd entered Stronghaven only this morning and had already run into trouble.

"Let's fetch the others from the tavern and get away from here," Avere said. "They might try to take me again."

Yanik nodded. "I wouldn't want to have to rescue ye twice."

Avere's eyes bulged. "Rescue me? If you hadn't come along, I would have handled them myself. They had to sleep sometime. Only one or two could stand guard, and I'm guessing it would have been one. I had a plan."

He didn't appear convinced. "The snake turned ye into a screaming shrew. What else are ye afraid of?"

"She has her daggers, you know," Erryn said. "And the snake wasn't just any snake. It was Iss." Irnys.

"I suppose you're not afraid of anything," Avere said to Yanik. "Don't bother answering, because I really don't care."

A smile played on Yanik's lips, but he remained silent. Erryn could sense the tension between him and Avere. Sometimes affection underlay teasing and bantering, but not in Avere and Yanik's case. She hoped they'd focus on killing those who threatened her, rather than on killing each other.

Erryn paced inside one of the rooms the group had rented at an inn far away from the Ferret base. "We have to find her."

Avere sighed. "I was afraid you'd say that. Millwood will have guards with him. He won't let her go without a vicious fight. She's his path to the throne."

"I'm not letting her hang."

"I know you believe she didn't do it, and—"

Erryn whirled to Avere. "She didn't do it. I know her."

Avere wasn't that naïve, but she didn't stand a chance of swaying Erryn. "I suppose the royal primate wouldn't have helped her escape if he believed her guilty," she said, lying.

"You haven't met Enkelo."

"Actually, I have, sort of. He wanted us to give him your head."

Erryn chuckled. "If they catch and hang him, I'll be there to watch."

"But they haven't caught him. So why hasn't he freed her? How did they take her without taking him?"

"We can ask her when she's free."

Renn and Asha had been watching and listening. Avere turned to them. "Millwood's estate is to the east. He'll be taking a route that passes through as many villages as possible. Do you know which way he'll be coming?"

Asha shrugged, but Renn pursed her lips. "Ye said his estate is to the east?"

Avere nodded.

"Then he'll be coming along the eastern trade route. There are lots of villages, and it's the most direct route."

"Then we search for them along there. We don't want them to reach the city with her. It'll be more difficult to free her here than it will be to handle a camp of guards."

"We go now, then," Erryn said. "We don't know how close they are. For all we know, they're almost here."

"Not you, Erryn. We can't risk you for this."

Erryn's mouth dropped open. "You expect me to sit here? I can help."

"Avere is right," Asha said. "Ye have to free the Six. That's more important than putting yer sister on the throne."

"I don't care about putting her on the throne. I can't let them hang her. She's innocent."

"She stood by and let her father run you out of Darroth." Avere said.

"There wasn't much she could do." Erryn's eyes narrowed. "You said there will probably be a vicious fight. You'll need the Fallen. How many are we?" She counted on her fingers. "Eight? I'm sure Millwood has more than seven guards."

"Which is why ye should remain here," Asha said.

"Let her come with us," Renn said. "If it was yer kin, ye'd want to be there, too."

"Exactly. I'm going." Erryn's mouth set.

They *would* end up with the most stubborn Beast Master in history. "Fine," Avere said. "We'll all go, except you," she said, turning to Asha. "Don't be offended. We need fighters."

"I'm quite capable of fighting. I didn't always wear the robe. But I'll stay, only so there's someone to tell yer story if ye don't come back. Is there anything I can do here while ye're gone?"

"You can protect Zhikinden's book." Avere pulled it from the bag she'd set on the floor and handed it to Asha. "We'll take it to a primate when we get back, unless we have to leave in a hurry." She didn't have to explain why she wasn't directing Asha to take the book to a primate herself. "That's the other thing. Be ready to leave at a moment's notice. If we can't re-enter the city for any reason, we'll get a message to you somehow."

"I understand," Asha said. "I'll go tell the others." Her gaze settled on Erryn. "Ye keep out of the fray as much as possible. Let the Fallen fight for ye. Ye can always summon them again, but if ye fall, we can't bring ye back."

Erryn barked a laugh. "Don't worry. I know to stay back." She absently grasped the bear hanging from the necklace she always wore.

"We'll meet in the common room in an hour." Avere picked up her bag and quirked a brow at Erryn and Renn. "We have a princess to rescue."

Fi staggered into the tent and collapsed onto the ground, grateful they didn't force her to raise the tent herself. It would be difficult when her hands were shackled. A guard would remove the iron bracelets when he delivered her meagre supper.

Jeena strode into the tent and stared down at Fi. "Only two days until Stronghaven now."

Fi couldn't tell if Jeena was pleased. Was she looking forward to seeing her charge dragged in front of a mob and humiliated? Millwood would likely place Fi in the stocks in a busy square. The merchants would sell spoiled fruits and vegetables. How long would she be on public display before they travelled to the next town and did it all over again?

Jeena had given her water twice more after that

first time, but she wouldn't be able to do it while Fi was surrounded by people who believed she'd killed their king. The coming days would be long.

A guard yanked the tent flap aside. "You, woman," he said to Jeena. "You're wanted. Give me your sword."

Jeena's eyes widened slightly, but she quickly masked her apprehension. She handed the guard her sword and left with him.

Fi closed her eyes, then jumped when the men around the fire outside roared. One of them—Millwood?—shouted. Fi strained to hear him, but his men were cheering, jeering, yelling encouragement? Fi's chest tightened. What were they doing to Jeena? She pushed herself upright and poked her head out of the tent, then quickly ducked back inside. Two guards were right outside the tent. She'd glimpsed Millwood's men ringing the fire, but that was all. She'd heard what sounded like a slap, though.

Another roar set her heart racing. Would she be next?

The ruckus around the fire died down. Footsteps thudded toward the tent. Fi shrank away from the tent flap. Jeena flew into the tent and landed on her side with a grunt. A guard burst in and grabbed her arm. "Get on your feet. You have a prisoner to guard."

Jeena struggled to her feet. Fi gasped. Blood ran down Jeena's left cheek from a gash just under her eye. Her nose bled. The skin around her right eye was an angry red, and would turn purple and blue. The eye itself was a slit and might be swollen shut on the morrow. Somehow her mouth had escaped the pummelling. The guard pressed

Jeena's sword into her hand and marched from the tent. Jeena wiped the blood from her nose and face with her left sleeve.

Fi wondered what to do. She wanted to ask why. Why had Millwood beaten her? He'd never laid a finger on her before. She searched the tent for something Jeena could use to wipe her face, even though she knew there'd be nothing. She wanted to do something! But she was afraid to offer sympathy or support. Jeena might take whatever she was feeling out on her. Then again, if she hurt Fi, Millwood would beat her a second time, and do who knew what else.

"Are you all right?" she said, then realized what a stupid question that was. Of course the wild woman wasn't all right.

Jeena's chest heaved, but she said nothing.

The guard who'd shoved Jeena into the tent returned, carrying a bowl. Another guard came into the tent and removed Fi's shackles.

"Here," the first guard said, handing Fi the bowl.

"None for you," the second guard said to Jeena. "You'll have to hope she shares her supper." His lips curled. "Like you share your water."

Fi suddenly understood. She waited until the guards had left, then said, "I'm sorry." She couldn't help but feel responsible.

Jeena ignored her, but her hands clenched. Her right eye made Fi's stomach roil. She took the crusty bread from the bowl and ripped it in half. "Here," she said, holding half out to Jeena.

The wild woman hesitated, then took it from her. Fi motioned for her to soak up more soup if she wanted to, but Jeena wolfed down the bread and stared past her. Fi forced the remaining bread and soup down. She hadn't had anything to eat all day, but her appetite had fled. She couldn't understand why Jeena didn't try to escape. When night fell, why didn't she use the sword to cut a hole in the tent and run? Maybe there were guards behind the tent, but even if there were, Jeena had a sword. She could cut down one or two, or make them kill her. Anything to free herself one way or the other.

Fi had wondered the same when the slavers had been her captors and had understood it even less then. Jeena had been one of them. She could have left the camp at any time, simply walked away. But instead she'd remained, a slave who wasn't chained.

"You never told me how you ended up with Devon and his men," she said, hoping that engaging Jeena in conversation would help the wild woman bear her pain.

Jeena stared mutely past her. Fi didn't try again. She dropped the empty bowl and waited for the guard to return and shackle her. The coming days would be long. Jeena wouldn't be sharing her water.

Erryn crouched next to Avere and peered at the light she could see flickering through the trees. A laugh pierced the still air. It must be past midnight, but someone was still up, and not afraid to be heard. The camp wasn't too far off the road.

Avere nodded. "You all stay here." She slinked away.

Erryn crept back to the others, who were crouched in the brush at the side of the eastern trade road. Nobody spoke. This was the second time Avere had left them to take a closer look at a group of travellers. But last time, the fire had been smaller and they hadn't heard anyone. Those at this camp were bold.

She lifted a hand to scratch her—Timor grabbed her hand. "Don't touch it," he said, referring to the brand Asha had painted onto Erryn's forehead. "Ye might smudge it, and then it won't fool anyone."

Erryn nodded. When they knew she'd likely call the Fallen, they'd decided that Asha would paint the brand onto her forehead. They didn't want word getting around that the Beast Master had somehow lost the warning seared into her forehead by the king.

The minutes stretched on. Erryn shot a glance at Renn, but wasn't nervous yet. There had been no surprised shouts from the camp's direction, and no men blundering through the brush, searching for others.

Avere suddenly appeared, startling Erryn. "It's them," she said calmly. "And I think I know which tent the princess is in."

Erryn's heart hammered in her chest. Fi was here, within reach! "How many are there?"

"Six around the fire. If all the tents are occupied, about thirty in total. There may be a guard or two in the princess's tent."

"How do you know which one is hers?"

"Two of the six are directly outside it."

"We're only seven," Toe said.

"An easy win, if we do this quietly. But I don't think we can. Three or four, yes, but not all six."

Erryn's shoulders slumped. "Then it could be seven against thirty."

"You're forgetting your powerful friends. Here's what I propose." Avere lifted two fingers. "I'll remove two of the six before we move in. Timor should be able to remove one or two with his bow. We should be able to take down the remaining two while the rest of them roll out of their bedrolls and fumble for their swords. I want Cheturrak, Lerxis, Sath, and Zayvang in that camp to greet them. Keep summoning them. Renn and I will get the princess, while Timor, Yanik, and Var fight alongside the Fallen. Toe, your ankle's still hindering you. Stay with Erryn. Protect her."

Toe solemnly nodded.

Var scratched her nose. "We're to kill everyone, then?"

Avere chuckled. "We're good, but not that good. They might take time to get out of their beds, but they will, and they outnumber us. That's why we'll retreat as soon as we have the princess." She turned to Erryn. "You'll leave the Fallen behind to keep them busy."

"I can't command them from a distance."

"You won't have to. Just make sure they're all summoned before you run."

"How will we know when to run?" Timor asked.

"We'll come to you when we have the princess. You'll blow your horn." Avere's gaze took in the others. "When you hear it, retreat. Remember that abandoned wagon we came across?"

Everyone nodded.

"We'll meet there."

"Millwood's men might come after us," Yanik said.

"Yes, so we won't be able to tarry long. Though if we kill Millwood, they might not chase us. Even if Millwood lives, they'll know Erryn's with us, so perhaps they won't come after us tonight. But we can't wait around to see. We'll wait at the wagon for five minutes, no more. Retreat as soon as you hear the horn. If we're gone, go back to the inn."

"We should kill Millwood," Yanik said.

"We want to get the princess and survive. Don't take your eyes off another because you're looking for Millwood. That will be the fastest way to end up with a sword in your belly." Avere paused. "Does everyone understand the plan? Fight, and when the horn sounds, run and meet at the wagon."

"What are we waiting for?" Toe said.

"To see if any of you has a better plan." Avere waited for a moment, then said, "All right, then. Let's go."

Erryn crept through the brush behind Avere, trying not to think of Fi being so close. She had to focus on calling the Fallen while doing her best to avoid the attention of Millwood's men. The moment Cheturrak, Sath, Lerxis, or Zayvang fell, she'd summon them again. She could keep doing it until all Millwood's men were dead, but eventually one or two smart ones would decide to hunt for the one summoning the Fallen. *The Seven. The Six and one beloved.* Enough. Fi's life was in their hands.

Avere motioned for everyone to stop moving. Through

the brush, Erryn could see several guards sitting around the fire. Timor murmured something to Avere and sneaked away. The others readied their weapons. Erryn crouched behind a fallen tree trunk, the best hiding place she could see. Toe crouched next to her. If only Millwood had camped farther off the road, where there'd be more trees and thicker brush.

Avere glanced behind her, then pulled a dagger from her belt. She drew back her arm. The blade flew from her fingers.

Fi went into Father's study and folded her arms. Father didn't look up from the parchment he was reading, even though he must know she was there. He would have heard the door bang open. But he'd make her wait, because she had to learn how to be more patient, apparently. She was on the verge of clearing her throat when Mother strode in.

Father looked up and smiled at the queen. "Is it two o'clock already?"

"I'm afraid so. He's waiting for us in the library."

Father set the parchment on the desk. "Very well. I'll—"

"Father! Am I invisible?"

Mother's failed attempt to hide a smile increased Fi's indignation. "I've been standing here for—" Movement beyond Mother caught her eye. The decorative suit of armour standing near the wall was tipping—

"Mother!" Fi shoved Mother out of the way, then raised her hands. The helmet wired to the rest of the armour hit her legs. She—

Her heart pounding, Fi opened her eyes and . . . there *was* something on her legs. She reached down her shackled hands, felt—something wet. And then . . . hair? Flesh? She screamed and pushed at the corpse pinning her legs.

Shouts from outside confused her further. The clang of steel on steel. Thudding footsteps.

Jeena grunted and rolled over. The tent flap opened and a woman entered. A wild woman with a broadsword. Fi froze. So did Jeena. Then another woman, shorter and lither, slinked into the tent, silhouetted in the light cast by the roaring fire outside.

What was happening? Were bandits attacking the camp? Were they another group of slavers? Or had word of her capture spread and another noble hoped to ride into Stronghaven with the disgraced princess? Fi stared helplessly at the two women. She was trapped. Her hands were shackled.

She shrank away when the shorter woman stepped toward her. "We're with Erryn," she said.

Shock rattled Fi to her core. Those were the last words she'd expected to hear. "Come with us," the woman said. "Hurry."

"What about her?" The wild woman's eyes were on Jeena, her sword ready to strike.

The short woman twisted—and lunged at Jeena, a dagger in her hand.

"No!" Fi snapped.

The woman's dagger was at Jeena's throat and her knee on Jeena's chest. "She has a sword, there," the woman said tersely, her eyes flicking to where the sword lay under the rolled-up shirt Jeena used as a pillow.

Fi's mind raced. If they left Jeena alive and any of Millwood's men survived, there was no telling what they'd do to the wild woman who was supposed to guard the princess. They'd blame Jeena, take out their own failure on her.

"We have to take her with us." Fi said. "Do you have any rope to bind her hands?"

"No."

"I'll help ye," Jeena said, her voice steady. "I'll fight."

The woman with the broadsword sneered. "She could cut ye down the moment she has the sword in her hand."

Fi was worried about that, too. She'd asked about rope because Jeena might attack the rescuers. It would depend on whether she wanted to please Millwood and his men, or throw in with the newcomers.

"We don't have time for this." The woman with the dagger studied Jeena's face. The bruises were a nasty red, and Jeena's right eye had swollen shut. "I think she'll fight with us."

"I'll fight with ye," Jeena said.

The woman lifted her dagger and straightened. "As soon as we're outside, we'll run. Take your sword and cut down anyone who gets in our way." She turned to Fi. "I'll deal with your shackles later. Stay with us and run as quickly as you can."

Jeena was on her feet, her sword in her hand.

"Don't kill any animals you see," the woman said. "They're with us. They won't touch you."

Animals? The Fallen? Fi didn't have time to think about it. The wild woman with the broadsword rolled the corpse away and hauled her to her feet.

"Stay with us," the other woman said again. They ran from the tent. Fi kept her eyes on the woman's back, but she glimpsed men fighting, bodies . . . Something large lumbered past her. It took Fi a moment to realize it was a bear . . . a huge bear . . . Sath. She would have turned and gaped, if she wasn't running for her life. Erryn was here. She was alive! But was she in her right mind? Fi wanted to search for her as she ran, but—

A yelp, behind her, then grunting and the sounds of weapons striking each other. Jeena and the other wild woman were fighting men who'd come after them.

"Keep running," the woman in front yelled.

Fi resisted the urge to look behind her and willed her legs to move faster. She'd had little to eat since leaving Millwood's estate. Fear powered her, and the desire to see Erryn. If she fell now . . . *Keep running!*

She could no longer hear the two women behind her, nor did she hear the thudding footsteps of guards in pursuit. Suddenly a wild man was ahead of them, sighting down an arrow he'd drawn. He released the bow string, letting the arrow fly.

"Sound the horn," the woman in front shouted.

The wild man didn't hesitate. He pulled the horn from his belt and raised it to his lips. A deep, throbbing wail permeated the night air. Fi ran past him.

"Yer arrow hit its mark," someone gasped between breaths. Fi thought it was the wild woman who'd come into the tent with the woman in front. She wondered about Jeena, but didn't turn around.

"Ye warriors always think ye're the strong ones, but it's often the bow that wins the day."

They'd reached the road. Fi's lungs laboured, and her legs ached. She couldn't keep up this pace forever, but when the woman in front dashed down the road, Fi mustered the strength to follow her. She stumbled. Someone grabbed her from behind and held on to her, pulling her along. It was the wild woman who'd come into the tent. Fi tried to keep pace with her, but by the time the woman in front stopped next to a rotting wagon at the side of the road and doubled over, the wild woman was practically dragging her along.

Fi's heart felt as if it were leaping from her chest, and she was too winded to speak. Her legs trembled. She plunked to the ground with an *oomph* and gulped down air. The others milled around her. Jeena was there. She'd survived. Fi studied the others. If they were with Erryn, they must be friendly to her.

The only other woman there who wasn't wild crouched next to her. "Let me get those off." She pulled what Fi assumed was a lockpick from a pouch on her belt and inserted it into the shackles' keyhole. Less than a minute later, the shackles fell from her wrists. She rubbed her raw skin and murmured a thank you.

The woman picked up the shackles and rose. "Now," she said, turning to Jeena. "Give the sword to him." She tipped her head toward the wild man with the bow.

"But I fought for ye," Jeena said.

"You did. But I don't know who you are and how you fit into this, and we're meeting someone you might be inclined to hurt. Give us the sword. We won't hurt you."

"Give it to him, Jeena," Fi said. When Jeena handed the sword to the wild man, Fi was only partly surprised.

The woman shackled Jeena's wrists in front of her. "Don't worry, you've just seen me get them off the princess." She stood in front of Fi and looked down. "Or should that be the queen?"

Fi met her eyes. "I didn't kill them."

"You can tell us what happened when we're somewhere—"

"A rider approaches," the wild man snapped. He raised his bow and nocked an arrow.

The woman motioned for calm. "It's too large to be one of Millwood's horses."

Fi could feel the vibration of the approaching horse's hooves. She pushed herself to her feet.

"It's Quon. She's riding Quon," the woman said.

The wild man lowered his bow.

"Quon?" Jeena backpedalled. "Ye're with the Fallener?"

Nobody answered her, but the wild woman with the broadsword moved closer to Jeena. Any other time, Fi would have gawked at the majestic horse, even though it was one of the Fallen. But this time her eyes were on the rider. A lump rose in her throat.

Quon trotted to a stop and lowered himself so Erryn could safely dismount. Another had been astride Quon's back—a wild man. Erryn supported him as he carefully dismounted, favouring his left foot. When he was on solid ground, Erryn patted Quon's side and stroked his muzzle. Quon faded away.

Fi's dear sister was thinner, but somehow stronger. Erryn held her head high and exuded a self-assurance she'd never had before.

Fi couldn't contain herself any longer. She ran to her and threw her arms around Erryn's neck. The tears she'd fought for months—wounded, humiliated, grieving—she didn't fight them anymore. She clung to Erryn and let it all out, and when Erryn's arms tightened around her, Fi's lagging resolve surged again. She would do it—take the throne, find out what had happened to Enkelo and Dann, avenge Father, Henrick, and Surann. Daros would crown her. It would kneel to her and beg her forgiveness. She was the rightful queen! Nothing would stop her from claiming what was hers and rooting out those who'd devastated her family and others she loved.

"You're safe now, Fi," Erryn murmured. "You're with friends."

"And family." Fi drew back, suddenly self-conscious, and gazed at Erryn. "I must look terrible. I know my hair is . . . " Her words died. With all the strength she could muster, she shoved the woman in front of her away, then howled, filled with disappointment and fear and weariness. Why? To soar so high, only to crash back down. She'd endured so much since that night at the castle, when she'd walked into the library expecting a boring conversation with the grand primate and primates from Westerfox. She'd endured accusations, sneers, humiliation, hunger, thirst. But this—this was the cruellest trick of all. The Seven had truly turned their backs on her.

"You're not Erryn!" she shouted. Tears, hot, devastated, resigned tears, poured down her cheeks. "You're not Erryn."

The woman's eyes widened. She reached for Fi.

Fi slapped the woman's hands away, then lunged at her and beat on the woman's chest, again and again and—

Alarmed cries rose from behind her, then strong arms restrained her and dragged her away from the woman. Fi kicked her legs and screamed again, this time in frustration. Once again a prisoner. The only thing that had changed were those who held the key.

The woman approached her but didn't try to touch her. "It's me, Fi. It's me."

She pushed against the arms restraining her. "You can let me go. I won't hit her again."

Erryn, or whoever she was, nodded. The pressure on Fi's chest eased. She took a step back. "It's not you. You don't have it . . . the brand. It's not real." She pointed at the smudged paint on the woman's forehead. "My father branded her. I saw it. I don't know who you are, but you're not my sister."

The woman's shoulders relaxed. "A lot's changed since we parted. My brand is gone. But it's me."

"How can your brand be gone?"

"Zhikinden removed it."

Fi's jaw dropped. "Do you honestly expect me to believe that?"

"No, but it's true." The others nodded and murmured

their agreement. "Do you honestly think there are two Beast Masters walking Daros who look exactly alike?"

This woman was thinner and more weathered than Erryn, but those were superficial changes. Still, Fi couldn't believe it. "Perhaps the two of you are Beast Masters because of how you look."

Someone tutted. "It's her," the woman with the daggers said. "She was branded. Zhikinden removed the brand. I saw it with my own eyes. I saw—"

Erryn, or whoever she was, raised her hand. Her eyes settled on Fi. "Do you remember when we caught Henrick kissing that girl in a laneway off the market, and he swore us to secrecy because he knew your father would punish him?"

Yes, but . . . "Erryn could have told you that story. And maybe somebody else saw him and we didn't know. Of course my father would be upset. Everyone would know that. The prince and heir kissing a common girl? He would have been furious." She drew a deep breath and continued to study the woman's face.

"Do you remember when you sneaked into your mother's dressing room and forced open one of her jewelry boxes? You were . . . nine. You took one of her necklaces. You showed it to me and laughed as you tried it on. When your mother asked us if we knew where it was, we said no, and you swore me never to tell. So your mother accused one of the servants, and even though the woman insisted it wasn't her, your mother dismissed her, because she was more willing to believe the servant had lied, than her daughter and foster daughter."

Blood rushed to Fi's cheeks.

"You told her the truth then, and she was so angry, she didn't speak to you, or me, for days. And she couldn't give the servant her placement back, because of the harsh words the woman had shouted at her. Too many people had heard them."

The woman in front of Fi looked down at her feet, then lifted her head and met Fi's eyes again. "The servant had worked for your mother since she was a girl, and our lies ruined that. We talked endlessly about how we could make it right, but we couldn't. When we were older, you said it was the first time you realized that being a princess didn't mean you could have everything you wanted, and you weren't referring to the necklace. You were referring to not being able to reconcile your mother and the servant."

Fi swallowed. She'd told herself that she was only nine, but it was one of the things she'd done that shamed her most. She'd always regretted it and wished she could change it. She'd taken and hidden the necklace. She'd told Erryn to lie. She'd begged Mother to take the woman back, but someone who'd disrespected the queen, even when right, couldn't come back. Erryn had been just as ashamed, perhaps more so. She'd always felt a debt to Father and Mother, and it was one of the few times she'd deliberately disrespected them.

The servant might have told someone about the incident, but couldn't have known how remorseful Fi was, or the lesson she'd learned. Erryn wouldn't have breathed a word to anyone.

"The necklace you took . . . you put it into her coffin. We went to see her together, remember? You asked your father if you could do it, and he agreed. You still felt guilty. It was your way of saying you were sorry."

The woman in front of Fi didn't have the brand, but it must be Erryn . . . somehow. "Erryn has a scar on her lower back, from a fall she took as a child."

"Come and look."

The woman with the daggers stiffened. "Are you sure—"

"Let her. She knows it's me."

Feeling the eyes of the others upon her, Fi walked behind Erryn and lifted her cloak, and her tunic, and her shirt, and . . . the scar was there. She traced it with her fingers. "I'm sorry."

Erryn turned around. "We were there when she took the brand away, and it was hard for us to believe. I forgot about it, about how you might react. I was just so happy to see you."

They embraced again. "I'm surprised you recognized me," Fi said, still holding on to Erryn.

"I'll always recognize you, Fi."

Her eyes welled again. Not everyone who knew and loved her was dead. And Erryn was herself and had seen Zhikinden. "Tell me everything."

Erryn let her go. "Not here."

"With all the screaming, we could have Millwood's men on us any minute," the woman with the daggers said. "Not that I'm blaming you, Your Majesty."

Fi snorted. "Just call me Fi. I'm not the queen yet. I'm nobody at the moment."

"If that were true, Millwood wouldn't have been bringing you to Stronghaven." She squinted up the road. "We'll give them another minute. Then we have to go."

The others exchanged glances. "Let me introduce you to everyone." Erryn gestured toward the woman. "This is Avere. She's a Ferret." Avere inclined her head.

A Ferret? "Did the spymaster send you for me?" Fi asked.

Avere's eyes sharpened. "Why? Should he have?"

"I—we'll talk later," Fi said, aware of the wild folk and not sure how they were involved with Erryn, just as they weren't sure about Jeena. Were they hired mercenaries?

"This is Timor," Erryn said, her gaze on the man with the bow. Timor nodded.

"This is Toe."

"Short for Toetril," the wild man said. "But everyone calls me Toe."

"This is Renn."

Renn grunted but kept her eyes on the road. Erryn stood a few feet away from Jeena. "Who's this?"

"Jeena." Fi pondered what to say. It was quite satisfying to see Jeena with her hands shackled and her shoulders hunched, but she quickly stopped gloating. With the amount of experience she had being in shackles, she couldn't be pleased at Jeena's predicament for long. "We'll talk about her later," she said, and had to admit to a stab of satisfaction at the apprehension in Jeena's left eye.

"They're not coming back," Timor said mournfully. "They're not coming." Toe patted his shoulder.

"We have to go," Avere said. "Millwood's men don't seem to be giving chase, but they could be regrouping. Planning."

"Yanik, Var . . . they'll meet us in Stronghaven," Toe said.

Fi doubted it. Whoever they were, they'd given their lives for her. The path to the throne was littered with bloody bodies. How many more sacrifices would there be?

It was a sombre group that trudged along the road. Renn stuck close to Jeena, Toe walked next to Timor, Fi remained at Erryn's side, and Avere kept an eye out behind everyone.

The sun peeked through the trees and cast shadows on the road. They pushed on, wanting to put as much distance as they could between themselves and Millwood's men before they stopped for something to eat. Sleep was out of the question.

Weaker than the others, Fi grabbed Erryn's arm and held on to her. Suddenly the air shimmered. Quon leaped into existence and bowed down.

"Get on," Erryn said. Fi hesitated, then mounted the majestic horse. "If Avere spots anyone, I'll ask him to bow and you'll have to get off."

Fi nodded, grateful for the respite.

"Do you mind if Toe sits behind you? He hurt his ankle."

How could she say no? Everyone here had risked their life for her. "I don't mind."

Erryn beckoned to Toe. He murmured something to Timor and hoisted himself onto Quon's back. "Only because I don't want to slow everyone down," he said.

Fi could feel him behind her. She was atop Quon with a wild man, but Erryn was there, and knew him and everyone else. Nobody seemed to care that she'd summoned one of the Fallen, except Jeena, who kept glancing behind her. Why was Erryn travelling with wild folk and a Ferret? How had she met up with Avere, and why did nobody seem to care that she was a Beast Master? Most of all, she wondered when Zhikinden had removed Erryn's brand. Zhikinden. Fi had cried out to the Seven many times since fleeing the Royal City, and couldn't help but wonder why the goddess had helped Erryn, but left her to rot.

Erryn knocked on the door to Fi's room and opened it when she heard Fi's muffled invitation to enter. Fi sat on the edge of the bed wearing a clean shirt and trousers, her hair clean and brushed. Steam no longer rose from the water in the washtub sitting in the corner. They'd only had a few hours of sleep since returning to Stronghaven, but without the blood and grime, Fi almost looked herself. She was thinner, her hair wasn't coiffed, and she was in clothes Erryn never would have imagined her wearing. A purple bruise marred her right cheek, and she had a small cut above her left eye. But otherwise, she was Fi. Erryn could hardly believe they were together again.

"Are you going to stand there gawking?" Fi said, making Erryn smile.

She closed the door. "Avere and Asha will join us in a few minutes. I said I wanted to talk to you alone first."

"Asha . . . she's the priestess?"

"Yes."

"You're going to tell me what happened? When you saw Zhikinden? Why you're with all these wild folk?"

"You're with a wild woman," Erryn said, using the words Fi would understand.

"I'm not chummy with her." Fi's eyes moistened. "I didn't kill them. I would never—"

Erryn sat next to her and took her hand. "I know."

"We went to the library, to—"

Erryn squeezed her hand. "Wait for the others."

"Does Avere ever sleep? She was awake when I dozed off and awake when I woke up."

"I don't know," Erryn said, chuckling.

"They killed Viren. He had nothing to do with it." Fi drew a shuddering breath. "Enkelo helped me escape."

"Enkelo?" Erryn winced at her shrill voice. "He did it so you'd owe him favours when you're back on the throne."

"I'm not so sure. It doesn't matter now anyway. He's dead. Dann's dead."

"Dann?"

"Tolin's third son." Fi rubbed her forehead with her free hand, then rested her head on Erryn's shoulder. They didn't speak again until Avere and Asha tapped at the door and came into the room.

Avere gazed at Fi and raised an appraising brow. "You look better."

Fi lifted her head from Erryn's shoulder and let go of her hand. "Tell me what happened with Zhikinden."

"All right, we'll start with our tale, and then you'll have to tell us yours." The Ferret leaned against the wall. "You tell it," she said to Erryn. Asha sank to the floor and sat cross-legged.

"I know you killed the guards who were escorting you to Rion," Fi said.

"Then I met a man called Rodney," Erryn said, skipping over the incident with Kell in the tavern in Moss, escaping from Persh on Quon's back, and the hunger that had driven her to petty pilfering. She told Fi what had happened after Rodney had taken her in—not everything, just about how she'd met Renn and Toe, how they'd helped her get to Stronghaven, how they'd gone to the Snowlake clan, and about their encounter with Zhikinden. "After that, we came here, to find a primate."

"Which we haven't done yet," Avere said.

"And then we heard about you."

"Thank you for coming for me," Fi said. "So when I was riding Quon . . ." She swallowed.

"You were riding Queyris," Erryn said.

"And the Seven . . . they haven't been able to hear our prayers."

"They hear them, but they can't do anything about them."

"But why are they bound? How?"

"We don't know," Avere said. "We need someone who

can translate the book, which might be blasphemous to everyone but us. But now it's your turn. Tell us what happened to the king, and how you ended up this far north and Millwood's prisoner."

Fi grabbed Erryn's hand again. As Erryn listened to Fi, her stomach knotted several times, usually at the same points Fi's grip on her hand tightened. She forced herself not to dwell on anything Fi said, to ignore the horror raging through her. If—*when* Fi took the throne and the Seven were freed, they'd make sure those who'd turned their backs so quickly on the rightful heir were punished. She hadn't cared about Millwood's fate, but now she hoped he lay dead, his throat ripped out by one of the Fallen. And the slavers . . . they'd traded their lives for coin, because they'd be hunted, and found, and killed.

"They could be alive," Avere said, when Fi fell silent. "The royal primate and Dann."

Fi heaved a sigh. "Then where are they?"

Avere didn't have an answer for her.

"This woman Jeena is one of yer captors, then," Asha said. "Why did ye bring her here? Why didn't ye let them kill her?"

Erryn had wondered about that, too. "Renn said you stopped Avere from cutting her throat."

"She was my guard, but also a prisoner."

"She abused you. She hurt you."

"I know, but it's more complicated than that. Let me deal with her. I want you all to go along with what I decide, not because I'm," she lowered her voice, "Filmona Lyos, because that doesn't count for anything right now."

Avere pushed herself away from the wall. "It's more complicated than that."

Erryn couldn't tell if Avere was mocking Fi. "Tell us what you want to do with Jeena, and we'll do it."

"We have to free the Six," Asha said. "No offence to ye, princess, but yer throne isn't as important as that."

Erryn was relieved when Fi smiled. She opened her mouth to respond to Asha, but Avere beat her to it. "Reclaiming her throne could help us with what we need to do. With the resources of the crown . . . though there will be forces working against us, of course." She tapped her chin. "I can't help but think the assassinations and the grand primate's apparent betrayal are somehow tied to the Seven being bound. If only the spymaster didn't want me dragged back to the Royal City. I sent him a letter, so I don't understand why he's being difficult."

"Our first step is to get the book translated," Erryn said.

"I'll go see a primate," Avere said. "I've consulted a primate here before. I have more questions for you," she said to Fi, "but I'll ask you later. We shouldn't tarry in Stronghaven. The sooner we know what to do next, the better." She inclined her head to Fi and left.

"Are you sure she's the best one to guard me?" Fi said.

"Does she make you nervous?" Erryn asked.

"No, but you could guard me."

"But you can't guard me. Fighting isn't one of your strengths," Erryn quickly added, when Fi frowned.

"So you'd rather share with Renn?"

"She's good with a sword," she said, silently apologizing to Renn. She'd have to tell Fi sometime—maybe.

"We can walk together, though," Fi said, lifting Erryn's hand.

"Yes, we can." Once Erryn would have loved holding Fi's hand, but now she was torn between seeing it as a friendly gesture and feeling as if she were lying to Fi. If Fi knew, would she want to cling to her foster sister's hand this way?

"Thank you for your people's help," Fi said to Asha. "I know you lost two of them. I'm sorry."

"I appreciate yer words, but ye have to understand, we're here for Erryn. We came for ye because she wanted us to, and we knew it would bolster her spirit." Asha rose. "I should see how Timor's doing. He and Var were close." She left, leaving Fi and Erryn alone.

"I like her," Fi said.

"You do?"

"She's honest. Sycophants are the last thing I need right now."

"Asha and her people don't care about the throne. They won't do anything against the crown, but they won't support it, either."

"They should. They're citizens of Daros."

"Citizens we've ignored."

Fi blinked at her. "You've been travelling with them for a while."

"I have. They're just like you and me. Their customs are different, that's all."

"If I take the throne, I'll want to include them more."

"In more than paying taxes, I hope." Erryn bit her lip. "They might not want to be included, not if it means you'll want them to be more like . . . us."

"After everything that's happened, are we still us?"

Erryn didn't know if she could go back to living in a castle, wearing fancy clothes and watching musical fencing while she stuffed herself with whatever dishes the cooks had prepared. What about Renn? What about Toe, and Asha, and the other Northerners she'd grown close to? She wasn't one of them, and they didn't see her as one of them, but did she belong in the Royal City now? She'd felt like an outcast when she'd been banished, and knowing she wasn't cursed by the Seven hadn't changed anything. She still didn't know where she belonged.

Are we still us? Erryn squeezed Fi's hand, then let it go. "We're together."

If Fi noticed Erryn hadn't answered the question, she didn't let on. "Where did you get that?" she asked, pointing to Erryn's necklace.

Erryn instinctively grabbed one of the animals hanging from the necklace and held on. "Oh, uh, I don't know—I mean, someone gave it to me."

"Who?"

"Just someone."

Fi frowned at her. "You wear it all the time. At the castle, you always grumbled when you had to wear earrings and a necklace. You didn't mind the rings, though you thought most of them were gaudy. Yet you wear that crude thing."

Erryn stiffened. "I like it."

"Well, I suppose that's all that counts. It's not as if

we're going to a banquet, is it? It doesn't matter what you wear," Fi said, making Erryn's jaw clench further. "I should go and see Jeena."

"What are you going to do with her?"

Fi shrugged. "Talk to her."

Fi squared her shoulders and approached the room where Jeena was being held. The door was ajar. She pushed it open. Jeena was sitting on the floor, her back against a wall. One of the wild men—Timor, she thought his name was—stood warily opposite Jeena. His eyes flicked to Fi when she entered the room, but then his gaze went to his prisoner again. They were treating Jeena well. Her wrists weren't shackled, and she'd eaten the same breakfast as everyone else. Still, she glared at Fi.

"I'd like to talk to Jeena alone," Fi said to Timor.

Timor frowned. "I don't know about that, uh, miss."

"I'll leave the door open. You can stand right outside." She didn't want him staring at either her or Jeena while they spoke.

"Are ye sure?"

"Yes."

He shot Jeena a warning look and went into the hallway. Fi closed the door halfway. She turned to Jeena and folded her arms.

"Look at ye, all pretty now." Jeena's mouth twisted. "Except for the bruises."

Fi was both irritated and amused. Were all wild women this stupid and stubborn? Asha seemed reasonable. Fi had only heard Renn speak five words, so she wasn't sure about her yet. And then there was Jeena, who seemed intent on cutting off her nose to spite her face.

"You can have a bath, if you want one," Fi said to her. "In fact, you'll have one when I've finished speaking to you."

Jeena's eyes brightened with interest, which she quickly masked. "Ye don't order me around."

"Yes, I do, actually. I'm only going to say this once. You serve me now. You're going to do whatever I tell you to do. First, a bath. Then you'll put on whatever clothes we scrounge up for you. Then you'll be my personal guard. You'll do what Millwood wanted you to do and gut anyone who threatens me in any way. Do you understand?"

They stared at each other. Fi tried not to blink. Unfortunately, she did, but she kept her eyes on Jeena's face and did her best not to smile when Jeena finally looked away.

"And then what?" Jeena said sullenly.

"What do you mean?"

"What will you do with me if ye get yer throne?"

"If you've served me well, nothing. You'll be free."

Jeena's gaze snapped back to Fi's face. Fi glanced around the room. "There isn't a washtub in here. Stay here while I sort out some hot water for you, and then I'll take you to my room. There's a washtub there. After you've had your bath, find me and make sure nobody kills me. I'll be wherever Erryn is."

She whirled and swung open the door, and—she almost bumped into Asha, who was about to enter the room.

"I couldn't help but overhear," Asha said. "She'll be working for ye, then?"

"Yes."

If Asha disagreed with Fi's claim over Jeena, she didn't show it. The priestess brushed past her and looked down at Jeena. Curious, Fi lingered.

"What clan do ye belong to?" Asha asked Jeena.

Jeena refused to look at her. "I have no clan," she muttered.

"Were ye shamed?"

"No."

"Ye left yer clan to work in the city?"

Jeena remained silent.

"If ye want to commune with us, ye're welcome," Asha said. "Tomorrow, before we leave, we'll gather and ask Zhikinden—"

Jeena snorted. "Ye're travelling with a Fallener. Zhikinden won't help ye."

"She doesn't know," Fi murmured to Asha. She raised her voice. "Do you remember when I attacked Erryn and she had to convince me it was her?"

Jeena didn't respond, and she didn't have to. She'd witnessed the incident.

"I didn't think it was her because the last time I'd seen her, she had an ugly brand right here." Fi pressed her right index finger against her forehead. "My father had it seared into her forehead, as a warning to anyone who saw her." Fi hadn't forgiven him for doing that, but she'd still loved him and wished he were here—so she could yell at him. "She's not branded anymore, and it's not possible to remove a brand. That's why I thought it wasn't her. But it *is* possible for one of the Seven, and that's what happened. Zhikinden removed her brand."

Jeena barked a laugh.

"It's true," Asha said. "I saw it with my own eyes. Zhikinden said the Fallener isn't cursed, but the Seven are bound to their beloveds, who we call the Fallen. The Fallener, who she called the Called and Caller, has to free them."

"And that's what we're going to do," Fi said. "You're on a holy quest now, Jeena. Maybe you should, er, commune."

Jeena appeared unmoved. "The Seven don't care about me, and I don't care about them."

Fi and Asha exchanged glances.

"Very well," Asha said. "If ye change yer mind, ye can always come and talk to me. Ye're with our group now. The Called and Caller said she would abide with the princess's decision about ye, and we abide with the Called and Caller." She left the room.

"I'll see about the water," Fi said, and followed her out.

"You don't have to guard her anymore," Fi said to Timor. She quashed her irritation when he looked to Asha for confirmation. She wasn't anybody right now. Even if she were the queen, he still wouldn't accept her authority over him. If—*when* she took the throne, the crown's relationship with the wild folk would have to change.

"Jeena has agreed to join us," Asha said. "She'll guard the princess. Go get yerself something to eat."

Timor nodded and bounded down the stairs at the end of the hallway.

"Are ye sure it's wise to trust her?" Asha asked.

"She'll be loyal to me," Fi said firmly. Truth be told, she'd first thought to give Jeena her freedom for the kindness she'd shown her with the water. She'd come to understand that Jeena had always been a prisoner of sorts, first with the slavers, and then with Millwood. But then Fi had realized that if she set her free now, Jeena would fall in with the first group of men that would have her. She'd let them rape her, and beat her, and treat her like a dog, and for reasons Fi was struggling to understand, Jeena would be loyal to them, and perhaps grateful. She might even think she loved them.

So Fi had come to a decision. Since Jeena so desperately needed to serve, she might as well serve the disgraced princess who wouldn't treat her like an animal. Fi's circle of trust was growing. She had Erryn and a wild woman who'd protect her at all costs. Satisfying, but also frightening. Everyone else who'd belonged to that circle was missing and probably dead.

Uneasy Alliances

Toe accepted the ale from Timor with a grateful nod and moistened his dry throat. He'd rather be downstairs in the rooming house's common room, but that would mean climbing up the stairs, too. He needed to rest his sore ankle. Tomorrow he'd use a walking stick. Right now, he closed his eyes to give them a quick rest, too.

After handing him the ale, Timor had left to join the others downstairs. When there was a light knock at the open door, Toe assumed he'd returned. Because Toe was close to Erryn and Zhikinden had spoken his name, Timor treated him with a deference he didn't deserve. "Come in, ye daft idiot. I told ye not to knock on yer own door."

"It isn't my door."

Toe almost dropped his ale. "I'm sorry," he said to Asha. "I thought ye were Timor."

"Do ye mind if I come in?"

"No. Come in."

Asha hesitated near one of the beds, then perched on its edge. "I came to see how ye feel. How's yer ankle?"

"It's feeling better already. I won't slow ye down, but I'll use a stick for a day or two."Asha grunted. She didn't say anything more and made no move to go, leaving an awkward silence between them.

"How are ye feeling?" Toe asked.

"Me? I'm feeling all right." Her smile quickly faded. "The princess is making Jeena work for her."

"That's good. Her spirit's broken."

Asha's brows rose. "The princess's?"

"No, Jeena's."

"And how do ye know this?"

Because he'd seen the same look in Renn's eyes all those years ago. "I've seen it in someone else." And . . . his heart sank. He leaned over the arm of the chair and set his ale on the floor. Asha's eyes didn't have the same haunted look, and yet . . . "We haven't spoken much since I came back to the stronghold. I didn't expect to see ye in a Mother's robe. Ye loved the hunt too much. When did ye give up yer sword?"

To his horror, Asha's cheeks reddened and she seemed to shrink in on herself. "I shouldn't have asked," he quickly said. "It's personal."

"No, it's not that. Do ye mind if I close the door?"

"I can—"

Asha was already on her feet and shutting the door. "Ye'll laugh now," she stated, perching on the bed again. "But I need to talk to someone, and Zheir and Lale aren't here."

Toe swallowed and straightened in his chair. He usually felt tense in the presence of a Mother, and Asha was no exception, even though he'd known her before and she was younger than him.

"A couple of years after ye left, I was out hunting with a few others and I split from the group. Ye know how I was."

He nodded. Asha had been a bold hunter who was as skilled with a sword and bow as Avere was with her daggers, but she'd also been reckless. The hunters teaching her had spent almost as much time scolding her as they did praising her, even though she'd always bagged more game than their other students.

"I was tracking a bear. The others were going too slow for me, so I left them behind. I found the bear—and three others."

"Four, then?"

"Aye. I was always quick with my bow, but not that quick. I was stupid. There was only one set of tracks, yes. I didn't consider that wherever the bear was going, there could be more. I was too focused on it to notice."

"But ye're sitting here, so ye survived."

"I stumbled into the middle of them. They were all staring at me, at their dinner. I could have run, or maybe taken down one with my blade, but I was frozen there. I didn't even try. One of them lumbered toward me. It was this close." Asha held her right hand a short distance away from her face. "And I called out to the Seven, and I said, I need yer help. I've been stupid, but I don't want to die for it. If ye save me, I'll serve ye. To be honest, I'd been thinking about it anyway. I always felt close to them." She shook her head. "Stupid now."

Toe leaned forward. "Why?"

Asha drew a shuddering breath. "Ye heard her. They haven't been listening. When that bear took a long look at me and turned away, and the others left, too, it wasn't them. It was luck. Or maybe something else caught their attention. It wasn't the Seven. They didn't save me."

Toe didn't know what to say. "Do ye regret taking the robe, then?"

"No, but was I meant to take it? And all those times we communed with the Seven and told others to put their faith in the Seven, we thought we were helping. We thought they were listening." She lifted her hands and dropped them to her lap. "What have I been doing all this time?"

"Helping."

"How?"

"Comforting folk. Being with them. Sometimes folk just need someone to listen, to care."

"I've been big-headed," Asha said, apparently determined to find fault with herself. "I've always thought the Seven wanted me to take the robe, because I thought it was them who saved me from the bears. But they couldn't have. They didn't even know about it."

"What's done is done. Ye said ye don't regret taking the

robe, and it suits ye, so don't spoil it for yerself. Ye didn't know. Ye're not the only one who thought the Seven were guiding ye, or comforting ye."

"But not many claim to commune with them and speak for them, as the Mothers do."

Toe thought back to the circular chamber and Zhikinden's words. "She didn't say they weren't listening. She said they couldn't do anything to help. And she called ye 'Young Mother.'"

Asha's voice rose. "Ye think that means something?"

"I do," Toe said, meaning it. He wasn't one to tell folk what they wanted to hear. "She could have called ye Asha, but to her, ye were 'Young Mother.'"

She nodded thoughtfully.

Toe hoped she'd find her footing again. As a man who considered his eyes and ears the best proof of anything, seeing Zhikinden had shocked and humbled him, but it hadn't made him question how he'd always related to them. He'd always believed in them. Someone had created Daros, the creatures who walked it, the beauty of the land, and his beating heart. But that was where he'd seen the Seven—in what was around him, not somewhere else. Erryn had challenged him more than Zhikinden's words had, by summoning the Fallen into existence from somewhere he couldn't see. But once again, he'd quickly believed his eyes and ears.

For someone like Asha, who'd not only put her faith in those she couldn't see and touch, but had dedicated her life to them and spoken for them, finding out they hadn't been responding and guiding would feel as if the ground under her feet suddenly wasn't there. Perhaps Lale and Zheir were also struggling.

"I've seen ye with the others," he said to Asha. "I've seen how ye are. Don't think ye've been wasting yer time all these years. Ye've supported folk in the clan, been their strength when they were faltering. They look up to ye. Ye haven't let them down."

"I'm not so sure about that." She bit her lip and lowered her head.

Toe could hear the sorrow in her voice and wished he could take her hand. But he didn't want to offend her, or have her think he wanted to take advantage of her when she was vulnerable.

"It's funny how ye didn't have any doubts about being a Mother when ye'd never seen her, but now that ye're sure she's there, ye're having doubts." The moment he said the words, he wished he'd chosen different ones, especially when Asha's shoulders heaved. "I'm sorry. I didn't mean it's funny."

"No, ye're right. It is funny." She lifted her head. Toe was relieved to see her smiling, though she did brush away a tear.

"Ye're doing what ye want to do. What ye're meant to do. Ye need to stop thinking about how ye came to it, or about what's past. Ye're doing Zhikinden's work now. There's no doubt about that."

"That's true, but it's still been weighing on me." Asha fell silent for a moment, then stood. "I should go. I told Timor I'd sit with him. Tomorrow he'll say a few words about Var and Yanik. I think he and Var would have pledged to each other eventually, but now . . ."

"They died doing Zhikinden's bidding. They're with her now."

"They are, but her gain is our loss." She went to the door, patting his shoulder as she passed him. "I'll find my way. Telling ye has helped. I couldn't tell anyone else."

"Ye can always talk to me," Toe said, even though her words dismayed him. He sat thinking about them after she'd left. *I couldn't tell anyone else.* But she felt safe admitting her doubts to him, because he was an outsider now, a visitor to the stronghold, someone who used to belong. She no longer saw him as Toetril of the Snowlake clan, and that saddened him more than he'd expected.

Avere slipped into the temple and paused to listen to the murmuring voice of the primate in the main worship room. Not long ago, she would have sighed and come back when the service was over, but now she quietly went into the room and knelt at the back. They were real. She'd believed in them before, but now she knew. She'd seen. Zhikinden had spoken her name. She'd never be devout, and she certainly wasn't going to give up her daggers. But she would no longer be dismissive and wonder why men wasted their lives wearing mitres. Her mind still wandered as the primate spoke, though, her thoughts turning to Arrick.

Fi had recounted her escape from Darroth, including how Arrick had greeted her when she'd emerged from the secret tunnel. *You're playing a dangerous game, Arrick.*

She wasn't angry with him for ordering his people to drag her back to Darroth. Surprised, but not angry. He must be concerned for her, as she was for him, making her even more eager to return to the Royal City. This was the longest she'd gone without seeing him. It wasn't that she missed him, not really, no, no—what was the primate saying?

Avere tried to focus on the service, but after seeing Zhikinden herself, the primate's words were even more boring than usual. Pretending she planned to rob the temple, she studied the main worship room for valuables, and entrance and exit points. Her eyes settled on one of the seven tapestries hanging on the walls, the one with the familiar image of Zhikinden woven into it. The goddess had looked just like it, but she'd also spoken of taking forms, so that wasn't what she really looked like. But it must have been how she'd appeared all those years ago, when they were all free and had walked Daros. Which meant the images woven into the other tapestries . . . Avere studied them with new eyes. If they succeeded in the task Zhikinden had given them, she'd see them all.

Rustling and chattering voices snapped her back to her surroundings. The service was over. Avere smiled at anyone who smiled at her. Most hurried past her, intent on returning to their lives outside the temple. Avere lowered her head enough to appear as if she were praying, but not so low that she couldn't see the primate at the front of the room, with several people clustered around him. Twenty minutes must have passed by the time the last person bid the primate good-bye. She waited another five, then went to the primate's study.

He was standing in front of the fire, a goblet in his hand. He'd already removed his mitre.

"Excuse me."

He frowned, then his eyes lit up with recognition. "You're the one who asked me about the cultist's cloak."

"And made a hefty donation to your carpet fund." Surprisingly, there *was* a new carpet in the worship room. "I'd like to make another donation to the temple."

"What do you want this time?"

Straight to business. She could like this man, despite the mitre. "I need something translated. It's written in an older tongue. I've been told you study ancient languages as part of your training."

He set his goblet on the fireplace's mantle and held out his hand. "I didn't specialize in languages, but I know the basics. Give it to me."

Avere fished the copy of the passage from the small purse on her belt and handed it to him. He read it. A vein in his temple pulsed. He crushed the paper and tossed it into the fire.

Avere kept her expression smooth. It was a good thing she'd had the sense to copy a passage, rather than give him the book.

"Where did you get that?" he snapped, his eyes hard.

"I—"

"Did the cultist give it to you?"

"No, I—"

"I heard the cultist was dead, and now I'm wondering if you ever crossed paths with her, or if you're one yourself."

"No! I—"

"Blasphemy! Blasphemy of the worst kind. I have a mind to call the guard and tell them you stole something, but I'll be merciful this once." He pointed to the door. "Get out! If I ever see you in this temple again, I won't be so kind."

Avere knew not to argue. A donation wouldn't work this time. She turned on her heel and marched from the temple. Outside, she stopped around the corner and caught her breath. Getting the book translated wasn't going to be easy.

"The closer we get to the Royal City, the more danger we'll be in," Erryn said. Her protective circle, as she'd come to think of them, were gathered in her room. One addition to the circle leaned against the wall. Jeena, Fi's personal guard, who appeared to take her job seriously.

"But we'll have the resources of the Ferrets." Avere looked down at the book on her lap. "The spymaster should be able to find someone who can translate the book."

"Not a primate," Fi said. "They're corrupt. Not all of them, but we can't tell who's working with Otane."

"We'll stick out in the Royal City," Asha said, gesturing to herself and the other Northerners. "Perhaps the three of ye should enter it by yerselves."

Avere's face lit up. "Yes, the Ferret, the Beast Master, and the fallen princess. There's a joke in there somewhere, with a very bad punchline. No, I'd go myself. You'd stay with Erryn and camp across the border in Rion."

"How long would it take ye?" Toe asked.

Avere pursed her lips. "To get there and back? A couple of weeks. But I'd wait for the translation, which could take a day or two. I could be gone a month."

"While we sit and do nothing?" Erryn shook her head. "No." She turned to Fi. "What about Cedric? If he's gathered some allies, maybe one of them would know a primate who'd help us, one outside the Royal City."

"I don't know how to get in touch with him."

"Didn't you have a plan?"

Fi frowned. "Yes, but . . . you have to understand, when we were in Moss, I was numb. I was grieving. I let them handle it all."

"Them?" Avere said.

"Enkelo, Cedric, and Dann. I wasn't listening. Enkelo and Dann would know how to get a message to him, but . . ." She grimaced and lowered her head.

Erryn patted her back. She'd talk to her about Dann when they were alone. Fi hadn't said anything to her, but every time she said Dann's name, Erryn could see her pain. Something had happened between them, but when? Fi had been betrothed to Viren when he'd died on the rack.

"Do we need the book translated?" Renn jutted her chin toward it. "We have the map."

"But we don't know the exact locations of the temples, or why the Seven were bound," Avere said.

"We don't need to know why. We freed Zhikinden without knowing."

"She's right," Erryn said, shooting Renn a quick smile. "But travelling to all those temples . . . it would take a while to reach each one, and we'd need local help to find them. And I'm not sure I want to go to Westerfox. Based on what you told us about your cultist, we could find help there," she said to Avere. "But based on what happened with the assassinations, we could also find ourselves in deep trouble. On the other hand, we'll be in grave danger if we enter the Royal City," she said, bringing them back to where they'd started. "If we decide to go there, we should all go. I don't like the idea of splitting up."

Avere studied her fingernails. "Let's look at the problems with the Royal City. Some of us are familiar there, though you could move around there now, Erryn. The guard might stop and examine you, but without the brand, they'd let you go. The one in the most danger would be the princess."

"She can't enter the Royal City," Erryn said flatly. "We need to find somewhere safe and leave her there."

"Excuse me." Fi's tone conveyed her irritation. "I'm right here. And I'm not staying behind. I'm not being separated from everyone." Her voice softened. "We just found each other."

"But entering the Royal City—"

"I know. But look at me, and I'm clean at the moment."

"Fi, every guard is on the lookout for you. It'll be dangerous getting from here to the gate out of town."

"But we'll do it. I'll be in a shirt and trousers, with a

cap on my head. I'm skin and bone. I'm with a group. And the last place they'll expect to find me is walking into Darroth."

"Once you're in the Royal City, you'll stay inside," Avere said.

If Fi didn't appreciate being given an order, she didn't show it.

"So you think we should risk the Royal City, then," Erryn said.

Avere nodded. "We're in danger no matter what we try. If we go to six other temples, that's six times the danger in my mind. The Royal City has unique dangers, but it's also big, and I know it well. The spymaster is there, too. Once we're inside, we'll contact him. He'll have somewhere to hide us." She paused. "There is one other big problem. If one of us is captured in Darroth, justice will be swift. There won't be much opportunity for a rescue on the ride to the square nearest the castle."

"Is that where they execute criminals?" Asha asked.

"Ones who have committed treason? Yes."

Everyone fell silent. Returning to the Royal City frightened and excited Erryn. If they found the temple quickly and freed the remaining Six, would Zhikinden and the others help put Fi on the throne? Did they care about such matters? Would they somehow give Erryn some semblance of a life, one in which she wouldn't have to hide? Would they tell her why?

"I'm willing to take the chance," she said. The alternative would be spending months travelling around Daros, into strange provinces where they'd need help from the likely hostile locals. "When we get there, our first step will be to find the temple."

"The book will tell us," Avere said. "We'll lie low until we get it translated." Her gaze swept the room. "Are we agreed, then?"

Murmurs and nods answered her.

"Then on the morrow, we leave for the Royal City."

To their salvation, or their doom.

"I can't believe it," Fi murmured as she stood next to Erryn, watching the guard question a woman on her way out of Stronghaven. After leaving the inn, they'd already run into a problem. This was the second gate they'd tried, to no avail. The guards were stopping everyone entering and leaving the city. Those waiting to be on their way grumbled and craned their necks. It was bad enough that Fi's scalp kept itching, making her want to rip off the cap she wore. She should never have agreed to let Avere cut her hair, especially when it wouldn't do them much good anyway, with the guards scrutinizing everyone.

Avere, who'd slinked into the crowd, emerged from the group of restless travellers and motioned for Fi and the others to follow her. They moved away from the commotion and gathered around the Ferret.

"It's Millwood. If there was any doubt he died in our rescue, there isn't now. A few of his men survived, but I doubt they could offer much of a description. But they know you were there." Her eyes met Erryn's. "You don't have a brand, but they'll pull you, and all of us, aside for a closer look." Now she looked at Fi. "We can't have that."

"I'll go through the gate alone," Erryn said.

"No," Renn and several of the others said in unison.

"Ye're the most important one here," Asha said, with an apologetic look at Fi. "We can't lose ye."

"But I'm not branded."

"Which doesn't mean they won't hold you for a while, because you look so much like you," Avere said. "They might want a noble to examine you, or they might send you to Darroth and let the Primacy have a look at you. I have no doubt you'd be freed, but you need to stay with us."

"If they sent me to Darroth, wouldn't that be good? It would get me into the city."

"It would, but who knows what could happen to you on the way. We can't lose you."

Fi wanted to scream. Thwarted already! "Perhaps we shouldn't go to Darroth."

"No, that part of the plan is sound," Erryn said. "But how do we leave Stronghaven?"

Toe scratched his beard. "They won't be stopping people at the gates forever."

"We could wait them out," Avere said. "But they won't let the killing of a noble go that easily. They'll search rooming houses and inns and watch the gates for a while. And I prefer to keep moving." Her expression grew thoughtful. "Let me speak to my colleagues. They might know a way out of the city that doesn't involve the gates."

Fi stared up at the stone wall that rose above the crowd at the gate. "How likely is that?"

"There used to be several underground passages out

of Darroth," Avere said, surprising Fi. Father had never mentioned them, and he'd always been concerned with how to get his family to safety in the unlikely event of an uprising.

"Queen Anthena collapsed them all," Avere continued. "Apparently she was concerned with troops getting in."

Fi could believe it. Anthena, Fi's great-great-great-great-grandmother on Father's side, had been paranoid. A few had whispered that she was mad. Even though Daros had been at peace during her reign, she'd almost bankrupted the royal treasury by quadrupling the number of guards and soldiers under her command, and she'd insisted on preparing her own food and drink. A queen, cooking for herself in the castle's kitchen! Anthena's eccentricities were the only reason Fi remembered the history lessons about her.

"And the Ferrets haven't dug any since then?" she said playfully to Avere.

"Not yet," Avere said with a smile.

Erryn gazed at Avere. "How are you going to ask anyone? They tried to capture you."

"I'll be prepared this time. I won't go to the base. I know where I can find a few away from home, but not until tonight. Until then, we'll take in the sights and sounds of Stronghaven."

Fi strolled away with the others, resisting the urge to glance over her shoulder at those waiting to leave the city. She looped her arm through Erryn's. Since they'd reunited, Fi had rarely left Erryn's side and couldn't stop worrying about being separated from her again. She expected to hear the shout of a guard at any moment, or to be grabbed from behind and dragged away. At least Erryn still wore a hat, even though the ugly brand on her forehead was gone. There was no point in taunting the guards to examine her closer. Fi wore a cap on her head, too, and was getting used to wearing a shirt and trousers, though she longed to slip into a gown and style her short hair. Erryn might not care about such things, but she did.

Jeena walked on the other side of her, as usual, and Renn always stuck close to Erryn. Their personal guards rarely spoke, at least in Fi's presence. She'd seen Erryn and Renn talking with each other, but always apart from the group. Erryn had told her that Renn warmed up to people slowly, but Fi had noticed the other wild folk didn't bother with Renn much, and surely she must know them well. They all came from the same clan.

"Can ye spare a coin for something to eat?"

Fi looked in the direction of the voice and cringed at the sight of a wild man huddled at the side of the road with his hand out. They were everywhere—beggars—and most of them were wild. They had beggars in Darroth, but not so many of them, and they were crippled, or addled, or old, or couldn't get work because they had a poor reputation. The situation here was different. Most of those hoping for charity were young and able-bodied, and wild.

She'd also witnessed the guard beating a wild man who'd been caught stealing food from a merchant's stall, seen them drag him away and pound on him. Outrage had clenched her fists, and she'd wanted to do something.

Guards were not supposed to beat citizens. But Erryn had quietly told her they couldn't get involved, so Fi had kept walking, her shoulders hunched and her nails digging into her palms every time one of the guards' fists thudded into the man.

She'd never been to Stronghaven before. Father had ignored it, had relied on the nobles in the region to maintain order and collect taxes. The roads were in disrepair, the guard had no respect for many of the city's people, too many houses and shops were falling apart. At the same time, the wild folk were a law unto themselves. They had no time for the crown, and their customs were foreign to her. Stronghaven certainly wasn't Darroth.

She'd seen Avere give to beggars a few times, always to children, and always when she thought nobody was looking. Fi couldn't figure the woman out, and was both impressed with and fearful of her. Fortunately, Avere was on their side.

As she had when the guard had beaten the man, she looked away again as they continued past the beggar without giving him any coin. She understood. If they pressed a coin into everyone's hand, they'd soon have nothing left to give. But it didn't sit well. If she took the throne, perhaps she could do something about it. Right now, if those begging on the streets knew who she was, they'd turn on her in an instant. The bounty on her head was high. She gripped Erryn's arm tighter and kept her eyes forward.

* * * * *

Avere entered the noisy inn and went straight to the barkeep, ignoring the leers of the men she passed. Most of them had a whore on their lap and would soon be in one of the rooms upstairs. Not wanting to remain in the hovel longer than required, Avere beckoned to the barkeep and held up several coins. His eyes widened. She'd bet his mouth was watering.

"About this height," she said, lifting her hand several inches above her head. "Sandy hair, thin, a bushy moustache, might be using the name Billy."

His eyes never left the coins in her fingers. "Upset that he ain't warming your bed, are we?"

Avere plucked one of the coins from her fingers. "Answer me now and I'll add it back."

"All right, all right. Just don't want any trouble. Already had someone dragging her husband out." He moistened his lips. "Upstairs, second door on the right."

She dropped the coins into his outstretched palm and bounded up the stairs. Stopping outside the second door on the right, Avere listened to the groans coming from within the room then, steeling herself, she threw the door open and marched inside.

The woman on top of Billy rolled off him, her eyes wide. Billy's mouth fell open, but he recovered quickly. "Do you mind?" he roared. "I'm in the middle of something here."

"I can see that." Avere snatched the whore's dress from the floor and threw it to her. "Get dressed and take a break." She tossed the woman a coin. "I'll let you know when you can come back."

Billy had pulled a blanket up to his waist. They waited

until the whore had pulled on her dress and left the room. "What in the blazes do you think you're doing?" he said.

"I need information, and I wasn't in the mood to be captured again. Is there a way to get out of the city without using the gates?"

"Why do you want to know?"

"Because I don't want to use the gates."

He scowled at her. "I'm not a fool. What have you done? The guards are questioning everyone because—" He swallowed. "You didn't do Millwood, did you? There was no order from the spymaster."

"Don't worry about what I've done. Just answer the question."

"You know he wants you back in Darroth."

"I gathered, and maybe that's where I'm headed. How do I get out quietly?"

He held her gaze, then relented. "There are a couple of ways out, but they're not pleasant."

Her nose crinkled. "Do you mean . . ."

He nodded. "The sewers. One will bring you out beyond the west wall, down near the river. The other one to the north."

"Tell me about the one to the west."

"All the entrances in the artisan quarter will take you there. If you keep heading west, you'll eventually make it through."

"Do you have a map?"

His eyes narrowed. "I might."

"Can I get a copy?"

"It's not here."

"I didn't think it was, but if I were to hang around the base in a few hours . . ."

"After what you did tonight, and before?"

"I'm leaving the city one way or the other. Do you think the spymaster wants me in the hands of the guard?"

"You'd die before you'd tell them anything."

"True, but you said the spymaster wants me back in Darroth, so badly that he ordered you to capture me." Avere still couldn't believe Arrick had issued such an order. "I doubt he wants me in a cell, or on the rack."

Billy nodded slowly. "You're probably right about that. But I've told you what you need to know."

Avere's fingers twitched, but gutting him would be stupid. A few strategic cuts, though. "I could get lost."

"You won't."

She studied his face. He wasn't going to give her more, and she wasn't going to plant a dagger in him. "I'll tell your whore to come back up."

He patted the bed next to him. "Or you could stay a while more."

She bit back a laugh, pulled out a dagger, and carefully ran a finger along its blade. "Maybe I will, but it's only fair to let you know that I like to play with my daggers when I'm excited. Most men leave my bed missing something important." She looked pointedly at his covered genitals.

Billy's face turned green. "Maybe another time, then."

"I think that would be best." She whirled and went back down to the common room, but couldn't see Billy's whore.

"Not dragging him home, then," the barkeep said when she returned to the bar.

"He's not worth it. I even promised I'd send his whore back upstairs. Where is she?" When the barkeep lifted his brows, she fished another coin from her purse and gave it to him.

"She's outside," he said. "Just left with another man."

Billy wouldn't be pleased, but that wasn't Avere's problem. She left the inn and walked in the direction of— Voices drew her attention, coming from the alley that ran next to the inn. She pressed against the corner of the building and peered into the darkness. Two shadowy forms stood several feet away. It was just the whore and the client, who must prefer it outside. Avere pushed away from the inn to leave, but then stopped.

". . . Ferret . . . trusts me," the whore murmured. ". . . working him . . . need to . . ."

Avere silently cursed when the inn door crashed open and two men tumbled out, wailing a song. Fortunately they were too drunk to notice her.

". . . leave after me . . ."

One of the shadowy figures loomed larger. Avere's mind raced. Should she stay with the whore, or follow the man? She darted away from the alley, bent over, and made retching noises until the man passed her. Then, her decision made, she darted into the alley. It must be a dead end, otherwise there would be no reason for the man to leave first. He'd just leave the alley at its other end.

In one smooth motion, she grabbed the whore, spun

her around, and pushed a dagger against her throat from behind. "Who was that man?" she hissed.

The woman whimpered.

"Who was he?"

"Just someone looking for a good time."

She pressed the dagger into the woman's skin. "I heard what you said to him. Who was he?"

"I don't know, I don't know," the whore said, the dagger and her panic straining her voice. "He pays me to pass information along to him."

"Who does he work for?"

"I don't know. He pays me good coin to listen to folk when they're inclined to talk. I don't know why. I didn't ask."

Avere believed her, but this woman had spied on a Ferret and passed along potentially damaging information. Billy didn't know anything about Erryn and Fi's whereabouts, but he was in charge of the Stronghaven Ferrets. He read the messages and gave the orders.

"I won't work for him anymore," the whore said.

This time, Avere didn't believe her.

"I won't tell him—" The whore's voice cut off. She gurgled and slumped to the ground. Avere wiped her dagger with a cloth she pulled from one of her pockets, then sheathed it. She dragged the woman's corpse to the end of the alley and propped it up against the wall. Then she crept back to the road. Only one man was about, teetering away from the inn. How long would it take Billy to realize the whore wasn't coming back?

Ten minutes later, he swaggered outside.

"Billy."

He turned to her and groaned. "What do you want now?"

"Walk with me."

"I could put a dagger to your back," he said, falling into step with her.

"But you won't, because I spared you once. Your whore . . . she's been spying on you."

His brows drew together, and he snorted. "What are you talking about, woman?"

"When I went back downstairs, she'd ducked out to meet someone in the alley. I couldn't catch everything they were saying, but what I did hear made it clear that she's more interested in what you have to say than . . . anything else. I don't know who the target really is. You, the Ferrets in general, or the spymaster." Or Erryn and Fi, but she couldn't mention them.

Billy whirled and marched back to the inn. "I'll gut that whore and—"

Avere caught his arm. "I've already taken care of that. Did you tell her anything?"

His eyes widened with indignation. "No. I'm not that stupid. It's not the first time a whore's been paid to spy on me."

"But you didn't know about her."

She watched him struggle with his ego. His shoulders slumped. "You're right. I should have been more careful."

"I won't tell."

He almost smiled. "You're a good one, mistress. But you've also upset the spymaster."

"I'm going back to Darroth. The first thing I'll do when I get there is see the spymaster."

Billy was silent for a moment. "Are you really going to use the sewers? What's the guard got on you?"

"It's best you not know."

He didn't press her. "If you come by in the morning, say eleven o'clock, I'll have a copy of the map for you."

Avere wanted to trust him, but . . . "Meet me in the tavern across the road. Alone."

"I wasn't crossing you. I was following orders."

"Orders that still stand, I'm sure."

He gave her a sly look. "You did say you were going back. Eleven o'clock in the tavern, then?"

"I'll be there." With a couple of the wild folk at another table, in case he didn't come alone. Without saying another word, she veered away from him and darted down an alley.

Erryn cringed when the floor creaked outside her and Renn's room. Since rescuing Fi, she and Renn could hardly snatch any time alone together. If they weren't sharing a room, they'd hardly speak. Erryn couldn't be happier about having Fi with her, and she understood Fi wanting to spend time together, but that didn't stop her from wishing she could have an hour alone with Renn, just to sit, and talk, and hold hands in comfortable silence. When Fi had said she wanted to bathe while they waited for Avere to return with a map of the sewers, Erryn had gotten two meat pies from the landlady and quickly brought them upstairs. That had been ten minutes ago. Surely Fi hadn't bathed already.

When someone knocked on the door, Erryn met Renn's eyes, then shouted, "Come in."

The door swung open. Fi bounded into the room, breathed in the air, and nodded. "Smells scrumptious. I should get one."

Erryn suppressed a sigh. "I thought you were going to have another bath."

"I was, but then I thought, the landlady will have to heat the water and have someone haul it upstairs, and I don't really need another one just yet. So here I am."

Renn rose and picked up her plate. "I'll finish this downstairs."

"You don't need to leave on my account," Fi said.

"Ye'll speak easier without me here," Renn said. Erryn couldn't tell if she was upset. She didn't sound upset, but . . . As Renn closed the door, Erryn glimpsed Jeena hovering outside.

Fi plunked into Renn's chair. "Why does she always do that?"

"What?" Erryn asked, after swallowing the last bit of her meat pie.

"Leave whenever I want to talk to you."

"I don't know," Erryn said honestly. Renn could be irritated, or not feel comfortable with Fi, or perhaps she was worried that she'd somehow alert Fi to their relationship.

"It can't be because I'm not a wild woman. She likes talking to you."

"Tell me about Dann," Erryn said, more bluntly than she'd intended because she wanted to change the subject. "I know he's Tolin's third son, but who is—was—is he to you?"

Fi's shoulders hunched, and she clasped her hands on her lap. "Tolin's dead."

"Oh. I'm sorry."

"I didn't know him well." Fi swallowed. "You're not going to think well of me."

"Because something happened between you and Dann?" Erryn said.

"Nothing happened. But I was betrothed to Viren, who was a decent man. He died on the rack because of me."

"You didn't kill him."

"No, but if he'd asked for another woman's hand, he'd still be alive, and might have been happier with her than he ever would have been with me."

"You don't know that," Erryn said softly.

"Yes, I do, because I loved Dann, and at my wedding I would have been thinking about him. We'd agreed nothing would ever happen and we were staying away from each other as much as possible, but—"

"You told him how you feel?" Erryn said, surprise lifting her voice. Viren had been an arranged marriage, not a love match, so she wasn't surprised Fi had been attracted to another man. But to admit to it—to the other man . . . Fi was usually more astute than that.

Fi fidgeted, her hands still clasped. "I said you wouldn't think well of me."

"You said nothing happened."

"But I wanted it to. If I'd had a choice, I would have chosen Dann."

"You didn't have a choice. You always knew you wouldn't choose who you'd marry." She reached out and covered Fi's hands, to still them. It was a friendly gesture, and Erryn felt nothing but concern and sympathy. There was a time when having this conversation with Fi, listening to her admit her love for someone else and hearing the longing in her voice, would have made her jealous. She would have resented Dann and hoped Fi's feelings for him would die. But no longer. She could be a better sister and friend to Fi now. "The men who qualified to be your husband made up a short list."

"Yes, and third sons weren't on it," Fi said with a hint of bitterness. "It doesn't matter now, anyway. He's dead."

"It matters because you feel guilty, and you shouldn't. Nothing happened. And it's not your fault that Viren died on the rack."

"He could have implicated me to spare himself a long, painful death, but he didn't." Fi's eyes glistened. "I think he loved me. He deserved better." She drew a shuddering breath.

"When did you realize you had feelings for Dann?" Erryn asked, wanting Fi to dwell on good memories, not bad. "You never mentioned him."

"I didn't notice him until after Father had banished you. It's your fault, really," she said with a thin smile.

Erryn knew her well enough to know she was teasing, despite her sombreness. "My fault? How could it be my fault?"

"I was missing you at a banquet, so I went up on the wall, to feel closer to you, I suppose. And there he was, escaping, like me. Perhaps if I hadn't been missing you so much . . . perhaps if I hadn't met him where we'd sat so many times . . . perhaps I wouldn't have instantly fallen in love with him."

"Or it would have happened anyway."

"Not there, because you would have been with me."

Erryn grinned. Her grin grew wider when Fi answered with a smile that reached her eyes.

"Talking to you about this has lifted my spirits," Fi said. "This is why I wanted to find you. Because I can tell you anything, and you listen to me, and you see me as me first, not a Lyos. You're my only family now, and I love you."

A lump rose in Erryn's throat. "I love you, too."

They hugged and held each other tightly for a minute. When they drew back, Erryn steeled herself. Fi was her only family too, and keeping a secret from her—a meaningful secret—would drive a wedge between them. Erryn wanted to keep their relationship honest. "I have something to tell you, and you might not think well of me," she said, forcing levity into her voice.

Fi's brows rose. "What is it?"

Erryn's heart hammered in her chest. She stood, walked a few paces and leaned against the wall. She didn't expect Fi to strike her, but . . . "It's about Renn."

"Renn?"

Erryn folded her arms. "We've become close. Very close."

Fi waited, her eyes shining with curiosity.

"We're involved."

"Involved in what?"

"Involved with each other," Erryn said haltingly. "We have feelings for each other that extend beyond friendship."

Fi blinked at her. "I read your diary," she blurted.

Erryn gaped. "You read it? I told you not to read it."

"And I wasn't going to. But then it was in my hands, and I'd just found out you were a Beast Master, and I wanted to see if there was anything in there that would help me make sense of it." She quirked a brow. "And I was curious."

Blood rushed to Erryn's cheeks. "What I wrote—I mean—I don't—"

Fi held up her hand. "I knew it would be a passing fancy, Erryn. But I thought it would pass and you'd fall in love with a man, not a woman." Her brow furrowed. "And certainly not a wild woman. Perhaps it's happened because you were lonely, or Renn was one of the few people who accepted you for who you are. Why didn't you get involved with Toe?"

"For the same reason you fell for Dann and not Viren!" Erryn winced at the same time Fi did. "Sorry. I shouldn't have said that."

"She could be a passing fancy, like I was."

"I don't know what the future will hold for us. But I do know that if for some reason we part, and I fall in love again, it will be with a woman. At the banquets and the teas and when we were out in the city, it was always girls, and then women, who turned my head, never a man."

Fi was silent for a moment. "Father would have chosen a husband for you."

"And I would have married whoever he chose, and maybe I would have grown to love him, but not with the passion a woman should have for her husband. And that's one of the few positive things that came out of the king banishing me."

"Not having to marry someone you couldn't love," Fi stated.

"That too, but I meant that I was able to admit it to myself that I'm one of those women the court whispered about."

Fi chuckled. "It's not a crime, but it's not an easy life, either. I suppose it's one of the few times that being a commoner would be more advantageous than being a noble. Commoners have more freedom in some areas." Her forehead creased. "But are you sure? It doesn't make me think any less of you, but it's not what I would want for you. Your life will be more difficult. It's not a crime, but it's not openly supported."

"I know love now. I'd rather live true to myself and forfeit those who disapprove, than deny myself for those whose friendship comes with conditions."

"Easy words to say."

"Right now, it doesn't matter. I'm a Beast Master. I'm not cursed by the Seven, but nobody believes that. Unless we can free the Six, and unless they somehow rewrite parts of the Holy Texts, I won't have to worry about what anyone thinks of me because I prefer the company of women."

"If we do free them and they make Daros understand that you saved them, what then? What if I take back the throne? You're my sister in everything but blood."

Erryn frowned. "What does that have to do with it?"

"You're avoiding the question. You know very well that if I sit on the throne and you free them, you'll be my sister, the Saviour, and you'll be titled. The people will demand it. And as my sister, you'll live at the castle. You know how many eyes are at the castle, Erryn. We had little privacy there. It's one of the prices we paid for all the luxuries."

"I wouldn't want a title."

"You wouldn't have any choice in the matter. Neither would I."

"What are you saying?" Erryn asked, not wanting to hear the answer. Fi had left out something significant—that Erryn would live at the castle until she was married. The queen would have to find a suitable husband for her sister, or tongues would wag. Fi knew that. Her omission had been deliberate. Perhaps she wanted to hear Erryn say it, as a way of admitting that her relationship with Renn would have to end.

Fi lifted her hands in a helpless gesture. "I'm saying to think ahead. You can do what you like at the moment. If—when I take the crown and you're redeemed in the eyes of the people, you'll be powerful, but not free. In some ways, you'll have less freedom than the poorest citizen in Daros. It's a paradox we Lyoses have lived with for generations."

"I'm taking everything one step at a time," Erryn said stubbornly.

"You'll have to face it sometime, Erryn." Fi's voice was soft and her eyes sympathetic, making Erryn feel worse.

"Maybe I'll leave Darroth. The moment you've taken the throne, I'll flee the city."

"No, you won't. You wouldn't do that to me."

"Then I hope they don't redeem me, because then I won't be able to stay in Darroth."

"No, you don't. You won't want to be on the run for the rest of your life."

Tears sprang to Erryn's eyes. "There has to be a way for me to be with someone I truly love, or at least to not be with someone I can't love. If you force me to marry . . ." Her throat tightened. "I don't want to resent you," she said, her voice a thread.

Fi's eyes welled, too. "I don't want that, either. But we might not have much choice. Remember that I was going to marry someone Father had chosen for me."

"It's not the same thing," Erryn snapped. "You could have grown to love Viren. I won't be able to love a husband who's forced on me, at least not in the way I should."

"There have been plenty of marriages among nobles in which love never grew."

"And that would make it all right? At least there was the possibility of love growing between them, unless one of them was like me. If you make me marry, you'll do so knowing you've sentenced me to a loveless life."

Fi grimaced. "I don't want to do that to you, and

perhaps you're right. There's no point worrying about it while we're both wanted by the guard."

Erryn almost wished she hadn't told Fi. Not only had it created tension between them, but Fi already had enough weighing on her mind. She missed Dann and still grieved for him. Millwood had paraded her through villages, and people had jeered and thrown rotten fruit and vegetables at her. She was a queen without a throne, and if she took the throne, she'd have to do something she hated. Erryn would have to remind herself of that if it came to pass—that Fi would be doing what she had to do. But every time Erryn had to lie with her husband, every time she had to pretend, she'd hate her. If she hadn't seen Zhikinden with her own eyes and heard the goddess's command from her own lips, she'd go to the nearest square right now, summon the Fallen, and let the guard take her.

She would do everything she could to free them. She would help Fi reclaim her throne. And then she'd . . . what? Fi was right. Erryn couldn't disobey her or run away, not because Fi was the queen, but because she was her sister, and Erryn was loyal to her. When Fi took the throne, she'd need her sister more than ever. There had to be a way to remain with her and avoid marriage. If there wasn't, she'd flee before her wedding, or perhaps take a sharp knife to her wrists, though if she could somehow make her death look like an accident to spare Fi any guilt, she would.

Fi had said there was no point worrying about it now, but they both knew they were delaying the inevitable.

Still, Erryn would go along with it, for her. Fi was pale, and her hands were clasped tightly again.

"Maybe it was selfish to tell you, but I didn't want a secret between us, especially one so important," Erryn said to her.

Fi smiled weakly. "No, I'm glad you told me. I would have been hurt if I found out you were carrying on right under my nose and hadn't bothered to tell me. I suppose I've been getting in the way."

Erryn managed a chuckle. "Just a little."

Fi didn't appear offended. "Who else knows?"

"Just Avere. Not because I told her. She notices everything."

"I have to admit to being surprised that it's Renn who has your heart."

"Because she's a wild woman?" Erryn wanted to say Northerner, but gently suggesting that Fi change the way she referred to Renn and the others would have to wait for another conversation.

"No, because she's . . ." Fi gave Erryn an apologetic look. "Yes, because she's a wild woman."

"That's the other good thing that's come out of being banished. I can't look down my nose at anyone. I had to accept help from whoever offered. Renn and Toe frightened me a bit when I first met them. I laugh about that now. They have paler skin and their own customs, but they're no different from us. And if we free the Six, it will be due to the wild folk. Without their help, I'd be dead."

"The first wild folk I met was Jeena. Hardly a good impression."

"She was one wild woman in a group of slavers who were all city men."

"Still, it wasn't the best introduction to their kind. But my knowledge of them is broadening. I have to admit to not being pleased with the state of Stronghaven. I know Father and those before him left this region to the nobles, all of whom are likely corrupt."

Erryn raised her brows. "If you think to bring the wild folk to kneel before the crown, you have a long road ahead of you, and it wouldn't be fair, given how the crown does nothing for them. They've been the most affected by the Seven's absence so far, driven from their strongholds and into the cities. Most of them here are poor. You've seen that."

Fi let out an exasperated sigh. "I didn't say I was going to beat taxes out of them. I'd like to pay more mind to them. I don't know what that means yet. Something else that's only a dream at the moment."

Voices outside the room drew both Erryn and Fi's attention. "Avere's back," Erryn murmured.

Fi looked at the door. "Before we go out, I have something to ask of you."

Erryn sat back down. She was closer to Fi, but felt more distant, and didn't like the feeling. "What is it?"

"When I was captured, we were on our way here, to Stronghaven. I want to go back to where I was taken. I want to see . . . I want—" Fi's voice choked off.

The tension between them immediately evaporated.

Erryn took Fi's hand. "It might be going out of our way, but it could make sense. Making a beeline for Darroth could get us killed. They'll expect me from the north. They might not be watching the other roads so diligently. Do you know exactly where you were?"

"Jeena should, or at least she'll know where the wagon was."

"I'll suggest it," Erryn said, meaning she'd suggest it to Avere and hope she'd go along with it. The Northerners looked to Erryn as the leader now. She usually wanted Avere to do the planning, because the Ferret was more experienced when it came to sneaking around without being seen. But they both knew Erryn had the final word. Even Fi would go along with whatever she decided. A queen without a crown and with a bounty on her head wasn't one who could give orders, especially to someone who'd been commanded by Zhikinden herself.

"Thank you." Fi suddenly embraced Erryn. "Let's not let anything come between us."

"We won't." It was the last thing Erryn wanted, but it meant she'd be faced with a tough decision, should she somehow be redeemed in the eyes of the people and Fi took the throne. How ironic, that she'd fight to survive and free the remaining Six, and by doing so, lose her own freedom.

Stumbling from the sewer, Fi fell to her knees and quickly untied the cloth that covered her nose and mouth. She wretched. Spittle hung from her lips. On the advice of Avere, she'd eaten nothing solid since midday and was now grateful for the Ferret's suggestion. The journey through the sewer had lasted only fifteen minutes or so, but the smells clung to her and infused her nostrils. She'd hung on to Jeena's belt and kept her head up, not wanting to see the clumps floating in the dirty water and the creatures swimming through it, or racing by her ankles.

The sounds of others wanting to empty their stomachs reached her ears, making her wretch again. Something touched her right foot. She shrieked and leaped to her feet, ready to flee whatever creature had emerged from the sewers. A hand landed on her shoulder.

"It's me," Jeena said sharply.

Fi turned to her. The wild woman had removed the cloth she'd tied around her head and lit a torch. She didn't look any worse for wear, nor did the others. Nobody had tripped and fallen. Fi's boots were wet; the rest of her was bone dry. But the stink . . . there had better be somewhere to wash nearby.

"Let's hope we don't have to enter Darroth through a sewer," she said hoarsely.

"Unlike here, there wouldn't be anywhere safe to emerge." Avere glanced around. "I'd say we're a safe distance from the wall, but we should move. We're too exposed here."

Those whose stomachs were as weak as Fi's were slowly rising to their feet and gulping down air. Fi drew a deep breath, but it didn't help much. How long would it take her nose to leave the sewer, too?

"Jeena, you said you kidnapped Fi about twenty miles northwest of Bexley," Avere said.

Jeena nodded.

"We'll head directly away from the wall for now."

"Is there a stream nearby?" Fi asked.

"I don't know." Avere's face scrunched up. "I hope so. When the sun's up, you'll guide us," she said, her eyes on Jeena. "Don't lead us astray." She whirled and headed toward Erryn.

"I wouldn't lead ye astray. I'm not stupid," Jeena said.

Fi didn't answer her. She trailed after Avere, confident Jeena would follow her, and hovered behind Avere when she reached Erryn. Renn was at Erryn's side. Fi had watched Erryn and Renn at every opportunity and had only seen their hands touch once. It must be difficult for them, and Erryn should realize it would always be difficult. Fi understood her not wanting to marry, but which life would be easier? Marrying a man she'd have no passion for, or being with a woman she'd love but in a relationship she'd have to hide? And would she have gotten involved with Renn, a wild woman, if she hadn't been on the run, despised by everyone, and expecting to die?

If she wanted a woman, one at court, or at least one who didn't stick out like a sore thumb, would be an easier relationship to manage. Both women would understand their marriages were their priority. Both would want it kept secret. Perhaps if Fi arranged a marriage with an understanding husband, Erryn would find the marriage a pleasing one, but how could she determine a man's feelings on the subject without telling him about Erryn?

". . . when we're in the forest," Avere said, bringing

Fi back to her surroundings. The group trudged away. Fi quickly followed, dismayed that she'd missed the conversation, but buoyed by the fact that she'd pondered a solution to a problem as if she were on the throne. Was it confidence, or denial?

"What are we doing?" she asked Jeena.

If the wild woman thought her addled, she didn't show it. "We're going to walk for a couple of hours and then find somewhere to camp. But tonight we'll only sleep until the sun comes up."

It must be about eleven o'clock. Wanting to enter the sewer when the streets would be empty, they'd left the inn at ten-thirty and arrived and entered the sewer fifteen minutes later, through an entrance located in an alley. Avere and Jeena had chased away the two drunks slumped against a wall. They were probably in their beds or in a tavern drinking more ale, and wouldn't remember anything on the morrow.

"Are you sure you know where you took me?"

Jeena nodded.

"The men you killed . . . they were good men."

"I didn't kill them."

"But you would have, if you hadn't been responsible for taking me. Didn't you care about what happened to the women you took? Didn't it bother you?"

Jeena's mouth set. She kept her eyes forward.

"If I take the throne, I'm going to hunt down every slaver in Daros, every last one of them. And I'm going to make sure the guard have Devon and Quinn's descriptions. I'll have special plans for them and everyone with them."

The wild woman's expression didn't change, frustrating Fi. "He didn't care about you. None of them did. He sold you to Millwood without a second thought. It was all about coin. I'm surprised he hadn't sold you earlier. How did you end up with him? You were the only free woman with them. Well . . ." Fi snorted. "Free in the sense that you weren't caged." She was about to ask why Devon kept Jeena around, then realized it was a stupid question. She'd gathered that the slavers' clients paid extra for wild women. Devon and his group had likely kept Jeena to impress, and to rape, though she didn't see it that way. She'd seen herself as one of them, perhaps loved them, or at least Devon.

"I don't understand why you didn't run away. You had ample opportunity."

"Why would I run away? My belly was always full."

Fi wanted to shout at her. What about self-respect? What about not selling people like cattle? What about wanting more from life than a stomach that didn't grumble? But she bit back her words. They'd do no good. The wild woman who was now a constant presence, who would willingly sacrifice her life for someone she'd formerly spat on, lived by a code Fi didn't understand. Jeena spoke about a full belly and must love coin, but loyalty seemed to be paramount for her. She could have tipped off the guard about Fi and Erryn by now. The bounty would set her up for life. But she hadn't, and Fi had known she wouldn't. It was as if Jeena needed to serve someone and couldn't make decisions on her own, not about anything important.

If—when Fi took the throne, she'd promised to free Jeena. She'd think it kind, but Jeena might see it as punishment.

At the sight of smoke rising from chimneys, Avere motioned for everyone to stop. It was too soon for Bexley, and she hadn't veered this far east on her way to Stronghaven. "Come to me," she said, and waited for everyone to gather in front of her. She looked at Jeena. "Can we pass through, or should we go around?"

"It's Woodpine. There's enough of my kind that we won't be noticed, but . . ."

Everyone waited.

The wild woman scratched her cheek. "They know me."

"How well?"

"I've stopped here many times."

"To do what? Steal their daughters?"

Jeena's face tightened.

"I suppose you wouldn't be stupid enough to drag people from their homes. You stocked up on supplies here?"

She nodded. "Enough times that some will know me."

"We can still pass through, as long as you don't think we'll run into your buddies. They'd recognize Fi."

"We won't. After Millwood's, we—they were going to head west."

"We need supplies. Pull up your hood."

Jeena did so. Everyone trudged along. A poster on a notice board next to the road caught Avere's eye. It wasn't the usual sketches of Erryn and Fi. She'd grown used to seeing those, and marvelled at how little they now resembled the two people she travelled with. Fi hadn't appreciated having her hair chopped off before they'd left Stronghaven. She almost looked like a boy. In contrast, Erryn had let her hair grow and hated it. If they survived and triumphed, and Erryn became the Saviour in the eyes of everyone, the first thing she'd do was take scissors to her hair.

No, it was the notice nailed to the board that sent a shiver down Avere's spine. The Primacy had called a meeting in Woodpine's main square for the next evening. All males between the ages of fourteen and thirty were strongly encouraged to attend. Those who didn't would be viewed as heretics.

"Are they building an army?" Erryn murmured.

"It appears like it. But why? They have the throne."

"Maybe they're not going to give it up to the noble who claims it. They wouldn't be building an army against Fi."

"Unless they've caught wind that she plans to fight for the throne. One of her men is gathering allies."

"Cedric."

"Yes, him. Though if he's as astute as she stated, he'd be quiet about what he's doing, especially when he doesn't know where the princess is and might be wondering if she's still alive. He must have set up a way to communicate with her group, and since the royal primate and the Tolin son are dead and he hasn't heard from them . . ."

"He might think Fi is, too." Erryn blew out an exasperated sigh. "If only we could get a message to him."

"We'll worry about that after we've freed the Six. We've

done all we can for Fi at this point. She's free. She's with us. We can't worry about the throne. It's not our priority."

"I just don't want him to give up."

"He won't. Even if he believes the princess is dead, he'll take the throne for one of her allies. He won't leave it in the Primacy's hands. He'll want to vindicate her of the accusations against her."

As they drew closer to the town, Avere walked casually and scanned her surroundings without being obvious about it. Woodpine didn't have walls, and only a single guard stood on the outskirts. Even if he'd wanted to challenge them, he was outnumbered, and he seemed more interested in watching two young women draw water from a nearby well.

"We could stay overnight and send one of the men to find out what the meeting is about," Erryn said.

"I think we should keep our eyes on our task," Avere said. "And I doubt they expect wild men to attend. They don't have to explicitly state the meeting is for city folk."

"You're right. They won't want Northerners."

Avere gave her a sidelong glance. If they managed to free the Six and the princess regained the throne, what would the woman walking next to her do? Avere had learned enough about her to suspect that returning to her former life wouldn't be easy for Erryn. She also knew Fi adored her, saw Erryn as her only living relative, and would expect her to remain at her side, figuratively speaking. If Avere were Erryn, she'd consider slipping away while everyone was celebrating, and ride as quickly as she could from the Royal City. But Erryn wouldn't do that. If they managed to take the throne, Fi's struggle would end, but Erryn's would only begin.

Erryn dabbed up the last of a scrumptious stew with a thick crust of bread and washed it down with a swallow of strong cider. The tavern hadn't looked like much from outside, but the food tasted better than some of the meals she'd eaten at the castle. If they weren't being careful with coin, she'd ask for one of the butter tarts she'd seen—

Avere suddenly pushed her bowl aside. "We have to go," she snapped.

Sitting next to Erryn, Fi said, "But I haven't—"

The back of Erryn's neck prickled. She hadn't noticed how quiet the tavern had become. A man swaggered into view, brandishing a sword. More joined him. Erryn cursed herself for sitting with her back to the door.

"We know what you are," the first man she'd seen growled. "Come quietly and we won't hurt you."

Were they talking about her, or Fi, who was sitting to her right? Renn was at her left. She hadn't moved, but Erryn could sense her tension.

"Don't try calling your beasts. There are too many of us."

He'd said "what you are," and now was speaking of beasts. Fi was safe. Avere was sitting across the round table. Erryn caught the Ferret's eye. She could see five men and could tell there were more behind her. The ones in view weren't in uniform and their swords didn't rest comfortably in their hands. They weren't fighting men, and they wanted the huge bounty on her head, so they hadn't summoned the guard.

Avere slowly twisted to face the one doing the talking. "Are you suggesting that one of us is the Beast Master walking Daros?" she said, sounding incredulous.

"I'm not suggesting it, I'm saying it."

"I'm no heretic. I wouldn't travel with one, either."

One of the men lunged and thrust out his sword. He held it an inch from Avere's throat. His obvious lack of experience with the weapon heightened Erryn's concern, but Avere appeared unruffled. Then Erryn noticed one of the Ferret's hands was under the table. She didn't have to see it to know what it held.

"You *are* travelling with one," the man said.

"Which one of us do you think is the Beast Master?" Avere asked.

Two of the men exchanged glances. The apparent leader gazed at Erryn and jutted his chin toward her. "She is."

Avere snorted. "I'm fairly certain the king branded the Beast Master. I think I would have noticed if she had the Beast Master's sign on her forehead."

"Her hair's hiding it."

"It isn't that long," Avere said.

Perhaps not, but Erryn's hair was now long enough that it would have obscured part of the brand, if it was still there. One of the men leaned closer and peered at her head. He carefully reached out. When Erryn didn't move, he roughly parted her bangs. His eyes widened.

The men who could see frowned and murmured among themselves.

"There's no mark," the one who'd parted her hair said, perhaps saying it to confirm what everyone except those behind Erryn could see.

"Me and Shona have been friends for years," Avere said. "How many, Shona?"

"Over ten," Erryn said. "I was a girl when we met."

"Yes." Avere chuckled. "Do you really think the Beast Master would be eating with wild folk?"

"We'd chop her up, put her in the stew, and feed her to the pigs," Renn said. A couple of the men guffawed.

The man with the sword at Avere's throat slowly drew the weapon back. "He said it was her."

Avere's eyes sharpened. "Who? I'd like to know who's making trouble for my friend." She raised her brows at Erryn. "Maybe it's Samson. He wasn't too pleased when you turned down his proposal after you'd courted for so long, but these men could have killed you." She shook her head.

"I don't know who he was."

"Are you in the habit of doing what people you don't know tell you to do? Didn't you wonder why he didn't challenge us himself? The bounty will make someone rich. Why tell you about her?"

"He was only one man, and an older one at that." The leader looked at Erryn. "I doubt it was this Samson, unless you were courting someone old enough to be your grandfather."

"It's good we listened to him and didn't set the tavern on fire," one of the other men said.

"Set fire to the place?" Avere gave the man a surprised look. "I was going to say someone was playing a joke on you, but if you'd burned down this tavern and everyone in it, you would have dangled from the end of a rope."

"He didn't want that, though. He only wanted her—well, who he thought she was. Said he was too old to take her himself. And we weren't going to burn the place down. It was only going to be a distraction."

"Fire can spread quickly, my friend. You could have killed us all, and everyone here is innocent."

"Sorry," the man murmured.

"Where were you going to take her?" Avere asked.

The man frowned.

"Weren't you supposed to take my friend here to this man?"

"Oh, right. He's waiting for us at the northern guard house. He'll be waiting a long time, now." He turned to the others. "Let's go."

"Before you do, what did this man look like?" Erryn asked.

"Grey hair, thin, a bit shifty, now that I think of it."

"Anything interesting about him?" That would distinguish him from the many thin and gray-haired men she'd seen on her travels.

They all shook their heads and shuffled away. Erryn looked over her shoulder and breathed a sigh of relief when the door to the tavern closed behind them. The others let out their pent breath.

"We should go," Avere said.

Nobody protested, even though some still had stew in their bowls. They didn't speak until they were well away from the tavern.

"We thought it best to watch and wait," Asha said, referring to herself, Toe, Jeena, and Timor, who'd been sitting at another table. "We could see they didn't know how to use their swords."

"That was the right way to handle it." Avere was silent for a moment. "I'd like to know who this old man is. He didn't want any of us killed."

"The bounty is higher if I'm delivered alive," Erryn said, as detached as if she were referring to someone else.

"But it's still a fortune if they deliver your body—or even just your head. The safer play for them would have been to burn the place down."

"I might have been unrecognizable."

"No, I'd wager they expected you to flee, and then they'd have you on your own. But the old man told them not to set a fire. I'm wondering if he recognized the princess."

"Me?" Fi squeaked.

"The bounty on your head will only be paid if you're alive. If he thought Erryn was the Beast Master, his first step to you would be to eliminate her."

"Or he could have just wanted me and didn't want to kill anyone else," Erryn said.

"I always work every possibility," Avere said with a small smile. "But yes, he could have been after you, and only you."

"We should go see who this man is," Fi said.

Avere gave her an indulgent smile. "Walk up to a guard house and potentially straight into a trap? No, let him wait, while we put distance between him and us." She paused. "Someone knows where we are. We must be extra-careful and keep our eyes open."

They continued on their way. Because of their hasty departure, they'd travel farther before the sun dropped behind the trees. Erryn deliberately lagged behind the others, hoping Renn would join her. Her spirits rose when she did. Only Fi and Jeena walked behind them.

"It was difficult not to do anything," Renn said.

"You did the right thing. There were a lot of them, even though it was clear they weren't mercenaries."

"I wouldn't have let them take you."

Erryn couldn't resist grabbing her hand and squeezing it. "I know." She reluctantly let Renn's hand go. Her feelings for the woman at her side weren't a passing fancy, like Fi had suggested. Erryn loved both women in different ways. She was tied to them both, and loyal to both. She shouldn't worry about anything beyond freeing the Six, but she couldn't help it. Perhaps the Seven would take her with them to the heavens. Otherwise she'd have to choose between the two women, a prospect that felt more impossible than freeing the Six and putting Fi back on the throne.

Fi sat inside the tent she shared with Jeena, rubbing her sore feet. She'd never walked so much in her life. Enkelo had set a slower pace and called for more rests, and Devon's gang had confined her to a wagon, not that she wished to be back with them. She'd rather wear her soles down to the bone than be in shackles. She glanced at Jeena, who'd just finished washing away the dust and grime from the day's travel.

"The wild folk gather together every morning before we set off," she said to her. They all sat in a circle around Asha. Fi had watched from a distance and strained to hear what was being said. She'd been disappointed. Apart from a few words from Asha inviting everyone to be still, nobody spoke. Everybody sat motionless with their eyes closed and heads lowered, until Asha stood.

Erryn always joined the circle, which interested and unsettled Fi. She'd gathered that everyone except Renn and Toe had wanted to kill Erryn, and only Avere's book had saved her. Erryn must have grown closer to the wild folk since the encounter with Zhikinden. Fi would have been cool toward them—tolerated them, but not embraced them. But all her life she'd had to deal with people who wanted to be close to her because she was a Lyos, people who didn't care one whit about her, but wanted to brag to their friends, or be seen sitting next to her at a banquet. She'd grown used to sycophants and learned how to deal with them. The situation with the wild folk was similar in that they'd despised Erryn until she was the Called and Caller.

Then again, Fi couldn't blame her for letting bygones be bygones. If she took the throne, she wouldn't be able to purge the nobility of those who'd called for her execution. Only those who'd made a point of publicly denouncing her would have to go. She'd have to forgive the others, invite them to the castle, serve them fine wine, and forget that had she been on the losing side, they would have watched her be cut open and hanged, and then celebrated.

"Why don't you join their circle?" she asked, her mind returning to the wild woman in the tent with her. "They'd welcome you. Asha talks to you."

Jeena hung the cloth she'd used to dry herself on the tip of a stick she'd stuck into the ground. "They're not my people."

"Are you saying you've always lived in the city? Asha told me some of you are born in the cities now, but I had the impression that's a recent development."

Jeena unrolled the bedroll the group had purchased for her in Stronghaven.

"Do you have family?"

"Why do ye want to know?" Jeena asked, her voice conveying her irritation. She lay on the bedroll and clasped her hands behind her head.

"We've been travelling together for a while now," Fi said, in the tone she'd use to speak to a child. "I'll admit to being curious about you. Aren't you curious about my life?"

Jeena snorted. "I know what yer life was like."

"I doubt it. Everyone thinks they know what it's like to be royalty, but they don't." She stretched her legs, then sat cross-legged on her bedroll. "You speak like them, so you must have grown up surrounded by them. In a . . . stronghold?" She thought that was what they called their settlements. "When did you leave? How did you end up with Devon?"

"Ye said ye didn't kill yer father," Jeena said, surprising Fi with the change of subject.

"I didn't. I loved him, and my brother and sister-in-law. But several primates, including the grand primate, swore that I did it with the help of my betrothed. Well, you know the story. You knew who you'd inadvertently captured." Fi remembered the jubilation, and the celebration around the fire.

"Not all fathers are like yers."

Fi was certain Jeena didn't mean that not all fathers were kings. "What was your father like?"

Jeena stiffened, and her mouth pressed into a thin line.

"Where is he? Is he still alive?"

"I don't know and I don't care," the wild woman muttered.

"You obviously do."

"I don't," Jeena snapped.

Not able to rein in her curiosity, Fi kept digging. "What did he do that made you angry with him? Because you *are* angry with him, aren't you? He must have done something. Are you mad because he didn't look for you when the slavers took you? He may have tried. Devon never stayed in one place for more than a night. I gathered he's been trading in women for a while. Your father could have looked for you and—"

Jeena was suddenly on her feet. She lunged toward Fi and stopped inches from her. Her breath came in quick gasps. Her hands clenched and her biceps strained against her shirt.

Fi wanted to slowly inch away from her, but she forced herself to breathe evenly and meet the wild woman's angry eyes.

Seconds ticked by. The charged silence in the tent was palpable. Fi blinked, but didn't look away. Outside, someone laughed. An owl hooted. Shadows cast by the lamp in the corner of the tent danced on Jeena's face.

Just as Fi wondered how long they'd stare at each other, Jeena slowly exhaled and returned to her bedroll. She lay on it again, but rolled over so her back was to Fi. "You didn't kill yer father, but if I ever see mine, I'll kill him with my bare hands. He didn't look for me," she said, her body stiff. "He always knew where I was. Now shut yer mouth so I can get some sleep."

How dare she! Fi opened her mouth to retort, then clamped it shut. She'd obviously hit a nerve. She thought about what Jeena had said. *Not all fathers are like yours. If I ever see mine, I'll kill him. He always knew where I was.*

Her mouth went dry. "How old were you?" she whispered, not expecting an answer.

Jeena's voice was barely audible. "Eleven."

Fi felt sick. "Why?"

"We left for the city, but he couldn't find work. Carting me around with him didn't help. We were hungry. He needed coin."

"What about your mother?"

"Dead."

Fi's throat was so tight, swallowing was difficult, but she forced another question out. "Did he sell you to Devon, or someone else?"

"Devon."

"How did he know him?"

"He heard whispers. Do ye think all the women Devon sells have to be captured? Ye're naïve."

Obviously. She'd never thought, never considered that someone would sell his own daughter. Rage coursed through her. If she took the throne—if, if, if! She must. She'd never wanted it, but it rightly belonged to her, and the more she travelled and lived among the people, the longer the list of what she hoped to accomplish grew. The list had been empty when she'd fled Darroth with Cedric and Enkelo.

"He decided to keep me," Jeena said. "Devon. But not as a slave. From the beginning, I stayed in a tent, not in a cage. He loved me."

Fi wanted to scream that Jeena had only been eleven years old and Devon probably raped most of the women he caged, but Jeena already knew. She'd try anyway, even though it would be futile. "He sold you to Millwood. You weren't in chains or caged, but he saw you as a possession, not a woman he loved. Men don't sell women they love."

Jeena didn't respond.

Suddenly feeling sorry for her, Fi doused the lamp and lay down. There was no point in continuing the conversation. Jeena had a distorted view of love, one that made Fi sick to her stomach. She'd thought she'd lost everything when she'd woken and discovered that the terrible dream hadn't been a dream, that Father, Henrick, and Surann were dead, and many she'd viewed as loyal had turned on her. But now she realized she'd still had her family's love, including Mother's. Without it she wouldn't be the woman she was, wouldn't still be able to hold up her head, and wouldn't be determined to stare them down as they led her to the gallows.

Jeena hadn't been hungry, or thirsty, or hunted, but she'd had nothing. Perhaps her mother had loved her, but nobody else had, and any memory she had of a mother's love had long since been replaced by the warped notion of love she chose to believe. Fi now had an inkling of why Jeena hadn't seized any of the many opportunities she'd had to leave Devon and his disgusting group behind. She existed to serve, to be patted on the head and told she was worth something. She should be as angry with Devon as she was with her father, but Fi would be wasting her breath if she pointed that out to Jeena. Perhaps being away from Devon and seeing relationships in which one wasn't abusing the other would help Jeena stand on her own again. Or perhaps she'd die pining for one of the men Fi would direct the guard to hunt down and capture. She didn't normally attend public executions, but she'd go to that one and direct the executioner to kill him as slowly and painfully as possible.

One of her teeth ached. She relaxed her jaw. Jeena was loyal to whoever held her leash. But not loyal like Erryn and Cedric. Jeena's loyalty wasn't earned. It was founded on fear, not respect. But for now, Fi would hold the leash. She didn't know what else to do.

* * * * *

At mid-afternoon the next day, Avere fell into step with Erryn and Renn and glanced over her shoulder. "We're being followed," she said, her voice low.

Renn's eyes grew distant. "I don't hear anything."

"They're a ways back. Timor picked them up first. I hung back a bit and heard them, too."

"How many are there?" Erryn asked.

"I heard two. There may be more. The two I heard are quite loud."

"They sound careless."

"Bumbling fools can still be a problem, and we don't know how many there are. We can look over our shoulder all the way to Darroth, waiting for them to strike, or we can force the issue."

"You want us to strike first."

"We should at least have a look at them. I doubt they'll do anything while the sun is up, so as soon as it sets, Timor and I will go. I want you and everyone else ready to fight, in case something goes wrong. Except Fi." Avere gave her an apologetic look.

Erryn didn't appear offended. "I know, she can't fight. If I wasn't who I am, I'd be useless, too."

"You left the sword." Avere remembered being puzzled over why someone being hunted would leave a perfectly good weapon behind.

"Jeena will stay with her."

Yes, the princess's lap dog. Avere didn't trust her. She didn't like that Fi and Jeena shared a tent, was afraid they'd wake up one morning to Fi bleeding all over her bedroll and Jeena gone. But the princess insisted, and she could become queen. Avere did not want to end up on her bad side. Frankly, she worried more about what effect Fi's death would have on Erryn than she did about Fi's life. Right now the princess was a liability.

"Asha won't fight, either, unless she's in danger," Erryn said.

Too bad. Avere understood the priestess was useful with a sword and bow. "We'll carry on as usual when we camp. While Timor and I are gone, the rest of you should stay in your tents. If there's trouble, you'll hear."

"It might be too late to help you by then."

"We'll go to scout, not fight. Unless we run into one of theirs scouting, we should be fine."

Erryn nodded. "I'll tell the others."

"Thank you." The wild folk listened to Erryn, and fortunately Erryn was reasonable and listened to Avere. She didn't go along with everything Avere wanted, but she listened to her.

A thought struck her. If Erryn freed the Six and became the Saviour in everyone's eyes, would the people of Daros take the opportunity to bring the Lyos dynasty to an end and crown her? It was an interesting notion, and one Avere immediately tossed aside. Erryn would never take the crown away from Fi. Also, as the queen's sister, she would be pressured to marry. She could resist, but the opposition would be strong. As the queen . . . she'd have to produce an heir, and a spare or two. So, no, Erryn would not try to take the crown. She'd choose love instead. Avere should think that silly, but in truth, she admired her for it.

Avere crept through the forest, aware that Timor was behind her only because she knew he'd left camp with her. If there was even the tiniest chance that Timor would leave his clan, Avere would suggest that Arrick bring him into the fold. Var, the woman Timor had hoped to pledge to, was dead. He might want to return to the familiarity and support of the stronghold, or he might be open to a change.

They must be close to where Avere had spotted a light through the trees. She slowed her pace and trod carefully, not wanting to snap a twig or startle a nocturnal creature. A shadow loomed, one she slowly came to recognize as a tent. With each step she expected to see more, but there was only the one, and now she could make out—

She stopped and signalled Timor to do the same. A figure sat outside the tent large enough to hold two men. Were there two more men inside it, or only one? She motioned for Timor to come to her side. "Only two, maybe three," she whispered.

"We could take them."

"I think we can, yes, starting with the one outside. I'll get him. You cover me."

Without waiting for a reply, she slowly skirted around the tent, making sure there wasn't another guard behind it. She crept toward the guard outside. Her dagger was at the old man's throat before he sensed she was there. "One sound and it will be the last one you make," she hissed. "How many are in the tent?" She grasped his hair and pulled back his head. Wide eyes stared at her. "How many?"

"One," he gasped.

There was something familiar about him, but Avere wouldn't allow herself to be distracted. Timor emerged from the bush, his bow drawn, ready to unleash an arrow.

"There's only one," Avere said softly.

Timor nodded.

"What do you want?" the man said. "We don't have much."

"I want to know why you've been following us," Avere said.

"Following—" His brows shot up, and so did his voice. "You're with her, with the heathen!"

"Quiet!" Avere snapped, pressing the dagger into the old man's skin. Movement, inside the tent. "The other one's up," she said to Timor.

Whoever it was would burst from the tent and end up in Timor's sights. Avere tensed.

"He won't hurt you," the old man said. "He's not a fighter."

The tent flap opened. A man's head emerged.

"Show me your hands, or I cut the old man's throat," Avere said. "And you'll end up with an arrow in your eye."

The newcomer was young, perhaps only twenty or so. On his knees, he lifted both hands. "He's not a fighter," the old man repeated. "Neither of us are."

Then what were they doing out in the forest, following Erryn? Avere peered at the grizzled face. Recognition suddenly dawned, followed quickly by shock. The last time she'd seen this man had been in Arrick's study. She was staring into the eyes of the royal primate.

Snakes and Sycophants

Fi strained her ears for any sound—a cry, a scuffle, the ring of weapons connecting. But all was quiet. She could barely see Jeena, who was poised not two feet away from her, ready to take down anyone hostile who entered the tent. She wanted to say she wished she was outside, not stuck in here where she didn't know what was going on, but she knew not to break the silence.

No sound. The camp wasn't being overrun. Everyone was safe. But her mind kept going back to another camp, the cries in the distance, and the strong arms around her, dragging her away from the man she loved. Jeena's arms. Fi tried to muster anger toward her, but couldn't. Things had been simple at the castle—or so she'd thought. They weren't so simple out here.

She stiffened. Footsteps. Voices. She wanted to move closer to the tent flap, but Erryn and Jeena's instructions had been clear. She was to stay here in the shadows.

Murmuring. Now she could hear Avere's voice, and Timor's, which must mean everything was okay. If only she could make out what they were saying! Why wouldn't anyone tell her what was going on?

Jeena lifted the tent flap an inch. A thin sliver of light—

". . . influenced. I insist—"

Fi's heart hammered in her chest. She knew that voice! "I'm going out," she hissed.

"No, ye have to—"

"I'm going out there with or without you." Fi brushed past Jeena and stepped outside the tent. She took a moment to digest what she saw. Two men sitting near the fire, their hands bound behind their backs. Avere talking to them. Timor alert, wary. Erryn crouched on the other side of the fire, behind the men, who may or may not be aware of her presence. Renn was next to Erryn, appearing relaxed, but Fi wasn't fooled.

Her eyes went back to the captured men. A lump rose in her throat. Her vision blurred. She wanted to run to him, but she couldn't, not in front of everyone. They'd listened to her tell how her betrothed had died on the rack for her. Only Erryn knew who'd won her heart. They'd both fallen in love with people the court would whisper about, love they had to hide.

She squared her shoulders and walked to the fire. Enkelo's eyes brightened. "You're all right," he breathed. Dann's head was lowered. He didn't lift it.

"Of course she's all right," Avere said. "As we've been telling you, she isn't a prisoner. She's travelling with us."

Enkelo snorted. "And as I've told you, I highly doubt that."

"Even though she's standing right in front of you, free."

"She could be under threat."

"I'm not, and I'm very happy to see you." If they were alone, Fi would have embraced him—both of them, though that would be difficult to do when their hands were tied behind them. "Why are they bound?" she asked Avere.

"We're not sure of their intentions," Avere said.

"They won't hurt me."

"It's not you I'm worried about."

Fi resisted the urge to gaze past them at Erryn. She wished Dann would look at her, but his head was still lowered.

"They've been following us because they believe you're our prisoner."

"You're travelling with the heathen, and that wild woman is often at your side, with a sword." Enkelo jutted his chin toward Fi's right shoulder.

Focused on Dann and Enkelo, Fi hadn't noticed that Jeena had followed her from the tent and now stood next to her. "She's my guard, but not in the sense you think. She serves me. As for Erryn, she isn't a heathen."

Enkelo's mouth twisted. "She has influenced you, twisted your thoughts. I deduced as much."

"We were looking for her," Fi said indignantly. "That's why we broke away from the others."

"You wanted to find her because you wanted to know what happened to her, not join her."

"I said I'd decide what to do when we found her and knew what state she was in." She silently apologized to Erryn, who was listening to every word. "She's herself, and she's not a heathen." She shifted her attention to Avere again. "Do they have to remain bound? It's clear they're not going to hurt us."

"What were you planning to do?" Avere asked Enkelo. Fi looked at Dann again, concern nagging at her.

"We hadn't decided," Enkelo said, the admission hunching his shoulders. "Once we'd found the princess, we were determined not to lose her again. We knew any attempt to rescue her would fail, so we followed you."

"It was you who riled up the mob in Woodpine. They said they were going to meet you at the northern guard house, but you had no intention of meeting them. You would have been captured. You had no interest in the bounty. You just wanted Erryn out of the way."

Enkelo didn't deny it.

"Where did you find us?" Avere asked.

"We heard word that the princess had been captured by a noble, and he was bringing her to Stronghaven. We were on our way there when we saw her—the princess. In Woodpine. And then we realized she was with the Beast Master." Enkelo's eyes met Fi's. "Are you all right? If you're not a prisoner, why did they capture you? Why do you look thinner?"

"They didn't capture me. They rescued me from the noble." Fi didn't want to talk about the slavers now. "But what of Mason and Duncan?"

"I'm sorry. The night you were taken . . ."

Fi swallowed. More men lost, protecting her. The road to the throne was awash with blood. But once assassins had struck down Father and Henrick, and framed her, it wasn't going to be any other way. "Untie them, please."

Avere pulled a dagger from her belt and cut the rope binding Enkelo's hands, then that binding Dann's. Still he didn't look up. Fi wanted to ask him if he was all right, but instinct stilled her tongue.

Enkelo rubbed his wrists. "The Beast Master may be herself, but she's still a Beast Master."

"But not a heathen," Fi said.

Behind Enkelo, Erryn straightened and rounded the fire. She passed behind Timor and Avere, who made room for her to Fi's left. Enkelo's face hardened at the sight of her.

"Should we tell them now, or in the morning?" Erryn said to Avere.

Fi was suddenly aware that Toe and Asha had joined the group. They must have been listening from inside their tents. Now that Erryn had joined the conversation, they'd emerged to protect her.

"It would be nice if we didn't have to guard them," Avere said, "though even after we've told them, I think it would be prudent to keep our eye on them."

"Told us what?" Enkelo snapped.

"That Erryn isn't cursed by the Seven, but loved by them."

Fi wasn't surprised when Enkelo snorted. "It's true. Zhikinden revealed herself to them," she said.

"Actually, Erryn freed her from bondage."

"Madness. You're all heathen." Enkelo narrowed his eyes at Fi. "Or your love for the heathen has allowed you to be misled."

"Show him," Avere said.

"You were there when I was branded," Erryn said. She sounded bitter, and her eyes were as hard as flint.

Enkelo's mouth set. "It had to be done." He surveyed those gathered. "Though I see some have ignored the warning."

Erryn crouched in front of him, her body taut. Everyone behind her inched forward, ready to strike. She lifted her bangs. "I'm not branded."

Enkelo's eyes widened. "But—then who are—no, it's you. I know you. But it's not possible."

"It is for the Seven," Avere said. "Zhikinden kissed her forehead and the brand was gone."

"You expect me to believe that Zhikinden appeared here, in the flesh, and to her?"

Avere stared down at him. "How else do you explain her forehead?"

He lifted his eyes to Fi's. "Were you there, Your Grace? Did you see Zhikinden?"

Fi hesitated, but only because her answer wouldn't help. "No."

Her reply hung in the air. The silence stretched out,

broken only by the crackling of the fire. Fi couldn't command Enkelo to believe what Erryn and the others had witnessed. Unfortunately her powers didn't extend to that, not that she had any at the moment.

Erryn straightened and stepped away from Enkelo. The tension defused for the moment, Fi's thoughts returned to Dann. Her heart leaped when she realized he'd lifted his head to look at Erryn's forehead. Then she gasped and covered her mouth with her hands. An ugly red scar split his left cheek from his eye to his mouth. He looked away and lowered his head again. She shouldn't have reacted so strongly! Worry gnawed at her.

"We have a story to tell you, about Zhikinden naming Erryn the Called and Caller, and telling us that she could become Saviour, and tasking us with helping her brothers and sisters." Avere's brow crinkled. "Ironically, because you're a primate, you might have a hard time believing it. We'll tell you the story on the morrow. For tonight, I want you to start entertaining the notion that Erryn isn't who, or rather what, you think she is, because I want to trust that you won't try anything foolish, so we'll only need our regular two guards when we sleep." She twisted and swept her arm at her allies. "Everyone here is loyal to Erryn and would skewer you without a thought. I hope we understand each other."

Fi winced. Enkelo was a good man, but would need time. "If I ask you not to hurt her, will you do that for me?"

"We're not addled, Your Grace. We understand the precarious position we're in."

"Thank you."

"We don't have another tent," Erryn said.

"They can sleep around the fire," Asha suggested.

"No," Avere said. "We want them in a tent. They can take mine." She gestured for Enkelo and Dann to go with her. Fi moved back to give them room. She tried to meet Dann's eyes, but he passed her without glancing her way, his head lowered. She kept her expression smooth, in case he glanced over his shoulder.

"They have a tent and some supplies," Timor said to someone. "We can fetch them in the morning."

Timor wasn't speaking to her, and Fi wouldn't have taken her eyes off Dann if Timor had been. She wanted to speak to Dann alone, and soon, to ask how it had happened, and to tell him it didn't matter. Her eyes welled with tears. She ducked her head and hurried back to her tent, aware of Jeena on her heels. She'd weep tonight, get it all out. When she spoke to Dann, she could be howling and aching inside, but her eyes must remain dry.

Avere looked over her shoulder at the two men eating breakfast near the fire under the watchful eyes of Toe and Timor. The younger one—the Tolin son—wouldn't be a problem. Enkelo, on the other hand, was determined and headstrong. They had to convince him they hadn't made up their encounter with Zhikinden, especially because he might be able to help them. She'd broach the subject of Zhikinden's book when she was confident he wouldn't throw it into the fire.

She headed toward the camp the two men had left behind, with Renn at her side. She'd asked Renn to go with her for a reason. "I wanted to speak to you alone," she said to her.

"What about?"

"Keeping Erryn safe."

Renn didn't turn to look at her, but Avere sensed her attentiveness. "I'm not worried about the younger scarred one, but the older man, the primate, could be a problem. The last time I saw him in the Royal City, he was hiring us—the Ferrets—to kill Erryn. He wanted her head—literally."

"We should go back to the camp and kill him first," Renn growled.

Avere smiled. "While that would prevent him from harming her, it would upset the princess, and we might need him."

"Why? He's old."

"And helped the princess escape. More importantly, he might be able to translate the book for us."

Renn shrugged. "The princess is with us now, and he might not be able to translate the book."

"We can't kill him, not yet. But keep Erryn close. If he does move to harm her, don't hesitate." She chuckled at the withering expression Renn tossed toward her. "I know, you wouldn't have. But now I'm telling you I'd support you, and that he's a threat. If he continues to doubt the story they're telling him while he eats his porridge, one of us will stick with Erryn at all times."

Renn nodded. They walked in silence until they reached the camp. There wasn't much in the tent. One bag with food, and another with some clothes. A pouch containing a small amount of coin had been on Enkelo's belt, but the two men had been running out of supplies. What had they planned to do? They couldn't have attempted a rescue and would soon have run out of food. She didn't believe Enkelo or the younger man were adept hunters, though she could be wrong. She wouldn't have thought Enkelo would throw his lot in with the princess, either, but he might have gambled that if the underdog won, his reward would be great. There was no mystery as to why the Tolin man had joined the princess. The Tolin name was now synonymous with traitor.

They took down the tent and carried everything back to their camp. When they arrived, Erryn was sitting at the fire, next to Enkelo. Renn dropped the tent and hurried over to her. Avere quickly followed.

Asha was seated at Enkelo's other side. ". . . were also hostile," she was saying. "But we saw what we saw, and heard what we heard. She isn't cursed. She's the Called and Caller, and the only one who can free them."

"I know it must be difficult for you," Erryn said. "It goes against everything you—we've—always believed. I went to the temple hoping to find something that would tell me why I was cursed. I didn't expect to find out I'm not, or to be in the presence of Zhikinden herself."

Enkelo grunted, his expression not giving anything away.

"Give him time to think," Fi said, sitting on the other side of Erryn. "I know you very well, and so I had a difficult time believing you were . . . that the Seven had rejected you. He's not close to you. Give him some time."

Enkelo didn't protest, and his eyes were thoughtful. Perhaps there was hope. "Where's Dann?" Fi asked.

"In the tent," Erryn said.

Fi stood and brushed off her trousers. "I should go and speak to him, to thank him for not giving up on me." She left without waiting for anyone to respond.

"You mentioned a book," Enkelo said. "Can I see it?"

Avere shook her head. "Not when you're right next to the fire. You might not believe it's sacred, but it is, and it's the only clue we have as to why and how the Seven were bound, and where the temples are."

"But you've decided to go to the one in the Royal City."

"Yes. Either path will be risky, but we're familiar with the Royal City, and we'll have at least one ally there."

"She's a Ferret," Erryn said. "We know the spymaster helped you and the princess escape."

"It would be madness to go back," Enkelo said.

"The only alternative is travelling all over Daros."

"The princess doesn't have to go with you. She has an army to lead. More men are rallying behind her, and Cedric believes there will be more still."

"The princess is staying with us." Avere paused. "You were running out of supplies, and perhaps you could handle one bandit, but not two. You won't alert the guard to our presence for obvious reasons, and you wouldn't stand a chance of taking Fi from us. Once you've looked at the book, you'll be free to go."

"My place is with the princess," Enkelo stated. "I'm not leaving her side."

"Then welcome to the group." Avere lifted a finger.

"But listen to me carefully. You move against Erryn, and you will die. You aren't important. You're expendable."

"Are you sure? I studied ancient languages when I was in the seminary."

Avere quickly masked her delight. "You aren't the only one who did that. But if you want to make yourself useful, you'll accept what we've told you about Erryn and translate the book for us, so we'll know where the temple is located in Darroth."

"I want to speak to the princess first. Alone."

"Nobody is stopping you." He might try to sway the princess away from Erryn, but it would be an act of futility. The poor man hadn't realized that Fi saw Erryn as royal, and him as a servant of the crown.

Fi stepped inside the tent Dann was using, aware that Jeena had followed her and would stand outside. She'd hear every word, but considering the tents and cell they'd shared, Fi didn't have anything to hide from her. Jeena had seen her at her worst.

Dann was lying on his back on a bedroll, with his arm across his eyes. He didn't stir, but she didn't think he was sleeping. "I thought I'd take the opportunity to come see you while everyone else is occupied," she said. Her breath quickened when he didn't respond. He wasn't dead, was he? No, his chest was rising and falling, and she'd glimpsed him when she'd come out of her tent that morning. He'd retreated into this tent at the sight of her. "You're avoiding me."

He slowly lowered his arm, but didn't look at her. "I don't want to."

"Then why are you doing it? I'm glad to see you." She snorted at her own words. "Glad? I sound like I'm greeting some noble at court. I'm delirious. Ecstatic. I thought . . . I thought you were dead."

"I am," he mumbled.

She was momentarily nonplussed. "No, you're not," was all she could say.

"I might as well be."

"Because of your cheek?"

He didn't respond. She wished he'd look at her. "What happened?"

"We didn't protect you, that's what happened."

His words confused her further. Was he avoiding her because of his disfigurement, or because he was ashamed that she'd been taken from him and Enkelo, or both? Talking down to him—literally—couldn't be helping. She'd clasped her hands when she entered the tent. Now she loosened them and knelt next to him. She took his hand and held on to it when he tried to pull it away. "You were only two. They were more, and when they grabbed me, I couldn't scream. I couldn't warn you."

At last he turned and looked at her. She cringed at how tired he looked. "Who took you?" he asked.

She hesitated. "Slavers."

He winced.

"They were going to put me into some type of auction, until they realized who I was. They decided to sell me to Millwood. I'd be on my way to the Royal City right now," *on the back of a wagon and tied to a pole,* "if not for Erryn and the others."

"They killed Millwood."

"They didn't set out to kill him, but they considered him expendable and he got in the way."

Dann's mouth turned up at the corners.

"Good. Your eyes can still shine." A lump rose in her throat. She tightened her grip on his hand. "I can't tell you how much I've missed you," she said, not caring that Jeena could hear. "My heart ached for you. At first, I didn't even care that I was in chains, because I couldn't feel anything. I was numb and felt there was nothing left to fight for. What would be the point of sitting on the throne lonely, or married to someone I'd felt obligated to accept, and who would always fall short?"

"You still feel for me, then?""Of course I do. Why wouldn't I?" Fi asked, even though she could guess the answer. When he didn't respond, she voiced her guess. "Your cheek doesn't matter. Well, it does, but it doesn't. Not to me. You didn't tell me what happened."

"The men . . . the slavers . . . they fought hard. If not for Mason and Duncan, I'd be dead. So would Enkelo. I had a sword, but . . . I'm better with books. I never should have gone with you. I should have stayed with the others." His mouth twisted in anguish. "I put you in danger. Because of me, they took you. They . . ." His eyes widened. "The slavers . . . they didn't . . ."

She could see the horror in his eyes. "No. Who I am actually saved me from that. They wanted me pristine. If they had, would it have mattered to you?" She held her breath.

"Yes, and no. Yes, because it would have been even more difficult to forgive myself for letting them take you than it is now. No, because I still would have loved you. Nothing will ever change that."

"Except your scar?" Fi said, keeping her tone light. "Did you get it because you were fighting the slavers?"

He nodded. "At one point I ended up on my back. One of them slashed my cheek."

Fi grimaced.

"He would have run me through, but Duncan near took off his head . . . and died for it. He should have worried about himself."

"Does it hurt?"

"Not as badly as it used to."

Fi slowly reached out her hand. He flinched. "Let me touch it."

"Why?"

"Because if I don't, it will stand between us." It still would, for a time, because of him, not her. But she also needed to touch it for herself. She ran her fingers along it, gently, afraid of hurting him.

"I'm no longer worthy of you."

She barked a laugh. "Do you really think me that shallow?" Perhaps she had been, but no longer. "You're as handsome as always."

A smile tugged at his mouth, warming her.

"No more of this avoiding me nonsense. I . . ." She instinctively stopped herself, then asked herself why. "I came here because I couldn't wait any longer to see you. I wanted nothing more than to tell you I'm so happy you're alive, but I didn't want to do it in front of everyone." She sighed. "But I'm tired of hiding my feelings for you. Time has passed, and I don't know how much time I have left. I want to live honestly. I want to hold your hand when we're walking. I want to tell you . . . that I love you."

His eyes moistened, and he swallowed. "I love you, too. I've loved you from the moment you appeared on the wall, even though I knew my brother would have your hand. But—"

Fi pressed her free hand against his mouth. "No. Whatever you were going to say isn't true. There's no reason we can't be in love with each other." She lifted her hand, then leaned in—no, she was a lady, and shouldn't be so forward. But she was also in trousers, in a tent, wanted for assassinating the king, travelling with someone just about everyone believed was heathen, and on her way to the city in which she'd be in the most danger. Who cared about formalities?

She touched her lips to his, and closed her eyes when he kissed her back. Heat and desire flooded through her, and the world melted away. Only they mattered.

"You're different," he said when they finally parted.

Fi took a moment to catch her breath. Now *that* had been a kiss. "Are you referring to my hair and the trousers?" she said, feeling lighter than she had since she'd fled the Royal City.

"No." He lifted his hand, which still held hers, and

touched her cheek. "You're stronger. You want to take the throne."

"I do. And I will." She tugged on his hand. "Sit up."

With his free hand, he pushed himself into a sitting position. She pulled him into a hug, and even though she knew her feelings for him were deep, she was surprised at how peaceful and content she felt in his arms, with her chin resting on his shoulder. Her mind went to Erryn and Renn. Could she deny Erryn this? It wouldn't be fair. Father had often reminded her that life wasn't fair, usually when she wanted something and he refused to give it to her. But could she ask Erryn to make a sacrifice she herself wouldn't be willing to make? Because she *would* marry Dann. Her royal counsellors would have to accept it. But after granting that large a concession to her, would they also agree to not marry Erryn off? What reason could Fi give?

She shared the burden with the one person she hoped to share everything with. "Erryn's in love," she said into Dann's ear. "With one of the wild folk. Renn."

"Is he the one who was sitting next to her in that circle? They were in a circle when I left the tent this morning."

"I didn't see the circle, but I can confidently answer your question with a no. Renn's the woman who's usually at her side."

He was silent for a moment. "I'm surprised she wants to go back to the Royal City and help you win the throne. If I were her, I'd stay in hiding."

"She can't. What they told you about Zhikinden . . . it's true. I wasn't there, but I believe it. They told Enkelo everything. I'll let him tell you." She didn't want to spend her time with Dann recounting the story. "If she does become the Saviour and the people see her that way, I'll have to grant her a title, which I'll gladly do. She's also my sister, and I want her seen that way, too. She'll be the most eligible woman at court, and she'll be expected to marry. But she won't want to take a husband."

"Surely she won't remain with the wild woman forever?"

"I don't know. Her feelings for the woman seem genuine, but if we succeed and her circumstances change, so might her feelings. Even if she decides to part with Renn, women catch her eye, not men." She drew back and gazed at Dann. "For her, marriage will be a prison of sorts. It will condemn her to a life without passion."

"I'm sure she would grow to love her husband."

"As a beloved friend, perhaps. But no more than that."

"There are worse fates."

She couldn't disagree with him. But right now, here, in his arms and gazing into his eyes, she would view it as most unfair to command Erryn to marry someone she could never love. But she would be queen. Father had also said that being the sovereign brought difficult choices, that some decisions kept him up at night.

A loud cough from outside made her jump. It took a second cough for Fi to understand. She let go of Dann and leaped to her feet. She no longer wanted to hide her feelings for him, but she wanted to tell the others, not shock them.

Enkelo strode into the tent seconds later. "Good, you're here. I need to speak with you."

"What is it?" Fi asked.

"Do you believe it, or are you saying you do because you're afraid of what they'll do if you deny their story?"

Surprise made her hesitate. "I believe it. You've seen her forehead." Even if Erryn had still been branded, Fi would have believed her. Erryn wasn't a liar, especially one who told such grand lies. "She's also herself and on the Seven's good side, which doesn't surprise me. We'll help them free the Six, and they'll help us take the throne."

"Free the Six." Enkelo scowled. "Why would the Seven need our help? They're powerful gods."

"I don't know, but apparently they do. Perhaps the answer is in the book they took from the temple."

"They want me to look at it."

"Aren't you curious about what it says?"

"Yes," he said, his reluctance to admit it making him sound surly.

"It will probably upset you. I suspect it will contradict some of what you teach."

"I suspect you're right." He slowly exhaled. "I know you love her . . . your sister . . . but you weren't there."

Irritation tightened her jaw, but sympathy won out. Enkelo had dedicated his life to serving the Seven. What he'd believed about Beast Masters was being tipped on its ear. "She's not the only one who saw Zhikinden," she said patiently. "So did the others."

"Wild folk."

"And Avere. And yes, the rest were wild folk. What of it?"

"They could be lying."

"Why would they lie?"

"They want power."

"No, they don't. I've travelled with them for a while now. They're doing this for the Seven, because of what they witnessed. They'd rather be at home." She could relate.

"I must remain skeptical."

"Then do. I won't dictate what you must think. I can't. But you won't harm Erryn. You must promise me that."

"So you want to go to the Royal City and put yourself in danger?"

"What would you have us do, Enkelo?" Dann said. "We're safer with the group. She's safer."

Fi smiled at him.

"Now that we're together again, we can go to Cedric. You've accomplished what you set out to do, Your Majesty," Enkelo said, his voice gaining vigour. "You found Erryn. We split away from Cedric and the others so you could do that, and now that you have, it's time to rejoin them. Next time we pass through a town, I'll send a message to him."

Fi took a deep breath. "Enkelo, now that I've found her, I'm not leaving her, especially since she's on a holy quest. Her task is more important than ours, wouldn't you agree?"

"If she's truly on a holy quest."

"I believe she is, and I think you'll come around to

believing it, too. Deny her words all you want, but you can't deny her forehead, or that she hasn't become a snarling, mindless animal, as the Holy Texts teach."

"Perhaps she will in time," he said, but Fi could hear his doubt.

"We can still send Cedric a message, and we should."

"We should," Dann echoed. "The last time we heard from him, he said he'd increased our numbers." He gazed at Fi. "We didn't tell him we'd lost you. We wanted him to continue gathering allies."

"That was wise, but what would you have done if you'd never found me again?"

"Put someone on the throne who would clear your and Viren's names and root out the rot in the Primacy."

The crown had no power over the Primacy, though Fi was sympathetic to the thought and would somehow have the grand primate removed from his position and executed, along with anyone who'd conspired with him. Otane would pay for his treachery.

"We'll send a message at the next opportunity," Enkelo said.

"You still haven't promised me you won't harm Erryn."

His face scrunched up and he inclined his head. "I won't harm her, Your Majesty," he said solemnly. "You have my word."

Fi almost giggled at his sour expression. "You don't have to like her, but she's my sister, and she's blessed by the Seven. Perhaps that's a bitter tonic for you to swallow, but I'm afraid you'll have to force it down. I would see any move against her as a move against the crown. It would be treason, and if her story is true, my wrath would be the least of your worries. Think on that. You are dear to me," she said, meaning it. "I wouldn't want to see you anger the Seven, not after all your years of loyal service to them."

Enkelo's face softened. "Thank you."

"I'll take my leave, then." She wanted to smile at Dann, but had to settle for nodding to both of them.

Outside the tent, Jeena fell into step with her. "I assume you heard everything."

Jeena nodded.

"When you serve the royal family, everything you see and hear stays with you."

Jeena snorted. "Who would I tell?"

Who, indeed. But Fi wasn't sure if Jeena had snorted for that reason, or because the woman she walked with was putting on airs by referring to herself as royal. Well, she was royal! And it was about time she claimed her birthright again, truly claimed it. She was a Lyos, and she should be in Darroth, on the throne, not sneaking around in trousers and limp hair. "Thank you for warning me about Enkelo's arrival. How did you know to do that?"

"I'm not stupid. Ye were betrothed, yet ye're talking soft to another man, and from what I've heard, he's yer betrothed's brother. And last night, ye kept looking at him."

Fi's heart thudded. Had anyone else noticed?

"I can tell when something's secret."

It was for now. She'd tell Enkelo soon, because she'd meant it when she'd said she wanted to walk with Dann and hold his hand. And she'd meant it when she'd said she'd take the throne. She wanted it now—the power. She had changes she wanted to make, and people she wanted to kill.

With Renn at her side, Erryn warily approached Enkelo and Dann's tent. In the five days since Enkelo had joined them, he hadn't spoken more than two words to her, but tonight, when they were eating supper, he'd asked to speak to her—alone. She'd briefly considered calling Lerxis to go with her, but now that she knew who she was calling, she avoided summoning them for trivial reasons. She sensed nothing but love from them, and she didn't want that to change. Renn's sword would be more than adequate. Worried Enkelo would sneeze and find a sword in his belly, she touched Renn's back and whispered, "Don't step in unless it's clear that he intends to harm me."

When she entered the tent, Enkelo was sitting cross-legged on a bedroll, with the book from the temple on his lap.

"You wanted to see me."

He scowled. "Just you."

"She's staying."

"I'm not going to hurt you. I promised the princess. I won't go back on my word."

"I'm staying," Renn said, her tone leaving no room for argument.

Enkelo shrugged. "Very well," he said, his eyes remaining on Erryn. She bristled at his dismissiveness, not only of Renn, but of all the Northerners. But to keep things civil, she bit her tongue.

"I understand most of this," he said, glancing at the book on his lap, its cover illuminated by the lamp at his side. "I can now provide some answers."

"Shouldn't we go to the fire, so you can tell everyone?"

"Some of it concerns you. I thought I'd tell you privately, so you won't learn about yourself in front of everyone."

"The book talks about me?"

"Yes."

She held her breath. "Does it say why?"

"Yes."

She swallowed. "Go on."

"Perhaps you should sit down."

His words alarmed her. She glanced at Renn, then sat several feet away from him and clasped her hands in her lap.

"I know how the Seven came to be bound—or rather, who bound them," Enkelo said.

Erryn leaned forward. "Who did it?"

Enkelo met her eyes. "They did."

His words hung between them. "They did?" she echoed.

He nodded. "This actually sounds plausible to me. I doubted it was possible for the Seven to be bound against their will."

"They did it to themselves." She was still trying to get her head around it.

"Yes. But . . ." Enkelo looked down at the book.

"Why? And what about me?"

"This book is a story." He lifted his head. "The story of

how the Seven came to be bound, and why. I'm not sure I believe it. If it's true . . ." He trailed off again.

"If it's true . . ." Erryn prompted.

"I said I have answers, but I'm not sure I believe the ones this book provides."

"Zhikinden told us to read the book. It must be true."

"I wish I'd been there," he murmured, the struggle within him plain on his face.

"Tell me what the story says," Erryn said evenly.

"They were bound long ago, when they last walked the land. Their . . . parents, or perhaps superiors, were displeased with them. They thought the Seven were growing too close to us, and that we weren't worthy of their love and attention. They also believed our love for the Seven wasn't true, that we were only interested in what the Seven could provide for us."

"Could those parents be the elder gods?" Erryn had listened to Avere tell him about Malina and her beliefs as they'd sat around the fire one night.

"Perhaps. That would be as good a name for them as any. They wanted to destroy us . . . Daros."

Shock stiffened Erryn's back. "Why?"

"Because they didn't believe us worthy. They gave Daros to the Seven to oversee and weren't pleased when the Seven grew close to us. So they decided to end us."

"We're still here."

"The Seven begged them to stay their hand. They insisted we were worthy, and that we loved them. To prove it, they proposed a test. A trial. A challenge. Call it what you will. Intrigued, their superiors agreed. But the superiors . . ." Enkelo shook his head. "They aren't wholly good. They insisted that if we failed the challenge, we would be destroyed . . . slowly. And they insisted on limiting the Seven's power to interfere. They wrapped it all into one and here we are. The Seven were bound to their pets. Without them to sustain the land, it would slowly die, and so would we. To survive, we had to free them.

"The Seven thought the challenge easy. The people loved them, and to free them, all they had to do was travel to their temples, or the One Place, and call them forth. They wouldn't be stumbling in the dark. The Seven were allowed to tell the people about the challenge and what they must do. But there was a catch. Only one person could call them forth—the Called and Caller. But that didn't matter, they thought, because all the people would help the Called and Caller on his journey to the temples or the One Place." Enkelo paused. "The Seven revealed all this to the faithful in Westerfox. That's where the Called and Caller's journey would start."

Erryn nodded, eager for him to continue. He still hadn't answered her most pressing question.

"Of course, we're fragile beings. We can become ill. We can be injured. The superiors agreed to two concessions: first, that the dying of the land would be slow, and second, that should the Called and Caller fall, he would be reborn again, and again, until he completed his task or the land died, and us along with it."

"Reborn? Do you mean I'm him, or . . ."

"Yes and no. Your essence, your identity is the same. Male and female exist only in the physical form."

"But how can I be him, or the Called and Caller from back then?"

"I don't claim to understand how the physical and spiritual are joined together into a human being, but they obviously are. You are the Called and Caller, and the only Called and Caller. You volunteered to undergo the trial. You expected to complete it back then, because the Seven spoke directly to the people and told them about the trial, and you had many allies who travelled with you."

"But I didn't free any of them," Erryn said, her head spinning. She'd go along with it, ask questions as if she believed it, even though it seemed impossible. "What happened? How did I fall?"

"The book doesn't say. If the Seven created the book, they did so just before they were bound. Since then, they've not been in a position to update it." Enkelo paused. "If the story is true."

"What about me? Why Erryn Fyler?" She *was* Erryn Fyler, daughter of Lord Garon Fyler and some whore, foster sister of Filmona Lyos, the rightful queen of Daros, beloved of Renn, of the Snowlake clan. How could she have been someone else, and many times?

"Your family resided in Westerfox and was close to the Seven. When they told the people of the trial and the need for a champion who'd free them, you volunteered, despite the sacrifice you had to make."

"What sacrifice?"

"The same one you always make, though unknowingly.

The Called and Caller always loses her parents before she knows them. The exception was the very first time. He—you—were nineteen when you and your parents agreed to pay the price. They were sacrificed, and then reborn, just as you are. The Called and Caller is reborn when her parents find each other and have a child. That's why there isn't a Beast Master in every generation, and there's only one at a time."

"So the passage in the Holy Texts that said Beast Masters gathered together . . . it's wrong, then." Another passage, the one that said only one Beast Master was born in each age, was correct.

Enkelo's voice hardened. "If the story is true."

"And my parents—"

"Were his parents, and have always been his or her parents. The three of you are trapped in the cycle, just as the Seven are bound, and Six remain bound. If the story is—"

"You don't believe it."

"It contradicts everything I've been taught and believe. You asked an important question. Why did you fall? If the people knew, why would they kill you? If the Seven view you as the Called and Caller and their and Daros's potential Saviour, why do the Holy Texts say you're heathen, despised and cursed by them? Why don't the Holy Texts contain any of what's in this book? Why do they record that the Seven said Beast Masters would walk the land, but say nothing about the Seven being bound and that only a Beast Master can free them?"

She had no answers for him, and according to the story

the book told, she'd been present for it all. She needed time to think. "What about freeing the Six? Does it say anything about that?"

"Just what Zhikinden told you and what you've already deduced from the map." Enkelo raised a finger. "Though it does include the location of the One Place, the temple that holds altars to all of them, where you can free them all at once. It's in Darroth."

"We know that already. Where?"

"In the most difficult place to reach." Enkelo grimaced. "It's under the Primacy's estate."

Erryn surveyed the pensive faces of those around the fire. She'd just finished recounting what Enkelo had told her and wondered what they were thinking. If she hadn't seen and heard Zhikinden herself, she'd regard the book the same way she'd viewed Malina's—the ramblings of some cult.

"It's a game, after all," Avere said, breaking the silence. "Everything that matters is. This one has the highest of stakes. Everything."

Erryn's chest tightened. It was on her shoulders. Her parents had agreed, too. Her father, and the mother she always dismissively referred to as a whore. Her mother had died in childbirth and her father soon afterward. They hadn't known who they were, but they'd found each other—again. Was that why her father had insisted she be born? Had he somehow sensed she should live?

"I wonder if the Primacy knows any of it," Avere said.

"Enkelo didn't know." He was inside his tent, perhaps

reading the book again and trying to convince himself of its veracity.

"As the royal primate, Enkelo might have been kept in the dark," Fi said. "But if the Primacy knows, wouldn't they try to help Erryn? What about the Holy Texts?"

Avere turned to her. "Why would they assassinate your father and frame you? To me, that's the more pressing question. They must know they can't hang on to the throne forever." When nobody offered an explanation, she shrugged. "Let's talk about the One Place, as it's called, that's underneath the vipers' nest. Do we still want to go to Darroth? We know where the temple is now, generally speaking, but will we be able to reach it?"

"You don't have to. Only I do." Erryn hugged her legs to her chest. "Maybe I could be disguised as someone else. If the spymaster could get me in—"

"He doesn't hold any sway with the Primacy," Avere said. "The only one who can try to influence them is the monarch, and even then, they don't have to listen." Her brow furrowed. "Could that be why they assassinated the king . . . but no, it doesn't explain why they left the princess alive, except to take the blame. I'm missing something."

"Where are we going?" Renn said, cutting to the core of the matter, as usual.

"I still think we should go to Darroth," Erryn said. "Figuring out how to reach one temple alive will be easier than figuring out how to reach six, and we'll be in familiar territory, with people who want to help us."

"And hang us." Fi gave her a wry smile. "Not what we're used to in the Royal City, Erryn."

Erryn smiled back at her. "You always said you wished you could go to the bazaar without drawing attention." Though Erryn had never believed her. Fi had always enjoyed creating a stir. "You'll have the opportunity to wander the city."

"As long as nobody recognizes her." Avere tapped her chin. "We're still agreed that we'll go to Darroth, then?"

"That's where we'll go," Erryn said, when nobody spoke against the idea. With that decided, most of the others rose and left the fire.

Renn remained at Erryn's side. "The risk grows every day," she said.

Erryn wanted to take her hand. She'd worried Renn might have trouble with the notion that the woman at her side had been others—well, not others, but not exactly herself. But Renn seemed to have taken it in stride, perhaps because she didn't believe it, or could grasp it in her mind in only a theoretical sense. Erryn could sympathize.

"What do ye think will happen if ye free them? Will ye live out yer life? They could want ye to go to the heavens with them."

She'd been trying not to think about that. "I don't know. One step at a time."

Renn nodded. "One step at a time."

They sat in comfortable silence, until a throat cleared behind them. Asha gave them an apologetic look. "Do ye mind if I sit with ye?"

"No," Erryn said, wondering if Asha knew more about her friendship with Renn than she let on.

Asha lowered herself to the ground. "What the primate told ye must be a shock for ye."

"Do ye believe it?" Renn asked.

"Do ye?" Asha countered. "That question is for both of ye."

"I asked ye first," Renn said. Erryn almost giggled. She'd heard this conversation before, and it must take place in the strongholds, too. People were people.

"It must be true," she said, so neither Renn nor Asha would have to go first. "Zhikinden told us to read the book. It must be true."

"But it's difficult for ye to believe, because of what it says about ye," Asha said.

"I wanted to know why. Now I know, and yes, it's difficult." She pressed her hand against her chest. "I'm only me."

"Maybe we've all lived before," the priestess suggested.

"That's not what the Holy Texts teach, but . . ."

The women flanking her murmured their agreement. They understood why she'd trailed off.

"I've been thinking about when I first became aware of the Fallen. I always wondered why I wasn't more shocked. I was afraid, and I knew to keep it secret. But it didn't feel as strange as it should have. And then there's Rodney. Did I end up in that area because I had some memory of it? I thought it was luck, or perhaps the aid of the Seven, that had set my feet on the same path as the last Beast Master, but now I'm supposed to believe it was me. I was him."

"Maybe ye have memories, buried deep," Asha said.

"I can't understand how ye're feeling, but ye know ye're always welcome to talk to me."

Erryn turned to her. "Thank you." She'd rather talk to Asha than Enkelo and any other primate, and not entirely because the Primacy hated her.

Toe gave Avere and Enkelo's backs a wary glance, then turned to Asha, who walked at his side. Only they four were heading into Bexley, while the others remained at the camp they'd set last night. The closer they came to the Royal City, the more they wanted to keep Erryn and the princess out of sight. They were also concerned that more than one or two of Toe's kind would draw attention.

The Royal City. Toe imagined castles, and streets lined with booths filled with silks and gold jewelry. He wasn't naïve. Beggars would be on some corners, drunks would stumble from taverns, and few people in the city would have the coin for silks. But the Royal City. He'd never expected to pass through its gates.

It would be filled with folk like the two in front of him. He was only with them because he didn't trust either of them. Avere had travelled with him for a while, but he'd never forgotten her admission that she'd been sent to kill Erryn, or how she'd quickly volunteered to do so if their visit to the temple in Loring had turned up nothing. She'd also gambled with Erryn's life by lying to the clan. The gamble had paid off, but still. As for Enkelo . . . the man was loyal to the princess above all else. He was suspicious of the book given to them by Zhikinden herself. And he only came out of his tent to eat and do his business. He looked down his nose at Toe and his kin.

When Avere had said she'd accompany Enkelo into Bexley so he could send a message to the spymaster, who would send it to the one named Cedric, Toe had insisted on going with them. "In case there's trouble, and we need supplies." He was a good haggler.

Asha had wanted to come along—to make sure he bought the right herbs, she'd said with a chuckle. She'd left her walking stick at the camp, so she could help him carry any bags.

"Do ye feel any better now, about what we talked about?" Toe had wondered, but hadn't wanted to pry.

She flashed him a self-conscious smile. "The story the book tells . . . it's disappointing the Seven didn't choose a champion from among us. We've always believed they came to us first when they last walked the land."

"They still could have."

"And what of our other teachings? We already know we were wrong about Falleners. Or perhaps I should say about the Fallener. There's only ever been one."

"She has no memory of it."

"No. If Zhikinden herself hadn't told us to read the book . . ."

"Aye." He hesitated. "Ye're not thinking of giving up the robe, I hope."

Her incredulous look said it all. "No! Though I did wobble. Yer words helped."

"I'm glad," he said, surprised at the flush of pleasure warming him.

"What will ye do when this is over?" she asked him.

"Run contracts."

"Truly? Ye would still do that now, after all this?"

"I need to eat."

"The land will recover. Game will be plenty again."

He appreciated her confidence, or rather, her refusal to acknowledge that they might fail. "I've been away from the stronghold for a long time. When I go back, I realize I've missed it, but . . ."

"Ye feel like a stranger there."

"Not a stranger. Just that time has passed, and I don't belong."

"Ye do. If ye came home, within a month ye'd forget ye were ever gone."

Home. The prospect of returning to the stronghold, of waking up to the sounds of children playing and the smoke of cooking fires wafting into the hut, drew him more than he'd expected. Heading off in a hunting party, feasting around the fire, sparring with his fellow clansmen . . . could he go back to that life? "Renn needs me to work with her. She's not good with folk, especially city folk. She'd have a hard time finding contracts."

"I expect Renn will come home."

Surprise raised his voice. "But she's shamed."

"She was named by Zhikinden and will have helped the Called and Caller free the Six. Yes, she's shamed. But I have no doubt we'll let bygones be bygones and welcome her home. Ian's family might object, but not loudly. Zhikinden accepted her."

But would Renn want to return? Whatever had driven

her to kill Ian might still be there to haunt her. "What about Erryn?" He wasn't blind. He couldn't say for sure that Renn and Erryn had grown as close as lovers, but he had his suspicions.

Asha snorted. "Erryn is on her way home. She'll soon be at the side of the queen, in silks, with rings on her fingers and Daros at her feet. Or perhaps the Seven will lift her into the heavens. Either way, there won't be a place for Renn. I hope she returns to the stronghold with us." She quirked a brow. "If she comes to ye for advice . . ."

"Ye think Renn would listen to anything I say?" Toe chuckled. "I can't tell her to return to the clan when I'm not sure if I will. And it's too late to tell her that growing close to Erryn will only hurt her in the end."

"She wouldn't have listened to ye, anyway. The heart goes where the heart goes. But she doesn't have to run contracts anymore, and neither do ye. Think about coming home. Ye'd be most welcome. We want ye back." She paused. "I'd like to see ye back with us."

Again, Asha's words warmed him. Before this business with Erryn, he would have refused. He didn't like to be hungry, and he'd grown used to travelling the dusty roads, delivering contracts and collecting coin. But it wasn't an old man's life. Still young and hardy, he hadn't given any thought to what he'd do when he hung up his sword. Perhaps he'd always assumed, deep inside, that he'd go back to the clan and die surrounded by his people. But with every passing year, there would be more strangers among those inside the walls.

But if Erryn succeeded and game would be plenty

again, perhaps he'd settle down and have children. He'd decided against it when he knew they'd have to grow up in the city and endure the superior looks of the city folk. But if children could grow up as he had . . . he'd think upon it.

"What about Jeena?" he asked.

"She's an odd one. Won't name her clan and has latched on to the princess." Asha's mouth set. "I'll talk to her again when the princess is the queen and Jeena has nowhere to go. Maybe she'll open her mouth then."

The trail they were walking joined the road. Bexley was visible in the distance. Avere stopped and turned to face them. "We'll stick together in the city. We'll go with Enkelo first, then we'll pick up supplies."

Toe nodded. He'd intended to stay with them. He trusted Avere more than he did Enkelo, but that didn't say much.

When they reached By Wing and Hoof, one of the two messaging companies that carried letters all over Daros, Avere turned to face Enkelo. "Remember to use code names for everyone."

He scowled. "I'm not an idiot. You forget my face is on all the wanted posters, too. All of you have forgotten that. I see how you all look at me."

"It would help if you didn't ignore everyone."

"I'm not used to them, like you are."

Avere gazed past him, to where Toe and Asha stood. If they'd heard him, they didn't show it. "If it weren't for them, Zhikinden would still be bound. Remember that."

Though she didn't know if Enkelo believed they'd freed Zhikinden. "What purpose would spinning a lie about freeing Zhikinden serve? What would it get us?"

He didn't hesitate. "The princess. The Beast Master's redemption."

"The princess was looking for Erryn because she loves her. We didn't have to lie to entice her to travel with us. As for Erryn, you've seen her. You've spoken to her. She doesn't need anyone to redeem her, though Zhikinden has—in person. I know that's difficult to believe, but one of the Seven actually spoke to and touched her. So if you have any ideas about hindering her passage to Darroth, or alerting the guard, get rid of them. Working against Erryn would be working against the Seven."

His stony expression didn't change. He gestured toward the door. "Shall we?"

Avere went to tell Toe and Asha they wouldn't be long, but they'd turned around and were watching a juggler walk past, with four—five balls in motion. She quickly scanned her surroundings, searching for an assassin or thief who'd strike while his targets were distracted, but only a woman stood nearby, with a child clutching her hand. Avere would long for the time when she could enjoy the sight of a juggler or bard without suspicion, except there had never been such a time for her. Even before joining the Ferrets, she'd been the thief, and sometimes the assassin.

Enkelo pulled the door to the messaging service open. When he waited for her to pass through, she almost shook her head, but then went inside. It wasn't that she thought he'd stick a dagger into her back as she passed him, but that she liked doing things for herself.

She waited while Enkelo wrote out the message he'd send to Arrick, resisting the urge to peer over his shoulder. He'd spoken the truth. It would be stupid of him to give away the game when he was one of the most wanted men in Daros. On the way, they'd discussed what he'd say: that he and his niece had met up with family, and now they were ready to join their dear friend. They would await a reply in Persh. Avere's heart beat faster. They were getting close.

Arrick would relay the message to Cedric, and a rendezvous would be arranged. It could take a while for Cedric's reply to reach them, and they were assuming Cedric was alive. Arrick's reply might inform them that Cedric had been caught and dangled at the end of a rope.

Enkelo handed his message and the requisite coin to the clerk, and joined Avere.

She went to the wooden counter for a quill and paper, then to one of the three tables people used to write their missives. She'd write this message in plain English, something she rarely did. Hopefully Arrick would understand.

She'd like to see the princess on the throne, but her priority was freeing the Six. The task from Zhikinden herself eclipsed everything else, including any orders that came from Arrick. If only she could tell him . . .

After taking a minute to ponder what to say, she dipped the quill into the inkwell and wrote: *On my way to Darroth with my friend who fawns over her pets. It would be a tragedy if she misses her meeting, not only for her, but for all of Daros. I adore her. Will await your reply in Persh. Avere.*

She wanted to roll the paper up, but nobody did that when using By Wing and Hoof. As she'd expected, the clerk glanced at her words before rolling the paper up for her.

"On the way to Darroth, are you?" he said. "You might want to change your mind."

"Why?"

"Haven't you heard?"

"I've been travelling."

He looked to where Enkelo stood. Perhaps he wanted to ask where the friend she'd referred to in her message was. "The city is under a curfew," the clerk said. "The guard can question anyone they want to—not that the law ever stopped them from doing what they wanted. I wouldn't go to Darroth now, not without good reason."

Avere's smile didn't wilt. She'd expected that getting Erryn—and Fi—into Darroth would be difficult, but she'd hoped altering their appearances and joining the streams of people constantly coming and going through one of the city's gates would be enough. They'd have to be more creative.

"By pigeon?"

"Please." She handed him the appropriate amount of coin and bid him good-bye, then went outside with Enkelo. They joined Toe and Asha and walked to the nearest market. The two wild folk went off to buy supplies. Enkelo dropped onto a bench. Avere remained standing.

"Do you believe the book, then, the one you took from the temple?" Enkelo asked.

Avere surveyed her surroundings. Nobody was within earshot. "Yes."

"If you hadn't seen Zhikinden and she hadn't told you about the book, would you believe it?"

She hated hypothetical questions that required one to rewind time. "I can't answer that now. I did see her. She did tell us to take the book and read it, that it would tell us what to do." She remembered Malina's book, the one that had remained on her belt since she'd taken it from the dead woman. "I understand it must be difficult for you. It goes against the Holy Texts. But we're not lying to you. We saw her. The book was in her temple. She told us to read it. No offence, but when it comes to the Seven, I'll take her word over anyone else's."

"I would, too, if I'd seen and heard her."

Avere frowned down at him. "Are you going to be a problem? Because you're expendable. If you were to go away, nothing would change. The princess would be sad—for a bit. But we'd still fight for her throne, and we'd still free the Six."

"You needed me to translate the book. You might need me again."

"You were convenient. We would have found someone else."

He sneered. "You're just a common thief and killer."

She smiled sweetly. "Yes, I am. What of it?"

"You call me expendable. What have you ever done?"

More than he'd ever know. "I helped free Zhikinden.

But I'm not interested in pissing contests, I'm interested in carrying out her wishes. If you get in the way, I'll remove you. Are we clear?"

"I have no intention of getting in the way. The princess has joined her fortunes with her sister's. I wouldn't do anything that would bring her harm. I want to see her on the throne."

Translation: he was loyal to Fi, which meant he had to be loyal to Erryn—for now. What would happen after Fi took the throne? When Avere finally spoke to Arrick, she'd discuss whether the former royal primate truly was expendable. If the answer was yes, she'd plant the dagger herself.

Arrick stared at the two messages on his desk and marvelled at how quickly circumstances could change. When the news about Lord Millwood's death had reached him, he'd hoped it meant the princess was free, and the message from Enkelo confirmed it. The princess was safe and wanted to meet with Cedric.

The message from Avere . . . his brow furrowed and he read it again. *Fawns over her pets . . . would be a tragedy for Daros . . . I adore her.* Further confirmation that Avere had stayed her hand and was not only travelling with the Beast Master, but was convinced the heathen was somehow important. Why hadn't she written a letter explaining herself? Was the Beast Master controlling her in some way? Avere sounded enthralled by the woman. He understood why she'd used By Wing and Hoof. A message from Stronghaven had told him about the botched capture.

Avere and her "friend" were on the way to Darroth, news that was both good and bad. He'd see Avere and be able to judge her state of mind, but only if she wasn't captured along with the Beast Master. What did she think she was doing, accompanying the heathen here? Fyler would be arrested the moment she approached the gates. Avere would try to sneak her in, but how? Darroth was the Royal City. There were no leaks in its walls. Guards patrolled the sewers and their number had been doubled at the gates. With the ugly brand on her forehead, it would be impossible for the heathen to slip inside. When she was arrested, Avere would swing, too. Arrick couldn't allow that, especially given how much Avere had done for Daros while its citizens slept comfortably in their beds.

He rubbed his forehead with a clammy hand. He should at least be honest with himself, let what he kept buried come to the surface, just for a moment. He wouldn't let Avere swing because if she died, the sun would never shine again, not for him. His chest ached because she'd been gone too long. Fear clenched his jaw because he was afraid he'd never see her again. If he'd known all those years ago, perhaps he'd have sent her to another city. No, he'd had ample opportunity to do so, but had wanted her close. Why had he sent her after the Beast Master?

The answer was swift, one he'd repeated to himself several times over the years. Because he'd promised himself he wouldn't treat her any differently. Because she was his best agent. Because she'd hate him for coddling her.

"Jack!"

Jack dashed into the study and slid to a halt in front of the desk. "Yes, sir."

"I have messages for you to deliver." And when Jack returned, Arrick would send him to the pigeon master with his replies to Avere and Enkelo. He'd direct Enkelo to Cedric, and instruct Avere to proceed to Darroth—not that she took orders from him anymore.

Forget about watching the gates for Avere. If she reached one, it would already be too late. He'd intercept her before then. As for the heathen . . . if anyone else but Avere had written the message, he'd leave her to fend for herself. But Avere believed Fyler was important and had made it clear she didn't want her harmed. Arrick would respect Avere's wishes until he could determine if she was thinking for herself. He'd send word that Fyler's head was to stay on her shoulders—for now. He'd even help her get into the city. But if he suspected she was manipulating Avere, he'd remove her head himself.

When Fi's shirt sleeve caught on a branch, she muttered a word her mother would have chided her for speaking and pulled her arm away. "I'm tired of trees," she declared to nobody in particular. Next to her, Dann chuckled. She glanced over her shoulder at Jeena. Her shadow's face wore its usual sombre expression.

A snail would probably make it to Persh before they did. It wouldn't be long now—less than an hour, Avere had estimated. But Fi wouldn't enter the city, wouldn't sit in a tavern's common room in front of the fire with a nice hot bowl of stew, nor would she retire to a proper bed. She'd have to remain at camp.

Chin up, she heard Father say. Tromping through the forest would be worse if she wasn't wearing trousers. She had to admit they were more suited to certain activities, but when she was queen, she could only ever wear them in private. And she should appreciate the trees around her more, because once she was on the throne, she'd have little time for idle walks.

Father had always been in his study, or in a meeting, or away from the castle on official business. She couldn't recall more than a few times when the royal family had managed several days in a row alone together with minimal interruptions. No interruptions had been impossible. Fortunately she liked being busy. And a warm bed, a feather pillow, hot water, clean clothes, and hair that wasn't tangled. One day her time as a hunted criminal would be a distant memory. She'd try not to forget the lessons she'd learned.

Dann tripped over a thick root jutting up from the ground. Fi caught his arm, and so did Jeena. Between them, they steadied him. His face flushed, but he murmured a thank you and they carried on.

Everyone walking in front of them suddenly stopped. Fi searched for Erryn and spotted her just in front of Asha and Toe. When Avere joined Erryn and pointed, Fi gathered they'd rest in this area. It was late morning, leaving plenty of time for Avere and Enkelo to go into

Persh and check for messages, so she wasn't surprised when the two of them set off together, with Toe trailing after them. Apparently he could talk down merchants, but Fi had overhead Avere telling him that she was just as good at haggling and would be better at it the farther south they were.

Everyone remaining behind followed Erryn to a spot not too far from a babbling brook. Two fires were soon roaring. Fi's stomach grumbled. She looked forward to whatever Asha and Timor would cook for the midday meal.

She'd just finished the last bit of rabbit in her bowl when Enkelo and Avere returned. Fi set her bowl on the ground and hurried to join them.

Enkelo could hardly get his words out. "Cedric is close," he said excitedly. "He has men, more than I would have expected. The tide is turning toward you."

"Even though I'm an assassin?"

"The nobles expected the Primacy to defer to them, but it hasn't, and it's ruling, if one can call it that, with an iron fist. Someone has also been circulating rumours that you were framed."

"Someone." Avere smiled. "We all know who started those rumours."

"Perhaps it will just be a matter of marching to Darroth's gates with an army," Fi said.

Enkelo shook his head. "A few nobles are still after the crown. We're still outnumbered. But we're not only four now."

They hadn't been only four—Fi, Dann, Enkelo, and

Cedric—for a long time. His dismissal of those who'd aided them, especially Erryn, rankled, but Fi wouldn't publicly rebuke him.

"What's the Primacy doing?" Erryn, who'd come over to listen, asked.

Avere gazed at her. "We already knew about the curfew. Apparently the bards took up the notion Fi was framed. Many have been arrested, one executed. A noble who voiced his opinion that the Primacy should name the successor rather than cling to power was put in the stocks."

Fi gasped. Nobles were never put in the stocks.

"That's upset other nobles. Many are looking for someone to latch on to, so they can direct their anger at the Primacy safely, through someone else. You're as good a person as any. You're a Lyos."

Fi didn't know whether to be pleased because they were willing to overlook that she may have killed her father, or upset because they were so quick to forget it. When she took the throne, she wanted a loyal nobility, not one that swayed with the wind.

"Where's Cedric?" she asked.

"About two days' travel away. He's waiting for us."

Her breath quickened. Only two days' travel? "Then let's get going. There's still hours of light, yet."

The others agreed. They were soon traipsing through the forest again, heading west from Persh, toward her army. It was beginning. She'd take the throne with the men they were going to meet, or die with them.

* * * * *

Hoping she looked halfway presentable, Fi turned onto the path that led to Duke Hampton's estate, expecting guards to burst from their hiding place and apprehend her. "Are you sure this is all right?" she asked Enkelo.

"This is where we're to meet him. Hampton has thrown in with us."

She nodded, wondering if the skin on her back was crawling because they were walking into a trap, or because she knew Jeena, Avere, Toe, and Timor were shadowing them, prepared to protect them. Jeena had wanted to go with them to meet Cedric, but until they were sure it wasn't a trap and that Hampton was, indeed, on their side, they wanted to keep the wild folk out of sight. Dann had remained behind at camp, at his request. He was a Tolin. He was tarred with the same brush as she, but while she could promise those who aided her a future reward, he had nothing. Erryn and Renn had also remained behind. Erryn was too valuable to bring into close proximity to an army. Renn had volunteered to stay with her, and Asha had also wanted to protect the Called and Caller, as she often referred to Erryn.

Fi jumped when the manor house's door swung open, then looked at Enkelo, feeling silly. A familiar figure stepped onto the path. A lump rose in Fi's throat. She wanted to run to him, but that wouldn't be ladylike, or the act of a queen. But when she reached him, she couldn't resist holding out her arms. He hesitated, then hugged her. "I've missed you," she said when they stepped apart.

"And I you, Majesty," Cedric said, his eyes bright. "Though I hardly recognize you." Blood rushed to his cheeks. He immediately lowered his head. "I'm sorry. I shouldn't have spoken."

Yes, she was thinner, and despite putting on clean clothes and managing to brush all the knots from her hair, looked more like someone who'd beg on the corner than a woman who'd sit on the throne. She'd asked Enkelo not to tell Cedric about her time with the slavers. She wanted to tell him and reassure him that she was all right.

"Lift your head, Cedric. You spoke the truth. I'm glad I don't look quite like myself. It'll make it easier to get into Darroth."

He met her eyes. "We're not ready for that yet."

"How many men do we need?"

"More than we have now, Majesty."

"Where are the men?" Enkelo asked, echoing Fi's thoughts. Not a single shout had drawn her attention, and smoke from nearby fires didn't wrinkle her nose.

"They're camped about fifteen minutes away."

"Someone must have noticed them."

"I'm sure they have," Cedric said. "Our numbers have grown as we've marched from estate to estate. But short of sending a force against us now, there isn't much the Primacy can do. It has always known its hold on the throne would be contested. It's always been a matter of who will strike first, not if anyone will strike. I suspect it will make its stand in Darroth and is gathering loyal forces there. The walls will help them."

A man emerged from the house and stood at Cedric's

side. He inclined his head. "Duke Hampton, Your Grace. We've met on several occasions."

Fi returned his nod. "I remember. I'm pleased you've joined us."

"As am I. A terrible miscarriage of justice. Well, justice was never done, was it? You were right to flee. You wouldn't have received a fair trial."

Had he believed that the day after the assassination? She opened her mouth to agree with him. It stayed open when another man stepped from the house. Eness! What was the snake doing here? Her first instinct was to flee, but she trusted Cedric's judgement. Still. "I'm surprised to see you here," she snapped. "Last time I saw you, you accused me of murdering my own father and were calling for my blood."

He had the good sense to cringe. "I beg your forgiveness. You have to understand how it appeared to us. You and Viren were the only ones in the room."

"With the primates!"

"Yes. But the grand primate said . . ." He trailed off.

His discomfort pleased her. The snake. "I said I didn't kill them. Do you actually believe I would have murdered my father, brother, and sister-in-law? You've known me since I was this high." She held her hand near her waist. "Had I ever shown any interest in ruling? Quite the opposite. I only seek the throne because I'm a Lyos and my father would expect me to do so."

"Yes, Your Grace."

"What changed your mind?"

He stared at her.

"Your mind, Eness. About me, my guilt. What changed it?"

"The way the Primacy is relishing the power. I thought it had taken on the regency to ensure the stability of Daros while we determined who had the most right to rule. But it has overruled the Royal Council to the point that we no longer meet."

Ah, so it wasn't so much that he believed her innocent, but that he was miffed about his loss of power.

"It made me reconsider its version of what had taken place in the library, Your Grace. Several ugly possibilities that had seemed unlikely became feasible." Eness had the audacity to smile.

"The lord's men are a welcome addition to our forces, Majesty," Cedric said. "They comprise about one third of our numbers."

He needn't worry. She knew enough to swallow her anger and resist the urge to slap Eness's face and clap in him irons. As much as it grated, she needed him—for now. "I'm glad you came around and want to see Daros's rightful ruler on the throne."

"Yes, Your Grace."

"Where's everyone else?" Cedric asked. "Your message mentioned you were travelling with a group."

"They're close." Closer than she'd admit. Hopefully he'd had the sense not to tell anyone they'd met up with Erryn. "Now that we've greeted one another, we'll return to our camp."

"You'll stay in the house, of course," Hampton said. "We've put aside several rooms for you."

"As Cedric said, I'm not travelling alone."

"How many are you?"

"About ten."

"We have room for everyone," Hampton said, twisting to gesture at his grand manor.

"Some of them are wild folk," Enkelo said.

"Oh." Hampton suddenly looked unsure of himself. "Will they want to stay—I'm sure we can—"

"Not all will want to stay in the manor," Fi said, primarily thinking of Erryn and Renn. Erryn wouldn't show herself, and Renn would stay with her. "My personal guard is wild. She'll stay with me. I'll speak to the others."

Hampton and Eness exchanged glances.

"Cedric, I'd like you to accompany us back to our camp."

"Of course, Majesty."

Fi nodded to Hampton and Eness. "We'll return soon."

They bowed. Fi whirled and strode away, trusting Cedric and Enkelo to follow her. "You know we found Erryn," she said, when they were a good distance away from Hampton and Eness. "Have you told anyone?"

"No, Majesty."

"Good. She'll stay hidden." She grinned. "She's herself, Cedric. Completely herself. Better yet, she's not cursed. Quite the opposite. We have so much to tell you. But before we do, you must see Erryn, so your mind will be open."

His brows drew together, but he nodded. Fi's spirits soared. Dann was alive and with her. Erryn was herself and would become the Saviour. Cedric was next to her and would offer her honest counsel. Tonight she'd sleep in a proper bed, after soaking in a hot bath. Ladies would brush her hair and file her nails. Eness had come around, which meant others could, too. The throne would be hers. All she had to do was take it.

Inside their tent, Erryn waited with Renn for the others to return. The imminent reunion with Cedric made her stomach churn. She'd last seen him that day at the market, when she'd revealed her secret to save Fi's life. He'd watched the guards march her away in disgrace. Fi had shrunk into him, her horror plain on her face.

Outside, Asha calmly greeted someone. "They're here," Erryn murmured to Renn. They both got to their feet. Erryn squared her shoulders. The tent flap lifted. Fi stepped inside, followed by Cedric. Erryn wasn't surprised that Enkelo wasn't with them. He still rarely spoke to her.

"I can't express how happy I am that we're all together again," Fi said, her eyes shining.

Erryn took a tentative step toward Cedric. His eyes widened.

"It's good to see you again." Erryn held out her hand, a magnanimous gesture considering he was a guard and she was foster sister to the rightful queen of Daros. They may be in a tent in the middle of a forest, but now that everyone had converged and a rogue court was forming around Fi, the hierarchies and niceties Erryn hadn't worried about since riding through the castle gates were back in play.

He gently shook her hand, his eyes never leaving her forehead. "I don't understand. The king and royal primate told me about your brand. It's on all the wanted posters. How can it be gone?"

"Zhikinden removed it," Fi said. "We have quite the story to tell you."

"This is Renn," Erryn said.

"Your personal guard, I presume," Cedric said.

"Yes," Renn said, before Erryn could reply.

"And where is the guard you mentioned?" Cedric said to Fi.

"She's in our tent."

Erryn kept her expression smooth. Fi had left out that Jeena hadn't been in their tent a minute ago. Jeena and the others had trailed Fi back from the Hampton estate.

"I'm sure Hampton can provide you with a personal guard." Cedric looked at Erryn. "He'd do the same for you, if you didn't wish to remain in the shadows."

"We want the ones we have," Fi said. "We trust them."

Cedric grunted. "I can see the wisdom in using people from outside his ranks."

"Sit down," Erryn said, taking the opportunity to sit cross-legged herself. "We'll tell you what's happened since I left the castle."

When everyone had found a comfortable spot, she told the tale, leaving out Fi's time with the slavers. Cedric asked few questions and appeared to accept what had happened, or at least kept his doubts to himself. It helped that Fi believed it all, even though she hadn't been there, and it would be difficult for Cedric to dispute Erryn's smooth forehead. Erryn agreed with Avere; out of all the gifts Zhikinden could have granted, the one she'd chosen had proven itself useful time and time again.

Still, Cedric didn't say much to her. He looked to Fi when Erryn had finished recounting what had led to them sitting together in her tent.

"I have to gather my things," Fi said. "Dann, Jeena, and I will be staying in the manor."

Erryn wasn't surprised. When everyone had discussed the likely invitation on the way here, she'd agreed with Avere once again. It would be safer for Fi to remain with them, in her ratty shirt and trousers. But now that they'd met up with nobles who'd tied their fortunes to Fi's, it was time for her to behave as the rightful heir.

"Everyone can stay in the house," Fi said, even though she must know that nobody else would. Their priority was to free the Six. Unfortunately, Erryn would be separated from Fi again. Not immediately, but soon. If they were to see each other again after that, Fi would be on the throne. Erryn couldn't bear to consider the alternative.

"Would you come with me to my tent?" Fi asked her. "I'd like Cedric to come with me, as well. And if Renn could stand guard outside with Jeena while we speak, I would be grateful to her. Dann and Enkelo are waiting for us there."

Rather than being upset because Fi was relegating Renn to outside the tent, Erryn was grateful. Fi, Dann, Enkelo, Cedric, and her. All from Darroth. All close to Fi, who wasn't asking them to her tent so they could watch her pack a bag. She had something to say regarding Daros and the throne. Renn would be out of place inside the tent but would overhear everything from her position outside.

Nobody spoke on the short walk to Fi's tent. Inside, Fi pulled a folded parchment from her pocket and held it up. "We hope for success, and I truly believe we'll achieve it. But I also believe in planning for all eventualities. If I fall, I expect you to continue to fight for the throne, on behalf of the heir I've named. Erryn. If I fall, the throne is Erryn's."

Erryn's mouth dropped open. "You can't name me."

"Why not?"

Because she didn't want it. Because she loved Renn. Because Zhikinden had kissed her forehead, but some would claim she'd never been marked in the first place. Only a few had seen the brand. They'd claim the description the guards had distributed had been based on rumour, that the king had intended to brand her, but his daughter had stayed his hand.

"I'm not a Lyos."

"You're a Lyos in all but blood and name."

She barked a laugh. "You have relatives."

"None of whom I'd trust with the throne. You're my sister. You were raised by my father and mother. If you're in a position to take the throne, it means you'll have freed the Seven. The people will know the truth about you. They'll want you on the throne."

"Will the people know the truth about me? We have no idea what the Seven will do once they're freed. They may destroy us. We didn't free them all those years ago. We turned on them. They trusted us, put their faith in us, and we failed them."

"If we free them and they destroy us, this parchment will be meaningless. But if there's still a Daros and a throne, and I've fallen, I want you to take it."

They locked eyes, and wills. Fi should have told her about this privately, when Erryn could speak her mind. She could remind Fi that if she was put on the throne, she'd have no choice but to marry and have children. But Fi would say that Erryn would have to marry, regardless, and that she must put Daros first. Today Fi was behaving like a queen. Queen Filmona Lyos. She truly was her father's daughter.

"You know I don't want this," was all Erryn could whisper. "I don't want it."

"But you'll take it. Because you're my sister, and you're my subject, and you serve Daros."

How could she counter Fi's words? Anything she said would sound disloyal and selfish.

"You've all witnessed this. You'll all support her, if it comes to that." Fi handed the parchment to Enkelo. "If I fall, your primary responsibility will be to ensure my wishes are carried out."

Enkelo inclined his head. "Yes, Your Grace." If he, Cedric, or Dann disagreed with Fi's decision, they kept it to themselves.

"Good. Thank you all. I'll collect my things now." Fi whirled, leaving Erryn seething. If she thought this conversation was over, she was wrong.

Erryn stormed from the tent and walked beyond the edge of the camp. Renn caught up with her.

"I don't want it," she said, when they stopped away from listening ears. "She knows I don't want it."

"But ye'll do it," Renn stated, her eyes unreadable.

"I don't want to do it."

"But ye will."

"I won't have to. She won't fall."

"But if she does."

She could run and hide. Instead of being hunted because she was a heathen, she'd be hunted because the queen had named her as her successor, and she'd abdicated her responsibility—after freeing the Seven and restoring Daros. "We don't know what will happen once I've freed them." About anything. Daros. The throne. Her and Renn. She'd avoided thinking about what would happen to them. Whenever her mind wandered to a future with Fi on the throne and the Seven freed, despair quickly chased such thoughts away. When she'd ridden through the castle gates, she would have given anything to be pardoned, to be welcomed back into the royal fold and for things to go back to the way they were. But now . . . too much had changed.

"I don't know. I honestly don't know," she said to Renn.

She expected Renn to bristle, to ask what would happen to them. But the woman she'd come to love pulled her into an embrace. Erryn rested her head on Renn's shoulder. Her tension drained away, but not her anger at Fi, who'd get it all, or die trying. Dann, the throne, as many gowns as she wanted. Why would she want to deny her sister love? Or was it that she believed the door to true love was already firmly closed for her foster sister? If Fi succeeded in taking the throne, Erryn would be in the queen's inner circle and under her roof for a time. She'd be expected to take a husband, to attend the balls and run an estate. Doing so seemed more impossible to Erryn than freeing the remaining Six and saving Daros.

Worse, Renn hadn't bristled. She hadn't protested, or shouted, or told Erryn to tell Fi to rip up the parchment, because they were going to be together. What had Erryn said in the beginning? We know it won't last? Were they both slowly accepting that? The thought knotted Erryn's stomach and provoked a dull ache in her chest. Her reward for freeing the Seven and saving Daros would be to live out her life in the shade.

The Road to Darroth

Fi studied herself in the mirror while a servant brushed her short hair. She could still feel dirt under her fingernails, even though she'd soaked in a tub for over an hour and another servant had scrubbed and cut her nails. But she was clean, she could run her fingers through her hair without pulling it, the pleasant aroma of rose petals filled her nostrils, and she wore a radiant maroon gown. Not trousers. Not a shirt. A gown that didn't hug her thin frame, but felt glorious. And she adored the gold necklace, earrings, and rings Hampton's wife had loaned her.

The servant set down the brush. Fi nodded. "Thank you. Would you send my personal guard in, please?"

The woman bowed and left the luxurious chamber

Fi would sleep in tonight. She rose and lifted her chin when Jeena strode in and stood before her. Jeena's eyes widened.

Fi smiled. "Do I look more like your idea of a queen now?" She didn't wait for an answer. "I see they managed to find you something, then," she said, taking in the spotless shirt, trousers, and boots they must have borrowed from one of the male attendants.

"I'd rather be wearing leather," Jeena said.

"Yes, well, this isn't Stronghaven, is it? Now, I called you in here so we can go over the rules."

"Rules?"

"Yes, rules. We're going in to dinner, or rather, I am." She assumed Jeena had already been fed. "You'll stand a discreet distance from the table, and you'll remain silent. I don't care if someone at the table comments on your clothes or your appearance, or insults you. You do not speak unless you are directly spoken to. You're to remain invisible. Also, anything you hear while you're with me stays with you. Most importantly, you are my guard. I am your mistress. You must never contradict me when we're with anyone. You can think I've just said the dumbest thing you've ever heard, but you keep it to yourself. When we're alone, you can say whatever you want, but when we're with other people, you agree or say nothing."

Jeena shifted her weight. "I'm confused."

"How can you be confused? The rules are perfectly clear."

"Ye said I'm not to speak unless I'm spoken to. But

then ye said I'm always to agree with ye. How can I agree with ye if I can't speak?"

"If you're directly spoken to, you can speak. I don't know why anyone would speak to you, but suppose I'm speaking to someone, and they say to you, 'what do you think?' You say, 'I agree with the, uh, princess,' I suppose. I haven't been crowned yet."

"So if someone asks me what I think about what ye said, I say I agree with ye. But if I'm invisible, why would someone ask me?"

Fi groaned. "Did you eat?"

Jeena nodded.

"Then your wits aren't addled because you're hungry. You're deliberately trying to annoy me." And she was succeeding. "You know what to do. And if you don't, here's an easier rule to follow. Don't speak while we're with anyone. If and when you should speak, I'll let you know."

Someone knocked on the open door. A man in livery bowed. "I'm here to escort you to the dining room, Your Highness."

Fi swept past Jeena, trusting her to follow, and the heavy footsteps behind her told her that the wild woman had. Jeena provoked furtive looks from the servants they passed. A wild woman in the manor. Fi could imagine the whispers.

The servant they were following stopped outside a doorway and bowed. "Your Highness."

When she entered the dining room, tears sprang to her eyes at the sight of the rectangular table laden with crystal, silverware, linen napkins, wine . . . Her throat hadn't tightened because she was attached to the trappings of wealth. Last time she'd seen a table set like this, Father had been alive. The king, with Prince Henrick as his heir, who would have Princess Surann at his side. Princess Filmona had been betrothed to Viren, the eldest son of Duke Tolin, and had looked forward to a comfortable life on an estate. She would have been a frequent visitor at court, her children would have had a doting grandfather, uncle, and aunt, and even though her heart still would have belonged to Dann, she would have learned to be content with Viren.

Father, Henrick, Surann, and Viren were dead. Dann was scarred for life, and not just physically. There would be no quiet estate and carefree life for Princess Filmona, no matter what happened. But she did have Dann, and Erryn, though her sister wasn't pleased with her at the moment.

"There you are," Dann said, entering the room and stepping to her side.

Without thinking, she put her hand on his arm and leaned into him, then quickly straightened when someone cleared his throat. Her eyes on the table, she hadn't noticed that Hampton and his wife, Eness, Enkelo, and Cedric were in front of the fire at the far end of the room. They'd seen, but they'd pretend they hadn't. Except perhaps Enkelo. He might broach the subject with her next time they were alone. The others would talk amongst themselves, discuss the nature of the future queen's relationship with the third Tolin son, and scheme about how to keep the two apart, should the relationship prove to be a romantic one.

"Shall we sit down?" the duchess said.

Fi found the dinner place card with her name on it and stood next to the appropriate chair. The others did the same. A servant pulled out Fi's chair, which was between Enkelo's and Eness's. The Hamptons would be at each head, so that meant Dann and Cedric would be across from her. She sat down, curious to see in which order everyone else would be seated. As the hosts, the Hamptons were next, then Eness. She pressed her lips together when Enkelo was the next one to take his seat, and then Cedric. Dann was seated last. So, it was to be like that. Viren had been innocent, so why were they treating Dann like a commoner?

The answer came as she was spooning a delicious vegetable soup into her mouth. Thus far, the conversation had touched on the banal, but just as the meal was about to get meatier, the conversation did, too.

"Now that we're alone, we have news to share with you," Hampton said with a grimace.

"Is it bad news?" Fi said.

"I would say so." He gazed at Dann. "Your brother Jared is alive."

Dann's eyes brightened. "Alive? Do you know where he is?"

"Unfortunately, we do."

Fi rested her spoon in her empty bowl and looked at Dann. His eyes were on Hampton.

"Your brother has thrown in with the Primacy's forces."

Dann's face flushed. So that was why they'd seated him last. Her first instinct was to rush to his defence and point out that he'd risked his life to find her, and the men who'd fled from the Royal City with him were part of the army camped not too far away. But Father had always listened, always observed, thought it through, and then made his move. It was doubly important that she do the same. She may be the rightful heir, but she was currently at the mercy of those who'd gathered under her banner and weren't hunted criminals. Plus, it wasn't her place to defend him. Not yet.

"How do you know this?" Dann asked hoarsely.

"He's not making a secret of it." Hampton sniffed. "I think he wants to prove his loyalty and redeem his family name."

"He should be proving his loyalty to the rightful queen," Enkelo said.

"There's also no need to redeem the name," Fi said, unable to remain silent. "Viren was innocent, just as I am."

"That may be, but it hasn't stopped the Primacy from seizing the Tolin assets," Hampton said.

Restoring them to one of the Tolin sons would be one of Fi's first acts when she took the throne. Everything should go to Jared, but if he was acting against her . . .

Eness pushed his soup bowl aside. "Your brother is ambitious. If not for the taint on the name, deserved or not," he said, glancing at Fi, "I believe he'd put his name forward for the throne. Since he knows the nobility would never accept him, he's doing what he can to earn favour with whoever eventually wears the crown."

"And who does he think that will be?" Fi asked.

"Duke Falkirk seems to have rallied a considerable number of nobles and men around him."

Falkirk? He must be in his sixties, and the last Fi had heard, his eldest son had a gambling problem. Was that the best the nobles could do?

"Why am I not tainted?" she asked. "I was with Viren in that room. Why is the Tolin name tainted but the Lyos name isn't?"

"The Lyos name isn't tainted, but yours is in some eyes." Eness steepled his fingers. "But people will quickly turn around when you take the throne. Nobody wants a change in dynasty. By blood, you're the rightful ruler, and you haven't been proven guilty of any crime."

"That's because she isn't guilty," Dann said, making Fi feel guilty for not coming to his defence earlier.

"It's a matter of believing whether the princess or a primate is an assassin." Eness shrugged. "Some can't imagine a primate, especially the grand primate, being involved in a conspiracy to seize power."

"I suppose princesses can be seen as greedy for power, as well as wealth." Fi was tired of this conversation. What did it matter who a sizable portion of her people wanted to see on the throne? She was the rightful heir, and the victim in this mess.

She leaned to her left slightly, to allow a servant to collect her empty bowl. "What are we doing to increase our numbers?"

"We've sent negotiators to meet with representatives of the Danvers and the Oakwoods. Both families have responded favourably to our overtures, and if they were to join us, we believe we'll have enough men to begin our advance. We expect more to join us along the way."

A servant rolled in the main course. Two others moved to the table, prepared to serve the next course to those seated.

"You're saying we'll be ready to march on Darroth?"

"To begin our advance, Your Highness. It may be some time before we launch an assault."

"And you believe the opposing forces will remain within—" A warm, red liquid sprayed across the right side of her gown. At first she thought it was wine, but—

The duchess screamed. Eness leaped to his feet. Hampton rounded the table, Cedric right with him.

Her heart hammering in her chest, Fi turned to her right. A servant lay on his side, a red stain blossoming on his back, between his shoulder blades.

"What is the meaning of this?" Hampton sputtered.

Enkelo crouched and removed the dagger clutched in the servant's fingers. He held it up. "We almost lost the fight right here, in this room."

Fi wanted to stand, but she couldn't move. *Father clawing at his chest, blood spraying from Surann's throat . . .* Jeena swam into view. Her sword . . . blood on its blade . . .

"Are you all right?"

Dann. She looked up at him, wanting to grab him and hold on to him and bury her face in his chest. But it was as if she'd lost all her wits.

"Perhaps it would be best if the princess retired to her chamber," Dann said.

If the others nodded or stated their agreement, Fi didn't notice, nor did she complain when Dann and Jeena helped her from her chair and led her from the dining room. The last thing she heard was Eness saying they'd get to the bottom of it, but she might have imagined his words.

Back in the guest chamber, she sank onto the bed. Dann brought her some water. Jeena remained near the door, her eyes wary.

Her hand shaking, Fi gulped down some water and carefully set the glass down. Dann sat next to her and took her hand. "What can I do?"

"Nothing," she murmured. "Just sit with me."

Slowly her shock subsided. Her mind cleared. She grasped what had happened, the terrible reality. "I don't want to stay here," she said, when the sun had gone down and the single candle Dann had lit struggled to banish the darkness. He'd only left her side twice, once to light it, and once to assure Hampton that she was all right and would speak to him on the morrow. If Hampton was wondering how close her and Dann were, let him. She didn't care anymore. "I want to go back to the camp."

"You won't be as comfortable there, and you'll be more vulnerable," Dann said.

"Will I? I know everyone there. None of them want to kill me. How many servants are in this house?" she asked, her voice rising. "How many have daggers up their sleeves? How many are handling the food I eat?"

The woman who'd brushed her hair could have slit her throat. The one who'd clipped her nails could have plunged the sharp scissors into her belly. If she took the throne, how long would she have to worry about those who buzzed around her? Would she ever be able to relax, to sit and have tea with a lady without worrying that someone had laced it with poison, or whether the new girl hired last week had taken a knife from the kitchen?

"I want to go back to the camp," she said again.

"You'll offend Hampton. You can't afford to do that."

She wanted to cry. She had less freedom than a beggar sitting in one of Darroth's many squares.

"But I'm sure he'll understand if you want to restrict who can be around you. He might suggest it." Dann squeezed her hand. "If he doesn't, I will."

She lay her head on his shoulder. "Thank you."

"He might not listen to me, though. I don't have any influence, especially now." She felt his sigh. "Why would Jared align with the Primacy?"

"He might truly believe Viren and I assassinated them."

"He doesn't know you well. I would be angry with him for believing that of you, but I would understand. But to believe it of Viren . . . they were always close."

"He might not find it difficult to believe Viren coveted the crown."

"But he didn't."

"Perhaps Jared believes I did and swayed Viren."

"But Viren wasn't a cold-blooded murderer." Dann's voice conveyed his bewilderment.

Fi lifted her head. "We can only guess at Jared's reasons."

Dann nodded, but his eyes were distant. "I should go. I'm sure Hampton and the others are already talking."

Part of her wished he could remain with her. The other part wanted to curl up into a ball and wish she was someone else, someone without the Lyos name, someone who could marry the man she loved, live in a nice, quiet cottage, raise children, and milk cows. She almost made herself laugh. She'd enjoy it for an hour and then wonder why she'd wished for such a life.

The only part she wouldn't grow tired of was Dann. When he let go of her hand and stood, she wanted to tell him to forget about Hampton and stay longer. But she was Filmona Lyos, and they weren't married. She had the strong suspicion the men she'd sat with in the dining room had some idea in mind of who should be at her side at her coronation, and Dann wouldn't be the name on their tongues. She would accept most of what they wanted. She had to. But she would not lose Dann.

"I'd kiss you, if it wasn't such a terrible moment to do so," Dann said softly. "Instead, I'll settle for saying good night."

Fi murmured a good night in return and waited until he'd closed the door behind him. "On the morrow, I want to visit the camp," she said to Jeena. "And I want to speak to Enkelo alone. We'll find him right after breakfast. You're not to leave my side. Apparently I'm not safe here. That servant could be one of many." He'd been so close to sticking a dagger into her and ending the Lyos dynasty. If not for Jeena . . . "Thank you. I'd be dead, if not for you."

"I'm sorry I didn't curtsy before I ran him through," Jeena said, her expression bland.

Fi's first instinct was to snap a response, but her better instinct held her tongue. "Yes, I'm, uh, sorry about the way I spoke to you earlier."

"Ye were putting on airs."

She raised her brows.

"Ye said I could say anything to ye in private."

"Yes, but . . ." She was a Lyos and would be queen, but she'd also spent more time in the company of commoners than any monarch before her. She hadn't achieved her position, fought for it, sacrificed, been judged the worthiest one. She'd simply had the right parents. Jeena had saved her tonight, and those in the camp had risked their lives and left their homes to help Erryn. They'd also rescued a princess they didn't care about.

She'd enjoyed herself since arriving at the manor, had savoured her hot bath and the many ladies buzzing around her. But lording her power over others was wrong. She could command without being surly and dismissive. She wanted true loyalty, not resentful acquiescence. She wanted what Erryn had—people who rallied around her because of respect, not fear.

"I'm sorry about how I treated you earlier," she said to Jeena. "I am a princess and will be queen, which I know you don't care about. But it does matter when you're with me, and when you're with other people who care. Still, I was wrong to speak to you so dismissively, and yes, you can say whatever you like when we're alone, as long as it's not too insulting."

She could swear Jeena almost smiled. "I agree with yer companion. Ye'd best take yer meals alone, or without servants."

Her companion. Now Fi almost smiled, especially since she wanted Dann to be more.

"No, Your Highness. I can't sanction it."

Fi blinked at Enkelo. She hadn't anticipated this. When Enkelo had entered the small sitting room attached to her bedchamber, she'd taken a deep breath and told him what she wanted from him. She'd expected to have to make a case, yes, but outright refusal at the outset? No. "It's what I want, Enkelo."

"You're not like others. You have freedom in some areas, but not in others."

Didn't she know it. "At the moment, I'm nobody. I'm simply Filmona Lyos."

"Poppycock. You're the rightful heir to the throne and have an army of men camped nearby," Enkelo pointed at the door, "ready to sacrifice their lives to see you crowned."

"All right, perhaps I'm not quite nobody. And perhaps I don't have complete freedom in all areas of my life. But I'm also not on the throne, and as you witnessed last night, many wish me dead. If I manage to take the throne, that won't stop, and the first year or two won't be easy. We'll still have to win people over to my side. I want to be with someone I trust, not someone I hardly know. I want to be with someone I love."

"You barely know him.""That's not true. And even if it was, you wouldn't hesitate to sanction whoever the Council wanted, even though I may only have ever seen him across a banquet table."

"You have a point." Enkelo rocked on his heels. "But Dann. His family name is tainted."

"Like you, he risked his life to find me."

"Some would say he did so to ensure that, should you become queen, the Tolin lands and assets will be restored to him."

"I don't care."

"You have to. You must agree to someone suitable."

Fi blinked back the hot, frustrated tears that sprang to her eyes. "I'm willing to take much counsel when I take the throne. I'm willing to be nice to men who are only supporting me now because the Primacy didn't turn out to be easily manipulated. I'll even reward them. But to be blunt, Enkelo, I'm not willing to be told who I take to my bed. Not after all this."

Enkelo's eyes widened slightly. "Hampton and Eness will have something to say about it."

"Hampton and Eness won't know. We'll have a quiet ceremony at the camp. Filmona Lyos will marry Dann Tolin. If I die before taking the throne, I want to die his wife." Her voice quavered. "And if I don't die, I want to be his wife so they can't make me marry someone else. I've lost everyone except him, and Erryn, and you, and Cedric. Do this for me, Enkelo. Give me your blessing and marry us. If I die, nobody ever has to know." But she would, and it would make all the difference. "If I don't die, they'll be upset when they find out, but it will pass. We'll have more pressing concerns than who I married."

"Your eldest son or daughter will rule."

"Yes, and they'll have Lyos blood, the same amount they'll have regardless of who I marry. Viren died for me. Dann has stood by me. You know he's honourable. You travelled with him. Would you rather see me marry the son of someone who was calling for my blood after the assassinations?"

"It's not a matter of who I want."

"No, it's a matter of who I want."

They stared at each other. "Are you sure Dann has no qualms about this? Not about you," Enkelo hastily added, "but about becoming your consort, knowing that some won't accept the news gracefully."

Dann didn't know. Yet. "Dann loves me."

"It's not that simple, Your Grace. But I'm not going to sway you from your position, am I?"

"No."

Enkelo slowly exhaled.

"I want you to marry us. If you refuse to do it now, then I'll assume you don't think he's suitable and won't ever want to marry us. And I'll fight for him. Make no mistake, I'll demand him when I'm on the throne. I'll give them a lot, but not this. So please, Enkelo, I want it to be you."

"Your wish is mine," Enkelo said, the diplomat—and politician—within him finally winning out. "I believe it will be a good match. It's not that I believe he's unsuitable. It's—"

"I understand. I also understand that you've always done what you felt would be good for me and the crown. You rescued me. You gave up everything, and trust me, should we succeed, you'll be rewarded for your loyalty. You know we can trust Dann, and you know there will be enemies lurking in every corner for some time to come. Most importantly, I've told you I love him. Having him at my side will help me face the challenges that are sure to come. I'm strong on my own, but with him, I'll be stronger."

"When do you want to do it?"

After she'd spoken to Dann. "He's going with me to visit the camp this morning. We'll discuss it along the way. But soon. Very soon."

"You'll want to be married there, I assume."

"Yes. We'll have to come up with some excuse for only you and Cedric to accompany me on a visit."

"I'm sure we'll think of something."

"Thank you," Fi said, wanting to hug him. "Your name will be in the history books." Hopefully because he'd helped to save the rightful heir and remained loyal to the end of his life, and not because he'd died trying to put an assassin on the throne.

"Do you want to get married?" Fi blurted, as she and Dann trudged away from the manor with Jeena on their heels. In a minute they'd be in the forest, where she wouldn't be able to look at him because she'd be busy making sure a branch didn't take out an eye.

"I always hoped to someday," Dann said. "Then things changed."

Fi glanced behind her. They'd rounded the curve in the path; only Jeena could see them. She stopped and turned to Dann. "The Tolin name will be redeemed. I'll make sure everyone knows Viren died heroically, and your role in all this will be sung by the bards."

"Things changed before then." Dann smiled. "And not in the manner you're thinking. I meant that I always hoped to get married and always assumed I would, but then I ran into you on the wall. Within an instant, I knew two things. One, that I was enraptured, and two, that you were betrothed to my brother. After that, marriage would have been an obligation and only for the purpose of siring children, to a woman who'd have been unfortunate to have me."

"But you would have been kind to her and loved her as best you could, because that's who you are," Fi said fiercely.

"I would have tried. Now I don't have to worry about it. Nobody will want me, despite the bards."

"I do." Fi gazed at him and willed her quaking insides to be still. "When I asked if you want to get married, I didn't mean it hypothetically. I meant soon, to me." She held her breath.

His brow furrowed, making him look angry. "We can't."

"Why not?"

"Because of you."

"Me? I'm the one asking."

"It should be me. But I wouldn't dare, because you're the rightful heir to the throne, and you'll need a strong man at your side, someone with influence and resources and a deft sword arm."

"I need—want—someone I can trust. The crown has influence and resources, and I'm quite strong myself." She sounded irritated, because she was, and reminded herself that she'd just sprung a proposal on him out of nowhere, surprising him and playing the man's role in this. "Viren proposed to me, yes, after my father and your father and who knows how many nobles had discussed it. By the time he was down on one knee, it had already been decided. Now I'm the queen waiting to be crowned. As far as I'm concerned, I get to decide now."

Dann shook his head. "You know as well as I do the Council will still decide. You'll have to accept whomever they choose."

"Not if I'm already married. Don't you see? Right now, I am just Filmona Lyos. Yes, I should be on the throne. Yes, I have an army rallying around me. But until I'm on the throne, I have some freedom, and I'm taking advantage of it. I want you to be at my side. I want you to be my consort. And . . ." She swallowed. "And if I die trying to claim what's rightfully mine, I want to die as your wife, and with you as my husband. I want to know they didn't take that away from me. But most of all, I want us to wed because I love you."

His face softened. "Have you told Hampton and Eness?"

"No, but I've told Enkelo, and he's willing to marry us."

"Soon, you said."

A glimmer of hope warmed her heart. "Tonight."

"Tonight?"

"Why delay? We'll get married at the camp."

He frowned, making her worry again. "You deserve a grand wedding, with a dress that will take everyone's breath away, and music composed for the occasion, and hundreds of people in the grand temple, and thousands outside."

"We can get married again and have all that." She hesitated, then pressed her hand against his scarred cheek. "I'll have what's most important to me. You. The man I love. I wouldn't have had that before. The music, the dress . . . it wouldn't have mattered. Marry me, Dann. Tonight, in front of the people who've risked everything and might die for me, for us, for Daros, for the Seven."

Her breath caught in her throat when he lifted her hand away from his cheek, but then he held it, and brought it to his lips and kissed it. Then she was in his arms, her heart soaring and the sun shining and everything seeming possible.

"Is that a yes?" she said into his shoulder.

He drew back. "Are you sure? I'll be everyone's last choice."

"But my first. And when they say I should marry Duke so-and-so's eldest son, I'll say, I'm sorry, but I'm already married." A giggled bubbled up inside her. She grinned, and he grinned back at her, and she glimpsed the carefree man who'd pirouetted on top of the parapet all those months ago.

"Tonight, then?" she said.

"Tonight."

They leaned in to each other. Their lips met. Fi forgot where she was and where she was going, until Jeena cleared her throat, making her jump.

"Ye said ye'd be back at the manor in an hour. If ye keep this up, ye'll be late."

"You're right. I don't want them asking questions. It's not that I want to hide our relationship," she said to Dann, "but that I don't want to have to argue with them. We have enough to worry about. I want them to focus on increasing our numbers and getting my throne back."

"Spoken like a Lyos and the rightful queen," Dann said.

One who'd marry the man she loved.

Erryn gaped at Fi, unsure of whether she'd heard correctly. "Married?"

Fi nodded, then smiled. "Tonight. And I want you to stand with me."

A multitude of thoughts raced through her mind. She wanted to be happy for Fi, she truly did. "I can't do that."

Fi's face fell. "Why not?"

"Because you've denied me love." She jabbed her finger at Fi. "You're marrying Dann tonight because you want to avoid fighting with the Council later."

"I'm marrying him because I love him."

"And you know the Council will want you to marry

someone else. So you're taking what you want. Love. I can't blame you for that. I admire you for it. But you refuse to allow me love. You've condemned me to do what you aren't willing to do: marry someone you don't love."

"I was going to marry Viren."

"But you didn't, and now you aren't willing to marry out of duty."

Fi slapped her thighs. "I don't know what you want from me. You can't be with a woman, Erryn, not overtly. You'll have to marry someone. I'll make sure it's someone kind, perhaps someone like you, who prefers the company of men. You'll have to have children, but otherwise it—"

"Are you listening to yourself? How do you expect me to stand next to you tonight with a smile on my face and be happy for you? I can't right now."

Fi's shoulders stiffened. "You've been away from the Royal City too long. You've grown too close to the wild folk."

Erryn couldn't believe her ears. "It's not that, Fi. I just want to spend my life with someone I love, just like you do. Look at what you're doing. Marrying Dann in secret, because you know that if you wait, they'll choose someone else for you. If you're going to defy the Council, why can't I? Why do I have to marry? And don't say it's because you're the rightful queen. Don't do that to me."

Fi opened her mouth, then closed it, then opened it again. "What do you propose to do then, Erryn?"

"Not marry."

Fi's face darkened. "And do what? Live on an estate by yourself? Or with Renn?" She almost laughed. Erryn wanted to smack her. "If you don't marry, people will talk," Fi said.

"I don't care." When Fi didn't respond, Erryn studied her face. "*You* do," she breathed. "You'd care."

"You're my sister."

"Shouldn't that mean you care about my happiness?"

"I do. I don't think you realize how difficult it would be for you."

"What do you think I've been doing since your father banished me? Living in a palace?"

Fi clasped her hands in front of her. "You've been free. Running, perhaps, but free. Back in Darroth, that won't be the case. If you don't marry, you'll be a spinster, and not because you haven't received marriage proposals from eligible nobles. People will whisper."

Erryn took a moment to collect her thoughts. When she spoke, her voice was softer. "If I—we—manage to free the Six, I don't know what will happen after that. The book says I've died and been reborn many times. If I succeed this time . . ." She shrugged. "Maybe I'll have fulfilled my purpose. Maybe that will be the end of this life for me. All the lives."

"Don't say that. I'll need you." Fi swallowed. "Surely they'll let you live out this one."

"If they were to ask me what I want, I'd need time to think about it. I'd miss you. I'd miss everyone. But facing a life married to someone I don't love . . ."

They stared at each other, their chests rising and falling.

"I want you to stand with me at my wedding," Fi finally

said, sounding subdued. "Let's not worry about what comes later. There might not be a later, for either of us."

Erryn wanted to agree to Fi's request. Of course she wanted to stand next to Fi at her wedding. She'd regret it if she stubbornly refused. But would resentment spoil it for her, the knowledge that Fi would deny her the same thing she wanted so much that she'd risk upsetting the men who'd rally around her when she took the throne?

"If I give you my promise that I'll do my best for you, that I'll try, somehow, to make things easier for you, will you stand with me?" Fi asked.

How could Fi make things easier? She wasn't wrong. Erryn *would* be whispered about, even derided, for not marrying, and Fi had admitted she'd care about the gossip. "You named me your heir. If you and Dann die, you expect me to fight for the throne. Then I'll really be trapped."

Fi waved a dismissive hand. "The moment Dann and I have a child, that paper will be worthless."

Erryn frowned at her. "You know there's a chance you'll both die before then. If that happens, I'm running. Enkelo isn't fond of me. He won't put forward the parchment you signed if I'm not around to insist on it."

"He will, because he's loyal to me. And you're not thinking, Erryn. If you were on the throne, you could choose your own husband, have two children, and then banish him from your bedchamber."

Erryn wanted to shake her head, her fist, gape, shout out in frustration. But it would be of no use, and despite Fi's pigheaded attitude and refusal to see things from

Erryn's point of view, she loved her. How much would she regret not standing with her tonight? She'd resent whoever stood in her place. "I'll stand with you, but this conversation isn't over."

"I suggest we continue it when all of the Seven are free and I have a crown on my head, because until then, we're arguing for no reason." Fi pouted. "I don't like arguing with you."

"I don't like it, either."

They stepped toward each other, and after an awkward moment, hugged, as they had many times before. But there was a distance between them. Fi had always understood. Fi had always supported her. Yet here Erryn was in Fi's arms, feeling more alone than ever.

Toe downed the last of his ale and wiped his mouth with his sleeve. Men from the manor house had brought two barrels to the camp, for the morale of those serving the rightful queen, Cedric had said when he'd arrived with them. Half an hour after the men had left, Toe had watched that rightful queen pledge her life to Dann, with Erryn standing next to her, Cedric on Dann's right, and Enkelo conducting the ceremony. The bride and groom had shared a meal with everyone and then returned to the manor, with Jeena on their heels. Were their bedchambers near to each other? One would have to stumble into the other's. Toe chuckled at the thought.

"What are ye laughing about?"

He looked up. Asha stood over him. "Have some ale," he said, raising his empty mug.

"How many have ye had?"

"Not many. This is my . . . third. Or fourth. Ye know how weak the city folk ale is."

"Do ye want to join those at the fire, then, instead of sitting alone in front of yer tent?"

He looked past her at the brave few dancing around the flames. "I'm starting to feel a bit light-headed," he mumbled. "I might not be steady on my feet. Best I not."

Her eyes narrowed, but she didn't insist. "I'll sit with ye, then."

"Do ye want some ale?"

She shook her head and lowered herself next to him. "Nice ceremony, if a bit dull."

Toe guffawed. When his people pledged, there was drumming and singing, and after the celebratory meal, the man carried his woman home. "She says she'll do it again when she's queen, in a grand temple."

"It will still be dull."

Toe nodded.

"Ye're getting older," Asha said, a curious lilt to her voice. "When will ye pledge?"

He wasn't surprised she hadn't asked if he wanted to. It would be a strange man who didn't want a woman and children. But . . . "I'll go back to running contracts."

"Ye didn't answer the question."

"Renn can't work alone. She's not good with folk."

"Are ye pledging to Renn, then?"

"Ye know I'm not." He eyed her appreciatively. She'd braided flowers through her long hair.

"Renn will be welcomed back by the clan. If we free

them, how could we turn her away? She was there, in the chamber, named by Zhikinden. She'll have travelled at the side of the Called and Caller, but she can't stay with her."

Toe looked for Renn but didn't see her, or Erryn. His suspicion about them was no longer a suspicion. He felt bad for them.

"I'll invite her to return with us," Asha said. "I hope ye do, as well. I would like it very much, if ye did."

He met her eyes. Desire flooded through him, and he had to stop himself from reaching out and touching her cheek. He was suddenly aware of how close she was to him. Their arms were almost touching. "If ye weren't a Mother, I'd ask ye into my tent," he blurted. Blood rushed to his face. His head buzzed.

Asha laughed, her eyes bright and her cheeks flushed. "Do ye think Mothers no longer want a man? How do ye think Renn came to be?"

"It's the wedding and the ale," he sputtered, though part of him knew it wasn't true. Mothers pledged. Mothers had children. But he'd been away too long. Asha would want someone untouched by the cities.

"If ye were to ask me into yer tent, I might say yes," she said.

Her words stunned him. He wanted her. He wanted to love her, and protect her, and ravish her. He leaned in, sought her lips—

She placed a gentle but firm hand on his chest. "I might not be able to say yes, so it's best we not start something we can't finish."

"What do ye mean?" Toe said breathlessly. "Ye said ye'd say yes."

She gave him an uncharacteristically shy look.

"What is it?" he asked, unable to take his eyes off her.

"I want to pledge—I want ye to pledge . . . us to pledge. Us."

He scrambled for words, but shock was addling his wits.

Asha's eyes glistened. "I'll understand if ye don't want to. It takes a strong man to pledge to a Mother. The clan has to come first, and the man second. And ye'd need to come home." She gulped down air, then touched his hand. "Ye're a strong man, and ye'll do fine at home."

"Me?" he finally managed to get out. "I thought I'd be the last man ye'd want."

Her eyes widened. "Why?"

"Ye said it yerself. I'm the only one ye could talk to about yer doubts. I'm an outsider now."

She rolled her eyes. "No, ye silly man. I meant I'm comfortable talking to ye. Ye listen. Ye don't make fun, or shout, or say I'm weak for having doubts. And I knew ye wouldn't tell anyone. That's important to me. That's what I want in a man."

Once again, he was speechless, his mind struggling to grasp what his heart had already accepted.

"I knew ye wouldn't ask, so I did." Asha lifted her chin. "I'm not meek. If ye want someone meek, ye'd best refuse me."

He took her hand. "I want ye. I accept." The smile that spread across her face made him smile, too.

"Then I won't be coming into yer tent," she said.

He leaned in again. She leaped to her feet. "It'll be all the sweeter the longer ye have to wait. My mother always says that."

Toe wanted to throttle her mother. "Stay and talk, then."

She shook her head. "I want to dance. I have something to celebrate." She held out her hand. "Ye can dance, too."

"No, I'll stay here."

She laughed again. "Typical. But hear this: ye'll dance at our ceremony, before ye carry me off." With a grin, she bounded away and joined those around the fire.

Toe watched her sway, vowing to survive whatever lay before him.

Erryn sat morosely a short distance away from the camp, on a tree that age had felled. Renn sat next to her, staring into the darkness. Faint notes from the lute Cedric was playing and the shouts of those who'd had too much ale rose behind them. Renn's fingers tightened around hers. The gesture deepened her anger. It wasn't fair. Fi would get everything she wanted. The Northerners would return to their stronghold and be hailed as heroes. Toe would be free to choose whatever path he wanted. She and Renn . . .

She quickly loosened her fingers when Renn yelped. "Sorry," she muttered. She'd expected to be upset when Fi married, but not for the reason her jaw was clenched tonight. And Fi would do it again! It would be even more difficult to smile when Renn was gone.

Her throat tightened. There had to be a way for them

to stay together. If not, she would ask—beg—the Seven to take her. What would be the point of remaining here, on the physical plane?

"Ye shouldn't be angry with her," Renn said. "She's yer family."

"I'm not angry. I'm . . . jealous. I envy her. And not because she's queen."

"Ye always said it wouldn't last."

"Because I thought I was going to die. Now I might live, knowing you're out there, which will be worse." She bolted to her feet. "I won't marry. I don't care what Fi says. I can't be expected to give up the person I love *and* marry someone else. I can't do it."

"Ye say that now, but they'll make ye."

She wanted to disagree, but would she withstand the pressure? What would she do? Where would she go? Fi would be the queen. One didn't defy the queen. Plus, her sense of duty was too strong. Even if she could run away, she wouldn't leave Fi in the lurch, especially in the beginning, when some would be sore losers.

At the same time, she didn't want to lose Renn. She didn't want to marry. She'd be no use to the queen if she resented her and everyone around her, and was grieving her loss of freedom. There had to be a way to satisfy everyone. But she'd be the queen's sister, and if she was back at the castle, it would mean everyone knew she'd freed the Seven, and so she'd also be the Saviour. The Council would not allow the queen's sister and the Saviour to do as she pleased.

Freedom for power. Love for luxury. The trades weren't

fair. Before being banished she didn't mind them, but now she saw them for what they were, and the knowledge would deny her happiness.

"I'll run away," she said, even though it was a lie. There had to be a way.

"They'll find ye. They'll want ye with the queen."

The queen would want her with the queen. Erryn sat on Renn's lap, laid her head on her shoulder, and closed her eyes when Renn's arms slipped around her. She shouldn't do this, not here where anyone could stumble from the camp and see. But right now she didn't care. Half the camp must suspect, perhaps all of it. Let them see. What would they do? Without her, the Seven would remain trapped. But to them, Renn was expendable.

With a sigh, she pushed Renn's arms free and slid off her to sit next to her again. Unless someone crept up on them, nobody would see them holding hands.

"There has to be a way for us." She paused. "Fi said she'd try to do her best for me." But Fi had wanted Erryn at her side when she joined her life to Dann's, and Erryn had seized on her words so she could be there. Regret would have dogged her otherwise, and she was glad she'd swallowed her resentment and stood with Fi, even though the ceremony had set her teeth on edge.

"Maybe it would be best if I went back to running contracts with Toe, and ye went back to being royal."

Erryn didn't believe her for a second, but admired the way she made it sound as if they had a choice. "That's not what you want."

"No."

"Then don't give up yet. I'm not."

Renn grimaced. "I must love ye, because I'm willing to tread a path of thorns after ye, even though I'll bleed and the path will never end."

Erryn blinked at her. Despite her mood, a smile tugged at her lips. "That's quite the declaration of love." Not caring about the camp for a second, she gently kissed her.

"You need to think more creatively."

They both leaped to their feet at the sound of the voice that came out of nowhere. Erryn's heart hammered in her chest. She glanced around, then relaxed slightly when Avere slinked into view. How long had she been nearby, listening?

The Ferret cocked her head. "While everyone's been busy getting drunk, I've been keeping an eye on things. Now, this is what I would do. Let the queen choose a husband for you. Marry him. On your wedding night, kill him. You'd be a widow. You'd be so overcome with grief at the loss of your true love that you wouldn't be able to even discuss marriage for years, or at least until you can no longer bear children and nobody will want you. As for Renn, I'm sure I can convince the spymaster to bring her into our fold, and to give her assignments that have her frequently crossing your path."

Erryn couldn't resist exchanging a bewildered look with Renn. "If you don't mind, I'd prefer to find a way that's a bit less violent."

Avere chuckled. "You wouldn't slit his throat. Poison, my dear. Have Fi marry you to someone frail or advanced in years. They'll all think he'd had a weak heart that couldn't withstand a night of passion. Nobody would have to know you'd killed him before either of you had removed any clothing."

"Uh, still. No."

Avere tutted. "Do you want to be with each other, or not? Desperate times require desperate measures."

"Even if I could kill the poor man Fi had chosen, I wouldn't want Renn slinking around in the shadows."

"All right, then. You could make her your personal guard. Our rightful queen has a wild woman at her side. Why not you?"

"I doubt Jeena will be around at that point, and I don't want to treat Renn like a servant."

"You'll have to do something better than hoping it will all work out for you. If it's a matter of not wanting to kill him, I'll do it for you. I'll add the poison to his drink."

"Why? Why would you do that for me? For us?"

"They spat on you, branded you, and sent you off intending to kill you. They have no right to ask more of you. She has no right." Avere shrugged. "And they tolerate your type of love in the shadows. Why not openly? I'm not one for silly conventions. Or silly laws."

"I appreciate your offer, but no, thank you. I don't want an innocent man to die for us. It would ruin it."

"Well, if you change your mind." Without another word, Avere skirted around them and headed in the direction of the camp.

Erryn turned to Renn. "You were quiet."

"I didn't know what to say. I don't want to have to kill anyone, but she's right. Hoping won't be enough."

But it was all they had. *Stay with Fi and not defy the Council and have Renn.* If Avere didn't think Erryn had been wracking her brains to figure out how she could do it all, she was wrong. The Ferret had suggested killing her future betrothed because she knew there was no easy solution to the problem. But they still had time, and Erryn still wasn't sure she had a future. All she knew was that if she lived beyond freeing the Seven, she wanted to be with Renn.

Fi sat at the table in one of Hampton's sitting rooms, wishing Dann wasn't across from her. This was an important meeting. The diplomats sent to speak to the sympathetic nobles had returned with news. But she couldn't resist sneaking looks at Dann and relishing the secret they shared, when she should be listening.

". . . will join us."

"That's fabulous news." On his feet, Eness clapped Cedric on the back. "With their men, we're almost ready to march on Darroth."

Knowing they'd expect it, Fi smiled. She didn't have to force it. Lately she was smiling all the time. "That's wonderful, gentlemen."

"While I agree that bolstering our numbers has brought the throne within our grasp, we need another thousand men, ideally two," Hampton said.

"That's the bad news, sir," said one of the diplomats.

Everyone turned toward him.

"Danvers has a couple of men inside the city. They reported that the Primacy is set to relinquish its regency."

Wide eyes and surprised murmurs greeted the man's words. "That doesn't make sense," Hampton said. "If anything, it's been tightening its hold."

"Yes, which is probably why it won't be putting a man on the throne, but a boy."

"A boy," Eness breathed.

Fi's mouth tightened. They'd give her throne to a child? "Who?"

The negotiator straightened and cleared his throat. "The eldest grandson of Duke Falkirk, Your Grace. He's twelve years old."

Eness scowled. "The Primacy will still rule in all but name for another four years. By then it might have hatched some scheme to eliminate its puppet."

"We must move soon, then," Cedric said. "If the people accept this boy, Her Majesty will be seen as a usurper, rather than the rightful ruler. Even if they don't, seizing an occupied throne will be more difficult than seizing an empty one. The nobles who've supported the boy will be compelled to defend his position."

Everyone fell silent. Fi looked to Dann and saw concern in his eyes, but he gave her a quick smile.

"When will the coronation take place?" Eness asked.

"According to the information we have, soon. Perhaps within a month."

His fists clenched. "We have to march now."

Hampton's brow furrowed. "We need more men."

"We'll gather more on the way. And our approach will perhaps delay the coronation they've planned."

"If we march, it must be to take the throne," Cedric

said. "Our approach could have them placing a crown on the boy's head sooner. We'll have to triumph before then, or soon after."

"We have allies inside the city who might be able to help," Enkelo, who'd been observing, said.

Eness gazed at him. "Who?"

"I can't say. Just know that we'll get a message to them."

"Our friends in the camp nearby will deliver it to them," Cedric said.

Not sure she could keep her expression bland, Fi looked down at her lap. Enkelo and Cedric were echoing the words they'd settled on when they'd discussed how to explain why the wild folk would continue on to the Royal City, rather than return to their land. Eness and Hampton remained unaware that Erryn was in the camp, and of the task she must perform.

"Are they mercenaries?" Hampton asked.

"No. But they'll be able to create distractions, perhaps eliminate key generals. I believe we'd be wise to let them signal when we should mount our assault."

"You mean camp outside the city until we receive word from them."

"Yes."

"You trust these men?"

"Yes."

Fi was glad her face was hidden. They knew the spymaster supported them, but that was all. Would his people obey when the orders he gave them worked against the Primacy?

Hampton huffed. "It sounds like we won't know what

they're doing. But for the moment, it doesn't matter. I regretfully have to agree with everyone. We must march, and hope that our numbers swell before we reach Darroth's gates."

"I'll visit the camp and tell the one who leads the wild folk they should proceed to the city," Cedric said. "By the time we get there, our people inside will have had time to throw some foxes among the chickens."

Fi lifted her head. "I'll go with you. I might not see them again, so I'd like to thank them for . . . everything."

Cedric nodded to her. "Very well, Majesty."

"Then you are in agreement with this plan, Your Grace?" Hampton said. "You wish us to prepare to march on the city?"

Cedric's face coloured. Fi scrambled to support him. "Yes. This morning I told Cedric it was time for the wild folk to leave. They never intended to join the main army. The more eyes we have in the city, the better." Her gaze swept those in the room. They didn't need to know that she'd said no such thing, and that she was taking direction about what to do from Cedric and Enkelo. And they certainly would never know that she'd go to the camp to say good-bye to Erryn. Again. The thought dampened her mood. They'd both be going into danger. If they were to die, at least they'd do it as sisters who'd reunited and put Erryn's banishment behind them.

"I'll inform our generals," Eness said.

"Thank you." Her eyes settled on Cedric. "I see no reason for us to delay visiting the wild folk."

"May I accompany you, Your Grace?" Enkelo asked.

"Of course." She looked at Dann. "And if you don't mind, I wish you to come with us, as well."

Dann inclined his head. "Of course, Your Grace."

Fi bit her lip.

Crouched near the fire, Erryn picked up a stick and drew a square in the dirt. "We'll go to Darroth," she said, tapping inside the square, "and rendezvous with the spymaster."

Avere nodded. "I'll go first. We know he's sympathetic to Fi, but we're not sure about you."

"We'll deliver your messages and enlist his help for my task," Erryn continued.

"Meanwhile we'll advance on the city," Cedric said. Erryn drew several circles that represented the army outside the square. "We've already told Eness and Hampton that we'll wait for a signal from you."

When Erryn and the Northerners were ready to infiltrate the Primacy's estate, the army would begin its assault to act as a distraction, even though it might not have the numbers to defeat the opposing force. She let the stick dangle from her fingers. "Are you sure about this?" she said to Fi. "If you lose . . ."

"It's more important that you free them," Fi said, sounding as if she meant it. But her expression was sombre. "I wish we could tell all those men what they're really fighting for, especially since they could sacrifice their lives for it."

"Our situation isn't as dire as all that, Majesty," Cedric said. "What we lack in numbers, we make up in resolve.

And I believe our numbers will grow on the way to Darroth."

"I believe they will, too," Dann said. "Support attracts more support. People who've been afraid to speak out on your behalf will be emboldened when your army marches through their town."

"Don't discount us, either," Avere said. "You'd be surprised what removing a few key people can do. The most important thing is that you wait for a message from us before you move. And don't forget my other suggestion when the time comes."

"We won't," Fi said.

"Then we're ready. We all know what to do," Enkelo said.

Everyone murmured their agreement.

"We'll leave right after we've had something to eat," Erryn said.

"Then if you don't mind, I'd like to have a private word with you," Fi said.

Cedric saluted her with a fist over his heart. "We'll wait for you here, Majesty."

Erryn pushed to her feet. "We'll go to my tent." Renn wasn't there. Erryn could see her sitting with Toe. Renn was madly gesturing and Toe's shoulders were slumped.

"Come on," Fi said.

Erryn fell into step with her, her mind still on Renn and Toe. She'd ask Renn about it later.

As soon as they were inside the tent, Fi said, "I wish we didn't have to part again."

"Me, too. I understand why the army has to move now, but . . ."

"It would be better if our hand wasn't being forced?" Fi nodded. "Unfortunately, they're right. This boy can't be crowned."

"Since the Primacy would still be behind him, he'd likely be unpopular."

"But still the king. It would muddy the waters. And frankly, I don't want a name in the history books between mine and Father's."

Erryn couldn't help but admire Fi's spirit. "I wish I was as confident as you."

"You've come further than anyone—well, further than your previous selves." Fi made a face. "Do you believe it? That you've been here over and over again?"

"I don't know. It doesn't really matter."

"No, I suppose it doesn't." She smiled. "I believe you'll do it, and I'm glad I'll be there to help, even though we won't be together. Don't worry about me. Don't pay any attention to the tide of the battle. Find the temple and free them. I have to believe that if they're freed, everything will proceed as it should. Those are my instructions, the instructions from your queen." Her voice dipped. "And your loving sister."

Lately, Erryn had envied and resented Fi, but none of that mattered now. "I'm grateful your father agreed to raise me. He didn't have to. He went beyond duty to my father, treating me as one of his own. So did your mother. I had a brother I admired, and I have you, who I love dearly." Her eyes welled. "Be safe, Fi," she whispered.

"Next time we see each other, you'll be queen, and—" Her voice choked off.

"You'll be standing next to me in triumph as the Saviour, or perhaps in the heavens, not because you perished, but because you freed them and they took you with them," Fi said firmly. "The Primacy should never have challenged the two Lyos sisters, and when you volunteered to free the Seven, they knew it would only be a matter of time."

They embraced. Erryn held on to Fi longer than she usually did and had to will herself to let her go, even though Fi showed no sign of wanting to be free. This would *not* be the last time she saw Fi in the flesh. The next time they embraced would be in Darroth.

Fi pressed her hand against her chest. "For the Seven. For Daros."

Erryn mimicked the gesture. "For the Seven. For Daros. For the queen."

They held each other's eyes for a moment, then Fi whirled and left the tent. Erryn stared after her for a long while, thinking of everything she wished she'd said, especially about Dann. She should have told Fi that she did like him, that her reluctance to stand with her at their wedding wasn't about him. She should have demonstrated a confidence she didn't feel. But that was what she'd always appreciated about their relationship, how they could be honest with each other. Perhaps if she'd told Fi about the Fallen earlier and not waited until she'd had no choice but to reveal herself, events would have unfolded differently. The king might still be alive. Fi could be at a tea party, not preparing to march on Darroth to claim the throne that belonged to her. Or perhaps things would have turned out exactly as they had, maybe worse.

She should return to Avere. It was time to gather everyone, explain the plan, and prepare to leave. With a heavy sigh, she steeled herself and—

Renn stormed into the tent, almost running into Erryn and knocking her over. "Sorry," she muttered.

"What's wrong?"

"Nothing." Renn's fiery eyes and tight face said otherwise.

"I saw you talking to Toe. It looked like you were arguing."

"Nothing's wrong," Renn said again.

Something obviously was, but Renn would tell her in her own time. Erryn lay a calming hand on Renn's arm. "We're leaving."

"Good. I'm tired of sitting on my bottom, doing nothing."

"When we get to Darroth, you'll wish you could be idle again."

Renn lifted her broadsword from next to her bedroll and strapped it onto her back. "I won't. And any soft bottom who gets in my way will lose his head." She stomped toward the tent's flap, then whirled. "What are ye waiting for?"

Erryn bit back a retort. "Nothing."

She followed Renn from the tent and didn't protest when Renn walked to the edge of the camp and stared into the distance. Given Renn's mood, it was best that she stand guard while Erryn and Avere met with the others

and everyone broke camp. Erryn didn't want any heads
rolling just yet.

Erryn crouched next to Renn and peered through the
trees at the campfire. The smoke curling into the noonday
sky had drawn their attention. Unfortunately the three
men sharing the meal they'd cooked on the pot hanging
over the fire weren't merchants, or a family on their way
to Darroth. Their breastplates glinted in the sun and
weapons hung at their sides.

She exchanged a glance with Renn. Avere had sneaked
away to get a closer look. Toe had wanted to come, but
Renn had waved him off. An icy cold had developed
between the two Northerners. Erryn had pleaded with
Renn to tell her what was wrong, but Renn remained
tight-lipped. She'd be angry if she found out Erryn
already knew that Toe and Asha planned to pledge to
each other. Was Renn resentful for the same reason
Erryn hadn't wanted to stand with Fi, or was it because
Toe would return to the stronghold and no longer run
contracts? Erryn suspected that Toe hadn't discussed it
with Renn before stating his intentions to Asha, not that
Renn would have tried to change his mind. She wouldn't
expect him to give up love and children for her. But to
find out he'd gone ahead without giving her the courtesy
of telling her first had slighted her, and perhaps made
her feel as if her loyalty to Toe, and their years working
together, hadn't counted for anything.

While Erryn understood Renn's feelings, her dismay
at them betrayed her spoken wish that Renn go back to

her normal life. If Renn had been planning to resume running contracts, it meant she'd given up on their relationship. Maybe she'd done so unconsciously, or truly felt there was no future for them. Renn had never expressed any desire to return to the stronghold, but she was shamed, or had been. The Northerners travelling with them had accepted her again, and if they freed the Seven, the rest of the clan would do the same.

But that was the future. For the moment, Erryn had to decide how long she'd pretend not to know why Renn was upset.

Avere was suddenly next to her, making her heart thump. "Only three, but there are signs that—"

"Five," a voice behind them said.

They whirled. Two guards brandished swords. Renn lunged. Avere's daggers flashed. Erryn instinctively called Zayvang and Lerxis. At the same time, shouts erupted from the direction of the guards' camp. Renn and Avere were on their own. Erryn sent the saber-tooth cat and the wolf to meet the guards rushing to join the fray.

The fight lasted no longer than a minute, though as Erryn remained crouched, hoping a sword didn't find its way to her belly or heart, it felt like an eternity.

Avere was next to her again, listening, her chest rising and falling. She tensed when Lerxis returned, her muzzle bloodied, then put a finger to her lips and crept toward the camp. Erryn looked for Renn and felt herself relax when Renn rejoined her. There was a new cut on her arm, but otherwise she appeared all right and held her broadsword at the ready.

"They made short work of the guards," Avere said, not bothering to lower her voice. "Three against two, but there's always that moment of confusion when they see the Fallen that costs them their lives." She sheathed the two daggers she held. "We should drag the bodies into the forest and hope animals get to them. We don't want whoever comes looking for them to know you're so close to Darroth."

Erryn stroked Lerxis and was about to dismiss her, but then decided not to. Since learning the Fallen were really the Seven—except for Zayvang now—she wasn't sure how to treat them. Zhikinden had said to use them, that they'd want her to do so, and Erryn had always sensed that the Fallen enjoyed walking the physical plane. If they were bound in the heavens, perhaps it was the only time they could taste freedom. She suddenly felt compelled to call the others, but it would be foolish. She wouldn't send Lerxis—Lleor—back just yet, though.

The wolf padded at her side when Erryn walked into the camp and surveyed the carnage. Her stomach didn't roil, which troubled her. If they freed the Seven and they allowed her to live out the rest of her last life, would she eventually forget? Would her stomach lurch again, or would she be forever numb to the sight of men ravaged by animals?

Return, she said to Lerxis, wishing the wolf could stay longer. Renn picked up one of the dead guards and slung him over her shoulder. A chunk had been bitten from the man's neck. His head lolled from side to side. For a moment, Erryn feared it would fall off. Not strong enough to carry a guard by herself, she followed Avere's lead, grabbed a guard's hands, and dragged him into the brush.

"We'll cover up the tracks," Avere said breathlessly, pulling along a guard who'd obviously eaten well. "We'll wreck the camp too, make it look possible that bandits killed them before any animals fed."

Erryn nodded, straining to pull the body she was dragging. A root had caught part of the guard's trousers. She had to let him go to free him, and though she tried not to, couldn't help but look at his face. The man had only been following orders. Did he have a wife? Children? How many more would they have to kill? How many had she killed in her past lives?

"Hurry up, Erryn," Avere said.

Erryn shook herself and grabbed the man's hands again. Five minutes later, they'd messed up the camp, put out the fire, and covered their tracks.

"The closer we get to Darroth, the more guards we'll run into," Avere said.

"How far away are we?" Renn asked.

Avere pursed her lips. "I'd say two to three days." She paused. "I shouldn't have missed the other two. I saw signs of more men, but I didn't see *them*."

"They came up behind you," Erryn said.

"That's no excuse."

"No, they came from another direction," Renn said. "They got to us after ye did, but they weren't following ye."

Avere raised her brows. "Are you sure?"

"I saw where they trampled."

"Still. I can't be sloppy. I don't like sloppy."

As soon as they entered their own camp, the others gathered around them. "What happened?" Asha asked. "Ye're bloodied."

"We ran into more guards than we expected." Avere turned to Erryn. "Maybe I should go on alone from this point."

Asha gave her a cursory nod. "Ye shouldn't have taken Erryn."

Avere frowned. "She volunteered to go. She—"

"Ye should have said no. She can't be killed." Her eyes angry, she turned to Renn. "And ye should know better. Ye risked her because ye're mad at Toe. Ye were foolish. If I hadn't been fetching water when ye left, I would have said so."

Renn's mouth pressed into a thin line and her hands balled into fists. For a moment, Erryn wondered if she and the priestess would come to blows. Being scolded would anger Renn at the best of times, but coming from Asha now . . .

"As Avere said, I volunteered." Erryn gave Asha an apologetic shrug. "I shouldn't have." She'd welcome not having to participate in bloody skirmishes. At the same time, the Fallen were useful in a fight. "From now on, I'll stay behind, unless we believe there are too many of them to handle without the Fallen."

"Better yet, let me go on alone from this point," Avere said. "I have to sneak into the Royal City alone, anyway."

"Will we be safe here? We just ran into five guards."

"I heard a couple of them talking at the fire. They were on their way to Moss, to temporarily bolster the guard numbers there. They weren't a regular patrol. There aren't any this far from the city."

"Maybe not when things are calm, but now . . ."

"You'll be keeping watch. You can always move. We'll work out what to carve on the trees, so I'll be able to find you when I return."

"We'll handle any guards." Asha gazed at Erryn. "But not ye. We can't lose ye."

"I won't be able to stand by if we're being overrun," Erryn said, wishing she could. She wasn't a coward, and she wouldn't let her friends and Renn die without a fight. But she didn't have the stomach for killing. It didn't matter that she was calling forth the Six to do it. When she'd stepped forward all those many years ago, had she understood what she was agreeing to do? It sounded like everyone had expected her to stroll to each temple, be welcomed by the locals with open arms, and free one of the Seven. What had gone wrong?

"How long should we wait for ye?" Asha asked Avere.

The Ferret drew back in mock offence. "Are you suggesting I might not return?"

"Not because ye'll leave us to fend for ourselves, but because something happened to ye."

"Nothing will happen to me. I'll be back within a week."

"Ye expect us to sit on our bottoms for a week?" Renn growled.

"Don't get fat," Avere said. "I'll gather my things and be off." She sauntered away.

Erryn lifted Renn's left arm and examined it. "I'll clean this for you."

"It's a scratch. There's no need."

Asha rolled her eyes. "Let her clean it. If it fills with pus, ye'll be no use to us when we need ye the most."

Renn scowled, but nodded. Erryn hung on to her arm as they walked to their tent, and after telling Renn to sit and wait, she heated water over the fire. Back with Renn, she rummaged through a bag for soap and a clean rag.

She lathered Renn's arm. "You seem angry at Asha. For more than what she said to you," she said, hoping Renn would bite.

Renn remained silent.

She tightened her grasp on Renn's wrist. "You know, being with someone means trusting them. You can talk to me. I won't think you're weak if you're upset about something." As she'd expected, Renn tried to pull her arm away. "I hope it's not always going to be like this."

"Like what" Renn snapped.

She rinsed the wound. "You refusing to talk to me about anything."

"Ye won't be there to talk to. Ye'll be married to some soft bottom."

Not wanting to meet anger with irritation, Erryn took a few deep breaths. "I'm not married at the moment. I'm here, right next to you. So are you going to tell me what you've been upset about since we broke camp near the Hampton estate?"

Renn stared past Erryn, her face stone. "Ye've heard about Toe and Asha."

Finally. "But I don't know what's upset you. I can try to guess, but I'd rather you tell me." She stopped patting at the wound when Renn's eyes moistened.

"I don't want to be alone," Renn said.

A lump rose in Erryn's throat. "You won't be alone. The stronghold will welcome you back. And that's only if we can't figure out a way to be together."

Renn brushed away a tear. "Ye still believe we can be together?"

"I'm not giving up yet. There has to be a way. If there is, we'll find it."

She lowered her head and focused on making sure she'd removed every bit of soap, so Renn wouldn't see her face. She'd like to believe that love always won, but she'd lived among the nobility long enough to know it wasn't true.

Fi emerged from her tent and looked wistfully over at Dann's. She couldn't wait for this charade to end. The men who ended up on her council would huff and rant and stamp their feet when they found out she'd had the audacity to choose her own husband, but they'd have to accept it. She'd push those who didn't aside. She wasn't a tyrant and would welcome those around her to speak their minds, but she wouldn't have time for those who didn't wish her to be happy.

"Good morning, Your Grace," the boy who'd been assigned to her said. He was always right outside her tent, waiting. She wondered if he'd be there if she poked her head outside in the middle of the night.

She smiled at him. "Good morning, Tommy."

"Would you like me to fetch breakfast for you and the lady?" he said.

She always wanted to giggle when Tommy called Jeena a lady. "Please." As usual, Jeena had left the tent before her, in case an assassin lurked outside. Not likely in the middle of the army's camp, especially when her tent was surrounded by those she knew and trusted, but she didn't begrudge Jeena's diligence. Quite the contrary.

Hampton was bearing down on them. "We may have found her, Your Grace."

"Really? Show me."

She followed him to a tent and went inside with Jeena when he motioned for them to enter before him.

Cedric and Eness were talking to a young woman. "Ah, you have arrived," Eness said to Fi. "This is Princess Filmona, soon to be our queen."

Fi's breath caught in her throat when the woman turned to her and bobbed a curtsy. Same height, roughly the same weight, similar enough hair colour, and though their noses and mouths weren't exactly the same, the shape of their faces and the position of everything that counted was similar enough. It would fool someone peering from a distance.

"What is your name?" she asked the girl.

"Miriam, Your Majesty."

"I'm pleased to meet you, Miriam." She looked past the girl. "Where did you find her?"

"She's sister to one of the men who joined us yesterday, Your Grace."

"She's certainly the best one we've seen so far. Do you agree?" she said to Jeena. The wild woman saw her more than anyone else did, including Dann, much to Fi's chagrin.

"She'll pass for ye," Jeena said, which Fi took to be an enthusiastic approval.

"Do you understand what you'll be doing?" she asked the girl.

"Yes," Miriam said shyly.

"You're sure you want to do it? Your brother isn't making you?"

"No, Princess. I want to do it for you."

Guilt tugged at Fi. This girl would be putting herself in danger. Fi would be doing the same, but she'd get a throne at the end. She'd remember to reward the girl and her family, assuming they survived. "Thank you. I won't forget your service to me, and to Daros."

Miriam bobbed another curtsy.

"You can't be seen together," Hampton said. "Once you've departed, she'll walk the camp."

"With guards," Fi said, inwardly cringing again.

"Of course, Your Grace."

"How long now?"

"We're about four days out, Majesty," Cedric said. "Once we're where they can see us, we'll wait for the messenger."

"But not forever," Eness said.

Fi gazed at him, her expression neutral. Eness and Hampton were skeptical about the "friends inside the city." If they knew about Erryn, they'd be even more so.

"The messenger will come, but I agree that we can't stay our hand too long. We don't want the young Falkirk crowned."

What to do with him was keeping her up at night. The boy was twelve—old enough to understand what he was doing, but young enough to be manipulated. For his sake, she'd better get to the throne before he did, or she'd have no choice but to execute him. Not the way she wanted her reign to begin. "Thank you, gentlemen. I'll leave you to prepare your charge."

She left the tent and looked to Dann's tent again. Her heart leaped. He was outside, perhaps looking for her. "I've just met my twin sister," she said to him. "If you see her, you might mistake her for me."

His mouth twitched. "I doubt that. If I did, the moment she opened her mouth, I'd know."

She grimaced. "I'm not sure I like this plan."

"You like it as much as they liked yours."

Fi's voice shot up. "I have to be there. I have to raise the standard."

"You don't have to be there."

"I do."

They stared at each other, but their conversation didn't have the heat of an argument. They both knew she'd have her way.

"I'm going with you," Dann said.

"No!"

"I'm your husband, and your consort. I should be there when the standard is raised."

"You don't—"

"—have to be there. Is there an echo?" he said with a smile. "If you must be there, so must I. If you think I'll sit in camp while you're in the city, I won't. I can't."

"I could demand that you stay."

"You could," he said mildly.

She sighed. "There will be six of us, then."

"Which isn't much different than five." He leaned forward so his lips were close to her ear. "Thank you, my darling."

All she could do while eyes were upon them was nod. She'd wanted to suggest that he go into the city with her and the others, but putting him into danger had stilled her tongue. "The girl—my twin—she'll be in grave danger. She could die for me."

"Many people are going to die for you, Fi."

"Don't say to get used to it, because I never will."

"Breakfast, my lady," a squeaky voice said behind her, making her jump. She turned around and looked at the two bowls in Tommy's hands. "Thank you. Would you fetch a bowl for the gentleman?"

He handed the two bowls to Jeena and scurried off. "Let's go to the fire," she said to Dann, wishing she were alone with him. She'd gotten used to Jeena hearing just about every word they said to each other. The wild woman's reticence helped. But never being able to take Dann's hand or offer him a sultry smile was grating on her nerves, and she missed him every night.

"I hope the messenger arrives quickly," she said. The sooner Erryn and the others were ready, the sooner she'd take back her throne, announce her marriage, and be with Dann as a wife should be with her husband. *Many people are going to die for you.* She'd need him.

Avere shuffled next to the family she'd met a day's travel from the Royal City. As soon as she'd spotted them, she'd known they'd be perfect, though now that they were approaching the gate, she wished they'd walk a bit faster. She wasn't worried about the guard, but about her own people, who must be watching for her. She knew Arrick well enough to anticipate his moves. He'd want her brought straight to him. Since the base in Darroth was exactly where she was going, she wouldn't have minded under other circumstances. But today she wanted to observe the base before entering it, to see if anyone else was doing the same. Then she'd slip inside and try to find out whether Arrick was going to do something silly like lock her in a room, before she revealed herself to him. She'd disobeyed his order. She'd tried to convey why in her cryptic messages, but whether she'd succeeded remained to be answered.

A little hand slipped into hers. She smiled down at Milly, the youngest of the family's three children. Avere had her cloak's hood up, she was hunching her shoulders, and she would appear to belong to this family. The eyes of any watchers should gloss over her. She wasn't doing anything amateurish like affecting a limp, which would only draw attention, not deflect it. Nor was she trying to spot anyone she recognized. She was doing what a member of this family would be doing—walking along the road, her eyes on the backs of those in front of her.

To her frustration, Mick and Janny, the mother and father in the Smithson family, slowed their pace further. She peered past them. The guard was taking a good look at everyone, which was slowing the line down. Five minutes later they were the next in line to be scrutinized. Avere glanced at the guard frowning down at her. Her natural instinct was to stare back at him, but a friend of the Smithson family wouldn't be so bold.

The guard moved them along without asking any questions, which told Avere that her face hadn't made it onto any wanted posters. They'd be looking for Erryn, Fi, Enkelo, and Cedric.

The family stopped when they reached the market square situated just inside the north gate. "You said you're visiting your aunt and uncle?" Janny said.

"Yes, I am," Avere said, wanting to hand Milly's hand to her.

"Where do they live?"

Mick skirted behind her. They'd stopped near a public board. "About half a day's walk, so I think I'll hire a horse," Avere said, wanting to be rid of the family.

"There's a stable not far from here. We'll go with you and leave you there."

"Thank you."

Janny had mentioned that she'd grown up in the Royal City and visited her mother about four times a year. She'd left when she'd met Mick, who lived in a village not too far from where Avere had left Erryn and the others two days ago. Five more days and the camp would move on. Avere had to return before then.

With Milly still clinging to her hand, Avere trailed behind Janny and the two boys who were only a year apart, and not much older than four-year-old Milly.

"I know a shortcut," Janny said, leading them into a wide alley running between two shops.

"Can we get sweets?" Milly asked.

Avere peered down at her. "You'll have to ask your—" A heavy hand was on her shoulder, and she could feel the tip of a dagger between her shoulder blades.

"We won't be getting sweets today," Mick said. "Go to your mother."

Milly let go of Avere's hand and went to Janny. The woman and her three children stared at Avere, no alarm in their eyes.

"What's the meaning of this?" Avere hissed, not wanting to kill anyone in front of children. "I don't have much coin."

"No, and I wouldn't try to steal from you. I know how good you are with your daggers."

Shock stabbed through her. "Who are you?"

"Someone the spymaster knew you wouldn't recognize. He wants to see you."

Her brain took a moment to catch up with his words. "You're one of us," she breathed.

Janny relieved Avere of her daggers—all of them. "Now be smart and come with us," Mick said. "He just wants to talk."

"I was going there anyway," Avere snapped, angry with herself. *Well played, Arrick.* She didn't know all his tricks after all. "You can put your blade away."

She whirled when she no longer felt the tip against her back, but only to glare at him. "You did well."

"That's high praise, coming from you." Mick swept his arm out. "Shall we?"

She considered thrusting a punch at his nose, but she'd probably break it, and Janny had her daggers. She'd humour Arrick. She turned on her heel and followed Janny and the three urchins hired to play her children.

Arrick kept his back to the door as the arrivals Jack had told him about filed into his study. He'd been eager for this day, and now it was here. He smoothed his features and turned away from the fire. Avere stood sullenly between the two Ferrets he'd tasked with bringing her here. It had taken them a week to come from Rochdale, a town he was certain Avere had never visited. He'd needed people she wouldn't recognize, despite spending a day or two with them.

He nodded to the one who'd taken the name Mick for this job, then to the one who called herself Janny. "Thank you. Jack will show you to the rooms we've prepared for you."

Janny handed Avere her daggers one by one, then the Ferrets Arrick had hired to play the married couple followed Jack from the study.

Arrick forced his eyes to Avere, relief battling anger. She'd failed at the job he'd tasked her with— spectacularly. How many times had a Ferret joined forces with the target? None that Arrick could recall. Perhaps it had happened, but history, and the Ferrets, had buried the turncoats. No, that word was too strong. He believed Avere was still loyal to him. Now, looking at her, curiosity overpowered everything else. She was thinner, her hair was longer, and her clothes were coated with the dirt and stains of a lengthy journey. But the fire in her eyes . . .

"You didn't have to drag me here," she said mildly. "I was coming to see you."

He swallowed. "It was for your protection, as well as to make sure you came." He waved his hand toward an empty chair. "Sit down."

She made a point of standing for a few seconds, then sat and crossed her legs.

Arrick went to the small selection of wine he kept in the study and chose a bottle that would bring him enough coin to buy a house, were he to sell it. He uncorked the bottle and filled two goblets, aware of Avere's eyes on him. When he turned and handed her a goblet, she didn't refuse it. If she knew the value of what she drank in one go, she didn't show it, but merely held out her goblet again. He refilled it, then took a sip from his own goblet. To business. He settled himself into his chair and gazed at her.

"I received all your messages. If I understood them correctly, you believe the Fyler girl has to remain alive. Why?"

"You obviously didn't receive the letter I sent explaining why I'd decided to go to Loring with her. If you had, you wouldn't be asking. You might have still tried to have me kidnapped in Stronghaven, but you wouldn't be asking."

So she hadn't meant to leave him in the dark. She was

still loyal. She still— He forced a frown. "The roads are more dangerous for messengers these days. We've lost a few. Pigeons are more reliable."

"It was too long for a pigeon."

"You haven't answered my question. Why do you believe Fyler has to remain alive?" Arrick repeated.

"When I tell you, you'll want more of your wine." She took another long sip of hers, surprising him. Avere rarely had more than one goblet and usually didn't finish it. "I've seen Zhikinden," she said.

He blinked at her. "What do you mean?"

"You know, seen her." She pointed at her eyes with the first two fingers on her left hand. "With these. In the flesh."

If it were anyone else, Arrick would have barked a laugh and told them to stop pulling his leg. "Start at the beginning."

"The story begins before then. I acted on a hunch, based on information from someone I trusted. She said Erryn—Beast Masters—weren't cursed by the Seven, but blessed by them."

"Based on what?" he said, careful to keep his incredulity from his face.

She downed the rest of her wine and leaned forward to set the goblet on his desk. "I know this will sound mad, but I met an old woman in Stronghaven, and she had this book."

As Avere recounted her journey from Stronghaven to the wild folk stronghold, to Loring, and then to the underground temple, he studied her face, her gestures, paid attention to every intonation and inflection of her voice. She believed what she was telling him. Either she'd experienced an elaborate hallucination, or she'd lived it.

"The entrance is somewhere on the Primacy's estate," she said. "The temple itself must be underground, like the other one was."

He shifted in his chair. "What you've just told me sounds like something a bard would sing and be laughed from a tavern for."

"If I hadn't been there, seen and heard it all, I wouldn't believe it."

"You stayed your hand because of what this Malina told you?"

"I stayed my hand because . . ." Her shoulders heaved. "I don't know. I suppose it was Malina's fervour, coupled with my own observations of Erryn. I didn't decide not to kill her, not then. I wanted to be sure."

"You're sure now."

She nodded. "I've been sure since the temple. We have to get her into the city. And I've only told you half the story. The princess you helped escape is on her way here with a sizable, but smaller army than the numbers we've heard the Primacy has amassed. Her forces will attack the same night Erryn tries to free the remaining Six."

He reached for the wine bottle and topped up his goblet. When he tipped the bottle toward Avere, she shook her head.

"I know it's a lot to take in," she said. "You weren't there. I was. I'm telling you it's the truth. Why would I make up such an unlikely story? If I wanted to deceive you, I'd come up with something you'd find plausible."

"You're telling me the truth as you see it."

"And as it happened. But frankly, it doesn't matter if you believe it or have doubts, as long as you help us."

"Tell me the rest of the plan," Arrick said, knowing they had one, since they'd decided to attack Darroth and infiltrate the Primacy's estate on the same night. "All of it. What will Fyler do? What will the princess do?"

"The first step is to get Erryn and those with her into the city. By then, the princess's forces should be camped within half a day's march. They'll wait for us to tell them the day and time. They'll act as a distraction while we go to the temple and free the Six."

He hoped his face didn't baldly show his dismay. "A lot could go wrong," he said quietly.

"Will you help us?"

His finely-honed instinct told him their plan was reckless and would end in ruin for all involved, but if she was speaking the truth about Zhikinden . . . He had no reason to doubt her. Perhaps it was his ego speaking, but it would take an event such as seeing one of the Seven in Daros for Avere to put someone else before the Ferrets and him. If he refused to help, she'd leave this study and return to Fyler, no matter how many rational protests he made.

His position was growing more precarious by the hour. A weekly visit from a Primacy representative had turned into a daily one. He'd had to become more creative with his lies and doubted they still believed him. The noose was tightening around his neck. His execution order might have already been signed. The plan cooked up by Avere and the others would likely end in failure, but it offered a chance, however slim, to defeat the Primacy and put the princess on the throne.

"It's a vague plan," he said to her.

Her eyes danced. She knew she had him. "We couldn't work out the details until we got here. Well, the armies will advance and attack as armies usually do, but how to get Erryn into the city and onto the Primacy's estate . . . we need your help."

Right now, he believed his people were safe. If he involved them in this, it could be the end of the Ferrets. A new organization would spring up to take its place, but it wouldn't be the one steeped in history and its service to the crown. It would serve the boy puppet and his heirs. "Getting her into the city will be difficult."

Her mouth turned up at the corners. "My favourite kind of challenge."

He couldn't help but smile. "Jack!" he called.

Jack bounded into the study, "Yes, sir."

"Fetch me the plans for the city."

He nodded and left.

"We don't have much time," Avere said. "I said I'd return within a week, and I've already been gone two days. If I don't get back in time, they'll move on and try to get her into the city themselves."

"You're going back? I assumed we'd send someone else."

"I need to keep her alive, Arrick. The wild folk with her

are capable, but my daggers have been busy." She lifted a finger. "Which reminds me of a little detail I haven't mentioned. When we make our move, our priority has to be getting Erryn to the temple. The princess and her army will be expendable."

He furtively glanced around the study, even though he was certain they were alone. "If you said those words at any other time, or in the presence of anyone else, they'd be treason."

"It can't be treason when she's not on the throne."

"It is to those who believe she's the rightful heir. Even for those who don't, asking them to support a Beast Master will be a tall order."

"Don't tell them it's her. Just tell them we're still loyal to the Lyoses, and when the army attacks, we're sending a group to the estate to assassinate the grand primate."

"Which wouldn't be a bad idea. Assassinating him, not the lie. I don't like lying to my people."

"Then choose those you believe will follow your order to aid Erryn, no questions asked."

"Which would still make it a tall order. We'd be helping someone they believe is cursed by the Seven, and we'd be telling them to protect her over the princess."

"Which is why the princess gave me this." She slipped her hand inside one of her pockets and pulled out a scroll.

Arrick took it from her and unrolled it.

For the spymaster and his Ferrets: Erryn Fyler, my dear sister, is not working against the Seven, but for them. She has a task to perform within the Royal City, the outcome of which is of greater importance than who sits on the throne. You are to give her all the help you can, and if you have to choose between helping your princess and helping her, help her. To do so will be to abide by the Seven's wishes, not to work against them. If necessary, you may work against any usurper on another day, but Daros may not have many more days if my sister falls without completing her task. It is vital for all of us that she succeed.

I remain your humble servant,

Filmona Lyos.

At the bottom of the letter, the princess, or someone else, had drawn the Lyos seal.

Arrick lifted his eyes from the scroll and set it on the desk. "This will quell the doubts of most, but not the pigheaded."

"Then we don't use them. Send those you suspect will act against Erryn on a task that takes them away from here. We'll have enough people working against us without having to sit at a table with them, too."

Jack returned and handed Arrick the city plan. "Thank you," he said. "I have another task for you now. See if we have any plans of the Primacy's estate. It doesn't matter how old they are. In fact, the older, the better."

Jack nodded and left the study again. Arrick unrolled the plan on the square table near his desk. He sensed Avere standing next to him. He hadn't heard her rise, even though he'd listened for it.

"Please don't tell me we'll have to use a sewer. I've had enough of those for now."

He chuckled. "They're all barred or grated, and the walls aren't porous, especially now. They've been inspected,

inspected again, and re-inspected. No, she'll have to enter the city like everyone else."

"Every guard will have memorized her face."

"Yes," he said absently, his mind working. He rapidly rejected the first few ideas that popped into his head, then one arrived that caught his attention. "She's northwest?"

"Yes."

"It will take longer, but bypass the city and come in through the south gate. The guards might be more lax there. They know she went north."

"All right, but there's still the tiny matter of every guard wanting the reward that will not only buy them some land, but allow them to retire. They might be lax, but there's no way she'll walk through a gate without one of them noticing it's her."

"Which is why I propose we do the following." Arrick described his idea to her and knew she agreed with it when she began to make suggestions.

"It's risky, but then every plan we come up with will be risky," she said when they'd settled on what they'd do. "The problem with this one is that if it fails, they'll have her. There won't be anywhere to run, and too many guards to kill."

"The too many guards will actually be an advantage this time." He hadn't welcomed the swelling of the lower ranks with mercenaries and volunteers out for blood, but now he was grateful for it. "But I agree, it's risky. We'll choose those who can think on their feet." He had several in mind who were in the city and who'd jump off a cliff if he ordered them to. They wouldn't have to read the princess's letter. "I'll—"

Shouts from the hallway turned his head. Heavy footsteps—many of them. He quickly reeled off a list of names, then hissed, "Hide."

Avere hesitated a second, then darted behind a tapestry hanging from the wall for the very purpose of concealing one of his people.

His heart pounding, he bent over the city plan. When the guards who'd entered the base without permission clamoured into the study, he slowly turned around.

"I didn't know we had a meeting today," he said.

"We don't." A captain Arrick didn't recognize nodded to two men. One grabbed his wrists and held them together, while the other chained them.

"The Ferrets work for the monarchy, not against it," Arrick said, more for show than anything.

"You can plead your case to the grand primate," the captain said. The two men who'd chained him grasped his arms. He shook them off and calmly left his study, surrounded by guards. A body lay down the hallway. Arrick steeled himself and glanced at the crumpled figure as they passed by. Albert, one of the cooks. The poor beggar had been on his way to ask what Arrick wanted for his midday meal. He would have been unarmed and wouldn't have protested the guards' arrival. Mercenaries and volunteers. These pigs now "protected" the people.

"This is a violation of an unwritten agreement between the Ferrets and the monarchy that has existed for centuries," he said.

"I just follow orders," the captain growled. "The grand primate wants to see you in chains, I put you in chains. Clear the way for the new spymaster, he said. Right away, I said. Don't know what you've done, but you won't be coming back here again."

They'd reached the main entrance. Arrick looked back at the building he'd called home since he was twelve, one that someone else would march into and violate. He couldn't help but think that the Seven had helped him today, despite knowing that if Avere's story was true, it was only possible for Zhikinden to do anything. Avere was here, inside. If the guards had come for him earlier . . .

He climbed into the prison wagon without protesting. The door thudded shut behind him, plunging him into darkness. The sharp odour of urine assaulted his nostrils, almost making him gag. The wagon lumbered forward.

He'd had a good run and regretted only one thing. He'd never told her he loved her. But he believed she knew.

Some Live, Some Die

Fi left Eness's tent with a sigh of relief. She didn't know how many more planning sessions she could bear. Grown men gathered around a table, pushing blocks that represented armies from one point on a map to another. Interminable discussions about who would go where, who would attack what, who would be killed and who captured . . . Had Father paid attention, or relied on his generals?

Jeena, who'd stood guard outside the tent, fell into step with her.

"You never sit down," Fi said.

"I have to be ready."

"You don't have to be as ready when there are other

guards," she said, glancing over her shoulder at the men in armour bearing the livery of Eness and Hampton.

"It could be one of them who tries to kill ye."

"There haven't been any attacks since the one in the dining room, but you're right. Your diligence is commendable." She accepted the water Tommy handed her and murmured a thank you. "Do you read?"

Jeena snorted.

Fi stopped walking to take a sip of her water, then sat down on the chair outside her tent. Jeena stood next to her, ready to challenge any strangers who approached.

"I only asked because it must get boring. Even when you don't have to guard me, you sit and do nothing."

"I train."

"Not all the time."

"I think."

Fi gave her a sidelong look. "About what?"

"Devon," she mumbled.

Fi groaned. "Still? If you're going to moon after someone, at least make it someone decent."

"I'm not mooning after him," Jeena snapped.

"Why are you thinking about him, then?"

When Jeena didn't answer, Fi sipped more water and then offered her glass to Jeena, who shook her head. "Are you sure? It's warm out today."

Jeena shook her head again, then surprised Fi by answering her question. "I think about the promises he made me."

"The ones he broke, or rather, the ones he never intended to keep."

"He had a rough life."

"So he turned around and made life rough for others? No, rough doesn't describe it. He takes women and sells them. Girls, too. That's despicable. It's monstrous. He's a slaver, the lowest of the low. And you think he's the only one who's had a rough life?"

"What do ye know about rough lives?"

"More than I used to." She handed her empty glass to Tommy, who always hovered a discreet distance away, and leaned back in her chair. She wanted to say, "You have a high opinion of Devon because you have a low opinion of yourself," but Jeena wouldn't listen.

"Devon respected you so little that he sold you for coin and never looked back," she said instead. "How long do you think you would have lasted if you'd refused to lie with him, or any of the other men who took you whenever they pleased? He would have gutted you and left you to die, because you would have been no use to him." She paused. "How many men have you bedded since you've been travelling with me?"

Jeena didn't answer.

"None. I can say that because you've always been in my tent or my chamber, or just outside it. Yet your belly is full, your clothes are relatively clean, and you've earned the respect of Cedric, Eness, and the others. Not because they drag you off at night and hump you like a dog, but because you've saved my life and demonstrated your skill with a blade. You're also discreet and loyal. That's true respect, Jeena, not the kind that lasts until you refuse to be used."

Nothing. Fi twisted in her chair. Jeena stared straight ahead, but her eyes were thoughtful. Maybe she was considering Fi's words, or maybe she was wondering where Devon was and wishing they were together. When Fi granted Jeena her freedom, she'd hate to see her use it to search for Devon and throw herself at his feet. She deserved better than that, but she had to be the one to realize it.

Avere stepped from behind the tapestry and surveyed the empty study, her mind in turmoil. Arrick, taken. She'd almost let her daggers fly; only her inner voice screaming that she must remain free had stayed her hand. Both of them in custody would have finished the game before it had truly started. But what now? Her first instinct was to find out where they'd taken Arrick and plan a rescue, but her head knew that path would be folly. She had to return to Erryn. She had to hold the Ferrets together.

Jack crept into the study, his shoulders hunched. "Albert . . ." His eyes latched on to Avere. He held out the plans he'd fetched. They shook in his hands. Thank the Seven he hadn't run into the brutes.

Avere collected herself. "Listen to me very carefully, Jack. The guards have taken the spymaster away."

His eyes widened with fear.

"I need you to help me. Can you do that?"

He swallowed, then squared his shoulders. "The spymaster would want me to help."

She smiled. "I want you to spread the word for everyone to go to their safe places. Tell them they have ten minutes, no more. Then meet me at the Crimson Crown. Can you do that?"

He nodded.

"Good. Give me the plans, and then go."

He stared down at the plans in his hand as if he were surprised to see them, then thrust them at Avere and hurried from the room.

Avere grabbed the letter the princess had written from Arrick's desk, then crouched near the desk and felt for the small latch near one of the legs. When she pulled it, a satisfying *click* reached her ears. She repeated the action with another latch on the other side of the desk. One final step. She sat in his chair, opened the left-hand drawer, and pushed on what looked like a carpenter's error. A softer *click* this time. The compartment near the right edge of the desk was now accessible. A key sat inside it. She grabbed it and opened a lockbox located in a hiding place underneath the floor. With no time to waste, she shoved the papers inside into her bag, enough information to blackmail just about every noble, primate, and wealthy merchant in Daros, with a few other influential men and women thrown in, too.

She didn't have time to glance around the study and wonder if she'd ever see it again. She raced down the hallway and was pleased to see others already leaving the base, with their most important possessions in bags on their backs. Only a few lived here, and all but one could take care of themselves. Twenty minutes later, she waved when Jack came into the Crimson Crown's common room. He dropped a bag to the floor and sat across from her. "Are you hungry?" she asked him.

"No, miss."

From the look of his face, Avere suspected he'd bring up anything he ate. Arrick and the Ferrets were Jack's life.

"Will they hurt him?"

She froze, not sure how honestly to answer him. She'd entered Arrick's world when she was just a year or two older than Jack and had looked up to him perhaps more than Jack did. If Arrick had been taken then . . . she'd have hated anyone who lied to her, because she would have deserved the truth, and Arrick would have wanted her to have it.

"They might," she said to him. "You have to prepare yourself." Her hands clenched under the table, and she had to force her next words out. "We might never see him again."

His chin trembled, but he mastered himself.

"I want you to carry out the last order the spymaster gave to me. Can you do that?" When he nodded, she went on. "I want you to get messages to the following people." She listed the names Arrick had reeled off to her before she'd darted behind the tapestry. "I believe they're all local."

"They are, miss."

"How long will it take you?"

He cocked his head. "Five or six hours."

"Have them meet me here at eleven o'clock tonight. That's the message."

"What about me, miss?"

"You too, of course. When you've delivered all the messages, come straight back here. We'll have supper together."

He swallowed. "And then what?"

"You'll stay with me. You can leave your bag here, unless you want to take it with you."

"I'll leave it with you."

"Good. And Jack . . ."

He waited.

"Be careful. Don't take any chances. If contacting anyone I've named will put you in danger, don't do it. Understand?"

"Yes, miss." He pushed back his chair. "Thank you for letting me stay with you."

"It's what the spymaster would want." She wasn't about to leave the boy Arrick considered a son to fend for himself. There was no blood relationship, but Jack had been a baby when he came into Arrick's care. When they'd lost one of their people, they'd discovered she had a babe at home, with no relatives to claim him. "I'll find a home for him," Arrick had said, and he had. Now it was up to Avere to care for him until she figured out what to do.

Jack was still standing at the table, looking at her. "Off you go, then," she said to him.

He rushed away. She stared after him, wishing she'd offered to do half the list herself. She wanted to be busy, not twiddling her thumbs, especially when the urge to forget about the Seven, and Beast Masters, and Malina, and usurped princesses, was strong. She wanted to use the people she'd summoned to rescue Arrick. But she'd thrown in with Erryn, and Arrick had thrown in with the princess. If he were here, he'd tell her to stick to the plan, that they served Daros and the monarch, not themselves. And when it came to Erryn, they were serving the Seven. Avere had seen Zhikinden with her own eyes. As much as she longed to, she couldn't abandon Erryn for Arrick.

He'd understand. They'd both chosen this life. They could be living in a cottage somewhere, collecting eggs and milking cows, and bored out of their wits. They'd always known they could be called upon to sacrifice themselves, but it didn't matter how much one understood the possibility in one's head. Now that it was happening, she understood that the pain of losing him would be far greater than any torture they might have inflicted on her, had they discovered her.

She'd get Erryn into the city, help free the remaining Six, and then kill every primate within the estate's walls. None of the bastards would escape alive. Not a single one.

Erryn stared up at the midday sun, then blinked in the direction Avere had taken when she'd left them.

"She's not coming back," Asha said.

Erryn blew out a sigh. Reluctantly, she turned to Asha. "No, it doesn't look like she is."

"Something must have happened," Renn said. "I didn't like her when I first met her, but she proved herself. She was there when Zhikinden came. Something's happened to her."

Which left them with no plan to enter the city, and

no eyes inside. "We'll have to continue on. When we're within a few hours of the walls, we'll come up with a plan."

Everyone nodded, but with doubt in their eyes. With the walls, and guards, and everyone looking for Erryn, how would she enter the city without help?

"I'll tell Timor to mark the tree." Asha walked away.

Renn gazed in the same direction Erryn had looked, perhaps hoping, like she'd been, that Avere would suddenly appear. "If she couldn't enter and leave without being caught, that doesn't bode well for us," Renn said.

"But nobody was looking for her. She's not wanted for anything. Something else must have happened."

"Something did."

They whirled.

Avere emerged from the trees behind them. "Sorry I'm late. We hit a snag, a rather large one. It took me a few days to pull together the people and gear we'll need to get you past the guards."

Erryn was so glad to see her, she had to restrain herself from rushing to her and giving her a hug. Avere would hate it. Erryn might even end up with a warning prick from one of the Ferret's daggers. "What happened?"

"They arrested the spymaster and took control of the Ferret base." Avere lifted a finger. "But not the people. Is everything all right here?"

"We'd just decided to leave."

"You haven't had any unwelcome guests?"

"No."

She nodded, then stuck her thumb and index finger into her mouth and whistled. More people emerged from the trees. Erryn counted eight, including a boy who couldn't be more than eleven or twelve.

Avere's whistle had attracted more than the people she'd brought from the city. Everyone gathered around Erryn.

"Welcome back," Asha said.

"Is there any stew going?" Avere asked. "We're starving. We can talk while we eat."

"Ye're just in time. We were about to break camp."

They all traipsed to the fire. While Avere and her people ate, everyone except Timor and Toe, who stood guard, listened to her account of what had happened at the Ferret base and afterward. Erryn wondered if the Northerners would appreciate the gravity of what had taken place. The Ferrets were supposed to be untouchable. Short of plotting against the monarch or actively working against his or her plans, they could do anything. Of course, if a Ferret was caught committing a crime, the monarch was free to let them rot in prison or be hanged, and often that was what happened, because he or she was never aware of the details of how the Ferrets worked on their behalf. A Ferret captured and tried would only be helped if the spymaster found out in time and intervened on their behalf, coin greased willing palms, or blackmail was used. For the spymaster to be taken from within his own base . . . the situation in the city was worsening.

Her concern grew when Avere described the plan for getting her into the city. "If it works, great. If it doesn't . . ."

"If anything goes wrong, you'll have to wait for your

next life to finish what you've started in this one," Avere said. A couple of those who'd arrived with her exchanged glances.

"I don't like that we'll be separated from the Called and Caller," Asha said.

"A group of wild folk will attract too much attention, and a city person travelling with them, even more. We thought about disguising you, but it'll be better if you simply enter the city on your own." Avere paused to spoon what must be cold stew into her mouth. "I'll draw you a map of how to get to the inn."

"And if ye're not there?"

"Then you can wait for the princess to arrive and help her, or go home. If we're not there, we've lost the game."

Asha's face made it clear that she did not want to have to make that decision.

"It's risky, but it's all we have," Erryn said.

"Entering the city from the south will mean an extra day's travel," Avere said. "We've already pushed ourselves to make it back here in time. I know you'd decided to leave, but we need to rest. I propose we leave early on the morrow." She gazed past Renn. "I see my tent's still up. Good. The one I brought with me is smaller."

When she put her bowl down and went to her tent, Erryn followed her. She felt the eyes of a couple of the newcomers on her back, and several had given her surreptitious looks while Avere was recounting events. Perhaps they were looking for the fur on her hands, or waiting for her to snarl. She'd travelled with her small group for so long that she'd almost forgotten how most people viewed her.

Avere stopped outside her tent and gazed at Erryn expectantly.

"Thanks for coming back," Erryn said.

"What do you mean? Of course I was coming back."

"You must have wanted to find out what happened to the spymaster." Erryn had noticed a slight change to Avere's voice whenever she'd mentioned him.

Avere ducked inside her tent. Erryn trailed after her. "We can't care for people in our business," Avere said, dropping her bag to the ground and crouching to rummage through it. "It would be folly to form attachments. We can find ourselves at the end of a rope at any time."

"What about Jack? You've taken him under your wing."

"He's useful. If he wasn't, I would have left him behind."

Erryn didn't believe her for a second. And Avere was still fishing through her bag, probably for nothing.

"He's also Arrick's foster son, I suppose. I never thought it was a good idea to keep him, but Arrick's always been a bit soft when it comes to children. When we're done, I'll find someone to care for him."

Erryn had enough sense to bite her tongue. "Do you think he's still alive? Arrick."

Avere's hand stopped moving. "I don't know."

"Where would they be keeping him?"

"Normally one of the dungeons, but it sounded like the grand primate wanted him." She gave up all pretense of searching her bag and sat on her haunches. "They're probably torturing him on the estate," she said, her voice steady, but weak.

"Depending on how things go, we could look for him."

"He'll probably be dead. He won't tell them anything. No matter what they do, how many times they burn him, how many bones they break . . ." Avere gulped down air. "If we do come across him, depending on . . . how he is . . . let me decide what to do with him. Trust me with that. I know him. I know what he'd want."

Her words chilled Erryn. "Of course it would be your decision. He's your spymaster." And, Erryn suspected, much more.

Three days later, Erryn held out her wrists and waited while Harry, one of the Ferrets, clamped them in irons. She could still call the Fallen, but hoped she wouldn't have to. The Ferrets surrounding her were attired in the armour of the city guard, and her hood would shield her face, especially since she'd be shuffling along with her head down.

"Excellent," Avere said. "You know where to meet us?"

Harry nodded.

"If anyone questions you, stay calm and stick to the story. Use the arrest order as a last resort. If anything goes wrong, you know what to do."

Fight to the death. They'd all take down as many as they could, including Erryn. She would not allow herself to be tortured. Burned, broken bones . . . she'd rather die. As long as she was conscious, she could keep calling the Fallen. If the guards captured her, she'd call them, and call them, until they had no choice but to kill her. But this plan just might work. Avere had told them about the surge of mercenaries in the guard. Unfamiliar faces among the ranks weren't uncommon.

"Jack and I won't be far behind you."

The Northerners would enter last, if at all. If Erryn and the others ran into trouble, they were to remain outside the city and help Fi.

Erryn searched for Renn, caught her eye, and nodded. Earlier, she'd been torn between saying a good-bye of sorts, and behaving confidently. She'd settled on the latter, though they *had* lingered inside their tent this morning longer than usual. They'd see each other again, inside the Royal City—or in the heavens.

"Shall we?" Avere said, sounding as if they were all about to go for an evening stroll. They'd waited until nightfall, hoping the dark would aid them, but the curfew time imposed on the city was drawing near. They had to move now.

Erryn walked, surrounded by her supposed captors. The fake arrest order wasn't for a crime so severe that she could hang.

Her heart leaped when she spotted the lights in the distance. Darroth. Last time she'd passed through its gates, she'd been on her way to the border with an escort that had orders to kill her. This time wouldn't be much better. A surge of panic almost stopped her in her tracks. This was madness! She was walking straight into the vipers' nest. But the alternative would be to let the Seven down, to leave them trapped and Daros dying. She'd return again, though her next life might not have allies, and she doubted she'd be born into luxury. How many times had she already tried and failed? This might be the best chance Daros ever had. She steeled herself and continued walking.

The lights became sharper. The dye Asha had rubbed into her hair was making her scalp itch. She desperately wanted to pull her hood off.

"Almost there," Harry murmured.

She hung her head. They waited while the guard questioned someone in front of them. *Where are you from?* and *What is your business in Darroth?* were the only questions the guard asked. Erryn shuffled forward, her heart pounding.

"Who's this, then?" someone growled.

"Caught half a day from here, relieving merchants of their coin." Harry.

"And you just happened to be there?"

"One reported it and Jellock sent us." One of the names Avere had given him.

"She was working alone?"

"She only went after the old, fat ones."

Several men guffawed. "I haven't heard about it," the guard who'd been doing the talking said. Erryn consciously slowed her breathing. The Fallen's scratching grew louder, more frantic.

"I don't hear about every ruffian," Harry said. "I'm sure you don't, either."

"Can I see the arrest warrant?"

Great, they had to get a busybody, probably a mercenary

throwing his weight around. Her escorts wore the livery of the rank and file. A commanding officer wouldn't leave the city to chase down a common thief. The curious guard was likely rank and file too, but it would be strange for Harry to refuse him.

"Why?" Harry said. "I told you, we're under orders from Jellock."

"And we're under orders to check people coming through this gate."

"Do you want Jellock to know you've been questioning his orders?"

"Come on, Cyrus." A new voice. "There's no point harassing our own people."

Silence, then, "Better that than to—"

A scream pierced the air, setting Erryn's heart racing faster than she thought it could go. Footsteps. Murmuring.

"Over there, in the bush." Avere. "Three of them dragging away a woman. They had swords."

"What should we do?" A guard near Erryn.

"Bollocks. You three, go. And you . . . take her through. Don't keep Jellock waiting."

Someone jabbed Erryn in the ribs. She walked forward, her eyes on the legs and booted feet of the escort in front of her. They turned several corners.

Erryn's hood was yanked off her head. She whirled— Harry grinned at her. "Take it easy. We're in." He dangled a key.

She held out her wrists, and glanced around while he unlocked the irons. They were in an alley, but she didn't know in which part of the city. When she and Fi had slipped out of the castle, it hadn't been to slink through alleys at night.

"This way," Harry said. They left the alley, crossed the road, and stopped outside the Crimson Crown. "You have coin?"

Erryn nodded.

"Then we'll see you on the morrow."

She pulled her hood up again and entered the inn's common room. Drunk patrons were howling along with the bard singing in the corner, the whores were working the tables, and those who weren't drowning in ale were shouting over the noise or playing cards. This could be any common room in any city, except for the men and women huddled in a corner, near a man holding a sign that invited his neighbours to a rally in one of the squares, a rally that would demand the curfew imposed on the city be lifted. As if mocking him, one of the serving girls shouted, "Drink up. Curfew's in fifteen minutes."

Erryn went to the barkeep. He hardly glanced at her when she dropped coin into his hand and he shouted a room number. As she climbed the stairs to the second floor, she couldn't help noticing how comfortable she was now. There was a time when the thought of stepping into a common room alone would have set her stomach churning. But now . . .

As soon as she was in her room, she gazed out at the city with mixed emotions. She'd never expected to be here again. When she'd envisioned returning, it had been to the castle, and to Fi, after receiving a king's pardon. It was a fantasy that had kept her going in the early days. There never would have been a pardon.

Ironically, she'd benefited from the assassinations but felt no guilt. She hadn't killed them, and while she'd always be grateful to the king, they'd never been close. In the end, when she'd truly needed him, he'd turned his back on her. She'd never truly been his daughter, just a favour to a friend. Instead of supporting her, of trying to understand, he'd banished her from the only home she'd ever known and the only people she'd ever loved. And now that she was back in the city, she wondered if she'd lost that home forever.

She shook herself and turned her thoughts to Renn and the others. Would that busybody guard at the gate kick up a fuss at a group of Northerners? They weren't wanted for anything, but that wouldn't stop the guard from harassing them, especially after they'd chased after the phantoms Avere had made up.

Someone rapped on the door four times, then paused, then knocked again. Erryn opened it to Avere and Jack. "They're fine," she said, before Erryn asked. "They waved me through quickly, and only two were there because the others were searching in the bush. I don't think they wanted to challenge a group of wild folk that outnumbered them."

"You didn't have any trouble, then?"

"Amazing what batting eyelashes and a boy can do to get you past guards." She looked down at Jack. "You could be useful on some jobs."

His eyes widened. "Really, miss?"

"No. The spymaster would have my head if I involved you in anything risky."

Renn hovered in the doorway. Toe appeared behind her.

"Let's go to our room," Avere said to Jack. "We'll speak in the morning."

Renn closed the door after them. Erryn pulled her into a hug, made awkward by the broadsword strapped to Renn's back, but she didn't care. They'd made it into the city. Their plan hadn't been scuttled at the start, and Renn was safe. "So this is where ye're from," Renn murmured.

Erryn let go of her to gaze out the window again. "The Royal City."

Renn stepped to her side and surveyed the view. "All cities are the same."

"Stronghaven is different. Not as many bureaucrats. More of you, and less of me. And it's . . ." she searched for the right word. "Bleaker. Tired."

"Because it's filling up with folk who can't get their food the usual way," Renn growled.

Erryn laid her hand on Renn's arm. "I'm stating how I see it, not how I'd like it to be. First we'll free the Six. Then, if I were on the throne, I'd forge a stronger relationship with your people." She lifted her hand. "Not make then kneel. But not neglect them. Millwood should have been advocating for Stronghaven. Fi needs to put someone there who will."

Renn exhaled slowly. "Which direction is yer castle?"

Erryn pointed to her left. "That way."

"And this Primacy estate?"

"The same. It's not too far from the castle."

Renn grunted.

"I'm not too familiar with this part of the city. We're south, so the castle and estate are northwest."

"Ye lived here all yer life and ye don't know the city?"

She smiled. "When we left the castle, we rarely ventured this far into the city, and when we did, it was with guards. They knew where they were going. We went with them. Whenever we left the city, it was to ride, or to visit some noble. When I got away—killed—the guards taking me to the border, that was the first time I'd ever been outside the castle by myself. Anywhere by myself, really." Her voice dropped. "It's hard to imagine it now."

"Ye're lucky ye survived."

"I had the Fallen, and then you and Toe. Without you, I never would have made it to Loring."

"There won't be a me and Toe anymore."

"I'm hoping there will be a me and you."

Renn frowned at her. "Ye still believe there can be?"

"We're about to take on the Primacy on its own estate. If we can do that, we can find a way to be together."

"Ye won't disobey yer sister."

"I'll convince her not to tell me to do anything I don't want to do."

Renn couldn't mask her skepticism, which would have irritated Erryn, if she didn't feel the same. First things first. She'd free the Six, then worry about her future—if she had one.

* * * * *

Fi entered Eness's tent and surveyed the men gathered around the war table: Dann, Cedric, Enkelo, Hampton, and Eness. "What is it?" she asked, sensing their tension.

"A messenger arrived from the Royal City, Your Grace," Eness said.

"And?"

"It's time."

"They made it into the city," Fi breathed.

Cedric nodded. "But the news isn't all good, Majesty. The spymaster has been arrested. The grand primate ordered it."

Fi's mouth dropped open. "But that's madness," she blurted. "Why would they want to get on the wrong side of the Ferrets, especially when they know where I am? They must know."

"Perhaps it's not you they're seeking, Your Grace," Hampton said.

"Who would—" Erryn. "The Beast Master? Why would they think the spymaster knows where she is?" she asked as innocently as she could.

"More likely, they're displeased that he doesn't know where she is," Eness said.

"What will they do with him, Enkelo?"

Enkelo shrugged. "I don't know. Living at the castle meant there was always some distance between myself and my colleagues. My loyalty was always to your family."

"We'll free him as soon as we're able." She didn't want to dwell on why those gathered exchanged glances at her words. If not for the spymaster, she'd probably be dead. "When do we leave?"

"First thing on the morrow, Your Grace," Hampton said. "Once we're close enough to knock at the gates, we'll get a message to our allies inside. They're ready to move when we are."

It was really happening. Excitement accelerated Fi's heart; fear clenched her stomach.

"I don't like the plan we worked out with these allies," Eness said to Fi. "There's no reason for you to enter the city. You should remain at camp."

"I can't. It has to be me who raises the standard."

"Begging your pardon, it doesn't. Your men can raise it for you."

"It will be me, Eness," Fi said, adding an edge to her voice. "I will raise the standard."

"Then take more men with you."

"The more we take, the more attention we'll attract. We've all agreed that we don't expect much opposition within the castle itself. They also won't expect me to be inside the city, especially with" —what was the girl's name?— "Miriam strutting around camp, making herself obvious." She wouldn't mention that she was expendable, that if they received word that Erryn needed help, they'd abandon the castle for the Primacy's estate.

"I still don't like it, but if it's what you want."

"It is."

"I believe the plan is sound," Cedric said. "Especially since we know the castle better than they do."

Including the location of all the hidden passageways built within the castle so her ancestors could cheat on their wives, and the Lyoses could meet with people in private, when not even their loyal servants were to know. Fi and Erryn had used them for a different reason. They hadn't spied on anyone, though the thought had been tempting. They'd used the passageways to while away time without servants hovering nearby or guards around them. They'd had some of their most heartfelt conversations while sitting in a musty passage. They'd always had to let Father or Mother know they were planning to disappear for a bit, so a search wouldn't be mounted for them.

The hidden passageways would help them, but Fi couldn't simply rush to the top of the tower and raise the standard. The guards within the castle loyal to the Primacy would quickly make their way to the top and cut it—and her—down. But her knowledge of *her* home should make it easier to quietly remove any opposition.

"If she's killed . . ." Eness said. "You should wait until our forces have triumphed."

"I'm not discussing this any further," Fi said. "I will enter the city. I will raise the standard." And hope the people of Darroth would rally to her, that many of the soldiers in the opposing force would throw down their arms, and that Erryn would join her on top of the tower with news that the Six were free. The men in this tent had stated several times that her army would be outnumbered, so she would not wait for a triumph that might not come. She would decide the battle by raising the standard. If the people didn't follow, then any victory she and her army might have achieved would be hollow. If the people didn't choose to follow her, she could not be their queen.

*   *   *   *   *

Fi studied herself in the mirror the servant held up to her. She hardly recognized herself. It helped that she'd lost a few pounds and Avere had chopped off half her hair. With the dirt the servant had rubbed onto her cheeks, and the stain on her teeth, and the cap she'd wear, along with the rags that passed for a shirt and pants, someone would have to look closely indeed to recognize her. Most would expect a princess, even a disgraced one, to be in an elegant dress, with her hair up and baubles hanging from her ears and neck and wrapping her fingers.

She handed the mirror back to the woman. Someone lifted the tent flap. Dann came in; his brows lifted. "Are you sure this is the princess?" he said to the servant.

Fi couldn't help but smile. "I think this will do."

"More than do."

She wanted to kiss him, but they weren't alone.

"Everyone is waiting."

"Then let's go." She rose and slung the bag she'd take over her shoulder.

The servant bobbed. "If I may, Your Grace."

Fi stopped and waited.

"May the Seven be with you."

"Thank you." The words still stirred her, even though she knew the Seven would be of no help, at least not initially. *Don't fail, Erryn. Don't die.*

Cedric and two guards chosen for their skill and loyalty stood waiting a short distance from the tent. Despite her anxiety, Fi smiled at the group of ruffians. A skilled observer might notice the swords hanging at their sides were of excellent craftsmanship and most of them had the bearing of military men. But most people would be cowering inside their homes, with the doors locked and windows boarded. Word that those who opposed the Primacy's regency were moving on the gates and scaling the walls would quickly spread. The faster she raised the standard, the fewer men would die by the sword, or from having burning pitch poured over their heads, or from falling a great distance when their grappling hooks and ladders were detached from the wall while they climbed it.

Fi searched for Jeena, then realized the wild woman was standing next to her. "I didn't recognize you," she said, a good sign. Jeena was in city clothing. With her dirty face and her hair in a scarf, she'd fool anyone.

Eness and Hampton were also there, to see the group off. "You'll have two hours," Hampton said. "Then we begin the assault."

Fi and her group would have to be inside the city by then, otherwise the gates would be shut tight. Assuming they entered the city without trouble, they'd rendezvous with a group of Ferrets near the castle and begin their journey to the standard flapping atop one of its towers.

"We'd better set off, then," she said.

Enkelo, who'd hovered nearby, stepped forward and raised both his hands to the heavens. "May our rightful queen reclaim her throne. May the Seven watch over you."

"Thank you," Fi said, more for what he'd done for her than for his words, which he knew could be empty.

Hampton put his hand over his heart, then raised his fist into the air. "For the Lyoses."

Eness mimicked the gesture and shouted the same words. The men camped the closest followed suit, and the cheer spread throughout the camp. The shouts still rang in Fi's ears as she wound her way through tents and broke free of the camp, leaving it behind. She would not see the camp again. By the time the sun rose on the morrow, she would be Queen Filmona Lyos, or dead.

Erryn paced the room at the Roaring Lion, waiting for a sign it was time to move. They'd left the Crimson Crown yesterday and moved to an inn closer to the Primacy's estate—and the castle. She'd walked these roads many times and gazed at many of the buildings from atop the wall, but seeing them yesterday, treading on cobbles she'd walked so many times before, had felt strange, foreign.

"Ye're going to wear down the floor," Renn said.

"Fi should be in the city by now."

"She was coming in quietly. The rest will come some time later."

True, but the curfew was fast approaching. Where were they?

"If she was captured, they'd still come," Renn said. "They'll be here."

A Ferret would have gone to the camp to let the others know, but Renn was right. The plan was for Fi's forces to wage their assault anyway. Erryn hoped with all her heart Fi hadn't run into trouble, primarily because she loved her, but also because of that stupid parchment Enkelo had. What if Fi fell, the army triumphed, and Enkelo revealed Fi's wishes? "I—"

A bell clanged outside, then another one. Erryn rushed to the window. People ran down the road, glancing over their shoulders. One shouted that the city was under attack.

The room door swung open. "It's time," Avere said.

Erryn pulled up her hood and followed Avere downstairs and outside. Everyone was already gathered there—Toe, Asha, and Timor. Without a word, they made their way toward the Primacy's estate, walking swiftly so they'd look like the many other people hurrying to secure their homes and protect their children.

When they were a block away from the estate, they joined four more Ferrets waiting for them in the shadow of a statue of Fi's great-grandfather. "Two at the southern gate, one at the northern," one said to Avere.

"Then we enter from the north."

"Do you have the plans?" Erryn said, for something to say.

"Yes. We shouldn't need them until we reach the room."

They'd all memorized the route they'd take through the administrative building to the room they suspected contained the entrance to an underground tunnel. "I bet only you can open it," Avere had said, pointing to a wall with a staircase behind it. Why have a staircase behind a solid wall? When they got to the room, they'd find out if the plans were in error, or the staircase led to a temple with seven altars.

They jogged to the estate's northern gate, matching the speed of those around them. "Go," Avere said when the north gate came into view. Two of the Ferrets broke from the group and approached the guard, blocking the man from Erryn's view. A moment later, one of the Ferrets slipped inside the estate. The other followed.

"Let's move." Avere led them to the gate and motioned for everyone to enter. Nobody shouted for them to stop. Everyone was too intent on getting home or to their favourite tavern, exactly what Erryn and the others had hoped for.

When Erryn passed through the gate, she didn't want to look at the crumpled figure the Ferrets had dragged to one side. The man wasn't part of the Primacy's treachery. He'd merely been standing guard so he could feed a family and had probably been worried about them when two men approached him. While one had distracted him, the other had slit his throat. "We can't leave anyone alive," Avere had said. "All it will take is one to raise the alarm." Erryn was already tired of the killing, and more blood would flow this night, rivers of it.

They reached the administrative building. The guard outside the side entrance they'd chosen to enter was swiftly dispatched. Inside, two thrown daggers cut short lives and shouts. Renn tussled with a guard who rushed into the main entranceway. Timor's bow sang. Toe and Asha, who'd left her walking stick at the inn and brought a sword, went to Renn's aid when another guard came running.

Quickly, the entranceway devolved into chaos. "Erryn,"

Avere snapped, another dagger leaving her fingers. "Call them. There are too many."

Erryn surveyed the fighting—and the carnage.

"Erryn!"

At the same time she called forth Zayvang, Sath, and Lerxis, she realized the Fallen hadn't been agitating to be released, nor was music calling to her, as it had when they'd approached the ruins near Loring. But she didn't have time to think about it. A guard headed straight for her—a sword cut through his neck, leaving his head dangling for a second. The man's body completed its step, then crumpled to the ground. Renn whirled and jumped back into the fray.

A guard banished Zayvang. Erryn called her forth again. Someone raced toward her and—an arrow thudded into his chest. He fell to his knees and then to his side.

No more guards spilled into the entranceway. Red pools soaked the wood floor. Erryn started to count bodies, then stopped. Sath lumbered over to her. She looked into Samshy's eyes. *I don't hear music.* The great bear stared back at her. Was Samshy frustrated because she couldn't speak?

"I think that's the lot of them—for now." Avere retrieved a bloody dagger and sheathed it. Toe inspected a gash on his arm. Asha went to him and peered down at it.

"I don't hear music," Erryn said, when Renn returned to her side. "When we were near the ruins in Loring, I heard music. If there's a temple here, it would be closer. I should be hearing something."

"Just because ye heard music once doesn't mean ye should be hearing it now."

Perhaps, but the Fallen weren't excited, either. Erryn didn't dismiss those in the physical plane with her. Guards could be lurking around every corner.

"Some must have retreated farther in," Avere said, mirroring Erryn's thoughts. "They'll know we're here now."

"We haven't seen any primates."

"It's late. This isn't a residence. And we're only in the entranceway." Avere motioned for everyone to follow her. "Let's go. I don't think anyone escaped, but if they did, we could have more guards on the way."

Erryn was certain nobody had. She didn't look down as she stepped over bodies.

Avere had pulled the sketch of their route from her purse. "This way."

They headed down the hallway off the left of the entranceway and turned a corner, then another one. A bang in a nearby room made Erryn jump. Avere pointed at her and Zayvang and then at the open doorway. Erryn and the saber-tooth cat followed the crouched Ferret into the room. Several books were splayed on the floor, next to a desk.

"Don't kill me," someone said. "I don't care who you are. I just work here. I won't tell anyone I've seen you. Lock me in."

Avere rounded the desk. Erryn stuck with her, wanting to see who it was.

A man crouched behind the desk, his hands clenched against his head. "Please. I have two young sons. They depend on me." His eyes widened when Zayvang brushed against Erryn's side. "The Seven preserve me!" he moaned. "The Seven look down upon me."

"Don't kill him," Erryn said.

Avere didn't turn around. "We can't leave anyone behind us."

"We'll lock him in."

"Please," the man said more urgently.

"He has children," Erryn said, almost shouting.

"He says he has children." In one smooth motion, Avere grabbed an iron figurine sitting on the desk and smashed it over the man's head. He fell to his side, silent as death.

"He has children!" Erryn said.

"I didn't kill him, but I should have. We'll have to hope he doesn't wake up anytime soon." She fished through the man's pockets and drew out a key. "As far as I remember, there are no passageways off this room, so locking him in should keep him here. Come on."

They rejoined the others in the hallway. Avere locked the door and took up the lead again. "I don't like this," she said as they made their way through empty hallways and passed empty rooms. "They might have all retreated to the same spot, which means we could face a large number of guards."

"Or we killed most of them when we came in," Renn said.

"No. Not for a building this size."

Avere stopped and turned to a closed doorway. "Here." She slowly turned the doorknob. The door creaked open. She slipped inside. "It's empty," she hissed.

The others filed in after her. "Look." Asha pointed.

A bookcase had been moved, revealing a door behind it, which stood open. "That's not possible," Avere said. "Only Erryn should have been able to open the door. It leads straight to the temple."

Erryn slowly shook her head. "I don't think it does. I'm not hearing anything. The Fallen aren't agitating. Look at the ones you can see." Everyone's eyes went to the two animals with them. "If the altars were just down those stairs, don't you think Lerxis would be eager to descend?"

"Be that as it may, we didn't come all this way to stop here." Avere raised her hand and listened. "I don't think anyone's down there."

"Then where are they?"

Avere peered through the doorway. "I can see light, from a flame." She descended the steps and stopped halfway down. After standing for a minute, she continued to the bottom. "There's nobody here," she called. "But you'd better come down."

Erryn stepped through the doorway.

Fi almost stumbled when Dann yanked her out of the path of a merchant fleeing the market she and Erryn had often visited. Though she'd expected an alarm to be raised, the bells had startled her. They'd passed through the gates without being challenged, buoying her spirits, but now the real test would come. The castle. But they weren't heading there. They were going to the nearby temple that housed the entrance to the passageway Enkelo had led her through when she'd escaped. They shouldn't have to kill the primate. Apparently he'd cooperated with the Ferrets for many years. He wasn't aware of the secret passage, but he'd been warned to be somewhere else this night.

Metal clashed on metal, behind her. She whirled. The two guards and Cedric were fighting with four guards who must have noticed their swords, or wondered why this small group of people weren't running for home. "Carry on," Cedric shouted. "We'll meet you there."

Fi hesitated. Jeena grabbed her arm and pulled her forward. The temple was just beyond the next turn, but they had to dodge panicked people fleeing for their homes. They raced around the corner—and straight into a man. Fi's eyes widened with shocked recognition. How could he be here?

A smile spread across Devon's face. "Well, if it isn't the little pig. Now I understand why the bells are ringing this night." His eyes raked Dann from head to foot. "You won't be any trouble."

Fi wanted to smack him. Devon's eyes moved to Jeena. "Look at you, darlin'. Love the scarf, but I'd know you anywhere. Are you delivering the pig to the primates?" He jangled a bulging coin purse on his belt. "I've just sold a few bitches. I'll split the coin with you, if you split the fortune you're going to get with me."

Jeena stared at him.

"No hard feelings about Millwood, eh? It was just business, darlin'."

"Jeena," Fi said.

The wild woman didn't move.

Devon drew his sword. "A pig and a spoiled boy. Not a pretty boy, though. Someone's already put you in your place." He gazed at Jeena. "Is he anybody? Should we keep him alive?"

Fi's heart pounded. "Respect, Jeena." She took Dann's hand. "Respect."

"You always were a mouthy one," Devon growled.

Jeena slid her sword from its sheath. Fi shrank away from her, making Devon grin. "It's time to show the little pig who's—" His eyes widened; his mouth dropped open.

In one smooth motion, Jeena kicked Devon away and pulled her blade from his belly.

He dropped his sword and fell to his knees. "What have you . . ." He toppled to his side.

Jeena looked down at him for a moment, then pulled the coin purse from his belt and added it to her own. "Let's go," she snapped.

Fi didn't need more encouragement. Still hanging on to Dann's hand, she broke into a run.

They reached the temple and stumbled into the main hall of worship. Fi doubled over and gulped down air. A minute later, Cedric and one of the guards strode inside. She didn't have to ask about the other man. Now they were only five, but seven Ferrets joined them in the cellar. They went into the room where the spymaster had been waiting when Fi emerged from the passage. "Behind that tapestry," she murmured to herself as she hurried to it. Dann lifted the cloth and held it aside. Fi felt the wall, pressing the appropriate ridges she'd memorized from a sketch Enkelo had drawn. The door swung open.

"Quickly," Cedric said. The Ferrets darted past her. Jeena followed them in, and Fi went after her. Dann, Cedric, and the guard entered behind her.

Two of the Ferrets had lit torches; one held a lantern. The lights acting as her guide, Fi walked the passage that had saved her life, but this time no monsters lurked in the shadows. She wasn't the same sheltered woman who jumped at mice. She was Filmona Lyos, the rightful heir, and she was here to take back her throne and avenge her father, brother, and sister-in-law.

When they reached what appeared to be a dead end, the tension in the air rose. With the Ferret holding the lantern so she could see, Fi pointed out the plates he'd have to press to open the door. If she did it, she'd be the one standing in the doorway when the hidden door swung open, an easy target for anyone in the worship room. The Ferret nodded.

Fi moved down the passageway to where Dann stood, putting Jeena and several men between her and the door. Wanting to grip his hand, she brushed hers against his.

"About to press the last one," the Ferret warned.

"Get ready," Cedric said. "We don't know what's waiting for us on the other side."

The men in front of Fi crouched, their blades in their hands. The door swung open.

Silence.

"It's empty."

She let out her pent breath. Everyone crept into the worship room. Fi had spent many hours here, staring at the mural of the Seven, contemplating the Holy Texts—at least, that was what she was supposed to be doing—and listening to Enkelo, usually with Erryn kneeling or sitting next to her, and sometimes the sons and daughters of visiting nobles. The last time she'd knelt here, she'd been in irons, disgraced. Now she was back. Home.

The lead Ferret crouched near the door to the hallway and raised his hand. Fi glanced at Dann, afraid she'd sneeze. Footsteps thudded past outside. It sounded like several guards, running. If they were heading out to help defend Darroth or to reinforce those guarding the gates to the castle, then the plan Cedric and the others had concocted was working.

Another Ferret was lifting tapestries. "It's the one of Grand Primate Jemen," Fi whispered.

The Ferret found it and only had to press a button to open the entrance to one of the few hidden passages Fi hadn't known about, but Enkelo had. This one led directly to Father's study, which would take them closer to one of the stairways that led up to the wall. Once she'd known about the passage leading from here to the temple, she should have realized there'd be a passage from the study. She'd known about the one leading here from the monarch's chamber, and she almost giggled when she recalled a conversation she'd had with Erryn about why a secret passageway would exist between the bedchamber and the worship room. Enkelo would not have approved of some of their answers!

Jeena slipped into the passage after two Ferrets. Fi followed them in. This passage was narrower and passed behind the walls of several rooms. They had to be quiet.

As they approached the study, muffled voices reached Fi's ears. She stopped behind those in front of her.

"I think there are three," one of the Ferrets murmured.

"I believe one is my brother," Dann whispered to Fi. "I recognize his voice."

She didn't know what to say. For his sake, she hoped Jared would surrender.

"The passage opens behind the desk," Cedric said. "That means at least two will probably see us right away."

"Then we'll have to be quick," the Ferret said.

"What are you going to do?" Dann asked.

"Try to subdue them. They may have information. But if they fight . . ."

Dann blinked at the Ferret, then nodded. "He joined the forces against you," he whispered to Fi. But she knew Dann still loved him, as she'd still loved Erryn when she'd thought her a heathen.

A Ferret and the guard squeezed past Fi to join Jeena and the two Ferrets with her. The door swung open, lighting up the passage. Thuds, grunts, steel meeting steel. Then the heavy breathing of men and women who'd just fought. One of the Ferrets motioned for everyone to come into the study.

When Fi emerged, Jeena and the others stood before two kneeling men whose hands were tied behind their backs. A third man lay on the floor, a dagger protruding from this throat. Fi recognized him as one of the members of the Royal Council. He should have followed Eness's lead.

"Ah, you're alive, brother," Jared said. "But not unscarred, I see."

Dann's eyes bored into him. "Why?"

"Why what? Why am I on my knees? Why am I defending the castle and opposing our brother's betrothed? Because she killed our king."

"You know that's not true," Dann snapped. "Perhaps you're misguided about her because you don't know her well, but you knew Viren. You believe he was part of a plot to seize the throne?"

"I believe women can bewitch men and persuade them to do all sorts of things. Look at you. She bewitched you, and here you are."

Dann lifted his hand. Fi thought he was going to backhand Jared across the face, but then he looked at Jeena and extended his hand.

Jeena frowned at him. "No."

"No, what?" Fi said, confused.

"He wants to kill him."

Fi's eyes flew to Dann's face. "Let someone else do it, and not yet. We haven't questioned these men."

"He won't tell us anything."

"Neither will I," the other man on his knees said. Fi didn't know him. A friend of Jared's, perhaps, or the son of some minor noble who'd seized his chance to become more important than he was. "By the Seven, I'll tell you nothing. Traitor!"

"We didn't kill your friend's brother because we thought you should make the decision," one of the Ferrets said to Fi. "We would have if he'd given us trouble, but we were on him before he could draw his sword."

"He has to die," Fi said, stating what Dann already knew. Anyone who publicly opposed her had to go, and not to the dungeon. There would be enough knives at her back from those who expressed their opposition privately, and those who would alter their allegiance as soon as they realized which way the wind was blowing and throw themselves at her feet, begging for mercy and forgiveness. She'd have to spare them. She couldn't be seen as a tyrant. "But I was hoping they'd tell us where guards are stationed within the castle, and especially upon its walls."

"We're loyal to your father." Jared's mouth set. "You took my brothers from me. I won't help you. I hope your life ends tonight at the end of a sword."

"Give it to me," Dann said to Jeena.

Jeena looked to Fi.

"Let her do it," Fi said. "Do you want this on your conscience? He's a traitor, but he's your brother."

"That's why I have to do it. For Viren. For your father. For what you went through."

Jared rolled his eyes. "You're terrible with a sword, brother. I want a clean death. Let the woman do it. She's more a man than you are."

Dann's face tightened and he stepped toward—Jeena's sword slashed through the air, slicing Jared's head from the rest of his body. The head thunked to the floor. Fi couldn't help but look at it, then her stomach roiled and she quickly averted her eyes.

"You should have let me," Dann growled.

"Ye have people like me to do it."

"You are a servant of the queen. You do what the queen tells you to do, and nothing more."

Fi lifted her hand. "We'll discuss this later." In private, where she could be honest without publicly humiliating anyone. "Take care of the other one."

The man spat at her, but she was too far away from him. "Lyos pig. The Seven curse—" His voice choked off and he slumped forward, Jeena's sword in his belly. The wild woman pulled out her blade and held it at the ready.

Again, everyone listened. Fi patted Dann's back, wanting to do more. One of the first things she'd do as queen was announce her marriage, so they could stop this charade. Dann's face was white, and his jaw clenched. She couldn't tell if he was angry, or struggling with grief. Both, she suspected. Her own grief had suddenly rushed back. She must have entered this study thousands of times, seen father with his head bent over a document, or speaking to Enkelo, or his manservant, the guard captain, or some noble. She'd always spoken a few words to him and then left, not wanting to sit in on a boring meeting. Now she'd give anything to plunk into one of the plush chairs and listen to Father discuss business.

After a minute had passed, one of the Ferrets pulled

open the door and peered into the hallway. He motioned for the others to follow him. They crept from the study and made it to the stairway without encountering anyone, but as they silently climbed the steps, shouts reached their ears. Guards were on the wall, one of the castle's last lines of defence against the rebels assaulting Darroth. Had her people made it into the city? Were the remaining Six free?

Near the top of the stairway, those in front of her stopped to gather their courage. This was it. There were no more hidden passages, nowhere else to hide. When they emerged onto the wall, those with her would have to keep the guards atop it at bay. She needed time to get to the top of the tower and pull down whatever standard was currently flying over the main courtyard. Then she'd raise the Lyos standard and implore those fighting in the courtyard and on the wall to lay down their arms. If those with her were overcome, it would only take one guard loyal to the Primacy to end the Lyos dynasty, and then the only hope would be that Erryn lived and Enkelo carried out Fi's wishes. Because if Erryn lived, then the Seven would be free. Surely they'd help the one who'd lived many lives trying to free them.

The lead Ferret glanced over his shoulder and nodded. Those in front of her rushed onto the wall. Her heart in her mouth, she raced after them, emerged onto the wall, and took a second to orient herself. "This way," she shouted, then ran behind Jeena, trusting that Dann and Cedric were taking up the rear, as they'd discussed. Three guards up ahead froze, then one shouted and charged toward them. Fi didn't see the dagger fly, but the guard went down, leaving two. Jeena and the Ferrets made swift work of them, but whoever was in charge of the castle's security hadn't spared any guards when it came to the wall.

Shouts, screams, and the ring of steel rose from the courtyard below. Her mind on her task, Fi didn't look down. Her protectors defeated another group of guards on the way to where the standard flew. Fi could see it now, a standard she didn't recognize flapping in the breeze. "We're almost there!" she shouted, adrenaline powering her legs. The Ferrets who'd fought at her rear rushed ahead of her now—most of them. One lay still. Fi pressed on. Another twenty feet and she'd be at the tower's entrance.

"Trouble," Cedric shouted.

She looked over her shoulder. Guards that had been on a different section of the wall had descended, run through the castle to this section, and were now in pursuit.

"More coming this way," a Ferret in front yelled.

Fi stopped when those in front of her did. At least ten guards were bearing down on them. Glancing over her shoulder, she saw at least as many racing toward them. They were trapped between two groups, with raising the standard almost at her fingertips.

Cedric raised his sword. "Protect the queen."

They encircled her, human shields that would take blows and cuts for her and eventually fall.

* * * * *

The moment Erryn stepped through the doorway, something rumbled behind her. She whirled, her mouth dropping open in horror. "No!" she shouted, grabbing the door and struggling to stop it from closing. Toe quickly dived inside, followed by Asha. Renn started to, but the door was heavy, and even though Toe grabbed it, they couldn't stop it from closing. Renn had jumped back, or she could have been trapped, maybe crushed. But that meant she was on the other side of it, along with Timor and the Ferrets.

"What happened?" Avere shouted.

"The moment I stepped through the door—how could I have been so stupid?"

Avere climbed the stairs, the light from her torch bobbing in the gloom. Past her, Erryn could see that some of the torches on the wall below were alight.

"Can you open it again?" Avere asked.

Erryn ran her fingers along the edges of the doorway. Toe helped her, but neither could find a way to reopen the door.

"Just like at the other temple," Avere said. "You couldn't open the entrance again. Once you're in, there's only one way out."

"It was open," Erryn said. "If I'm the only one who can open these doors . . ."

"Apparently, you're not." Avere gazed down the stairs. "Which leads me to believe that either someone's waiting for us down here, or they used this route to escape the building when they realized it was under attack."

"But who?" Erryn asked, not expecting an answer.

"The Fallen didn't follow you through."

"I can still command them." A wall couldn't break the mental bond they shared. Erryn dismissed them. She'd call them again when she needed them.

"Renn," she shouted.

A muffled cry answered her.

"Go help Fi. Go help Fi! You can't do anything more here. Go help Fi."

Renn's response could have been "no," or "we'll go." Erryn hoped it was the latter, because those on the other side of the door could only wait around helplessly, which wouldn't do anyone any good.

Before she turned away, she pressed one hand against the stone and held the necklace she always wore with her other. *If I don't see you again on this plane . . . live a good life. I'll be waiting.* Maybe she should have said good-bye to her earlier, rather than insisting on optimism.

Avere had descended the steps again. "I thought perhaps the torches had burst into flame when I entered, but now I think it's more likely someone came through here not too long ago. Look." She pointed down at the ground.

Erryn crouched next to her and examined the footsteps in the dust.

"There's a trail." Toe's brow creased with concern. "Many men have passed through here."

"At least we know which direction to go." Erryn slid one of the lit torches from its sconce and followed the footprints to another opened stone door.

"There are skulls here, but none of the symbols for the Seven," Asha said.

Erryn went to where Asha stood next to a lit torch. Her eyes confirmed what Asha had stated.

"Maybe we're in the wrong temple," Avere said. "This isn't where we can free them, but a temple for this Death we've heard about."

"But the other temple had skulls, too," Toe said.

Asha nodded. "And the door responded to ye," she said to Erryn.

"And to someone else," Erryn pointed out. She'd been separated from Renn and was trapped under Darroth until they found a way out, but the indications that people had passed through here recently unsettled her the most.

"Our only choice is to move forward." Avere transferred the torch to her left hand and slid a dagger from its sheath. "Let us go through any doorways first," she said to Erryn.

They went to the open door Erryn had noticed. She waited until the others were through, then stepped over the threshold. The door rumbled shut behind them. Why hadn't it done so for those who had passed through earlier?

"Perhaps only you're trapped inside once you enter," Avere said, obviously wondering about the same thing. "When we were at the other temple, you mentioned music. Are you hearing any?"

"No," she said. And the Fallen weren't agitating any more than usual. What if this was a temple to Death, and its intention was to trap the Beast Master inside it? She'd slowly die in here, along with the others, her task unfulfilled. She could almost believe it, except for the book Zhikinden had told them to read. Unless Enkelo had translated it incorrectly, this was the temple that would free the remaining Six.

"We're descending," Asha said, bringing Erryn back to her surroundings. The priestess had grabbed Toe's arm and was hanging on to it.

"Just like the other temple," Toe said. Except this one only had skulls.

Avere stopped and turned around. "There's a doorway up ahead, and light coming from whatever's beyond it." She snuffed out her torch. Erryn did the same with hers. The light from up ahead prevented the passage from being plunged into darkness. Avere crept forward. The others silently followed her.

At the doorway, Avere stopped and listened, then stepped through—

"Slowly, now." A foreign voice. "Drop the daggers and you won't be hurt. It's not you we want."

A sick pit formed in Erryn's stomach. Daggers clanged to the ground.

"Now for the rest of you," the man continued. "Come out where we can see you."

"Go," Erryn said, desperate to believe the man's words that he wouldn't harm them. She followed Toe and Asha through.

The moment she stepped into the circular chamber, music assaulted her, and the Fallen screeched, scratched, clawed. She grabbed her head. Her knees buckled, but through sheer force of will, she remained standing. The sounds soaring through her mind matched those at the other temple. It was their suddenness and loudness that shocked her. She battled to hear herself think, and to see.

They were in a circular chamber with a domed ceiling far above their heads. It could have been the same chamber in which they'd freed Zhikinden, except this chamber was much larger, and Erryn counted three altars. The remaining four must be hidden by the line of guards and the primates facing her. More guards had pulled Toe, Asha, and Avere away. Erryn stood alone. She recognized one primate. She'd exchanged polite words with him at several banquets and special services: Grand Primate Otane. Three of the primates standing with him wore mitres with a distinct style she didn't recognize.

Otane stepped forward. "At last, we meet." He swept out his arms. "Welcome to the temple of my master, Beast Master. Welcome to your tomb."

Fi slipped the bag from her back and fumbled to open it. Inside was a hunting horn, but first she pulled out the rolled-up standard and handed it to Dann. "Unroll it." Then she grabbed the hunting horn, and blew it as loud and long as she could, and pushed her way through two Ferrets so she could see what was happening.

The guards rushing from the direction of the tower faltered. She glanced to her right. The other group was still coming. "Hold the standard high," she said to Dann.

"Get back behind us," Jeena shouted.

"No. I've had enough of hiding." She squared her

shoulders and raised her voice. "I am Filmona Lyos, your rightful queen."

The guards rushing toward them stopped, but her throat tightened with fear when laughter reached her ears. Then she remembered how she looked. They didn't recognize her.

She searched the guards' faces, then stepped away from the tower, toward the group of guards who'd rushed along the wall from the other direction. "Captain Evan, don't you recognize me? I recognize you. When I was twelve, my father rewarded you for helping me out of the water when I fell off my horse and banged my head. If not for you, I might have drowned." The mare had suddenly balked at riding across the stream.

Evan scowled. "You knowing about that doesn't mean you're the princess. You could have been at the ceremony. There were lots of folk there."

"Yes, but afterwards, in the king's study, I presented you with a new pair of boots. Leather, for when you were out of uniform. I did so because I'd heard you complaining about the holes in the pair you had at the time. The only people who were there are all dead, except for you and me."

He blinked at her.

"You asked me how I knew your size, and I said I'd had one of the men ask your wife. I want you to go home to that wife tonight a hero, not a traitor."

"Traitor?" another guard shouted. "If you're who you say you are, you're the traitor."

"She speaks the truth," Cedric shouted, "And she isn't a traitor. She is your rightful queen."

"Is it her?" a third guard asked Evan tentatively.

Evan took a step—Jeena raised her sword. Fi touched her arm. "Let him."

The guard captain moved closer and peered at Fi's face. "I believe it is."

"Then—"

Evan motioned for the man to remain silent. Fi listened for sounds of fighting behind her, but the only shouts and grunts she could hear were coming from the courtyard. The other guard group on the wall must also be listening. If she could sway this one man . . .

"I didn't kill them," Fi said. "I know you're up here because you're loyal to the throne, but I'm telling you that if you kill me, you'll have acted against it."

"Anyone in your position would claim their innocence."

"In my case, it happens to be true. That's why many of the nobles have joined forces to restore the throne to me. That's why they're assaulting the walls. They know I didn't kill my father, brother, and sister-in-law.

"You saw me often. You know I had no interest in the throne, and I never would have gone along with another's scheme."

"Viren was innocent, too," Dann said.

"You were in the room with them," the skeptical guard next to Evan said.

"So were foreign primates," Fi said, knowing that accusing the grand primate wouldn't be the right move. "I believe they want to place someone from Westerfox on the throne. I've heard rumours that the seat of rule will be moved to that province. That's one of the reasons we've launched the assault tonight. You've heard of the child puppet they plan to sit in my seat, someone they can control. What do you think the child's first royal decree will be?"

Fi had heard no such rumours, except the one about the puppet monarch. But there were always rumours flying around Darroth; gossiping about the monarch and court was the Royal City's primary pastime. Plus, Westerfox primates had killed the king. They were involved. She'd added only a smidgen of baseless speculation to the mix. Westerfox was in Daros, but far away from the Royal City. Its people spoke with accents and its primates wore different mitres. Nobody on this wall would want Darroth to lose its status as the jewel of Daros and the home of the monarch.

"I am the rightful ruler of Daros," she said, quickly filling the silence created by the doubts of the captain and his men. "My father was assassinated, and I was framed. You all served him well. Serve him now. Put his daughter on the throne. The crown belongs to the Lyoses, not to a boy who will be controlled by Westerfox."

"The primates *have* been acting more like kings than regents," shouted a voice from behind her. "We were talking about this in the barracks just this morning. When they took over, it was supposed to be temporary and they'd leave ruling to the Royal Council, but most of the Council is gone. We said they must know something we don't."

"I never thought she was guilty," another guard said.

Cedric stepped to Fi's side. "You all know me. I've stood next to most of you, protecting our king. I dedicated my life to serving him. Do you think I'd have helped the princess escape if I'd had even a smidgen of doubt about her innocence? I'm here ready to die for her. If I'm cut down, I'll go to the Seven knowing I fought for the rightful heir, for the Lyoses, for the family the Seven have blessed and trusted for generations."

"If she's innocent, why didn't they kill her?" the skeptical guard said. "They killed the king, but left her alive. Why?"

"I've wondered about that too," Fi said honestly. "I can't answer for the assassins. I can only speak for myself. I didn't kill my father. I wish with all my heart he was here, alive, and on the throne. I'm only here to raise the Lyos standard because he would want me to do it. They took his life. They will not take his throne. It belongs to the Lyoses. Join with me. Come with me while I raise the standard and stop my people from killing each other."

The last word she spoke rang out in the tense air, punctuated by the shouts and clashing of steel from below.

The captain and several guards lifted their swords. Fi shrank back and cringed.

"For the Lyoses," the captain roared, thrusting his sword into the air.

"For the Lyoses," several echoed, their swords raised in allegiance. But not all swords pointed to the sky. One of the guards who'd shouted his support suddenly fell to his knees. Evan whirled. Men who'd stood with each other a second ago now lunged at each other.

A guard leaped toward Fi. Jeena cut him down. Fi grabbed Dann's hand and searched for a path to the tower, but there was none, and the men who believed her a traitor outnumbered the men who'd raised their swords. Her heart sank when one of the Ferrets fell only a few paces away from her. She was still trapped, and her men were dying.

Erryn dragged her eyes away from Otane and focused on the three altars she could see—those for Samshy, Lleor, and Irnys.

Otane stared coldly at her. "I won't waste your—"

She called the three Fallen. *Go to the altars! Quickly!*

The guards swiftly cut the Fallen down. Otane's mouth pressed into a thin line. "It's done, Beast Master. How terrible for you, being so close, but utterly defeated. Daros will have to wait yet again, but I'm afraid the land will die before you walk the land again."

"Why would you want Daros to die?" Erryn said, wanting to keep him talking.

"Because it deserves to. It . . ."

She stopped listening, her mind consumed with how to get the Fallen onto the altars. The numerous guards were blocking the way. Even if she were to call all six at once, and Zayvang for good measure, they'd cut them down. Then again, if only one of the Fallen made it, one of the Seven would appear here, in this chamber.

". . . time for this to end. You—"

She called Sath, Lerxis, Zayvang, and Cheturrak. They burst forth, charged—one by one, the guards cut them down. There were too many of them.

Otane smiled. "Enough! Step forward and kneel, Beast Master."

When some of the guards had moved to cut down the Fallen, two more altars had come into view. Cesernys's and— An idea sprang to Erryn's mind. If she could get Otane and the others to come closer to her . . . She called the four Fallen again and commanded them to remain with her.

Otane shook his head. "This is pointless. Though I must say, I get great satisfaction from knowing how the Seven have been humbled. Look at them."

"Seven." Avere snorted. "I'm afraid you've fallen behind. Zhikinden walks free. That truly is Zayvang."

Shock tightened Otane's face. He quickly smoothed his expression. "Then where is she? I don't see her." He turned to the other primates. "Do you?"

"Finish this, Otane," one said.

Otane turned back to Erryn. "Get rid of the beasts," he ordered the guards. "Leave her for me."

The guards rushed forward. Their swords swiftly banished the Fallen from the physical plane, though Sath managed to bite a chunk from one's arm. He sank to the floor, his face white. The rest of the guards remained near Erryn, ready to dispatch the Fallen again.

"I'll just keep calling them," Erryn said.

Otane and the other primates moved closer to her. "Then it's time for you to die. Kneel."

Erryn stared at him. *Rachagha. Quietly. Quietly.* She couldn't see the great bird, but she felt her entry into the physical plane. She kept her eyes on Otane. "I won't kneel to you."

Otane nodded to a guard. The man clamped his gauntleted hand on Erryn's shoulder and pushed her down. Her knees connected with the stone floor. She looked defiantly up at Otane.

"Ye will rue the day ye worked against the Seven," Asha spat.

"The Seven will no longer rule Daros, and you won't be alive to care." Otane held out his hand for a sword. "Move the others farther away."

"Don't look at them. Look toward the heavens," Erryn shouted, hoping Asha, Avere, and Toe would lift their eyes and understand. "Look toward the heavens."

Otane took the sword a guard offered him and planted himself in front of Erryn. "You have lost, Beast Master. I give you a merciful death."

Avere screamed, her piercing voice making Erryn and a few of the guards wince. Asha began to pray, loudly. "Don't do this," Toe shouted. "Don't kill her."

"I'm sorry I've failed you," Erryn shouted. "I'm sorry. Forgive me. Forgive me, please. I'm sorry."

"Silence," Otane yelled, but their voices continued to echo around the circular chamber.

Beyond Otane, Rachagha came into view, descending from where she'd materialized high up near the domed ceiling, the sound of her flapping wings overcome by the cacophony Erryn and the others were creating.

Otane drew back the broadsword. Erryn's voice faltered, then she shouted, "For the Seven! For the Seven." Rachagha landed on the altar.

Her shirt splattered with the blood of those dying around her, Fi pressed into Dann. She was tempted to squeeze her eyes shut so she wouldn't see the sword that would end her life, but all wasn't lost yet. More of the men who'd rallied to her had fallen, but there were enough still on their feet to hold those trying to kill her at bay. Running for the tower was out of the question. They'd swiftly be cut down, and more guards could be waiting for them inside the tower, waiting to kill anyone who reached it. Dann still held the standard high, making her love him even more. If they died here, it would be as husband and wife, but history would be oblivious.

"More are coming onto the wall," Evan shouted.

Fi's heart sank, but then Jeena twisted to her left and Fi glimpsed those running toward them. It was Renn and the others!

"They're with us," Dann yelled. "They're with us!"

"We outnumber you now," Evan roared. "Who will you fight? Turn to our allies and we'll cut you down. Keep fighting us and they'll cut you down."

"Drop your weapons and join me," Fi shouted as loudly as she could, hoping to be heard over the fighting. "Drop them."

"Do it." Another voice. "They're too many now."

Swords clattered to the ground. The few men alive

who still opposed her dropped to their knees, their breath ragged.

Evan turned to Fi. "Should we kill them?"

"No." They'd been following their orders and wouldn't be a threat to her when she was on the throne. She jutted her chin toward Renn and the others and noticed Timor had raised his bow. "It's all right," she shouted. "They're with me." Her relief turned to dismay when she realized Erryn wasn't with them.

She motioned for the new arrivals to close the gap between themselves and the guards. "Where is she?" she said to Renn.

"I don't know. We got separated."

"Where?"

"She went through a door and it closed behind her."

Fi did a head count. Avere, Asha, and Toe were missing, too. "The others are with her?"

Renn nodded.

At least Erryn wasn't alone, but . . . The standard was so close. Fi would raise it and then go to Erryn's aid. "To the standard," she shouted,

"My queen."

Cedric. His shaking voice set her heart racing. No. Not Cedric.

She turned around—and gasped.

Brilliant light forced Avere's eyes shut. Her head felt as if it would explode. She struggled for breath, then gulped down air when the pressure on her chest eased. Swords clanged to the ground. She opened her eyes. Still holding the sword, Otane had turned around to face the altar. But he'd lost the guards' loyalty, and the primates with him were backing away from Roosad.

"Call them!" Roosad's voice rang out, its force making Avere sway.

She looked to Erryn. Otane whirled and swung back the sword. Still on her knees, Erryn rolled to her right and—

Avere drew one of the daggers the guards hadn't found and threw it.

It dropped to the ground before it reached its target, as if it had hit an invisible wall.

Otane's sword was ripped from his hands and flew across the chamber. The grand primate's eyes widened, then rolled back in his head. He crumpled to the ground. "We will deal with him." Roosad looked at Erryn. "Call them, and become the Saviour."

Erryn knelt again and closed her eyes. The air shimmered, and then they were all there—Lerxis, Sath, Quon, Cheturrak, and Iss, running, lumbering, slithering . . .

One by one, they reached their altar. Searing brilliance made Avere lower her head. A breeze ruffled her hair; the air crackled with power.

"It is done," a female voice said, caressing Avere.

"Lift your eyes, Saviour."

Then the ground rumbled under Avere's knees, and even though her head was lowered and her eyes closed, a blazing light enveloped her. A glorious moment of ecstasy, then all was dark and silent.

She listened, then slowly opened her eyes. The guards and the Westerfox primates lay still. Otane was gone . . . and so was Erryn.

She pushed herself to her feet. "She's gone," she said to Toe, who was lifting his head. "Erryn."

Asha's eyes opened. She glanced around the chamber. "They took her. They took her with them to the heavens."

Avere wondered if that would have been Erryn's choice. Poor Asha would have to tell Renn. Avere certainly wasn't going to do it. She had a more pressing concern. "You two should go to the castle. I want to find the spymaster."

Toe nodded. "A door opened over there," he said, pointing.

"Just like at the other temple." Avere retrieved the dagger she'd thrown and the ones the guard had taken. She led the others through a short passage and wasn't surprised when they emerged into the same room from which they'd entered.

They retraced their path through the administrative building. When they reached the first guard the two Ferrets had killed, Avere stopped and lifted her hand. "Listen."

Toe and Asha cocked their heads.

"What do you hear?"

Their brows furrowed. "Nothing."

Exactly. Nothing. No shouts. No screams. No fighting. Silence.

At the same time Fi's mouth dropped open, her heart soared. The Seven stood in front of the tower. The Seven!

They weren't alone. Erryn stood with them. Fi quickly dropped to her knees and lowered her head, and sensed those with her doing the same.

"Rise, Filmona Lyos, Queen of Daros," a female voice boomed.

She scrambled to her feet but kept her head lowered.

"Hold your head high."

Fi raised her head and blinked at the towering figures in front of her. Zhikinden stepped forward. "Come with us to the top of the tower, young queen. Bring your husband and your personal guard."

Her personal guard? Did she mean Jeena?

"Yes, Jeena," Zhikinden said, startling Fi.

Her eyes wide, Jeena stood.

"Come," Zhikinden said.

Fi took Dann's hand, and after a moment's hesitation, took Jeena's, too. Her legs trembled as she went to the Seven. When they turned and entered the tower, she couldn't help but feel a bit slighted, then realized how foolish that was.

Erryn trailed after them, but slowed down enough that Fi caught up to her. "You freed them," Fi said.

"Yes, and then suddenly I was on the wall, looking at you." She sounded bewildered.

"Did the others survive?" Dann asked.

"As far as I know. Are Renn and the—"

"They're fine," Fi said. "They were with us on the wall."

They reached the top of the tower. Fi's eyes went to the strange flag flapping in the breeze, then to the man kneeling next to it. Otane. Her grip on Dann and Jeena's hands tightened, so she let go. She'd love to put her hands around Otane's neck and squeeze.

The Seven went to the edge of the tower closest to the courtyard. "People of Daros," Zhikinden said, her voice as loud as thunder.

Screams and shouts reached Fi's ears. The faint sounds of fighting faded away.

"Fight no more. Your queen has come home."

Suddenly Jeena was at the standard, lowering the strange flag. She fumbled as she removed it from the line, then held out her hand. Dann handed her the Lyos standard.

"Come to the standard and raise Dann's hand." Zhikinden's voice inside Fi's mind was clear and firm. Dann must have heard something too, because he took her hand and stepped forward at the same time she went to do the same. Now Fi could hear sobs and shouted prayers coming from below.

Jeena raised the Lyos standard. Fi lifted Dann's hand.

"Welcome your queen and her consort, whom the Seven have blessed," Zhikinden said.

A few ragged cheers rose, then more, then a roar, and clapping, and the strains of a flute.

Erryn went to Zhikinden's side. The goddess lifted one of her hands, and Roosad lifted her other. "This is Erryn Fyler, who has saved Daros this day," Zhikinden roared. "You know her as Beast Master, but she is the Saviour, and the Called and Caller, and loved and blessed by us, the Seven. You will thank her."

Another roar, one that shook the stones under Fi's feet.

"And now, the traitor Otane, who worked against the Seven. He killed your king and your prince, and he accused the princess of the crimes he committed. What should we do with him?"

Fi couldn't make out the shouted replies, but was certain "kill him" was at the top of the list. She gazed at the seven larger-than-life men and women in front of her. They looked normal, maybe a little taller than most, but they seemed to shimmer, as if standing in a light that wasn't there.

"Do you agree that we should kill the traitor, Your Majesty?" Zhikinden said to her.

Fi blinked. They were asking her? Then she understood. "Yes, kill him," she shouted.

"We will respect your wish." Zhikinden lifted Otane as if he were a sack of potatoes and hurled him off the tower to the mob below.

The grand primate's scream abruptly cut off. Bloodthirsty shouts rose from the courtyard. Fi tried not to relish the thought of what was happening to him. He'd be beaten, and cut, and torn limb from limb. But she couldn't stop the glow of satisfaction that swelled within her.

"We must speak with the Saviour. You may go," Zhikinden said.

Fi realized the goddess was talking to her. "Yes, of—of course," she stammered. She lowered her head. "Thank you."

"Rule well, young queen."

She wanted to look at Erryn, but instead she descended the tower steps, with Dann and Jeena trailing her.

"Where's Erryn?" Renn said, as soon as Fi reached those waiting on the wall.

"Still with the Seven." Her stomach was still in knots, and her mind swirling from her encounter with the Seven. She glanced over her shoulder at the tall figures still atop the tower, then forced herself to turn away. She couldn't stand here gawking. *Rule well, young queen.* She had work to do. "Let's go to Father's—my study."

"Of course, Majesty," Cedric said.

Majesty. Tears prickled at her eyelashes. Not because of the power and the luxury. For them. Father. Mother. Henrick. Surann. *I did it. I took back what's ours.* And she would give it back in a second if it returned them to her.

Fi hoped Erryn would eventually join them in the study. She hoped she hadn't just missed her only chance to say good-bye.

"Lift your eyes to mine, Saviour," Zhikinden said.

Erryn met the goddess's eyes with some trepidation.

"That which you set out to do long ago is finished. Do you wish to live out your last life?"

"You're giving me the choice?"

"It is your life, Saviour."

"I have questions."

"You may ask them."

"Why would Otane oppose you? Why would he let Daros die?"

"Pride and petty jealousy, and the interference of one

who should only have watched. Those from whom the Primacy sprang were upset that the one chosen to become the Saviour was not one of them. One of our elders felt that Daros should not have been given a chance to redeem itself, so it offered those who were jealous great rewards if they prevented the Saviour from becoming Saviour."

"It was close," Lleor said. "But we had no doubt."

"Perhaps you didn't," Samshy said. "I was beginning to get restless. But given the rules we'd agreed upon and how quickly those who wanted us to fail rewrote our words, I am amazed that we stand here free, and that our beloved Daros survived."

"Rewrote your words?" Erryn said. "You mean the Holy Texts?"

"Yes," Zhikinden said. "Not all of them. Not most of them. But the words about you are untrue."

"Can you tell me about my other lives? What was my name in my first life, when I took on the task of freeing you?"

Zhikinden exchanged a glance with Iryns and Cesernys. "You must believe us when we tell you that it would be better for you not to know. Do you really want to hear about the lives you've taken and the ways you've died? Trust us when we say that you should be content to only remember the life you have now."

Erryn nodded. She had enough blood on her hands in this life. "Is it true what the book said? That my parents were sacrificed and then always sacrificed?"

"Yes."

"My father and mother weren't Beast Masters," she said, wanting to confirm it.

"Not every generation was blessed."

Blessed. She hadn't seen it that way in the beginning. "The Northerners believe you went to them first. They don't follow our Holy Texts, but they also believed Beast Masters were cursed."

"The eldest of our children can be influenced as much as our younger ones. When we were bound, those who opposed us did so quickly, and poisoned the minds of all kinds."

"Do you mean Death?"

Zhikinden frowned. "We defeated death long ago. You will die on the physical plane, but you will not die."

"But what about the skulls?"

"Those represent Daros, Saviour. From the moment we were bound and the temples created, Daros was dying. Malina, like all, had only half the truth."

Erryn had other questions, but realized all but one didn't matter anymore. The Seven were free. Daros would survive. But . . . "What will happen to the Holy Texts?"

"That is an interesting question, Saviour. Your scholars and primates will discover that they have changed."

"Been corrected, you mean," Queyris said with a chuckle.

"I suppose I do."

Erryn exhaled slowly. "I don't have any more questions."

Zhikinden nodded. "Will you remain, or depart with us?"

If she remained on the physical plane, she'd be caught up in the machinations of the crown. She'd never be in rags again, her belly would never grumble, she'd sleep on soft feathers, never on hard ground. But what about Renn? What about Fi's determination to see her sister married? If she stayed, would she be condemning herself to a life filled with anger and resentment, and one devoid of love?

"This is a difficult decision, I see," Zhikinden said.

The worries and fears that immediately surfaced when she pondered the question made it feel that way. But in her gut, she'd always known. Every time she'd thought about what she'd do if they asked, she'd argued both sides, but her heart had desired only one.

"I'll remain." She couldn't selfishly leave Renn behind, even though they might have to part. Fi also needed her more now than ever.

Zhikinden grasped her shoulders. "If you wish to continue to call our beloveds, we would all agree, but I can remove our gift, if you prefer."

"I'd like to keep your gift," Erryn said, surprising herself a little, but knowing it was the right choice. "When I start wondering if this actually happened, they'll assure me that it did."

Zhikinden's smile warmed her more than the sun ever had. "Then the gift remains yours. We must leave you now. We have much work to do. We have a land to revive, and beloveds to greet." She kissed the top of Erryn's head. "Go now, Saviour. Live well, until we see you again."

Then they were gone. Erryn stared at where they'd

stood, then descended the tower stairs to the wall, as Saviour, Called and Caller, and with the pressure of Zhikinden's hands still warming her shoulders.

Avere crept down the dank steps leading into the dungeon, the moans already reaching her ears setting her teeth on edge. The dungeon marked on the old plans of the Primacy's estate had no longer existed. If Arrick wasn't here, in the castle dungeon, she'd go to every dungeon in Darroth until she found him. Many guard towers housed cages in their basements.

She hadn't sneaked onto the castle grounds, and no guards had stopped her when she'd pulled open the dungeon's thick metal door. They must have abandoned their post to join the crowd gathered in the courtyard. Prisoners didn't remain in the castle dungeon for long. Those locked up here were usually destined for the gallows or headsman. But times had changed. Avere would bet most of those here had supported Fi or spoken out against the Primacy, nothing more. They'd soon be liberated. She'd arrived at the castle in time to catch a glimpse of the Seven and see the Lyos standard flapping atop the tower.

Her nose wrinkled at the stench. She peered into the first cell. The prisoner inside rushed to the bars. "Are you here to let me out?" he said.

She studied him. His clothes were clean, and his face unblemished. "How long have you been here?"

"Since this morning."

"Why did they arrest you?"

"I spoke up for the princess. Someone reported me."

"Well, today's your lucky day, friend. Sit tight. I predict you'll be back at home before you know it."

She moved to the next cell. The man inside was curled up, moaning. Blood spattered the thin shirt he wore. Perhaps his release would come in time for him; perhaps it was already too late. The prisoner in the next cell was also bloodied and mumbled to himself. As she progressed down the cell block and turned into the next one, her mood sank. Only the first prisoner remained untouched. The others . . .

She smelled him before she saw him, the unmistakable odour of infection assaulting her nose and making her cover her mouth. He was lying on his side, his back to the cell door. Needing both hands, she steeled herself, then uncovered her mouth and pulled out a lockpick. A minute later, the door creaked open. She went to him and fell to her knees. "Arrick!"

He grunted. She helped him roll over. Two of the fingers on his left hand were gone. Multiple bruises and swollen lumps marred his face, and he'd never see out of one of his eyes again. But it was the festering wounds that tightened her throat and made the blood pound in her ears, so loud that she thought she'd pass out.

"Avere," he whispered.

She swallowed. "I'm here." They could take off an infected arm or hand or leg or foot, but Arrick had been racked, and the wounds on his torso . . .

"The princess?"

"On the throne."

"The Seven."

"Free."

"We did it."

Her vision blurred. "Yes, we did."

His eyes slid shut. She covered her nose and mouth with her sleeve and gulped down air, then sat cross-legged behind his head. "Lie on my lap," she said, grasping his shoulders.

He helped her as best he could, the effort of moving a few inches making him pant. She looked down at him. His eyes were still closed. "Jack," he whispered.

"He's safe." She squeezed her eyes shut, gathered her courage.

"Do you remember the last time we did a job together?" he said. She could only nod, which he couldn't see, but he didn't wait for her to reply. "The last morning, we sat next to the lake. We talked about what we'd be doing if we weren't Ferrets."

That conversation was burned into her memory. It was the only time they'd almost told each other. "I said I couldn't see myself doing anything else," she said, struggling to keep her voice steady.

"And I said we weren't the . . . type to set up house. We'd be . . . bored."

Her fingers closed around the hilt of her favourite dagger. How many times had she silently slid this dagger from its sheath? Usually anticipation quickened her heart, but tonight her chest ached, and her hand felt heavy.

"We were younger then." His marred left hand was moving. She realized what he wanted, and what she needed. She grabbed it and held it tight, and took a few seconds to steady herself.

"We're older now, Arrick, but I still think we'd be bored. We were born to be Ferrets, and—" She couldn't say it, couldn't say they'd die as Ferrets, still serving the monarch, still slinking in the shadows and sacrificing, their names never to be in the history books despite the role they'd played in every historical event. "We'll always work together." She blinked away tears. "Always be together."

"That time, sitting by the lake with . . . you . . . I think of it often, go . . . back there in my mind."

She readied the dagger.

"I'm back there now. The sun is . . . reflecting off the clear . . . blue water. There are swans swimming—"

In one smooth motion, she cut his throat. The dagger clattered to the ground. She cradled his head with her right hand and felt his grip slowly loosen on her left. Mercifully, he didn't struggle, or kick, or gurgle. He quietly slipped away.

Be at peace, my love. Be at peace.

Unforeseen Choices

On her way to the study, where she guessed Fi would be, Erryn rounded a corner and almost bumped into Toe and Asha. She gaped at them.

"Erryn. Ye're alive!" Asha enveloped her in a hug.

Erryn hugged her back. "You got out, then."

"Another doorway opened," Toe said, patting her shoulder.

"Where's Avere?" Erryn asked, looking for her.

"She went to find the spymaster."

"What happened?" Asha said. "We thought we heard Zhikinden."

"The Seven were with Fi when she raised the standard." Erryn stared at them, wondering why she couldn't believe they were here, and then realized they were standing in the castle, next to a portrait of some former council member and near a table with a priceless vase on it.

"We were coming to help her," Toe said. "We wanted to go up onto the wall, but we got lost in all these passages."

"She's not on the wall anymore. I'm guessing she's in the study. Come on."

They fell into step with her.

The study door was closed. Erryn rapped on it.

"Who goes there?" someone shouted.

"It's Erryn."

"Erryn!" Fi.

The door swung open. Erryn stepped inside. Fi rose from the desk, rushed to her, and threw her arms around her. As they hugged each other tightly, it occurred to Erryn that she was hugging Fi in front of everyone without a second thought, but when it came to Renn . . . Fi was the queen. Or was it that they were sisters, and the hug was chaste? Or perhaps that Renn was a Northerner, and they were in Darroth now?

Fi let her go. "It's done. I'm the queen, and you . . ."

"She's the Saviour," Asha said.

"I thought you'd go to the heavens with them," Fi said.

"They gave me the choice." Erryn looked past her and met Renn's eyes. "I chose to stay and die one final time." Bloodstains on the carpet drew her eye. "What happened?"

"We came through a passage that leads here and—"

A commotion in the hallway made Erryn turn around. The Northerners and guards drew their weapons. Footsteps tromped toward the study—many of them. Erryn prepared to call the Fallen.

"Lower your weapons. It's Eness," a voice bellowed.

The Northerners looked to Erryn. She looked to Fi, who nodded. Eness wound his way through those gathered and dropped to one knee in front of Fi. "The city is yours, my queen."

Enkelo and Hampton joined Eness and mimicked his gesture.

"Rise, gentlemen," Fi said. "Eness, you know who on the Royal Council supported me and who didn't?"

Eness straightened. "Yes, Your Grace."

"When you leave here, send word to those who were with us that we'll meet on the morrow, here in my study, at nine o'clock. I would have a servant do it, but they've all understandably fled for their lives. They'll come back eventually, but I want this message sent immediately, or they won't receive it in time."

He nodded. "The crowd is calling for you. They want to see their queen."

"Then they shall. Let us all go to the wall."

Eness and the others turned. Eness looked at Erryn and did a double-take. "Your Grace!" He drew his sword.

Four sword tips stopped within an inch of his throat and belly.

"I gather you weren't here when the Seven presented my sister to the people as the Saviour of Daros," Fi said. "My sister isn't a threat. Quite the opposite. Believe me when I say that if you harm her, you'll incur the wrath of the Seven."

"It's true, Eness," Enkelo said, surprising Erryn. "She has their favour."

Eness slowly sheathed his sword. Renn, Jeena, Toe, and one of the guards lowered their weapons, but their wary eyes remained on Eness.

"To the wall, then," Fi said.

Everyone parted to let her pass. Erryn trailed after Fi, and wasn't surprised when Jeena reached Fi's side two seconds after she did and took up the lead. What would become of her now? Fi would keep her word and grant her freedom. Asha had said the Snowlake clan would accept her, but she'd never mixed with her own folk.

Thinking about Jeena made her turn around and search for Renn. Too many people separated them—Eness, Hampton, Dann, guards, and then Renn, in the back, with the rest of the Northerners.

Anger clenched her hands. If it weren't for Northerners, she wouldn't have freed the Seven, and Fi probably wouldn't be on her way to the wall to wave to her subjects and truly begin her reign. There would be banquets to honour those who'd supported her, and Fi would be generous with her rewards. She'd better not forget those relegated to the back of the line.

Erryn emerged onto the wall at Fi's side. Jeena was still in the lead. The crowd below roared. Erryn waited for Fi and Dann to step to the wall's edge, then joined them when Fi beckoned to her. Eness, Enkelo, Hampton, and Cedric were also invited to stand with her.

The cheers washed over Erryn. It was done. She was back in Darroth and no longer cursed. She was standing with the queen, the royal consort, the royal primate, and two men who would definitely sit on the Royal Council. The city had already ensnared her.

Erryn waited while one servant cleared away her empty plate and a second one placed another full plate in front of her. Meat and eggs. She waited for the servants to serve those eating breakfast with her—Renn, Toe, Asha, and Timor. The Northerners had agreed to have their clothes washed, but had refused to be fitted for new garments. Fi hadn't quibbled. "I won't force you to do anything you don't want to do," she'd said, setting Erryn's teeth on edge. She wouldn't force them to wear something they didn't want to, but she'd force her sister into a marriage she didn't want, and she'd assumed Erryn would have her measurements taken. After all, the queen's foster sister, the Saviour, couldn't roam the castle's halls in rags.

So here she sat in a shirt and trousers two servants had probably been up all night sewing. When she'd examined herself in the mirror, a stranger had gazed back at her, one in fine clothing and wearing a Lyos family ring. The clothes fit, but they didn't.

"What do ye think they'll be discussing?" Toe asked.

Erryn picked up her knife. "You mean Fi and the Council?"

He nodded.

"She's probably told them when she married Dann. They're probably upset, but she's the queen, and the Seven called him her consort. They'll have to decide what to do about the Primacy. The monarch doesn't usually meddle in its affairs, but given what happened, I suspect she'll choose the next grand primate." It wouldn't be Enkelo. He'd expressed his desire to remain the royal primate, and Fi had agreed. As for Cedric, he'd turned down everything Fi had offered him—except an apartment in the castle. He'd no longer sleep in the barracks, he'd take many of his meals with the queen, and when he finally retired, he'd live out his days as one of the queen's family.

"What will she do with the boy they were going to put on the throne?" Asha asked. "She won't kill him, will she?"

Should Erryn tell them about Fi's decision to execute the boy's parents and grandfather and appoint one of her most ardent supporters as his guardian? Leaving him alive and under the influence of those who'd agreed to put him on the throne because they lusted after power wouldn't be acceptable. Fi had chosen not to kill the boy, but he'd never be allowed near her or anyone she cared about.

Erryn surveyed those around the table, those who'd never sat in a room and listened to powerful people decide who lived and who died, who prospered and who struggled, who counted and who didn't, all without blinking an eye. The few council meetings she'd sat in on hadn't bothered her. Now just thinking about it was putting her off her food.

She drank some water. "She won't kill the boy," was all she said. Fi had taken Jeena into the meeting with her. What would Jeena think about the men around the table?

For the umpteenth time that morning, Erryn wanted to look at Renn, but she couldn't bring herself to meet her eyes. They'd slept apart last night. She'd woken up in a soft bed, her head on a feather pillow and her body cozy under thick blankets, but had felt chilled, lifeless. She'd walked the familiar hallways with a sense of detachment. She no longer felt connected to this place. *We're home.* She didn't feel it. She'd asked herself where home was. The answer that had immediately sprung to her mind had both surprised her and made her nod. But it was moot. She was Erryn Fyler, the Saviour, and foster sister to the queen. She was trapped.

"Has anyone seen Avere?" she asked.

Everyone shook their heads. Erryn was worried about her. When the guard had freed those in the dungeon, they'd found the spymaster, his throat slit. Nobody had voiced what they'd all guessed had happened. "Hopefully she'll be at the banquet," she said to the others.

Toe cleared his throat. "After the banquet, we'll be going back to the stronghold." He smiled across the table at Asha. "It's time for us to go back to our people."

Erryn swallowed. "All of you?" She looked at Toe, but . . .

"I'm only speaking for us, me and Asha."

"I'll be going, too," Timor said.

Erryn steeled herself. "And you?" she said, forcing her eyes to Renn.

"Ye should speak about this privately, I think," Asha said. She changed the subject. "Do ye think ye'll be able to come see us pledge? We'd like it, if ye did."

So would she. But she suspected Fi would want to marry her quickly to some noble. Would her husband want to travel up north to attend a "wild folk" wedding?

Probably not. Why had she told the Seven she'd remain? At the same time, could she have left with them, leaving Renn and Fi behind, and all the new friends she'd made?

"I'd like to, but I don't know if I'll be able to." Panic suddenly gripped her. She gulped down more water. "May I speak with you privately after breakfast?" she said, not to Renn, but to Asha.

Asha inclined her head. "Of course."

Then she'd force down her food and try to stop wishing that she was dreaming, that she'd wake up in a tent, dirty, hungry, on the run—and free.

"I can't do this," Erryn said, as soon as Asha shut the bedchamber door.

Asha's brow furrowed. "What?"

"This." She pulled on her shirt and looked down at the clothes she wore. "This." She swept her arm out, at the four-poster bed and the armoire crafted by a master carpenter, the carpet that cost more than most people would earn in a year, the velvet curtains . . .

She went to the window and gazed out, her back to Asha. "You'll laugh, but I wish I was going with you. To the stronghold."

"Why would I laugh?"

"I'm not one of you. I'm a spoiled soft bottom who has everything anyone would want."

"But ye don't," Asha said. "I know ye don't."

Her eyes welled with tears. "No," she whispered.

Asha stepped to her side and stared out the window. "If ye could convince the queen, ye know ye'd be welcome."

Erryn's throat tightened. "The queen's sister living among wild folk," she said mockingly. "She'd never allow it. She'll let me visit you, but . . ."

"Can't ye just leave? Would she stop ye?"

"It would hurt her and publicly embarrass her. I do love her. She is my sister." Erryn turned away from the window. "And she's right. I'm a Lyos in all but blood. I can't just walk away. I'd lose as much as I'd gain, and I'm not referring to the wealth. I'd lose Fi. I'd know I'd turned my back on my duty. I wouldn't be happy. The problem is, I won't be happy here, either." She gave Asha a rueful look. "I don't expect you to solve my problem. I guess I just wanted to get it out, to hear someone say they understand. Renn's too involved. She can't see it objectively."

"I do understand yer problem." Asha paused. "Why did ye come to me instead of going to one of yer primates? Don't misunderstand me. I'm glad ye're talking to me. But is it because I know about ye and Renn? Or is it because ye don't want the primates to think ye weak, or disloyal?"

"It's because I care more about what you think and say than I do about them. And not because they framed Fi and cursed me. Most of them are good people and weren't involved with Otane's plot, and they were only following the Holy Texts when they cursed me. No, I . . . I feel more comfortable with you now."

"Ye said ye're not one of us, but ye're wrong. Ye've travelled with us, eaten with us, fought with us, laughed with us, loved with us. But ye also have one foot in the city. Don't be so quick to disregard that. It's part of ye."

"I know," Erryn murmured. "That's why I can't just leave."

"Ye say the queen won't listen to ye, but speak to her anyway. She may not want ye to live among us, but I doubt she wants ye to be miserable for yer entire life."

"She said she'd try to marry me to someone like me, as if that would make it all right." She blew out an exasperated sigh. "I want to be with Renn."

"Renn won't stay here. She loves ye, but if ye feel out of place here, think about—""I know. And I would never ask her to hide in the shadows while I'm married to someone. I would never ask that of her."

Asha was silent.

"It's a problem without a solution."

"Speak to the queen. Now that she's back on the throne and in a position to marry ye off, she might reconsider. I have no doubt she loves ye. Thinking about marrying ye off is different to doing it. One is easy, the other hard."

"I won't have much time to try to get her to see my point of view. The banquet is in a week. She'll want to announce my betrothal then."

Asha's brows rose. "That quickly?"

"She'll title me at the banquet," Erryn said, marvelling at how she would have welcomed it once. Now she didn't want it—another shackle. "A noblewoman my age, with my pedigree, even a foster one, and the Saviour . . . she'll announce it at the banquet."

"Then I would speak to her and plead yer case again."

She'd already pleaded her case. Doing so again wouldn't change anything. Renn would return to the stronghold, and Erryn would remain here in Darroth, watching musical fencing, drinking tea, and trying to be some noble's wife.

Fi finished signing her name and handed the paper to Edward, who was acting as her secretary, to affix the royal seal. "I think that's all of them." She turned to Jeena, standing guard off to her left. Edward kept glancing at the wild woman, reminding Fi of the bet she'd made with Dann. Within twenty-five minutes of the council meeting ending, one of the counsellors had asked to speak to her alone and suggested that she didn't need a personal guard, especially a wild woman. She'd said it would happen within thirty minutes; Dann had said an hour.

"The order I just signed is going to the guard," she said to Jeena. "It's for Quinn's arrest, and anybody with him. We'll find them and free any women." She turned to Edward. "Please leave us."

He bowed and closed the door behind him, leaving her alone with Jeena.

"I said I'd grant you your freedom, and I meant it." She pulled out a drawer to her right, lifted out the coin purse Edward had delivered to her earlier, and plopped it on the desk. "I assume you'll be going north, perhaps with Asha and the others?"

"No."

"No to going north, or to going with Asha?"

Jeena shifted her weight. "I'm not going with them. They're not my people."

"What do you intend to do?"

"I don't know."

"I can grant you a piece of land near Stronghaven." She now owned Lord Millwood's estate. Eness had shown her a map of it. There was land to spare. She hadn't decided yet which of her supporters would win that particular prize. Whoever it was might not want it, given its location. "You could build a house."

"Don't ye need someone to guard ye?"

Fi leaned back in her chair and folded her arms. "I have the guard."

"That's not enough. Ye told me what happened in that room. If there'd been a personal guard with yer father, he might still be alive."

"It's true that poisoning the wine wouldn't have worked." A personal guard on duty wouldn't have drank any.

"Ye need someone to be honest with ye. I've seen how they simper in front of ye. If ye said horses have six legs, they'd all agree with ye."

Fi chuckled. "It's not quite that bad, but I am aware that most nod their heads when I'm around, some without hearing what I'm saying. As for honesty, I have a husband." Who couldn't handle a sword. She didn't care. She loved his gentle and thoughtful nature. "You do realize I'm giving you your freedom. You can take this coin purse, which contains a generous amount of coin, and I'll give you a deed to go with it. You can leave this study, the castle, Darroth. You can do anything you want."

"Ye're the only people I know now."

"You can make new friends."

Jeena frowned. "Ye don't want me to guard ye."

She hadn't given it any thought. She'd assumed Jeena would be chomping at the bit to leave and would be gone the morning after the banquet, if not before. "You're a wonderful guard. You've saved my life several times. But your debt to me is paid. You no longer have to serve anyone. Your life is yours."

"I can do whatever I want."

"Yes!"

"I want to guard ye."

Fi stared at her. "Why?"

"Because ye need me to."

She searched Jeena's face for any hint of deception or amusement, but found none. The woman was serious. Fi could tell her no, to go build a house and a life, but she couldn't bring herself to do it. First, Jeena was right, having a personal guard she could trust and who'd proven herself would be prudent, especially during these early days of her reign, when there would be poor losers about. Second, the woman had grown on her. She'd almost forgotten Jeena's cruelty toward her—almost— and given everything that had happened since then, she couldn't bring herself to be cruel in return. If she insisted on Jeena leaving the castle, the woman might fall in with the first man who'd have her, and Fi would bet it would be someone abusive and demanding who treated her like an animal. Jeena seemed to attract, and be attracted to, those sorts of men. She wasn't Fi's responsibility, but a friendship had grown between them, and friends looked out for each other.

She unfolded her arms and clasped her hands on her desk. "I suppose I could use a personal guard, and you would serve well in the role. But understand this . . . you would not be my prisoner. You would be working for me. There's a difference. I'll pay you, in addition to this coin purse, which is yours for your service so far. If you ever tire of being my personal guard, you merely have to tell me. You aren't bound to me. Do you understand?"

Jeena nodded.

"Then you'll have the apartment next to mine and Dann's. It goes without saying that his life is as important as mine, and when he's present, I expect you to guard it as diligently."

Jeena nodded again.

"And as usual, anything you overhear you keep to yourself. You'll be bribed, Jeena, many times, to divulge what you've heard in here or during council meetings. People will want to pay you to arrange a meeting with me. You may even be asked to kill me."

"Good. It'll save me trouble. I'll kill them right there and then. I won't have to wait until they try to kill ye."

Fi almost giggled. She was already liking this arrangement. "Then it's settled. Here." She lifted the coin purse and dropped it into Jeena's hand. "Can you ask Edward to come back in? He's hovering in the hallway."

Jeena opened the door and grunted for him to enter.

Fi peered at the servant. "Tell the maids to prepare the

apartment next to mine for Jeena. I've just engaged her as my personal guard."

"Yes, Your Grace," Edward said, the look on his face almost bringing on a giggling fit again. "There's another matter we must discuss."

"What is it?" Fi asked.

"Your sister, Your Grace. Fifteen more gifts have arrived in the last hour, and I have several letters with offers. You must make a decision soon."

Fi's mood plummeted. "Perhaps I can wait a bit. After everything she's been through, she needs a rest."

"I wouldn't advise a delay. Everyone is expecting an announcement during the banquet, and there will be negotiations to complete before then. We only have a week."

A week to decide the course of the rest of Erryn's life. "Bring the letters to me."

He bowed and left the room. Fi blew out a sigh.

Dann strode in and stopped short. "What's the matter?"

"Gifts, letters, and surely more on the way. For Erryn."

"Oh." He grimaced. "What are you going to do?"

"Something I don't want to do." She forced a smile. "I'm sure I'll say that many, many times, now that I'm queen."

"Not like this, though."

"No." She would be hurting someone she dearly loved. She was the queen! Surely there must be something she could do, but what? "Oh, I've just engaged Jeena as my personal guard," she said evenly, catching Dann's eye and giving him a warning look. "She used her freedom to offer me her service."

"To guard ye, too," Jeena said.

If Dann had anything to say about it, he had the good sense not to say it in front of Jeena. "We know we can trust you," he said, making Fi want to hug him for what was a difficult admission.

"Can I say something about yer sister?"

Fi looked at Jeena. "What?"

"Ye should pledge her to a wild man."

Fi gaped. "Why would I do that?"

"Because she's the Called and Caller. A wild man would treat her like a goddess, not like a toy he owns."

Fi wished she could pledge Erryn to a wild woman. It would make her choice an obvious one.

"She's the Saviour," Jeena continued. "She doesn't need a husband."

"I'm afraid things aren't that simple."

"Ye gave me my freedom. Ye can give Erryn hers."

"I'd like to. If there was a way . . ."

"Let's put our heads together," Dann said. "You too," he said to Jeena. "Perhaps we can think of a way to satisfy everyone."

She admired his optimism and envied his naiveté. Come up with something that would satisfy her, Erryn, the Royal Council, the primates, and the people? Did he have anyone he wanted her to raise from the dead while she was at it? Being queen would mean making decisions that would keep her up at night. Unfortunately, she'd begin her reign by harming someone dear to her, and would cringe every time she saw Erryn and her husband, because she'd know, and hate herself for having done it.

Erryn strolled into the garden and went to the male gardener pruning a rose bush. He looked up and immediately straightened. "Good afternoon, my lady."

"Good afternoon," Erryn said. "I was told Renn came out into the garden. Have you seen her?"

"Is she one of the wild folk?"

"Yes," Erryn said, wanting to snap at him.

He pointed. "She went down that path."

"Thank you. Can you see that we're not disturbed? If anyone else comes along, can you direct them down another path?"

"Yes, my lady."

That way of addressing her was starting to grate. They used to call her Erryn. With respect, but still. She wasn't a lady or a duchess or the queen. But Fi would title her within days, and then everyone would bow and scrape and never say anything interesting to her.

"What's your name?" she asked him.

"Pardon me?"

"Your name. I don't know it."

The servant gave her a queer look. "Andrew, my lady."

"That's a beautiful rose bush, isn't it?"

"Yes, my lady."

"Have you been a gardener long?"

"Yes, my lady."

She sighed. "Thank you." She strode down the path he'd indicated, feeling his eyes on her back.

It didn't take her long to find Renn, who was sitting on a bench, staring at one of the numerous fountains that dotted the garden. Erryn plunked down next to her.

"This is stupid," Renn said.

"What?" Erryn asked, wishing she could take her hand, but it would be too risky.

Renn jutted her chin toward the fountain. "I've always thought they were stupid."

"Fountains?"

Renn nodded.

"I don't mind them." She paused. "I figured I'd find you outside somewhere."

"My bottom's had enough of velvet."

Erryn chuckled. "I guess that's why you call us soft bottoms, though most people don't sit on velvet, you know. They sit on wood."

"But not ye. Everything for ye is soft."

Did she detect a sneer? "These clothes don't fit me anymore."

Renn's brows drew together. "They look all right to me."

"I meant this doesn't feel like home anymore. The castle. The luxurious furnishings. The five course breakfasts. The clothes."

"Where does?"

She forced out the answer that sounded ever more futile, and hurt more each time. "With you."

"Ye can't be with me. I can't be with ye," Renn said, her hands clenching and unclenching. "Ye'll have a husband to coddle, and care for, and bed."

"You know that's not what I want. I want to be with you. I wish I was going back to the stronghold with you, because that's what you'll do, isn't it? Return to the stronghold with Toe and the others. You're not shamed anymore."

Renn shook her head. "Ye'd last five minutes at the stronghold before ye'd be crying for yer soft bed."

"After all the time we've travelled together, that's what you think?" She tried to keep the hurt and tears from her voice, but she couldn't. Her fingernails dug into her palms. "Why have you loved me all these months, then?"

Renn was silent for a moment. "It's not what I think," she said softly. "It's what I have to tell myself. It's the only way I'll be able to leave this place without ye."

"You don't have to leave."

"Ye know I do. Ye can't expect me to stay here and watch ye fawn over some man and give him children."

She brushed away her tears. "If I had the choice—"

"Leave. Come with us."

"I can't. Some of us are born into a life we can't escape. I—"

Footsteps. Anger clenched Erryn's jaw. She'd told the gardener—Andrew—to stop anyone from coming this way. The gardens had many paths. It should have been a simple matter of pointing people to another one. But then the person making the footsteps came into view, and Erryn's anger died.

"I was told I'd find you here." Fi frowned down at Erryn, but if she noticed Erryn's moist eyes, she didn't say. "I've come to discuss your future."

"You mean my marriage."

Renn stood, her jaw set. "I'll leave ye to talk."

Fi quickly held up her hand. "Stay. This concerns you, as well."

"Oh, so now ye think it concerns me. Ye haven't talked to me about this before, but now ye want me to be here and find out who she'll share her bed with."

Fi's cheeks coloured. "Shut up and listen to me."

Now Renn's face flushed. Erryn could see the storm brewing and pulled Renn back down onto the bench. "I want you here," she said, still holding Renn's arm.

Renn muttered something under her breath but remained seated.

"Tell us, then," Erryn said to Fi, shrinking inside. Some noble was about to have the best day of his life. He'd won the grand prize: her life.

Fi sipped her wine and set the goblet down on the table. At one time, she would have been on her third glass, but tonight her first glass was still half full. Never again would she drink herself silly.

She glanced behind her. Jeena was only inches away, appearing relaxed, but Fi knew better. Anyone who so much as twitched the wrong way would find a sword at their throat, or suddenly be a body without its head. She had to admit she was pleased Jeena was staying. She truly was a woman Fi could trust, and those would be in short supply, especially since Erryn would no longer reside at the castle, but on another estate.

She turned to her left and smiled at her sister.

Erryn smiled back, but Fi could see the tension around her eyes and mouth. It was almost time to make the announcement. Renn wasn't here. Considering how many men Erryn had politely danced with tonight, Fi hadn't insisted she attend, especially since she wouldn't have been seated at the royal table, but elsewhere. Erryn wasn't dancing with anyone now because Fi had told the three men vying for the privilege that she was about to make an announcement regarding her sister's future. Word had quickly spread, and only a few couples danced to the music. The rest had returned to their tables or stood drinking their wine, gossiping about who would be named, become the second most influential man in Daros, and step forward to kiss Erryn's hand, to claim her as his.

Fi had endured frosty looks from nobles who'd expected her to summon them or their sons to the castle to tell them Erryn would join their families. Eness, in particular, must have expected to be rewarded, and he would be, but not by becoming that powerful. She'd forgive that he'd initially sided against her, but not forget. And she would never have slighted Lady Vivien. Eness hadn't proposed, but everyone had always expected them to marry, and Vivien loved him. She'd suggest to Eness that he get on with it.

She beckoned to a nearby servant and whispered instructions to him. He hurried away. A minute later, the musicians finished playing and set their instruments aside. The anticipation in the air was palpable. Fi squeezed

Erryn's hand under the table, then stood. Dann rose with her, and now she took his hand.

The hall grew quiet. She'd already welcomed everyone to the banquet and said a few words after supper, so she got straight to the point. "I know you've all been wondering about my sister's future. You know she aided the Seven, freeing them from bondage. She lifted a curse that was ravaging the north and would have done the same to Darroth. We all greatly wronged her." Fi paused. "She is now known as the Saviour, and as the Called and Caller. It's time to reward her for everything she's done, and to grant her what was already rightly hers, because she is a Lyos in all but blood. She must be titled. My father had planned to do the same when it was time for her to marry." Plans he'd changed when he found out she was a Beast Master, but Fi wouldn't mention that.

She turned to Erryn and nodded. Erryn's chair scraped against the floor. She stood and faced those gathered.

"Erryn Fyler, I hereby grant you the royal country estate near Redstone, which is within a day's travel of Darroth. It won't be your main residence, but you may wish to use it when you come to Darroth for more than a few weeks and grow tired of the castle."

A few chuckles reached Fi's ears, but she could sense the tension in the room. Erryn still wasn't titled, and the astute listeners would have gleaned that Erryn would not be living in Darroth.

"But, of course, you must have your own estate and your own title. I hereby name you Lady Millwood. You will receive all the former lands and assets of the former Lord Millwood."

Surprised whispers and murmurs buzzed around the hall. Fi waited for everyone to quiet down. She'd just granted Erryn a title everyone would consider an insult, given that the nearest town to the Millwood estate was Stronghaven. Indeed, when the Millwood estate was up for grabs, the monarch usually granted it to someone he or she wished to see the back of. But since Erryn would marry, receive her husband's title and reside on his estate, they'd view the title Fi had just bestowed on her as secondary—just one of the many prizes she would shower upon the Saviour.

Fi widened her smile. "When I was travelling back to Darroth, I had the opportunity to spend some time in the northern lands, including Stronghaven and the villages and towns in its vicinity. The crown's relationship with the wild folk has been a weak one." Non-existent, actually. "I've been told I should refrain from calling them wild folk, that the more polite term is Northerners."

Laughter rippled through the crowd. Fi wouldn't quibble. She'd start saying Northerners, and soon everyone would be saying it. As Jeena had said, if the queen said the sky was green, soon everyone would swear it was. "We have neglected the north. I want to change that, especially given the role our honoured guests," she nodded to the table where Toe, Asha, and Timor sat, "played in saving Daros and restoring me to the throne. I will never expect Northerners to adopt our ways, as they live off the land and will now return to living off the land. But the Northerners will be neglected no longer.

"I have created the post of Overseer of Stronghaven and the North. The overseer will be the crown's representative in the north and the crown's liaison with the Northerners' strongholds. I can think of no better person to fill the role than my sister, who has travelled extensively with the Northerners and has their respect. She also freed the Seven, and they do not expect someone who can summon their beloveds into the physical plane to sit idle. In her new role, she will have much work to do. This means, of course, that she will leave Darroth."

Fi's heart ached. What she was about to say . . . she knew she wasn't offending Erryn, but everyone would see it differently. Then again, only Erryn should matter now. Only Erryn did. She drew a deep breath. "Now you are expecting me to give my sister's hand to one of our fine and loyal men." She could see the smug looks on the faces of a few nobles who'd struggled to hide their disappointment all evening, and the slightly lifted brows of many others. All Erryn had received was a royal manor, which didn't come with much land, and the Millwood estate. Not only that, it sounded as if she, and whoever married her, would have to live in the north.

Fi could almost see the nobles' thoughts. The queen's sister had gone from the most coveted prize in the land to an undesirable one. She must have done something to offend the queen. Despite the queen's kind words, there must be a rift between them. Receiving her hand would now feel like a punishment. Erryn had been right. When

Fi had wanted to at least return her father's lands and title to her, Erryn had turned them down, saying it would make her too attractive a marriage prospect. She wanted to shut the door on marriage for good. Fi had known Erryn didn't want to marry, but to refuse to become Lady Fyler . . . at that moment, Fi had understood how strongly Erryn wanted to avoid a husband and be with Renn.

"I know you will all be disappointed," she said, knowing full well they'd be relieved, "but I will not be announcing my sister's betrothal tonight. She has asked me to give her some time to grow into her new role, and I have agreed to do so. But not for long, Erryn. We have agreed to a two-year delay, and two years it shall be." Now Fi smiled inside. In two years, everyone would know the Overseer of Stronghaven and the North took her role seriously, to the point that she actually did visit the strongholds, sometimes spent weeks within them, and that one of the first things she'd done when she returned to the north was purchase a house within the city of Stronghaven, where she resided several months of the year. Nobody standing in this room would want himself or his son banished to Stronghaven, living in a stronghold for even a day, and meeting with wild folk inside common rooms. They'd all conveniently forget about the queen's sister, except for those times when they'd politely dine with her on the annual visit Fi had made Erryn promise to make.

Nobody would nag Fi in two years' time, and once Erryn was past child-bearing age, it would be moot, anyway. But oh, how Fi's chest tightened at the thought of Erryn leaving again! She'd expected to have her sister at her side, at the banquets, often in the council room, though only there to watch her husband, and at the many tea parties. The Fi who'd flitted around the castle would have insisted she stay and marry. But the one who'd had rotten vegetables thrown at her and been humiliated and spat upon couldn't humiliate and spit upon Erryn. Fi wanted Erryn to be happy, and so she was willing to give her up, but she'd miss her terribly. Though she took comfort from what Erryn had said when she'd hugged Fi after hearing her plan. "You haven't given me up, Fi. Quite the opposite. If you'd made me marry, I would have been here, but you would have lost me."

She realized everyone was waiting for her to speak. "Thank you, everyone. Please congratulate my sister, Lady Millwood and the Overseer of Stronghaven and the North."

Polite applause filled the room. Fi let go of Dann's hand and hugged Erryn. "Thank you," Erryn whispered to her.

Fighting tears, Fi nodded. "If you don't come visit me at least once a year—frankly, I'd prefer twice—I'll have you arrested and dragged here."

She felt Erryn's smile. "We'll come every year."

Yes, we. It probably wouldn't take long for people to notice the wild woman who was often at Erryn's side. Not a guard. Perhaps a representative the wild folk had assigned to deal with the overseer. Whatever story they came up with, nobody would openly question it.

Fi sat back down and sipped her wine again. For the first time since returning to the castle, she felt as if the crown fit nicely.

* * * * *

Staring into the fire in Arrick's study, Avere didn't turn around when the footsteps of two—no, three—people stopped just inside the open door. She turned around moments later. "A member of the royal family inside the Ferret base," she said to Erryn. "If it wasn't you, I'd rush to a window to see if pigs are flying past it." The woman may dress like a Lyos and when warranted sound like a Lyos, but her time away from Darroth had fundamentally changed her. Avere had thought that once Erryn was back among the servants, silk, gold, and fawning, she'd revert to her old self, but no.

"You weren't at the banquet last night," Erryn said, with Renn standing at her right and Asha at her left.

"Are you sure? Perhaps you just didn't see me." She didn't feel her smile. "I wasn't there."

"Then you don't know—"

"That you're now Lady Millwood and the Overseer of Stronghaven and the North, and you only have a glorified guest house near Darroth. No, I didn't know." She almost smiled an empty smile again. "They're saying you must have offended the queen somehow, or that even though you're clearly on the right side of the Seven, the queen doesn't want you close, not with your . . . abilities. Of course, it's nonsense. We all know the real reason." Her eyes flicked to Renn. "Well done. Now, why are you here? Surely you don't need our services so soon?"

Erryn chuckled. "Not soon, no, but I will need them. That's why I'm here. Are you the spymaster now?"

She'd been asking herself the same question. When she'd told Arrick's trusted circle about his death, they'd all looked to her, waiting for orders. But she was like Erryn. She'd never wanted to sit at the head of the table. She was best out there, slinking in the shadows, getting things done. She didn't have the time for politics. She only fawned over someone when it would help her get close to them so she could slit their throat.

"I don't know," she replied. "The others seem to think I'm the natural successor, but the role doesn't suit me, something I'm sure you can relate to."

Erryn's eyes brightened. "I was hoping you'd say that."

"Why?"

"I have a proposal for you. Come with me to Stronghaven."

Avere didn't bother to mask her surprise. "Why would I go with you to Stronghaven?" she asked out of curiosity.

"Because I'll need you. Don't be offended, but I got the impression the Ferrets assigned to Stronghaven aren't the best of the bunch."

She barked a laugh. "Offend me? It's no secret among us that those who screw up are often shipped off to Stronghaven. Nothing interesting happens there. Or I should say, nothing used to. Now that the queen's sister will be there, acting on behalf of the crown and actually taking an interest, I suspect that will change."

"Which is why I'm asking you to go with me. I need someone I can trust, who can listen where I can't, and talk to people who won't talk to me."

To give herself time to think, Avere turned back to

the fire. This time last year, she would have laughed at anyone who suggested she move to Stronghaven.

"You could act as a Ferret, or you could work directly for me."

"I'd still be a Ferret," she said. "I'd want to retain a certain . . . independence."

"You're considering it, then?" Erryn said, surprise lifting her voice.

What was left for her here? The study Arrick would never return to. Memories that would haunt her at every turn. Protecting the queen and her interests. Avere suddenly realized that she needed to work for someone who meant something to her. She liked Fi, but the queen was merely one sovereign in a line of many. Erryn, on the other hand, was the Saviour, the Called and Caller, could still bring forth the Fallen . . . and Malina had wanted to find her. Malina had been right. Avere had disobeyed Arrick to help the woman standing behind her because for once in her life, her cynicism hadn't won. "I'm responsible for Jack. I know he's almost a man, but he's lived here all his life."

"Bring him with you."

"The Ferret base in Stronghaven isn't as civilized."

"The residence I'll purchase in Stronghaven will have to befit my title." Avere caught a hint of contempt in Erryn's voice. "It will have plenty of chambers. He'll live there and still be able to go to the base every day."

"I don't want him in this life," Avere blurted. "I want him out. He needs a trade."

"Then we'll find him an apprenticeship. We can also

engage a tutor for him. He can take his time and decide what he wants to do. If he doesn't have to be at the base, he can move with us. We'll split our time between the Millwood estate and Stronghaven. You won't have to worry about him."

"I'm not worried about him," she snapped. "I'm responsible for him."

"I'm just saying he'll be all right." A pause. "Are you accepting my proposal, then? You'll come with us?"

"I need a change of scenery, so yes, I accept." She turned back to them once again. "I'll need time to close my affairs here and make sure there's a solid chain of command in place."

"We'll leave in—"

"Five days, yes, I know. That should be enough time."

"It's settled, then. We'll meet you and Jack in the castle courtyard at seven o'clock. Or no, join us for breakfast at six o'clock. The queen will be there. I'm sure she'd love to see you. She's asked after you several times."

"All right, then." She'd like to see Jack's eyes pop out of his head at the heavily-laden table and all the silver.

"We also want ye to come to the stronghold and see us pledge," Asha said.

"Someone will have to be there to protect Erryn on the way, I suppose. The guard can only do so much."

They all grinned at her. She smiled back, and for the first time since she'd left that dank dungeon, almost felt it. Life would be all right again. The void, the ache, wouldn't go away, but she'd get used to it.

"We'll take our leave, then," Erryn said.

"Good-bye. Oh, and next time, don't chatter my ear off, Renn. You always do, and you just have to stop."

The wild woman's mouth turned up at the corners. Avere wished she were near a window, sure now that pigs would be flying by.

The three women left the study. When Avere could no longer hear their footsteps, she gazed at the fire again. "It's the right thing to do," she said, to the one whose presence still pervaded this room. "It will be better for Jack, and protecting Erryn's interests in a savage city like Stronghaven will be quite the challenge."

She could almost hear his chuckle and see the look he'd always given her when she wasn't telling the whole truth. "And what is the whole truth, Arrick?"

That Erryn wasn't the only one who'd changed.

Erryn led her horse over to where the others waited in the castle courtyard. The clomp of the mare's hooves rang out on the wet cobblestones. They would set out for the Millwood estate in drizzle, hopefully not an indication of how the rest of the journey would go.

She stopped next to Renn, who was eyeing her horse with trepidation. "You can ride, right?" Erryn said.

"I can, but I don't like it. I always rode in the wagon. If anyone rode, it was Toe."

"We won't be racing there." For the first time, the group would travel without looking over its shoulder. She surveyed those standing next to their horses, waiting for Fi and Dann. There were only two horses for Toe, Asha, and Timor. Toe and Asha would ride on one. Timor would ride, or try to, on the other. He'd never ridden a horse, another reason they wouldn't ride at a swift pace. Erryn would make a point of riding close to him the first few days. After that, Timor would be managing all right.

Avere was standing next to Jack. Seeing the boy brought a smile to Erryn's lips. He hadn't spoken much over breakfast, except when Fi had addressed him directly. Given how red his face had turned and the few words he'd stammered out, she probably wished she hadn't—not unkindly, but because she'd embarrassed him. But he'd been among friends. He wouldn't hang for it, nor would his fortunes plunge. In fact, his fortunes had just shot up. He'd been taken in by the queen's sister. Avere could slink in the shadows and do her work without worrying about her charge, who'd be tucked up in a soft bed, either on the Millwood estate, or in Stronghaven. Erryn owed it to her. She'd suffered the greatest loss.

Fi strode into the courtyard, with Dann next to her and Jeena behind her. She stood before them and smiled, but Erryn could see it was forced. "Seeing you all now . . ." Fi swallowed. "I wish you were staying." She turned to Toe and Asha. "And I wish I could come for your ceremony. I hope you understand that I would, if I could. I can't leave Darroth so soon."

"We understand," Asha said. "Erryn will be there to represent ye."

"I have no doubt that she'd be there whether she was my representative or not." She paused. "Well, let's not prolong our good-bye. It will only make it more difficult."

She and Dann spoke a few words to Toe, Asha, and

Timor, then to Avere and Jack. The boy managed not to faint. Finally she came to Erryn and Renn.

"I wish we didn't have to part again, but it was the only way for you . . ." Fi's voice caught. "I had to do it this way."

"You didn't have to do it at all," Erryn said. "So thank you."

"I couldn't have seen you . . ." Fi shook her head. "You know I wanted to give you the Arlington and Falkirk estates. Most of all, I wanted to reinstate the Fyler title and give your father's land back to you."

"I didn't want any of that."

"You would have, once."

"But not anymore, and not only because of Renn."

Fi's eyes moistened, and she nodded. "But we're still sisters."

Now Erryn's eyes welled with tears. "Of course we are. I believe we know each other now more than we ever did, and because of that, our love for each other is truer."

Fi managed a smile, but her eyes were dull. "I'll say good-bye, then." She looked at Renn. "Don't let anyone kill her. And be happy." Then she reached for Erryn. "I thought once we reunited, we'd stay united."

"We *are* united," Erryn murmured into Fi's ear. "And remember, I'm only a bird away."

"I'll see you at the coronation. Do come a few days early."

She smiled. "I will."

Fi let her go. Dann gave Erryn a quick hug. "Thank you," was all he said, but his voice conveyed more.

Fi stepped back. "You have my most heartfelt thanks,"

she said, her gaze taking in the Northerners and Avere. "Daros, and I, will always be in your debt. You're always welcome here. Are you sure you don't want that donation I offered?"

"We thank ye, but with the land awakening, we won't need the coin," Asha said. The others nodded and also murmured their thanks.

Erryn mounted her horse, and so did everyone else, including Timor. But then his horse started to fuss. Toe leaned over and steadied it.

Fi raised her brows at Erryn. "I wish you all a safe journey," she said, amusement brightening her eyes. "May the Seven keep you."

"And you," Erryn said. The others murmured the same. Toe and Asha trotted forward. Even though six of the royal guard would ride with them to the Millwood estate, and Erryn didn't have to worry for her life—not too much—the others still insisted she ride in the middle of the group. Avere and Jack were behind her, Renn at her side. Timor was where she could see him.

As she rode through the castle gates, she glanced over her shoulder one last time at her dear sister, her brother-in-law, and the Northerner who was now the loyal personal guard to the queen. Erryn recalled the last time she'd passed through the castle gate on a horse, in disgrace and banished, with guards who planned to kill her. This time she was leaving by choice, something she'd never thought she would do. But she was no longer Erryn Fyler, foster sister to the queen. She was Erryn Fyler, the Saviour, the Called and Caller, Lady Millwood, the Overseer of Stronghaven and the North, adopted by Northerners, and foster sister to the queen. Most importantly, she was herself.

Epilogue

Erryn swung off her horse and patted the purse on her belt, to reassure herself it hadn't fallen off. Renn handed her the sack of apples she'd ridden with since the last village they'd passed through. The others took the opportunity to dismount and stretch their legs. The royal guards' breastplates reflected the afternoon sun.

"I won't be long," Erryn said.

She fished the land deed and the invitation to an audience with the queen from the purse, then strode up the path to the humble cottage and rapped at the wooden door.

It swung open. Rodney peered at her.

"Hello, Rodney. Remember me?"

He smiled.

Author's Note

Thanks for reading *Fate or Folly*. If you enjoyed the Daros Chronicles, please consider leaving a review for *Pawns and Puzzles*. It will help other readers feel more comfortable about taking a risk and buying the first book in the Daros Chronicles.

To learn more about my books, visit my website at www.sarahettritch.com. While you're there, you can sign up for my email list, and I'll notify you when I release a new book. I won't share your email address with anyone, and you can unsubscribe at any time.

Thanks for reading!

In the mood for more epic fantasy? In *The Salbine Sisters*, an apprentice mage discovers that she can't do magic and sets out on a quest to find out why. Of course, things don't go according to plan.

She gave up everything to become a Salbine Sister, member of a religious order of powerful female mages. But when Maddy nearly dies while trying to draw forth elemental fire, she learns that Salbine has withdrawn from her the gifts every sister works to master. Feeling trapped in an order to which she no longer has any right to belong and believing herself unworthy of the love of Lillian, one of the most powerful mages in the sisterhood, Maddy begs the abbess to let her travel to another monastery to research her condition.

On her journey, Maddy's faith in both herself and Salbine are tested to their limits.

"I have no idea what century this story was based in but it has horses, swords, magic, and women who are intelligent, strong and capable: the last bit being the most important for me personally." – reader review (CAB)

"I really enjoyed the characters and the story got me hooked and had me on the edge of my seat till the last minute." – reader review (Lisa)

Other Titles by Sarah Ettritch

The Salbine Sisters

The Missing Comatose Woman

The Rymellan Series

Threaded Through Time

The Deiform Fellowship Series

The Voice in My Head

The Perfect Christmas Gift

9 781927 369548

www.ingramcontent.com/pod-product-compliance
Lightning Source LLC
Chambersburg PA
CBHW032158180726
48284CB00001B/93